CW00543968

DON'T GO BACK

An absolutely gripping psychological suspense
thriller

MARK WEST

THE
BOOK
FOLKS

Published by The Book Folks

London, 2022

ISBN 978-1-913516-37-6

www.thebookfolks.com

For Mum and Dad

Prologue

The night Kate Marshall died, she prepared for yoga as usual.

She pulled her hair into a loose ponytail, checked her reflection in the mirror on the dressing table and touched the small picture there of her mum, taken before the cancer drained her vitality and life. Three months now and still a raw wound.

Shaking the emotion away, Kate walked along the landing to her son's room. Nine-year-old Lewis was sitting on the bed watching a Pokémon film on his tablet and gave her a heart-warming smile.

"I'm going to yoga, then to see Grandpa."

"Can I come?"

His words tugged in her chest. Lewis had taken Nanny Cheryl's death badly and now fretted after Grandpa, asking if they could go and see him every day after school to make sure he was okay.

"We talked about this last week," she said patiently. "You don't want to sit in the church hall with all the ladies doing yoga, do you?"

"I can take my tablet."

"I'll tell Grandpa you give him your love and we'll FaceTime him tomorrow."

"He knows I love him," Lewis said with a sense of resignation. "I love you too, Mum."

"Love you, buster."

She went downstairs, put on her trainers and walked out into the yard. Her husband John was in the shed, humming along to music only he could hear, leaning over the guts of a laptop spread over his workbench.

Kate waved to get his attention and it made him jump. He pulled out his earbuds.

"Didn't mean to scare you," she said, "but I'm going."

"You didn't scare me," he said with a smile. "Don't tie yourself in knots, and say hello to Richard."

"I will. Lewis is watching Pokémon but keep an eye on the time, yeah?"

"Always do."

She thought he'd lean over for a kiss but his mind had apparently already gone back to the laptop and he put his earbuds back in. She blew him a kiss and left.

* * *

The yoga class, in a small community centre that smelled of feet and old meals, cleared her mind as she hoped it would. The sun had dipped below the horizon by the time she walked to her car with the usual crowd, feeling tired but happy.

Kate said her goodbyes, got into her car and drove to the entrance. A teenager, clad in black with his hood pulled up, cycled along the pavement towards her on a BMX, the saddle so low his knees were almost to his chest. Since he was staring at his mobile, she waited for him to go by, uncertain if he'd noticed her.

He stopped right in front of the car, tapping the screen before putting the phone to his ear.

Surprised, she watched him for a moment or two then tapped the horn.

The rider, startled, nearly fell sideways and when he'd recovered his balance, threw her a glare and bared his teeth.

"Get out of the way," she shouted, gesturing at him to move.

He didn't pause in his conversation. She honked the horn again and he looked away, slowly cycling on without even glancing at her.

Shaking her head at his stupidity, Kate turned left and drove past him. She glared but he didn't look, slowly pedalling on, his hands draped over the handlebars.

She took the 'old route', as John called it, out of Seagrave towards her dad's house in Radnor, singing along with the radio as she drove. The bypass was quicker but she preferred the old coast road, past the Gothic All Saints Church and up Duncan Hill to Julia's Point, Crozier's Farm buried deep in a thick wood to the right, with glorious glimpses out to sea on the left.

The heavy twilight had shifted into evening gloom by the time she reached Julia's Point. Suddenly, her headlights shone on a baby seat in the middle of the road and Kate stamped on the brakes. The car shuddered to a stop half a dozen or so feet from it. She blinked, breathing heavily, gripping the steering wheel tightly enough to whiten her knuckles.

The seat was turned away, handle up. Kate looked around, taking in the empty road and the black mass of trees to her right. She hadn't followed any cars up the hill and none had passed her, so where had this seat come from? It had to be empty, surely? She looked towards the trees again, the depths of them dark and forbidding, capable of hiding anything.

Surely it was a trap, the kind of urban legend she read about on Facebook, wondering how anyone could be stupid enough to fall for it. A baby seat, on a little-used road, at night? She'd get out of the car and someone would rush out of the trees at her.

But what if it wasn't a trap and there was a child in the seat and she drove away and someone else hit it. How could she live with herself? She checked her mobile, saw it had no signal and looked back to the seat, thinking of Lewis and how safe he'd been strapped into his Maxi-Cosi but how utterly vulnerable he'd be out here. If she couldn't ring for help, she'd have to at least check the seat was empty before driving on.

Palming her keys, she got out carefully, alert to any noise or movement and locked the door, so no one could sneak in while she wasn't looking. She turned a full circle, taking in the dense trees, the empty road and the waist-high wall on the sea side, the solitary lamp post in front of it festooned with dying floral tributes.

She heard the sea and a light wind caressed the trees, making the upper branches whisper. Kate stepped away from the car, senses alert for any sign she wasn't alone. A bird called from high in the branches and she looked for it, her body aching with tension. The big crow came out of the trees, startling her, and flew off over the sea.

A baby cried, the high keening of a newborn. Definitely coming from the child seat in front of her.

Kate moved quickly, trying to focus on both the road and the dark woods at the same time, the lusty cries keeping her moving. She knelt in front of the seat and the baby squirmed against the straps, face screwed up in distress.

"Hey," she said.

The baby briefly stopped crying but its bottom lip continued to wobble. The tiny infant, perhaps only a handful of weeks old and wearing a filthy all-in-one, looked terribly grubby with dried snot around its nose and cheeks. The acrid stench from its filled nappy drifted to her.

"How did you get up here?"

The baby looked at her for a moment and then over her shoulder.

She heard a light footstep, the soft crunch of gravel and half-turned towards the woods.

Heavy plastic covered her head, smothering her scream. She tried to grab it but the bag, or whatever it might be, was pulled down past her shoulders, pressing her arms into her sides. Hard fingers grabbed her shoulders, pulled her to her feet and spun her around. She staggered, trying to stay upright.

"Mind the baby, Kate," a voice called.

Terror and claustrophobia rattled through her, tears coating her cheeks, the air suddenly hot and fetid. Shoved forward, she fell, knees burning as they scraped the road. Hands lifted her up, pushing her forward again.

She couldn't breathe, panic closing her throat as she tried to grab for the bottom of the bag but couldn't quite reach.

Another shove and she took five steps, now completely disorientated. The bag was pulled off and she gasped for air, rubbing away the tears smearing her vision. The wall was less than a foot away, the sea dark beyond it and blending into the night sky.

She hit the stonework, rough chips digging into her knees and thighs.

Her assailant pressed against her back, kicking at her feet to unbalance her.

"Please stop!" she screamed.

A push on her shoulders and she felt her centre of balance shift, her feet leaving the ground.

"Please!"

Kate fell.

Chapter 1

Even as Mondays went, Beth Parker's morning started badly.

Up before dawn so she could get to Birmingham for a nine o'clock meeting, Beth crept out of the bedroom so as not to wake her husband Nick. She made her way to the bathroom and sat on the toilet, planning out her day. As she got up, she glanced into the pan and sat down again, head in her hands, and cried.

There was blood in the water.

Beth didn't wake Nick because she didn't want to face the conversation. Instead, she showered and dressed, had a light breakfast and was on the road before the first light of the day cast pink and orange rays across the sky.

Another month gone.

She stared at the road, trying once again to work out just what was wrong. Her GP said it was neither of them and the hospital consultant agreed. They'd both been checked thoroughly and there was no outward sign they should have difficulty conceiving but that was the absolute fact of the matter. A little over four years now, of hopes and broken dreams, of romantic dinner dates and dirty weekends away and, latterly, an ovulation calendar as unerotic as it was apparently useless.

She blamed herself and Nick blamed himself and sometimes they talked about it but mostly they didn't. Beth was thirty-three, plenty of time yet – as people kept reminding her, seemingly unaware of the casual cruelty of their words – but it didn't change the facts. Nick's sperm was active and strong but they weren't conceiving, so how could it be anyone's fault but hers?

Pulling onto the A14, she switched on the radio, trying to distract herself. Time had proved this kind of negativity didn't help, only inspiring arguments and stabs of self-loathing and anger at her stupid body, even if those feelings wore off through the month. And she had plenty to focus on today.

* * *

The meeting room, a dozen floors up, looked out over Snow Hill but Beth's view of office blocks, busy roads and high-rise flats in the distance was obscured by the persistent drizzle freckling the windows.

Rosie, her managing director, had called a natural break when they reached page four of the contract – which had taken them more than an hour and only represented half the document – and the meeting dispersed quickly. The two solicitors facilitating the meeting disappeared into the warren of offices after taking orders for fresh hot drinks. Rosie went to make a call and the other attendees went for a nicotine fix. If Beth leaned back in her chair she could see them sheltering under an ineffectual umbrella on a terrace, grimly enjoying their smoke even as rain speckled their shirts and blouses.

Beth's mobile, placed on the heavy wooden table next to her notes, buzzed and she activated the screen. The Messenger app had a notification and she opened it to a warning.

> *You have a new message from Wendy Shaw. Do you want to connect?*

The name jolted her, a shock of recognition pulling her sharply away from the present. Could it really be Wendy? Beth put her glasses on to check the profile picture. The face might have been Wendy Shaw but fifteen years was a long time, people changed. Should she accept and open another door to a past she'd worked hard to distance herself from? It wasn't even as if she and Wendy had been good friends, so what could the woman possibly want?

Curiosity won out and she accepted, opening the message.

> *Hi Beth*
> *I don't know if you'll remember me, but I hope you do, we were friends in Seagrave before you left for university. It's been a long time, hasn't it? Anyway, I unfortunately write with bad news about Kate Crenshaw. We've been talking for a while and I know she was happy you'd reconnected on Facebook but, well, I'm sad to say she's gone.*

Beth felt a thick wave of emotion clog her throat. It must be a mistake, Wendy getting it wrong somehow. She read on.

> *There was an incident at Julia's Point. She lost her mum a while back and was full of grief over that, obviously, but she was married and they had a little boy and her dad's still around, so nobody is quite sure what happened. But it doesn't seem like Kate really. Had she said anything to you? She talked about you a lot, said she hoped you could get together soon and I'm sure she'd want you to come to the funeral. Would you? I know it would mean a lot to her – it'd mean a lot to her dad, I'm sure, and me as well, to see you again. Please say you will. Hope to speak to you soon.*

In a fuzz of disbelief, Beth logged into Facebook and checked Kate's profile, the background photo a view of Seagrave beach, the sun low on the horizon painting streaks in the water. The profile picture was Kate and her son, faces pressed close as they smiled broadly for the camera.

Her wall was full of glowing tributes grieving the loss of 'a great woman and friend', 'a loving mum' and a 'truly gentle soul'. Beth stopped reading after the first dozen, her eyes hot, the back of her throat dry. She couldn't allow emotion to get the better of her here and reading these tributes didn't help. A quick flick down the screen showed many more friends and relatives striving to get their thoughts and feelings known.

To stave off the hot tears behind her eyes and nose, Beth went back to Wendy's message. What did incident mean, had there been an altercation or a car accident? When she lived there, people didn't walk up Duncan Hill because it had no path, they cut through the woods and the abandoned holiday resort at Crozier's Farm instead.

And what did Wendy mean when she wrote it didn't seem like Kate? Was there a suggestion she'd jumped off Julia's Point? The place had been a notorious suicide spot in her teens but why would Kate leave her husband, not to mention her son and dad?

Rosie came into the meeting room, rubbing her hands briskly and sat next to Beth with a big smile that slipped when she looked at her. "Everything okay?"

Beth blinked and smiled, putting on her best face as she put down her phone. "Of course."

Rosie looked as if she wasn't entirely convinced then nodded and opened her folder. "Let's hope we get through the next part quicker than the first, eh?"

* * *

The meeting finished an hour or so after the catered lunch – clearly expensive but with little substance – and Beth went down in the lift to the underground car park with Rosie.

"Are you sure you're okay?"

Beth hoped her smile worked. "I just had a bit of bad news from an old friend."

"Nothing serious, I hope?"

"No," Beth lied, not wanting to talk about it.

Rosie touched Beth's arm. "I'm glad to hear it. And I'm really pleased with what we accomplished today, Beth, you did a bloody good job in there and that deal could set us up for the next eighteen months."

"We did it together, Rosie."

The lift doors opened.

"Just take the damned compliment," Rosie said as she stepped out. "Go home, enjoy the afternoon and I'll see you tomorrow."

Beth's mind was a tumble of thoughts as she drove home, thinking of Kate and their lives together, of Jenny and Wendy, that awful summer fifteen years ago and their estrangements.

She hadn't focussed so clearly on it in a while and the effect was overwhelming, bringing fresh tears, pushing her back into a past she didn't want to remember.

Kate had made the first move, her friend request coming out of the blue just before last Christmas with a short and sweet message.

> *I hope this is the right Beth (who might have been called Kennedy in an old life) because you look like this girl I used to be best friends with. Do you know the fabulous seaside town of Seagrave, did you go to Montsaye Community College, were you best friends with Kate Crenshaw? If yes, thank God, hope you're well. If not, sorry to bother you. Either way, let me know, okay?*

The message made her smile and she replied instantly, trying to use the same light tone Kate had – her attempt to sync back into their teenaged patterns not as hard as she thought it might be.

Kate got in touch because, she said, she'd missed the friendship and Beth did too, though the past towered over everything. As their chats progressed they even tried talking about that summer but the conversation stalled because they both understood what the past meant, what they'd done and what they should have done. Guilt was an invisible third wheel in the messages.

The conversation got easier the less they focussed on the past and they laughed more. They'd planned a meet-up in London that summer and Beth was looking forward to it. She'd made some good friends since Kate and was still close with the girls she'd met at uni but the bond of childhood friendships was strong – they'd done a lot of growing together, shared so many secrets and lies.

Yet now that meeting in London would never happen. Which meant saying a proper goodbye was something she had to do, even if it meant returning to a town she'd long since turned her back on.

Beth stopped at Corley Services, bought a coffee and sat on a picnic bench to drink it. She checked Kate's Facebook again and saw more messages of condolence, some now directly addressing her widower John, all of the posters as surprised as the next by what had happened.

Beth opened Wendy's message, re-read it then typed.

> *Thanks for your message Wendy and of course I remember you, I hope you're well. Thanks for letting me know about Kate, I'm honestly stunned and can't believe it. You said there was an incident, did you mean like an accident or do they think Kate went over the wall? I'd like to come to the funeral, can you keep me updated when it is? Thank you.*

Nick was still at work when Beth got home.

She went up to the bathroom and caught a glimpse of herself in the mirror, saw the haunted look in her eyes and didn't like it at all.

The past had barbs that cut deeply and pulled her back to a time she'd tried to shut away in a box never to be looked into again. A box full of a life she'd never talked to Nick about.

Now she realised the past couldn't be outrun, especially the bad things you'd done. There were stains that couldn't be washed away, a taint from the version of you that didn't exist anymore.

When she left for university Beth made the decision to put that summer behind her, embracing the fresh start she'd been given where people only knew her from now, not from decisions she'd made or actions she hadn't taken.

People like Nick.

After it became obvious there was more to their relationship than a casual fling, she'd spent a sleepless night trying to decide whether to tell him everything. In the end she'd chosen, for better or worse, to keep quiet. It hadn't been as difficult as she'd imagined – she only had to ignore that last summer – and her mum's attitude and absence from their lives meant it wasn't often discussed.

Her guilt was a wound so deep nothing could suture it, the best she could ever hope for was that she'd forget it for a while, until she heard a snippet of music, the caw of a gull or saw someone who looked similar to Kate or Jenny, then it would open again and hurt. The wound explained the woman Beth had become.

Her tears came then, tracking silently down her cheeks.

If she went home for the funeral, Nick would want to come along for moral support and they'd be back in that environment, with her waiting for the past to trip her up.

Nick had been part of her life for the best part of fifteen years, her husband for twelve, and if everything came out now, how would he react to the news that she'd kept these awful secrets from him? Worse, how would he react to finding out she'd let one of her best friends die?

Chapter 2

Clouds the colour of bruises filled the sky over All Saints Church.

The tension Beth had felt on the journey to Seagrave got worse as Nick drove up the bypass and across the top of town. It had been so long since she'd been here she felt like an outsider.

"How're you holding up?" he asked, joining a queue of cars waiting to turn onto the old coast road to Radnor. Offering to come with her straight away, he'd accepted her explanation that Kate was part of her old life, before university, without pressing the matter and she loved him for it.

"Not good, all things considered." She felt like shit, there were no two ways around it. Funerals were never good but one for an old friend she'd fallen out with so badly fifteen years ago, in a hometown that held bad memories, promised to be worse than most.

He nodded, clearly unsure of what to say. The traffic moved and he turned into the junction.

All Saints Church, encircled by a low stone wall, its lychgate flanked by large trees, sat a hundred yards or so along on the right and several cars were waiting to turn into The Slips, a narrow lane that ran alongside it.

"Do I follow them?" Nick asked.

"Yes, the road stops just after those trees behind the graveyard." She, Kate and Jenny used to cut through them to the small meadow that led to Crozier's Farm, sitting in the grass, listening to music and talking. For a moment, she closed her eyes and saw Kate with sunlight brightening her hair, blossom filling the air around them. The memory seemed to pull the air out of her lungs and she blinked the images away.

Both sides of The Slips, the grass verge on the left and the thin pavement that separated the road from the church wall on the right, were crowded with cars. Traffic cones marked out a space in front of a double-width gateway, where a handful of people sheltered under umbrellas.

Nick parked in the first available spot. "Ready?"

"Not really." Tension pressed on Beth's chest. "But let's go."

She got out, opened her umbrella against the drizzle and waited as Nick walked around the car, pulling up the collar of his coat. He took her hand and as they walked to the coned-off area she scanned the faces of the people but didn't recognise any of them. She wondered if Wendy was already here.

Through the gates, they walked up to the path that looped around the church, passing headstones so old the elements had eroded the inscriptions. Mourners stood in groups and a few nodded towards her and Nick. Beth nodded back without recognising them.

At the east end of the church, they stopped under the stained-glass window and looked out over the cemetery. It stretched down to the trees where the newer plots were and she saw an open one, the mound of earth hidden by a green tarpaulin. The last burial she'd attended was her dad's and it had rained then too, though her overwhelming memory was standing beside his grave and feeling the weight of her mum's disapproval.

Movement in the trees caught her eye and she saw an indistinct shape there. For the briefest of moments, she thought it was a person, medium height and thin, hair pulled into a ponytail.

Jenny.

But it couldn't be.

"What's wrong?"

"I thought I saw someone in the trees."

Nick followed her gaze. "Perhaps it was a rambler who didn't want to cross the cemetery with all of us here."

His answer made more sense. As much as she'd have loved it to be her much-missed old friend Jenny, that wasn't going to happen.

"The hearse is here," someone said.

Beth turned to see a man in a top hat lead the vehicle into The Slips. Someone moved the cones and the hearse parked in front of the gates, a black car with darkened windows pulling up behind it.

Half a dozen men got out of the hearse and made their way to the back of the vehicle. Nick squeezed her hand and Beth squeezed back, tears prickling her eyes as the coffin was slowly taken out. The pallbearers settled it on their shoulders as the doors of the second car opened and a man and boy got out. Beth recognised Kate's husband

John from Facebook and assumed the child was her son Lewis. He stared at the coffin with wide eyes, standing behind his father's legs.

An older man got out and it took Beth a moment to place him, his hair white in the sour light. As he turned, Beth felt jolted back to that summer.

"Is that Kate's father?"

"Yes, that's Richard."

He looked so old and broken, the sadness coming off him in waves, that even though he was only in his early fifties, he seemed twenty years older.

The man in the top hat nodded at John then led the funeral party up the path. John stared resolutely at the coffin and Richard looked as if every step filled him with unimaginable pain. Lewis's cheeks were slick with tears.

Beth and Nick went into the church with the other mourners.

The interior was small and packed, almost more mourners than pews. Beth and Nick sat near the back and she looked at the photograph of Kate on the cover of the order of service. The teenager she'd known was clear to see in the features of the woman smiling in some sunny location. Beth felt like a fraud and looked around for Wendy, but there was no sign of her.

A celebrant led the short service. A few anecdotes made people laugh, some elicited sobs but Beth felt strangely aloof from the words, hearing them without properly taking them in. Most of the stories were of Kate as wife and mother, but Beth's tears were for the young woman she'd known and the adventures they'd shared.

They stood for a hymn, knelt for the Lord's Prayer and listened to a reading by a young woman who spoke clearly even though her voice wobbled on a couple of occasions.

Finally, the celebrant touched the coffin and the pallbearers lifted it, the congregation standing as it was carried out through the south door. Nick took her hand and gave it a light squeeze as they waited to move.

* * *

He'd booked the hotel room without telling her. "Since we've both got Friday off work, I thought we could stay in Seagrave and…"

"Make a weekend of it?" she asked witheringly. "It's a funeral."

"I know, but being away from home might take your mind off things, give us a few days to get some quality time together."

She could see he was trying and knew a break would give them a chance to enjoy each other's company without any pressures, but it meant going back. "We've never been to Seagrave, Nick, because I couldn't wait to get away."

"It's been a long time."

"I won't fall magically back in love with the place." Even as she said it, she knew it was too cruel. He didn't know and how could he if she'd never told him?

"I know, but I thought you might see some old friends, have a pleasant time." He looked like he knew he'd made a mistake. "I'm sorry, this sounded a lot better in my head."

Perhaps he was right and if he wasn't, surely that was her fault for not explaining enough about that summer. She puffed out her cheeks and looked at the sincerity and hurt in his eyes. "You're an idiot, Nick Parker, but so am I. We've never talked about my problems with Seagrave so how could you know?"

"I should have asked before I booked."

"And I'd have probably said no."

"I'll phone and cancel, it's fine."

"Don't," she said quietly, "we'll go. It's a lovely gesture."

* * *

The rain had stopped by the time the mourners crossed the cemetery and huddled around the open grave. Beth watched the trees, hoping to see the person with the ponytail again but whoever it was had gone.

Crows cawed as the celebrant began the committal. Richard started to cry and Lewis held his hand tightly as John put arms around both of them, biting his lip as he looked into the grave.

The coffin was lowered into the ground. John and Lewis silently dropped in roses, Richard dropped a handful of earth. Beth wiped away a tear.

Nick put his arm around her shoulders and squeezed. "This is terrible," he said, "such a tragedy."

"I know, I don't know how her little boy is coping with this."

"It is hard and I didn't know her."

The undertaker in the top hat led the procession back towards the church and took Richard's elbow, as if afraid Kate's dad would collapse. The family lined up beside the south door and Beth swallowed hard, remembering the pain of the same thing from her dad's funeral. Nick's presence gave her comfort. If she'd come on her own, she'd probably already be driving home to escape the grief.

They joined the line, moving forward slowly and she watched others shake the men's hands and touch Lewis gently on top of his head or on his cheek. When they reached them, Nick touched the small of Beth's back to guide her on.

"Thank you for coming," John said, looking at her as he shook her hand, an actor reciting lines he barely understood.

"I'm so sorry for your loss." She looked at Lewis as John stroked his hair with his free hand. "For both of you, it's tragic."

"Thank you."

She moved to Richard and he tried to smile but the emotions at war in his face clouded it. She felt sorrow well up, her vision shimmering with anguish for the man who'd lost his wife and daughter in quick succession.

"Thank you for coming," he said then paused, holding her hand still, his eyes narrowing.

"I'm so sorry for your loss, Richard."

"Beth?" His voice cracked, fresh tears rolling down his cheeks. "I thought it was you."

"It is. I can't imagine the weight of this, so soon after Cheryl but I'm really so sorry."

"Oh my God," he said in little more than a whisper and pulled her into an embrace.

She gladly hugged him back and he seemed too skinny, diminished by his loss.

They stood for a few moments before he slowly let her go, as if reluctant for them to part.

"I'm so pleased you came, it's so good to see you."

"I wish it could have been under better circumstances. I had no idea about Cheryl."

At the mention of his wife, he closed his eyes briefly. "I understand," he said after a moment, "it's been so long since you went."

"Fifteen years."

"Oh so much time, so much life," he said and looked at Nick.

"This is my husband," she said and introduced him.

"I'm sorry for your loss, Mr Crenshaw," Nick said and shook his hand.

"Thank you, but please call me Richard. I appreciate you showing your respects and bringing Beth back to see me."

Nick nodded, clearly unsure of what else to say.

"Are you coming to the wake?" Richard asked.

She hadn't planned to, scared for feeling a fraud – the runaway come home – but how could she say that to him, his hurt and anguish so obvious? "I hadn't really thought…"

"I wish you would, I'd love to talk to you, introduce you to John and Lewis."

"Then I will."

He touched her shoulder, as if to seal the agreement. "You remember the Conservative Club?"

"Of course, we'll be there."

She heard raised voices, looked towards John and saw him throw a punch. A woman screamed as a man staggered back a couple of steps, stumbled off the edge of the path and fell onto the grass. John was already moving towards him, face like thunder.

"John!" called Richard.

Nick grabbed John's arm, pulling him back. The widower turned on him, fire in his reddened eyes.

"No," Nick said, "not here."

John's expression softened when Lewis grabbed for his legs, clearly frightened.

"John," Richard said, putting his hands on his son-in-law's shoulders. "Please."

A heavyset pallbearer rushed towards them.

"He can't say that kind of thing," said John, "it's not right."

The punched man got up, holding the hand of the woman who'd screamed. The pallbearer looked from him to John and back again, then led the man away from the funeral party.

"He said she'd jumped," John said. "How could he say that at her funeral?"

Chapter 3

Fifteen years ago

Running late, Beth was relieved to see Kate had already staked out their usual spot on the beach.

She stopped in front of a busy arcade, waiting for a break in the traffic. It was hot, the sky bright and clear, and she wore her one-piece, denim shorts and a sloppy T-shirt.

The holidaymakers around her wore less, their exposed skin already reddening.

Normally, the mass of tourists annoyed her but not today. With sixth form now over, she had the freedom of summer to look forward to before university life took her away from the town she'd lived in her whole life.

A car crawled by, filled with a red-faced family and two dogs. A little kid in the back stuck out his tongue and she returned the gesture, laughing as his face dropped in shocked amazement.

"Hello, Beth."

She turned to see Clare, one of her mum's friends, a clipboard clutched to her chest. Excited children rushed by her to the grabber machine on the arcade apron, next to an electric chair machine currently occupied by a grimacing man, his girlfriend urging him to hold on.

"Hi, Clare, how're you?"

"Not as good as you, I imagine. Your mum said you broke up yesterday?"

"That's right, just off to the beach."

Clare nodded, smiling. "I remember those days – me and Diana were just the same."

Beth smiled, not knowing quite what to say. Things had been strained with her mother for a while now.

"Are you looking forward to going away?" Clare continued.

"A bit nervous." The thrill of going away, starting a new life and meeting new people, was overshadowed considerably by the prospect of leaving her friends behind. She held her hand out flat and rocked it from side to side.

"Perfectly normal," Clare said with a light laugh and held out the clipboard. "Listen, love, I don't want to keep you, but I'm collecting signatures to keep the pier as it should be, would you mind?"

The 'Pier Saga', as her dad called it, had raged since spring when shady local entrepreneur Hugh Cowley suggested renaming the Empire Pier, saying 'The Sunshine

Pier' would tie in with the town symbol and become a marketing success. That Cowley owned The Sunshine Arcade along the front and wanted to re-open his pub, The Sunshine Smile, on Regent's Row as a gentleman's club was entirely coincidental. There were plenty of opposition but the council, whose newly elected mayor was Cowley's golf partner, had pushed ahead with the plan.

"Of course," said Beth.

Beaming, Clare handed her the clipboard and Beth signed in the slot. The person before her was apparently called IP Knightley.

Clare took the clipboard back, raised her hand to draw someone's attention and gave Beth a big smile. "Thanks, love, I appreciate it. Now get over to the beach and have some fun."

Beth spotted a gap in the traffic and rushed across Marine Drive. A small amusement area, with zorbs in a paddling pool and a pirate-themed crazy golf course, lay between the pavement and beach, enclosed by a plastic fence painted to look like a wooden stockade. Beth walked alongside it towards the Winter Gardens, an entertainment complex with lots of glass panels reflecting the sun. A large sign outside proclaimed the 'Final Year Prom' would take place tomorrow. Beth's prom had been held there two years ago and she finished the night by losing her virginity to Ronnie, her first serious boyfriend.

Just thinking of him caused a moment of sadness before Sam's Place came into view. A long, single-storey building with Moorish Towers, the amusement arcade had been around for years and now sported an American theme. Three flagpoles over the porch carried the Union Jack, St George's Cross and the Stars and Stripes, and a wooden replica of the Las Vegas Marlboro Man rose from behind the clock. It might be a poor copy but Beth thought the neon flourishes on his arms and hat were a nice touch.

The Empire Pier reached out into the high tide between the two buildings. It looked as though the wood and metal structure had never been modernised but Beth liked the fact it only had lights and benches, as if removed from the cheap thrills of the amusements around it.

Staircases led to the beach on either side of the pier where it joined the pavement and Beth made her way down the one nearest the Winter Gardens.

Kate lay on a raffia mat a dozen or so feet away, equidistant to the wall of the crazy golf and the pier supports. Empty mats lay on either side of her and she looked out towards the sea, her rucksack on the sand between her bare soles. Beth slipped off her flip-flops and made her way across the warm sand. Kate, even though she had earbuds in, rolled onto her side, shielding her eyes with her hand, sunglasses pushed on top of her head.

"Hey, you."

"Hey." Beth dropped her flip-flops on the sand, lay on the mat to Kate's right and smiled at her oldest friend. They'd known one another since the first day of juniors, their friendship surviving everything growing up could throw at it. "Been here long?"

"Most of the morning."

"I can tell. Did you want me to put cream on your shoulders?"

"Bugger." Kate moved her shoulders, trying to check herself. "I thought they were getting hot."

"Hot and red."

Kate pulled her long dark hair, thick and wavy, away from her shoulders as she knelt up. She wore a homemade tankini which looked as good as anything Beth could have found in a shop, paired with Adidas shorts. She reached into her rucksack for the cream and handed the tube to Beth, who applied the lotion diligently.

"Thank you. Did you want some?"

"I'm good," said Beth, rubbing the excess lotion across her cheeks. With strawberry blonde hair and fair skin, she was always well prepared for the sun, able to burn, it seemed, just by looking out of a window.

"You smell good too."

"I smell of fresh bread." She always did after a shift in the bakery.

"That's what I mean."

The girls laughed at the old joke and laid on the mats, Beth happy and content as she laced her fingers and rested her chin on them. She took in the big sky and almost endless beach, small family groups dotted along the sand, most concentrated near the shoreline where tiny figures played in the surf.

Tradition dictated they meet here, the day after school finished, to eat and make plans for the coming summer months. It had come out of the upheaval of the first year at Montsaye Community College, which saw Kate and Beth separated in class for the first time. Beth was with the equally nervous and lonely Jenny, their shared worry bonding them completely. Thankfully, Jenny and Kate got on well too and what had once been the 'Dynamic Duo' – as Kate's dad christened them – became 'The Three Musketeers'.

"I'm going to miss this," said Kate in a tone that made Beth turn to her.

"Me too." Hearing level-headed Kate voice her own worries made Beth feel a little better at her own concerns, of being so far away from family, home and old friends. Not, as her dad kept telling her, that Derby was all that far away. She'd told him it was far enough, though closer than Jenny, going to London, and Kate, heading for Liverpool.

"No, it's not the time to be down," Kate said, admonishing herself. "Today's our day to come up with plans, assuming Jen ever bloody gets here."

"Her shift ended at midday, I think."

"Yeah, she said when I called in on my way here." Kate paused, as if she wanted to say something else.

"And?"

"Nothing."

"What else were you going to say?"

Kate looked as if she'd just sucked a lemon. "I bumped into Ronnie."

"Oh." Beth felt the familiar chilly weight in her belly, a horrible combination of anger and sadness.

"He was picking up some bits and trying to avoid Jen, I think, but walked right round the corner into me." She touched Beth's arm. "He said to say hi."

"Uh-huh," she muttered, her throat too tight for proper words.

"Have you still not spoken to him?"

"No." The split itself hadn't been too bad but his rebounding straight into the arms of Chrissie Ford, of all people, had been awful. Chrissie had been a bitch since the first day they met and Beth still had absolutely no idea why.

Kate wasn't a fan of Chrissie either. "She," she said disdainfully, "wasn't there."

"Let's not, eh?" said Beth, feeling her mood sink.

"You're right, I'm sorry, I didn't know if I should have said."

"You're fine, it's not your fault. But tell me something good, to take my mind off it."

"I saw the Goose Fair setting up." An annual event, it was always fun but Kate seemed a little more excited this year.

"And?"

Kate raised her eyebrows and smirked. "I saw some of the lads putting the Waltzer together and one of them was…" She made a long breathy sound. "He looked well fit and you know I promised you a summer of singles' fun."

"So what were his mates like?"

"I only saw one, who was something like seven feet tall."

"Hey, ladies."

Beth looked over her shoulder as Jenny bounded down the stairs, blonde ponytail bobbing, smiling broadly. She wore her work clothes from Scott's, a bright green polo shirt and black jeans and stopped on the bottom step to pull off her trainers.

"Your shoulders are burning," she said as she flopped down next to Kate.

"I know. You're late," said Kate.

"Sorry about that. Did she get you to put the cream on, Beth?"

"Uh-huh."

"So why're you late?" asked Kate.

"The manager put the yellow stickers on early and there was a stampede for out-of-date sarnies," Jenny said.

"You lead such an exciting life."

"We all have to work," Jenny said, raising her eyebrows at Kate who'd delighted in telling her friends that her summer job, helping out in her mother's office, didn't start until Monday.

"And work builds character," said Beth, parroting one of her mum's favourite sayings.

"That's what she said," Kate said, "but you're here now and you know the rules, the last two to arrive get the goodies."

"When did you get here?" asked Jenny.

"I came straight down after breakfast."

Shaking her head, Beth got up and helped Jenny to her feet then led the way up onto the pier and into Sam's Place, the air conditioning prickling their skin. They crossed the brightly lit interior, noisy with electronic sounds, music and laughter, to the food court and waited for their order, watching grown men looking furtive as they fed slot machines in the cordoned off 'adults only' section.

When the food was ready – hot dogs with everything plus fries and Diet Cokes – Beth took the meals and Jenny got the drinks. They went outside, the sun hot on their chilled skin as they went down to the beach. Kate took the bag Beth gave her, dishing out the hot dogs to her friends and Jenny ripped open the bag of fries for easy access. They never took an individual pack, always sharing from the pile.

Kate raised her cup and smiled at her friends in turn, eyes full of warmth, and Beth was hit, yet again, by the melancholy that this was slowly coming to an end.

"To us," Kate toasted.

Beth and Jenny held their own cups up, tapped the rims gently. The Coke fizz glittered in the air.

"All for one," Beth said.

"Always," said Jenny.

"You know what?" Beth asked. She loved these girls, her sisters and what they had between them. She never wanted it to end. "I don't care what we do this summer, so long as we do it together and have a laugh."

Jenny patted her shoulder. "And I agree."

"You're so melodramatic," Kate said, "we'll be doing this again next year, you'll see."

"But we'll be different," Beth said.

"And so will life," Jenny said and raised her cup. "Come on, all for one."

They toasted once more, unaware of just how bad the summer would become.

Chapter 4

"Well," said Nick as he got into the car, "that was different."

Beth tried to repair her mascara using a tissue and the sun visor mirror. "I feel so bad for John."

The line-up had broken down as the man and his wife were escorted away, Richard taking John to one side, to try and calm him as Lewis tagged after them. The mourners, all thrown by the insensitivity they'd just witnessed, drifted back to the cars.

"Me too. I mean, even if you thought she'd jumped, why would you say it to her widower at the funeral?"

"No idea."

"Do you think she jumped?"

Beth finished dabbing under her eye then looked at him. "Honestly? I don't know. We'd only been speaking again for a while but it doesn't seem likely."

"Did you want to go to the wake? I know Richard asked but…"

"We ought to," she said, because it felt like she'd be letting Richard down if they didn't. Make-up repaired as much as possible, she bunched the tissue and flipped the sun visor up. "It was good to see him, it's been too long."

He smiled. "Do you remember how to get to the Conservative Club or shall I satnav it?"

"Cheeky bugger," she said, returning his smile. "Turn around and head into town."

He followed the other mourners out of The Slips and into Seagrave.

"So who was Cheryl? Kate's sister?"

"No, her mother. She died a few months ago, before Kate and I picked up on Facebook."

"Ouch, that must be really hard for Richard."

"I can't even imagine." Beth looked out the window, trying to distract herself and the fresh tears that threatened to fall.

"How old is he?"

"Early fifties, same as her mum, they had Kate very young. When we were teens, me and Jenny thought they were so cool because they listened to music we knew. It was great. Kate didn't think so, of course." A group of women carrying yoga mats came out of a community centre they passed. "I liked them, being at their house."

"Was it just Kate?"

"Uh-huh, only child like me. Jenny had a younger brother and sister."

It felt better than she'd expected to be talking about the past. Maybe coming back here hadn't been such a bad idea after all.

"So that was your little gang, you and Kate and Jenny?"

He wasn't being nosy, she knew that, just trying to establish a picture of a life she'd never told him about. "That was us," she said.

"I'll bet you had some adventures, living at the seaside."

"A few." There were a lot of good times, with plenty of laughs and sisterhood but the darkness of that final summer had shadowed them badly.

"Are you glad you came back?"

She watched the town roll by. "Ask me later."

"I will," he said, "if you promise to give me a guided tour."

"Of course."

He crossed the roundabout that marked the edge of town as she remembered it and she was hit with a rush of nostalgia. Time away did things to memory, as she knew from revisiting Derby, but Seagrave seemed to have aged poorly. They passed weathered shops, petrol forecourts that now hosted car washes and streets of narrow terraced houses in need of love and attention. A corner shop was boarded up, another had been turned into a booze market. They passed the wide market square and it now looked painfully small, with only a dozen stalls set up, a handful of people wandering through them.

At the lights, the old Fair Deal general store on the corner had gone. The site was split into two units with a vape shop in one half, the other was something called the Glow Street Mission, where patrons could 'seek help and grab a coffee'. 'Everyone can glow' proclaimed the poster in the window.

"How's it feel, seeing the old town?"

"Odd. So much has gone."

"That's progress for you."

* * *

Nick turned into Carey Street, composed of neat rows of small, terraced houses on either side. The Seagrave Conservative Club was midway along, facing towards the sea. Its distinctive double-fronted building was exactly how she remembered it, with the small balcony between the upstairs windows and an ornate main doorway that never seemed wide enough. A soggy St George's Cross flag drooped from the flagpole.

"Shit!" Nick jammed on the brakes, the car coming to a shuddering halt as Beth saw a flash of motion to her left.

A teenager on a BMX executed a perfect half-turn in front of them, left foot planted as the rear tyre skidded around. The saddle was so low it looked impossible for him to sit down.

"Are you okay?"

"I'm fine," she said, heart racing, "how about you?"

"Been better."

The teenager, his black T-shirt emblazoned with a big cartoon sun, tilted his head as he looked at them and when Nick honked the horn, he slowly raised both hands and pointed finger guns at them. He made exaggerated 'pow' movements with his lips as he 'shot' first Nick then Beth, before spinning the bike around and riding away at speed.

"What the hell was that?" Nick asked, shaking his head.

"I don't know."

"I could've killed him, fucking kid." A horn honked and Nick checked the mirror, raising his hand to apologise. "I'd better move."

"No harm done," she said, glad it hadn't been her making the emergency stop. "If you go up the alley by the club, you can park back there."

He did as she directed and pulled into the small gravel area that was half full. They got out and she walked around the car to his side.

"So," he said, jutting his chin towards the building, "did you ever come here?"

"A few times, it was the venue of choice for eighteenth birthday parties."

"Happy memories?"

"Most of them."

Hand in hand, they walked towards the club.

"We'll stay long enough to say hello to Richard and John then slip out," she said.

"Whatever makes you most comfortable."

"Thank you," she said. "And thanks for being so understanding."

He kissed her cheek. "I'm trying, but you know you can talk to me, don't you?"

"I know," she said, wondering how he'd feel if she told him her guilty secret – that she was complicit in Jenny's death.

* * *

Kate's wake was in the upstairs ballroom and bar, where the eighteenth birthday parties had been held. Beth pushed open the door and a pensioner in a tired red steward's jacket, his thinning hair neatly combed, stood up quickly.

"Afternoon, love, here for the wake? Everyone's through there," he said and gestured towards the ballroom on the left, "and there's tea and coffee in the bar, compliments of the family. You can buy something stronger if you prefer though."

"Thank you."

"You're welcome, love," he said as he sat back down.

"Are you ready?" Nick asked.

"No."

She led him into the ballroom that hadn't changed since she'd last been here, with tables and chairs set along the walls around the wide wooden dance floor. The small stage at the end was curtained off, a buffet table set up in front of it. A piece of tinsel stretched across one corner of the panelled ceiling.

The room hummed with muted chit-chat, as people stood around in small groups. Beth looked for Wendy but didn't see her. John stood with a group of men, someone's arm hooked over his shoulder. Lewis was with Richard and an older couple beside the buffet table. When Richard saw her his face brightened and she gave him a little wave. He said something to the couple, ruffled Lewis's hair, then crossed the dance floor with his arms out. If it was possible, he looked even more tired now than he had at the cemetery, his eyes rimmed red.

Beth hugged him. "I'm so sorry for what happened with John."

"I'm sorry you had to witness it."

He let go and stepped back, hands on her shoulders, and looked her up and down. "It's so good to see you." He shook Nick's hand. "You too, Nick. Thank you for what you did to help John."

"No problem, I just wish we could have met under better circumstances."

"Indeed." Richard gestured towards the stage. "We've got food, if you're hungry, though I think Lewis is making his way through the sausage rolls solo." He gave Beth a faltering smile. "There's people too, a lot of them." His voice wobbled. "I only saw some of them recently and they all want to say the same things."

"I wish I could say something that would make things better."

"Bless you, Beth. Sometimes, it's better not to say anything at all."

She knew exactly what he meant, from what had been said to her after her dad died. People unloaded their grief and sense of loss without seeming to make the connection they were lamenting to the deceased's daughter.

"I miss the noise," he said quietly. "Seeing you reminds me of how you three tore through the house like whirlwinds. Me and Cheryl, we were convinced you kept us young." He glanced at Nick and smiled. "I'm sorry, going back into the past, I don't mean to cut you out of the conversation."

"I understand, Richard, honestly. Listen, I'll have a wander, give you two a chance to catch up."

"Thank you," she mouthed to him.

Richard watched him walk away through to the bar. "He seems a good man."

"I think he is."

"You deserve that." He gave her a small smile and gestured towards a table behind her. "Shall we sit?"

"I'd love to."

They sat across from each other and he took her right hand in both of his.

"It feels like we have so much to catch up on." He looked at the ceiling briefly, as if trying to keep his emotions in check. "I've been clinging to the past a lot just recently and seeing you reminds me of your teenage years. I'd come home from work to find you three in the lounge or sunbathing in the garden, all full of news and noise and I'd have to find a quiet area to have five minutes before dinner."

"I remember those days too."

His eyes filled with tears. "I'd give anything to have them back. Lewis is wonderful but he's making me realise I didn't take as much notice of Kate as I should have." He let go of Beth's hands and rubbed his eyes distractedly. "I thought I wanted peace and quiet but now I've got it, it's not what I wanted at all."

"You were a great father and I loved spending time at your house."

He nodded slowly. "You're very sweet. I wish we could talk all day but there's so many people."

"We're here until the weekend so why don't we have dinner and catch up?"

"Would you mind? That would be so lovely." He took out his wallet. "My brother printed these cards up," he said and handed her one. "I think they're tacky but they've got my name and number on and were so helpful after Cheryl. Lots of people wanted to keep in touch and I kept forgetting my number so I just handed these out."

"I'll ring you."

"I would love that. And, by the by, I was really sorry to hear about Gordon. Your dad was a good man."

Beth nodded, afraid to speak in case her voice and her resolve cracked.

"He and I kept in touch for a while after they moved but you know how life goes and we didn't hear about his passing until much later, unfortunately. How is Diana these days? It's been a long time since I last saw your mum."

"She's as well as you would expect. So do you know what happened with Kate?"

He worried at something on the tabletop with his finger. "Misadventure is the official verdict."

"What does that mean?"

"They don't know and nor do we. It was a normal Thursday, she went to yoga and was coming to see me, which she did every week, for a cuppa and a catch-up. When it got to nine thirty I rang to make sure she was okay but her mobile went to voicemail so I rang John and he said she'd gone out as usual." He chewed his cheek for a moment. "John rang the yoga teacher who said Kate left the class with the others so we knew it had to be something on her way to Radnor."

Beth put her hand over his. "Don't tell me if it's too painful."

He shook his head, eyes glistening. "It feels right you should know. Lewis was in bed so I said I'd drive to theirs but the police arrived while we were on the phone. They found her car at Julia's Point." A single tear slid down his cheek. "They found poor Kate early in the morning; said she went over the side. It was awful, so many questions, so many horrible theories but there was no note and we all know about Julia's Point and…" His voice tailed off and he forced a smile, gestured towards the buffet table. "I mean, look at him." She looked at Lewis, munching his way through a plate of Wotsits. "Why would she take her own life? Losing her mum hit her – hit all of us – hard but she had a good marriage, a beautiful son, a wonderful home. It doesn't make any sense."

"And you clearly made them see that in the end."

"Eventually. John gave them her diary and they interviewed us and there was nothing to suggest she was having dark thoughts so the coroner recorded misadventure."

"For what it's worth, I never got a sense she was unhappy, other than grieving her mum."

"Thank you." He held her hand again. "It's the not knowing, that's what hurts the most."

She stroked the back of his hand, feeling the weight of his pain. To lose a spouse would be life-changing, to lose a child within months of that would be overwhelming. She wondered how he managed to make it through the day.

A man Richard's age came to the table. "Sorry to interrupt," he said, "but we're going to have to head off."

"It's okay, I've been monopolising him," Beth said and stood up. "I'll call you."

Richard stood and hugged her. "That would be really nice."

"Take care," she said and kissed his cheek, before he walked away with the man.

Beth surveyed the ballroom. She couldn't see John or Wendy and, deciding they were probably in the bar, made her way across the dance floor to the foyer. As she passed the men's toilet, the door opened and John came out, almost bumping into her.

"I'm sorry," he said, without properly looking, "I nearly knocked you down."

"That's fine, John."

She saw recognition, then embarrassment, cross his face. "Oh bugger, sorry, you're the wife of the poor sod who had to break up my fight. Belle, isn't it?"

"Beth Parker, or Beth Kennedy as was."

"Of course," he said and shook her hand. "I'm John Marshall, Kate's husband." The words pinched his mouth tight and he tried to smile his way through it. "Widower. Bollocks, I'm never going to get used to saying that."

"I thought you held up very well, as did your little boy."

"Lewis is taking it well. He seems to have a better grasp on things than me and Richard." He let go of her hand. "Kate was excited about getting back in touch with you. To be honest, it surprised me I hadn't heard of you before, but suddenly she was full of news about you."

It made Beth feel slightly better to know Kate had kept her husband in the dark about that awful summer too. "I was so pleased she got in touch."

"Yes and now she's gone." His eyes widened as he realised what he'd said. "Shit, that sounded awful."

She shook her head. "No, it sounded real."

"I keep messing up, either talking like she's still here or has been gone for years."

"It must be so hard, she was so young."

"It still doesn't make sense to me. Did Richard tell you what happened?"

"He did."

"So what was she like, back when you knew her?"

"She was lovely, my best friend in the whole world but it was fifteen years ago, you knew her much better than I did."

He leaned towards her. "To be honest, Beth, I'll take the clues anywhere I can find them. The police have done their work, cause of death is identified and unless anything else comes up, all the facts are known." A little tremble quivered his chin. "And yet," he said, emotion thick in his voice, "her son and her dad and me, we have no idea what happened. She was cut up badly about Cheryl but she loved us, loved Lewis with a passion and was worried sick about how Richard would cope. That's not the kind of person who'd jump off Julia's Point, is it?"

"Doesn't sound like it," she admitted. "Could it have been an accident?"

"No damage to the car."

"Maybe she got out to get some air? It's been a long time since I was last up there, is the wall still only waist-high? Maybe she sat down and…"

"Fell, you mean?"

It sounded unpleasant and disrespectful said out loud. "Sorry, that was an awful thing to say."

"It's the only explanation I can come up with. There was no sign of a struggle, nothing was missing from her car. They checked her phone but the last call was to me and Duncan Hill is a mobile blackspot." He rubbed his neck and grimaced, as if massaging out knots. "She went to yoga every week, called in to see Richard then came home and had been doing it since Cheryl died. I got used to the routine and that night, I was so absorbed in repairing an old laptop when she came to say goodbye, I didn't give her a kiss. I'm not even sure I said goodbye but I know for a fact I didn't give her a kiss and that's killing me." He rubbed his forehead hard. "All I had to do was lean over."

"You couldn't have known, John."

"Everybody tells me that," he said, lips trembling, "and I'd tell other people the same thing but it doesn't make it any easier to stomach." He wiped his eyes and cheeks with a handkerchief. "I'm sorry for going on, you don't need to hear this."

"I wish there was something more I could do."

"You've done enough, coming here, honestly. How did you know about it, did you see on Facebook?"

"No, Wendy messaged me."

He frowned. "Wendy?"

"Someone else from back in the day." He clearly didn't know her. Hadn't Wendy said she and Kate were friends, or had Beth got that completely wrong?

"I don't remember Kate mentioning her so she obviously didn't make as much of an impact as you."

He waved at someone and Beth turned to see a woman in her mid-forties standing by the door.

"My sister," he explained, "I'd better go and see what she wants."

"I shouldn't have held you up."

"You didn't and thank you for listening."

She watched him walk away, emotion rolling through her. Her best friend hadn't told her husband about that summer and now she was gone, leaving him with a gap in knowledge he couldn't fill. Could she do that to Nick? Perhaps if she'd told him on that wintry afternoon in the coffee shop when they decided to give this new relationship of theirs a go, he might have absorbed it easier, perhaps accepted her secret. But now? She read somewhere a marriage is based on trust and secrecy was the enemy. Beth had kept her guilt a secret because she genuinely thought it was for the best, even as it festered and tormented her over the years. So what should she do now?

Chapter 5

Then

Beth woke early as sunlight crept over the top of her curtains. Her dad walked along the landing grumbling and her mum hummed tunelessly to herself in the bathroom, before the pair of them shared breakfast. Beth heard the sounds of crockery, cutlery and light conversation.

When her dad trooped back upstairs, he knocked on her door. "Are you decent, Sprout?"

"You can come in, Dad," she said.

"Lovely day," he said and opened the curtains with the economy of movement he'd employed since his heart attack. "I was talking to Mum over breakfast."

Beth could tell, from the tone of his voice, that something was wrong. She put her book down and sat up, leaning against the headboard. "Oh?"

"She's worried about you, love. We both are."

"I know, Dad, but she assumes I'm going to do everything wrong and get into trouble."

He gave her a wry smile. "And you think you're not?"

"Not if I can help it."

"She's only looking out for you."

"I know." She didn't enjoy arguing with her mother but, on the other hand, she didn't enjoy the fact she sometimes treated her like a twelve-year-old.

Her father, on the other hand, was easier to deal with, an easy-going presence with a core of steel, utterly dependable and currently the major cause of her worry.

When her mother picked her up from school the day he had this heart attack, her eyes a mess of smudged mascara, it knocked Beth sideways. In that sad ward filled with other middle-aged men surrounded by their families, he'd seemed too grey, a ghost of himself, and for one awful moment, she was convinced a nurse would rush in, tell her mum they'd made a mistake and her dad had died but they hadn't been able to move him.

He recovered slowly and the heart attack brought on some good changes. He exercised more – he and Beth enjoyed early morning walks – but something in his personality had changed and she couldn't quite put her finger on it. He still told the same stupid jokes and embarrassed her in front of the girls without understanding how but he seemed to struggle with the pressure of processing what had happened. The brush with mortality scared them all but he seemed now to be planning for a time he wouldn't be here, trying to smooth the troubled waters between Beth and her mother.

The thought of him gone frightened her; made her cry.

"Things are changing," he said.

"I know, Dad, I'm trying."

"I see that, Sprout." He gestured towards the bed and she moved her feet so he could sit on the corner, the mattress compressing. He'd lost weight but not enough and the lack of progress was getting to him. "It's a big year. First me, then you heading for university. It's a lot for her to take in."

She felt the familiar rankle of annoyance, of putting her mother at the centre of the stresses. Her father had the heart attack, Beth had to deal with the aftermath as much as her mother did, and her dad also had to cope with Beth going away. How did it only come back to her mother? Beth saw the compassion in his eyes and knew she couldn't say anything other than "I know".

He patted her duvet-covered foot. "So how does it feel then, starting off the summer holidays?"

"Odd. Like we've got all these weeks to look forward to without knowing what happens after."

"What happens is you go off to uni and have a wonderful time and your lives really open up."

He'd taken her to most of the open days and told her to go far enough away that she couldn't come home for the night, so she could enjoy the full experience. He'd never gone to university and she could almost feel his regret at that sometimes.

He got up, hands on his knees to give him extra leverage, and stopped at her door. "Just take care, okay? It's a big world out there, Beth, and I want you to explore it."

"Thank you."

After he left, she picked up her book but couldn't focus. She listened to him get dressed for work and he tapped the door as he walked by.

"See you tonight, Sprout."

"You will. Love you, Dad."

"Love you too."

He went downstairs and, as soon as the front door closed, her mother came up. She tapped Beth's door but came straight in.

"Okay, love?"

"I am, are you?"

"Busy day. The ladies rang. Mrs Goodbody had a bump on her bike and can't make the backgammon game so they've asked me to go in."

"That'll be nice. Is Mrs Goodbody okay?"

Her mother nodded absently. "You know what she's like, that big bike and sidecar, she probably whacked someone's door or something. So I need you to do me a favour."

"Of course."

"I need you to pick up Nan's watch."

"Right," Beth said cautiously. Her grandmother lived on the other side of town, a flat in a big old house facing the sea, and wasn't the nicest old lady Beth had ever met. Childhood visits were fractious, her grandmother looking concerned any time Beth moved in case anything got knocked off a shelf or damaged in some other way. She also clearly disliked her dad. By the time Beth hit her teens and could make the choice, she'd cut down on her visits, popping in once a month – always with her mum – as well as the obligatory Christmas. For her part, her grandmother seemed to tolerate her granddaughter rather than enjoy her presence.

Beth's mother folded her arms tight across her chest. "I'm sorry, am I intruding on your plans?"

"Not at all, I was only going to meet the girls for lunch."

"Well that's fine, you can do my little favour first, there's plenty of time to spend with your friends."

How had it come to this, that they could slip so easily into a potential argument? "Did you need me to take anything over for her?"

Her mother frowned. "What do you mean? I need you to pick up her watch from the jewellers."

"Ah." Had she been told about this before and forgotten? "I didn't realise. Shall I take it to her?"

For the first time, her mother smiled genuinely. "Would you?"

No, Beth thought, she really wouldn't want to. "I'd love to," she lied.

Her mother's smile got wider. "Well that's lovely but Nan's gone away with her man friend, so bring it home for now and you can drop it in when she gets back."

Marvellous, Beth thought. "Lovely," she said.

* * *

The sun was hot, heat rising from the pavement as Beth rode away from the house. Fergie, next door's horribly yappy little brown furball of a dog, patrolled his front garden with vigour and looked at Beth, as if to decide whether she was the enemy or not.

"Stupid dog."

He ignored her and went back to his patrols and Beth cycled into the old town.

Market Street was almost empty, looking as if time had left it behind. A few of the shops were boarded up, 'for sale' signs showing their age as they hung over bolted front doors.

Fennell's Jewellers stood proudly amongst them, as it probably had since her grandmother was a little girl. Double-fronted with narrow leaded-pane windows displaying various treasures, its only concession to the seaside trade was a wire pot of cheap handheld foil windmills next to the front door.

A bell over the door tinkled to announce her presence. A short man in a dark suit came through the door behind the main counter, light catching his pate through thinning grey hair. He smiled at Beth and clasped his hands together. "Good morning, miss, how can I help you?"

"I've come to pick this up," she said and handed him the receipt her mother had given her.

"Ah," he said as he read it. "You're surely not Mrs Freeman's daughter."

"No."

"She doesn't seem old enough to have a granddaughter." He chuckled at his own joke and didn't seem phased that Beth didn't laugh in response. "Of course, you look so much like Diana you can understand my mistake."

She didn't look that much like her mum surely?

"Well please remember me to her when you see her, I'm Mr Fennell. We go back a long way, your Nan and I." He smiled again. "Anyway, if you'll just follow me."

He led her to a glass case with a small set of narrow drawers on top. He took a pair of thick-rimmed glasses from his breast pocket and put them on as he smoothed the receipt out on the glass top. The case contained a china cast of a hand with necklaces hanging off the fingers. In a small wicker pot next to it was a pile of colourful friendship bracelets threaded with beads, another small concession to the tourists. They'd make perfect gifts.

"Could I have a look at those friendship bracelets too, please?"

"Oh yes, certainly," he said, his eyes heavily magnified by the lenses.

He unlocked the back of the case and reached over the necklace hand for the basket. He caught one of the fingers, making the necklaces clack together and stopped, as if waiting for everything to fall over. When it didn't, he pulled the hand out first and then the basket, putting them side by side on the counter while he went back to the drawers.

Beth picked out a bracelet with a lot of red thread for Kate and one with a lot of yellow thread for Jenny. Pleased with herself, she looked at the hand and the necklace closest to her moved slightly, catching the light. A simple thin chain, the silver pendant seemed to be formed of letters. She put her hand behind it, to hold it steady so she could read it as 'JR', linked in cursive script. The one behind was the same.

"Are these initials?"

"Not my good lady wife's finest moment," Mr Fennell said carefully. "She bought them at a trade show but didn't think they looked like initials." He picked one of the necklaces up. "It's just a pattern but looks like JR, you see. Now, if it was just the J, you could have any number of Janets being possible purchasers but how many Janet Rogers are likely to come in?" He shook his head.

"Perhaps you'll see a coach tour of Janet Rogers this summer," Beth suggested.

Mr Fennell laughed. "If there is, young lady, I'll get in touch and tell you."

Beth thought of Jenny, the perfect recipient. The necklaces were clearly at the cheaper end of the jewellery on offer, only slightly more than the bracelets. "Actually, I know a JR."

"Then, my dear, you could be my perfect customer."

He slid a watch into his palm from a long, thin brown envelope. After a quick check, he put it into a paper bag which he handed to Beth.

"Mrs Freeman has already paid."

Beth handed him the necklace and the friendship bracelet. "I'll take these too, please."

* * *

Beth put the Fennell's bag into her rucksack as a gull wheeled overhead, turning lazy circles before dropping to grab at an abandoned pasty in the middle of the road.

"Hi, Beth."

With an inward groan, Beth turned around. "Chrissie."

Chrissie Ford, her two sycophants standing just slightly behind her, gave a big fake smile, her eyes wide. "Been shopping?"

Collectively known as The Barbies, with Chrissie their clear leader, they'd ruled the roost during school and Beth, secure with her own friends, had maintained an uneasy alliance with them. She had expected things to change during the sixth form but Chrissie had still led the in-crowd; her BFFs Ali and Toni doing her bidding and boys falling over themselves for this trio of well-dressed, tanned blondies. Except Chrissie absolutely wasn't a natural blonde and never had been.

"Picked something up."

Ali, next to the kerb and chewing gum, perked up. "What's that?"

"A ring?" asked Toni.

"It can't be a ring," said Chrissie.

"It's my Nan's watch," said Beth.

"So not a ring then." Ali giggled.

Chrissie tapped Ali's hand, a joke admonishment. "You're naughty, Ali. Beth might have someone who wants to buy her a ring." Chrissie's smile dropped. "But not Ronnie."

Even though Beth knew the jibe was coming it still felt like Chrissie had driven a knife into her guts and was now debating which way to turn it for maximum pain.

Chrissie cocked her head. "Nothing to say?"

There was plenty to say but Beth didn't want to give any of it a voice. Ronnie had always been a good runner and, when he started racing for the county, achieved a level of celebrity in school that had surprised Beth. As exam pressures and training regimes increased during sixth form, things between them got strained. Words were said that couldn't be retracted and tears were shed. On parting ways, she was gutted at how quickly Chrissie moved in on him even though their partnership – Queen Bee and Star Athlete – made sense. Weirdly though, she became determined to rub Beth's nose in it.

Chrissie folded her arms, clearly looking for some kind of conflict. A moment later, her cohorts mirrored the move. Beth rubbed her temple, knowing the longer she left it, the more frustrated Chrissie would become.

"Nothing to say?" asked Toni, her voice a little high.

Chrissie glanced over, brows furrowed, and Toni looked at the floor.

Beth watched the exchange, silently amazed. How could they still be acting like this?

"Nothing?" Chrissie asked, finally.

"What do you want me to say, Chrissie? Are you squaring up to me?" She wasn't, of course. Chrissie was all talk, enjoying an ability to press everyone's buttons while maintaining a perfect reputation with adults. Sometimes it was good to wind her up.

"Is that what you want?" Chrissie turned to Ali. "Did she just threaten me?"

Beth laughed sourly. "No, you stupid cow, I asked if you were squaring up to me."

Chrissie's mouth was a perfect 'O'. "Stupid cow, eh? Now that's not very nice, is it?"

"Pleased me to say it."

"Well it would, it has that common element."

Beth laughed and shook her head.

"What's so funny?" Chrissie asked, a flash of annoyance crossing her face, as if she'd been caught out somehow and didn't understand it.

"You, this – these idiots."

Ali and Toni raised squeals of indignation but Chrissie silenced them with a wave of her hand.

"We're adults now," Beth said, "you and I are going to university, I don't know what Tweedledum and Tweedledee are doing. You're not at school anymore."

"You think you're so clever, don't you?"

"No, but I'm eighteen and I'm not standing in the street arguing with you like we're twelve."

Clearly on the back foot, Chrissie looked frustrated for a moment. "You're just jealous."

"Of what? You and Ronnie?"

"Yes."

As annoying as it was, Chrissie was right – Beth was jealous, and it did hurt. She'd lost the first boy she'd ever properly loved, the first boy she'd slept with and, worse, lost him to someone who acted like a real bitch about it. Beth felt hot tears gather behind her nose but she couldn't cry – she wouldn't give them the satisfaction. "Oh, Chrissie, grow up."

"Fuck off, Beth, you know it's eating you up inside that we're together and I'm better for him than you could ever be."

"Jesus, Chrissie, what are you getting out of this?"

Chrissie smiled sweetly. "The happiness of knowing I'm in a loving relationship."

"Fuck's sake," Beth muttered and got on her bike. "If that's what makes you tick, you go for it."

Beth rode away, feeling Chrissie's glare burning a hole in her back and tears running down her cheeks.

Chapter 6

The toilets looked tired. Water dripped steadily into a cistern and the room smelled of cleaning fluids strong enough to wrinkle Beth's nose.

She shut herself into the furthest cubicle, thinking of what Richard and John had said about Kate, questioning why she would kill herself. If only Wendy was here, Beth could ask if they'd had any conversations that might shed some light on things.

The outer door opened, letting in a quick burst of conversation, and heels clip-clopped over the floor tiles. A tap squeaked and water ran.

Beth finished, straightened her clothes and opened the door. A young woman in a white blouse and black skirt leaned over a sink, touching under her eyes with a tissue. Beth crossed to the sink nearest the windows. The woman's reflection glanced at her briefly as Beth washed her hands.

"Good turnout," the woman said with a quick smile then went back to dabbing her eyes. "As these things go."

"It is."

"Not a big fan of funerals, myself."

"No, me either." Beth dried her hands then checked her own reflection, her eyes red and puffy, colour high in her cheeks.

The woman straightened her skirt against her thighs. "I thought it was you," she said into the mirror.

Beth glanced at her, unsure she'd heard properly. "Sorry?"

"Beth Kennedy," the woman said. It was a statement not a question.

"That's right, Beth Parker now."

The woman had a soft pretty face and pale blue eyes and something about her looked very familiar. "It's been some time, hasn't it?"

"I'm sorry, do I know you?"

"You did once," the woman said.

Beth looked at her properly and the familiar element swam into focus. "My God, Maggie?"

The woman's eyes brightened. "I didn't know if you'd recognise me or not."

Beth might not have recognised Jenny's little sister but could clearly see enough of the little girl now to spike a memory of those times when Maggie wanted to tag along on whatever adventure they were heading out for. Kate and Beth welcomed her presence, but Jenny always overruled them with a terse "you don't have to spend time with her at home, I never get away."

"Sorry, but it's been a long time." Beth stepped forward, expecting Maggie to open her arms for an embrace but the woman didn't move and Beth stopped awkwardly. "Are you okay?"

"Not really, just been to a funeral." She shook her head. "I'm sorry, I'm all over the place. I'm okay, all things considered, how're you?"

"Feeling similar, I think."

Now Maggie opened her arms and Beth responded, holding Jenny's younger sister tightly for a moment or two.

Letting go, Maggie stepped back and looked Beth up and down. "Where does fifteen years go, eh? So, what've you been doing, any kids yet?"

"Not yet, still planning. You?"

"Two, with a husband who seems to spend his life giving me a headache."

"How old are your kids?"

"Sam's five, we had him early doors, and Izzy is two."

"Lovely ages."

"So what's the wait with you?" Maggie asked. "Are you with someone?"

"I married the man I met at university."

"Isn't your clock ticking?"

Maggie's bluntness surprised her but then, fifteen years had passed and she'd last seen her as an eight-year-old. "It is, but we're working on it. We travelled for a bit after uni then work got on top of me and time just goes, like you said. And what do you do?"

"I help out at Sam's school at dinnertimes and do some reading sessions with the kiddies in nursery. It fills my day." Maggie leaned on the sink, looking at Beth in the mirror. "So why did you come back?"

The question was framed innocently but the words curdled as Beth processed them.

Maggie laughed, as if she'd been misunderstood. "I'm sorry, Beth, that sounded horribly rude. I meant, why did you bother to come back?" The innocence slipped away.

"I'm here for Kate's funeral."

"But you haven't been back since, when, that horrible summer you left?"

Beth felt a flush of shame run through her as she saw Maggie's anger build. "I'm sorry, I wanted to come back for my friend's funeral."

"When did you last see her? Was there a fifteen-year gap with her too?"

The best thing Beth could do was leave, before anything more was said. Maggie was clearly angry and Beth could understand it but now wasn't the time or place. "We stayed friends," she said, cringing inwardly with the realisation that telling the truth would just make her seem worse.

"Odd, Kate told me you lost contact before you left for uni."

Beth bit her lip, unsure of where this was going, annoyance and worry overriding her shame. "You know a lot, Maggie."

"Enough. So did you come back to find out what happened, worried history was repeating?"

Annoyance warmed Beth's veins. "All I know is what's been reported and what Richard told me."

"You asked him?" Maggie said, incredulous.

"Of course I didn't, he told me. It's misadventure."

"Yeah, woman who's just lost her mum, who lost her best friends fifteen years ago, goes over the wall at Julia's Point and it's misadventure."

Beth took a deep breath. "Maggie, I don't want this."

"Who does?" Maggie leaned on the sink. "You got away once, Beth, why come back?"

"To say my goodbyes."

"You did that fifteen years ago." Maggie's head drooped. "You and Kate, you fucked off to university and never gave a second thought to those of us who couldn't leave. Mum and Dad were desperate to, they didn't want to be reminded of Jenny everywhere they went, they didn't want people constantly expressing their sympathy. They wanted to get away for some peace and quiet but couldn't afford it and had to stay here. It ground them both down."

"I wish it could have been different, but it's not like I ran away, we were already going."

"And that makes it right?"

Beth had asked herself the same question time and again. It seemed unfair, even cruel, and the fact she wanted to go away made her cry. It was her dad who pointed out the summer had already taken a dreadful toll so why should she add to the tally? He sat her on the patio and, as the night air grew chillier around them, talked through things calmly and persuaded her to go; making her see it was the right thing to do even if it felt like she was deserting everyone.

"It depends on your point of view," she said.

Maggie smiled sourly. "That's a good way to put it. It worked from your point of view, I suppose?"

"No." The events hung over her like a dark cloud for months, made worse by her father's deteriorating health and the increasingly difficult relationship with her mother. Beth didn't want to tell any of her new friends what was wrong and thus was stuck in a painful bubble of her own making. "You don't know anything about me, Maggie. You don't know how I felt."

"I wanted to, I really did." Now Maggie looked on the verge of tears. "You knew how much I looked up to you, Beth. The three of you together were the coolest people I knew, and you were the only one who properly had any time for me. When you went, it felt like you'd betrayed me."

"But that's not true."

"I was eight and whether it's true or not, it's what I believed." She pressed the tissue against her eyes then examined it. "Shit." She dabbed more gently this time.

Beth stretched her neck, trying to straighten out the kinks she could feel forming. "I don't know what to say."

"I can imagine."

The door opened, letting in a fresh burst of chatter from the foyer, and the woman who came in didn't glance at them as she went into a cubicle.

Beth looked at Maggie and knew there was nothing she could do or say to make the situation right. "I'm sorry you feel like this."

Maggie nodded and Beth left.

* * *

Nick stood by the window on his own, nursing a glass of Coke, and she felt a rush of love for him.

"Hey," he said as she walked over.

She hugged him quickly. "Sorry, I got caught up."

"That's okay," he said and dropped a kiss on her cheek. "How're you holding up?"

"I feel like shit. Can we go?"

"Of course." He put his glass down and, holding her hand, led her through the bar to the door.

"Thank you for coming," said the steward as they passed him.

Chapter 7

Then

Jenny lived on New Street; a narrow road filled with small terraces.

When Beth pressed the bell, someone inside shouted. The latch clicked, a little voice said "Dammit" and then the door opened.

"Hey, Beth." Maggie, Jenny's little sister, was eight and impossibly cute, peering up at Beth through her blonde fringe. Her Disney Princess dress had seen better days and a dozen spangly bracelets rattled on her arm. "You look pretty."

"Thank you, but not as pretty as you."

The little girl seemed to collapse in on herself with embarrassment.

"Maggie?" Jenny called.

"What?" The cuteness disappeared for a moment as she bellowed upstairs.

"Stop hogging Beth, let her come up."

"I'm not hogging her. She's talking to me."

"Beth, come up."

Smiling at the exchange, a usual occurrence when she called for her friend, Beth stepped into the front room. The TV played to a small gathering of dolls, sat around a rug filled with cups and plastic plates.

"Did you want tea?" Maggie asked.

"Maybe later, when I come back down."

"Okay. I didn't want you to take it upstairs anyway, I don't want to make smelly Jen one."

"But maybe she's thirsty."

"Good." Shyly, she took Beth's hand and led her towards the picnic. "Your lips look nice."

"Do you think?"

Maggie nodded. "When I get bigger, I want to look pretty like you."

"Maggie, you already look pretty."

"Oh I know, but I don't want to look like Jenny. You're far better."

Beth laughed and opened her bag. "Here," she said and handed her ChapStick to Maggie, who grabbed it eagerly and looked at it with something approaching awe.

"Wow, thanks. What is it?"

"You put it on your lips, makes them look pretty."

The little girl's eyes widened. "This is your lipstick?"

"Well, it's yours if you want."

"Really?"

"Of course. Enjoy tea with the girls, I'm going upstairs."

"Uh-huh," said Maggie, turning the ChapStick over in her hands. "Okay."

When she heard her name called from the kitchen, Beth poked her head around the dividing wall. Mr Reid sat at the small dinner table, a spread of papers in front of him. "Hi, Beth."

"How are you, Mr Reid?"

"I'd be a lot better if you started calling me Len instead of mister."

Pete, Jenny's baby brother, waved from his highchair, spaghetti sauce all over his T-shirt.

Jenny's mum, Joan, turned to smile. She had dark circles under her eyes. Her ash blonde hair was pulled into a loose ponytail and she had speckles of sauce across her shoulder. "It's good to see you, Beth."

"You too, Joan."

Mr Reid held out his arms in mock indignation. "See?"

"She sees more of me," said Joan, waving her hand at him, "leave her alone."

Len went back to his papers and Joan fed Pete another mouthful without looking. "All set for uni?"

"I think so, everything's sorted and I'm just trying to compress my bedroom to fit into two suitcases."

"Your mum must be getting frantic with the time running away like it is."

"Some days better than others," Beth said, trying to be diplomatic.

"I'll bet. I haven't seen Diana in ages and wouldn't mind a catch-up to compare notes on sending our firstborns away." Pete called for more food, then found some pasta on his tray and fed himself. "Jen's worked hard for this and deserves the chance but I'm not looking forward to her not being about. Though the house'll feel less full, that's a fact." She turned her attention back to Pete. "You'd better go up."

"I'll see you in a bit," Beth said and walked through the lounge, where Maggie was delicately applying ChapStick to her dolls, and up the stairs. Three Babygros were draped across the top banister and a clothes horse full of clothes almost filled the small landing in front of the bathroom. Mr and Mrs Reid's bedroom was at the front of the house and she saw the edge of Pete's cot next to their bed. Beth tapped on the closed back bedroom door and went straight in. Jenny sat on her bed, pulling on socks. Sunlight was streaming through the window and making her glow.

"You escaped Maggie then?"

The bedroom was divided evenly in two, Maggie's stuff on the left. Somehow, Jenny had fitted as much stuff into her side as Beth had in twice the space, the stereo on a rickety shelving system over a narrow desk at the end of her bed, more shelves on the wall filled with books and folders. The remnants of her early teens, posters of bands and handsome actors culled from *Smash Hits*, were conspicuous by their absence, rectangles of unbleached wallpaper their legacy. Posters featuring Disney Princesses crowded over Maggie's bed.

"She's alright."

"You're an only child. When you've slept in the same room as someone ten years younger than you for eight years, then you can comment."

"She's fine with me," Beth said and sat on Maggie's bed.

"Because she loves you."

"She loves you too."

"I know and it's just got worse because she's figured out what it means with me going to university. We had the tears I expected, the declarations of love, but now she's working out what she's going to do with all the extra space she thinks she'll have."

"Will your mum and dad put Pete in here?"

Jenny looked up, face pale. "I bloody hope not. If they get some privacy, I'll probably end up with another sibling. I mean, a decade gap between your first two is bad but excusable. To wait another six years for the next is, well, it's unreasonable is what it is."

They both laughed and it felt nice and easy.

"I have something for you," Beth said and slipped her bag off her shoulder. She took out the necklace, now neatly wrapped, and handed it to Jenny.

"For me? Thank you."

"You don't know what it is yet."

"True." Jenny carefully undid the wrapping paper, smoothed it on her lap and put it on the bed.

Beth wondered if she was going to save it for Christmas then despised herself for thinking it.

Jenny's eyes lit up as she opened the Fennell's bag. She took the necklace out as if it was made of precious stones and laid the pendant in her palm.

"It's lovely," she breathed.

"It's a necklace, Jen, not the Crown Jewels."

Jenny's gaze seemed to bore into Beth with love and affection. "Are you kidding, nobody's ever bought me anything like this before." She touched the curving letters then got up, motioned for Beth to stand and hugged her. "I love it, thank you."

Beth enjoyed the closeness, trying to quash the realisation her opportunities for these hugs lessened with every moment of the summer holiday. "Come on, you weirdo, we have to meet Kate."

"Right, right," said Jenny, "as soon as you put it on me." She gave Beth the necklace and turned around, holding up her ponytail so Beth could attach the slim chain.

* * *

The Jupiter Cafe had been their meeting place of choice for a long time and all three girls loved it. Set on the corner of Andrews Street and Page Road, long windows stretched across both elevations and the handwritten sign over the door had a few stubs of neon attached to it.

Kate sat at their usual table on the far right of the Andrews Street window and waved as they went in. Mrs Jones, tall and broad with a white trilby perched on the back of her head, smiled at them from behind the counter.

"I knew it," she said. "If you get one of the musketeers in here, the other two can't be far behind."

Beth grinned. Mrs Jones was loud, a bit brash and had a cutting sense of humour, but always treated the girls with respect and occasionally slipped an extra Kit Kat onto their tray. Beth liked her.

"Can't do without your cuppas," she said.

"Away with you," Mrs Jones said with a dismissive wave.

Jenny led the way to their table. The ones in the middle of the room were free-standing, the ones by the window were attached to the wall. All had bright red plastic tablecloths, condiment bottles and shakers forming a cluster in the centre of each.

Jenny sat across from Kate, Beth slipping in next to her. Over Kate's shoulder, the lower part of the white-tiled wall was covered with multiple picture frames showing Mrs Jones and various celebrities who'd graced the Seagrave Hippodrome. Beth didn't recognise any of the actors and singers who pointed at the Jupiter sign. Above these were postcards sent from around the world by regulars and newspaper clippings that mentioned the cafe. Amongst them was their picture taken when, aged thirteen, they'd represented the Jupiter Cafe in a pram race. They hadn't won but Mrs Jones gave them a complimentary Coke each for taking part.

"Bitches," Kate said and leaned back as Mrs Jones brought over a tray with three cans of Diet Coke, three tumblers with ice and a heaped plate of chips.

"Ladies," she said as she set it down.

The girls thanked her as one, so she grabbed a chip and walked back to the counter eating it.

"Nice bling," Kate said, "where did you get that from?" She leaned forward on her elbows, touched Jenny's pendant. "Does that say JR?"

"It does, isn't it lovely? Beth just gave it to me."

Kate looked at Beth in surprise. "Very nice."

"It's a gift," Beth said, "for being my best mates."

"I don't think a JR necklace would suit me, somehow."

"Idiot, I got you something else." Beth took Kate's package from her bag and slid it over the table.

"Oh," Kate said, all melodramatic, "you shouldn't have."

She tore into the wrapping paper, effectively shredding it, and Jenny looked on, aghast. Kate spread the friendship bracelet flat on the tabletop.

"It's lovely," she said, smiling widely. After a quick check to see how it tightened, Kate slipped it onto her wrist. "This is lovely and now I feel bad because I didn't get you anything."

"No need, honestly." Beth looked at her friends and felt the warmth.

"Did you nick them?" asked Kate with a squint.

"No."

"Did someone else steal them and offload them to you to get rid of?"

Jenny choked a laugh at that which, of course, simply spurred Kate on.

"Have you given them to us because you knew we'd be impressed with shiny things and not ask questions?"

"Yes."

Kate nodded in appreciation. "Fair enough. Your mum must have bought good crackers last Christmas."

That one surprised a laugh out of Beth. "If you must know, I got them from a respectable jewellers shop not two hundred yards from this cafe."

"You robbed old man Fennell?" Kate asked, eyes wide, her grin giving her away.

"I did."

Jenny shook her head. "You see what happens when we're not there to supervise you. If you do a job like that, you need lookouts."

The jokey comment pulled her up. "I wish you'd been there, I bumped into Chrissie and the Barbies."

"Shit," said Kate, snapping out of joke mode. "What happened?"

"Not much." Beth ate a chip slowly. "She tried to wind me up. I bit a little – we had an argument."

"She's such a bitch," said Kate.

"And anyway," Jenny pointed out, "you let him go."

"You did," said Kate as she put her hand over Beth's.

It wasn't strictly the truth, but it was the story the three of them stuck to.

"You're right," Beth said after a moment. "I did." She took a deep breath. "Didn't mean he could rebound straight into Chrissie-fucking-Ford though, did it?"

Kate laughed. "Nope."

"The bitch," said Jenny and took some more chips. "So, what're our plans for this evening?"

"We could see if they're still working on the Goose Fair," said Beth. She leaned in close to Jenny. "Kate's spotted some talent."

"They've packed up for the night, I already checked," Kate said. "I did see the talent again though and he whistled at me. I spun around to give him a mouthful and he stood there grinning at me, all lean and mean and moody-looking. I swear, I felt my ovaries explode."

"Really?" asked a clearly surprised Jenny. "That good?"

"Oh yes."

* * *

In the end, they called into a pub on Regent's Row. It was filled to capacity with a lively band playing. They drank with friends, danced badly and laughed a lot.

It was almost eleven o'clock when Jenny looked at her watch. "Shit, I've got to go."

"It's not that late," Kate pointed out.

"Early shift tomorrow, in store for eight."

"Bad luck," said Beth.

Jenny shrugged and made a "huh" sound then hugged them. "See you tomorrow, what time are we hitting the fair?"

"Not too early or we'll be over-run by kids."

A promise to meet in the cafe for seven and she was gone.

Kate tapped her glass as Beth realised the noise level had increased. "Did you want another or shall we walk?"

"Let's go."

They walked down to Marine Drive, weaving through the partygoers, tourists and kebab eaters. Out of the clammy pub, the night felt pleasantly cool as they walked towards the pier. A horse and carriage clattered past, the young couple in the back looking deep into each other's eyes.

The Winter Gardens were brightly lit and a few people milled around outside. Sam's Place had closed for the night.

At the end of the pier, the sea lapping at the supports below them, they leaned on the railing and looked out at the horizon where lights on a boat flashed.

"I'm going to miss this," said Kate, "finishing off our night looking out to sea."

"Me too."

"I feel like I have to go though, or this place'll end up suffocating me."

Although the thought of leaving behind everyone and everything she knew terrified her, she knew exactly what Kate meant. "I'm looking forward to all the new faces and places."

"Away from the kids we've gone through school with, the boys we know."

"Absolutely."

"It'll be hard, like starting over."

It felt like Kate had read her mind and that was so reassuring. Beth was ready to spread her wings, even if the thought of letting go of her anchors – friends and family, the Jupiter, Sam's Place, their spot on the beach – frightened her a little.

"I'm going to miss you," Kate said.

"Same here," said Beth as something tugged in her chest. "You and Jen make Seagrave for me."

"But we can visit all the time."

"And we will."

"We're just being silly, aren't we?"

Beth looked out towards the ship on the horizon. "Maybe."

Chapter 8

Beth didn't say anything as they went down the stairs.

The rain had stopped when they got outside, the dark clouds fading. Nick took her hand as they walked to the car. "How are you holding up?"

She shrugged. "I've been better."

"For what it's worth," he said, when she didn't elaborate, "I thought you held up well in there."

"Thank you for coming with me," she said and hugged him. "I'm not sure I could've done it on my own."

He cupped her cheek. "You'd have coped, although I'd have missed a funeral where I had to break up a fight."

"There is that," she said with an awkward smile. "Well, it's all over now."

"It is. So what did you want to do, head for the hotel or go for a walk?"

"I'd like to get some air. I feel like I need to blow some fog away."

"Would you mind if I walked with you?"

"I was hoping you would."

"Do I get a guided tour then?"

She laughed in surprise and it sounded magical. "It's been a long time, I probably won't recognise parts of it," she said but there was an upbeat tone in her voice.

"You'll know more than me."

"We'll leave the car here," she said and, taking his hand, led him towards Carey Street. "This is the Conservative Club alleyway."

"Fascinating."

She tutted. "Dad brought us here for special meals when the Goose Fair was on, it was always a big treat."

"Wait, you live in a seaside town which presumably has a funfair near the beach and you still got a town fair?"

"We did. Are you jealous?"

"Too bloody right I am."

She laughed as they reached the pavement and turned right. "The old town first, I think."

* * *

The few stalls dotted around Market Square looked dreary and tired, a handful of customers milling around them. Only a mobile chippy seemed to be drawing business. A stallholder in front of his mobile phone stand looked up from his own handset as they approached but his expression slipped quickly from hopeful to resigned as they walked by.

"The Market Square," she said, "site of the fabulous Goose Fair."

"Is it something about Seagrave that everything has to be fabulous?"

"So the town council would have you believe."

The southern end of the square was closed off by shops, older buildings ahead and along the road to the right. The shopping centre on the left, a brick-built piece of Brutalist architecture, looked out of place and its lettering was in need of a clean. Three units were visible on the ground floor, one boarded up and Boots occupying the other two. People ate fish and chips from cardboard trays on benches and a small child rode a plastic elephant, clearly enjoying himself although none of the adults nearby paid him attention.

It looked less than pleasant but he couldn't tell her that. "Does it look how you remember?"

Beth turned in a complete circle, taking it all in. "Kind of. The shops are all different though."

"Did the market used to be busier?"

"It's Thursday," she said as if that explained everything, and stopped.

He followed her gaze towards a fruit and veg stall in the corner plot, far too much of its stock left for the time of day. The proprietor, wearing a jumper and bodywarmer, lugged boxes of produce into the back of a panel van.

"That kid on the bike," she said quietly.

To the left of the stall, a teenager on a BMX with the saddle set low leaned against a bench, his attention glued to his mobile phone. He wore a black T-shirt with a shining sun on it and his black hair was styled in a scruffy Mohican.

"What about him?"

"Isn't he the one from outside the Cons Club?"

Nick thought back to the incident, but didn't remember the haircut. "I don't think so but there must be hundreds of kids here who ride bikes."

"But look at the saddle, it's set so low he can barely sit on it."

"Maybe that's trendy."

The teenager looked up, as if he'd heard them – which was surely impossible – glaring at Beth then Nick, before smirking and shifting his attention back to the phone.

"Friendly natives," said Nick.

"Do you think he heard us?"

"I doubt it."

"He glared at us."

"Maybe he's short-sighted and was trying to focus?" It didn't even sound convincing to him.

Beth gave him a sour look. "Really?"

The teenager slipped his phone into a pocket, stood on the pedals and pulled away from the bench quickly enough to do a wheel spin. With a final glance over his shoulder, he disappeared around the corner of the shops at the end of the square. A horn sounded in his wake.

"That was weird," she said.

"It's just a kid, nothing to worry about."

"No," she said, shaking her head as if something was on her mind, "it's…" She bit the inside of her cheek, drifting off in thought.

Nick touched her shoulder, trying to draw her back. She'd done this a lot recently.

"Are you sure you're okay?"

"Yes," she said and kissed him quickly on the lips, "I'm being silly." She pulled a face to make him laugh and succeeded. "That's better."

"So you were going to show me the delights of the old town?"

"Sounds more exciting than it is. It's the part of the town that's been here forever and not just the seaside-y bit at the front."

They crossed the square, the fruit and veg man looking up hopefully as they passed to the street beyond. The buildings were old and grand, their architectural flourishes belying the fact they now housed coffee shops and bookies'. A charity shop with an overflowing tub full of cuddly toys by its front door, occupied a tall narrow building that had apparently once been a cinema.

She led him past old arcades with ornate glass ceilings and shops that got tattier the further they went. Narrow alleys between every second or third building led into gloom.

"Where do these go?"

"Some lead up to other streets, some are for shop access. We used to explore them."

Nick heard a scuffle as they passed one alley and saw what seemed to be two bodies, one on the ground, one leaning over them, fifty yards away from the pavement. It was difficult to make out but was he witnessing a mugging?

"Hey," he called.

The person leaning over the body turned, raising himself on one knee, his broad muscular back and bald head catching some of the poor light. Nick suddenly felt horribly exposed.

The man moved his head and Nick saw a cross scarred deeply in his right cheek.

"Oh my God," Beth gasped and pulled Nick away from the mouth of the alley. "We have to go."

Chapter 9

Then

The Goose Fair almost filled Market Square with its rides, stalls and food stands.

An annual staple, Beth looked forward to it because it was different. She shared the funfair on Marine Drive with the tourists but saw it all year long, not just in its summer finery but in the off-season too, its gaudiness paled by peeling paint and blown bulbs. In town for just a week, that wasn't the case with the Goose Fair.

They met at the Jupiter, Jenny last as usual, all dressed in time-honoured fair outfits – jeans, T-shirts and trainers. Skirts and slip-on shoes were definite no-nos. Tonight, Kate's T-shirt looked a size too small, perfect to highlight her boobs and flat belly, and her shorts showed a lot of thigh. She also wore more make-up than usual, eyes perfectly lined, her lips a startling red.

Beth gave her a wolf-whistle and Jenny did the same and, both times, Kate had the good grace to blush.

"Ready then, bitches?"

"To see the man who blew up your ovaries?" Jenny asked with a smile.

"I'm curious to see this hunk," said Beth, touching Jenny's arm conspiratorially. "What do you think? I'm imagining a humpback, advanced balding and a few missing teeth."

"I went by this afternoon," Kate said as she swatted Beth's arm. "He was on the roof of the Waltzer, wearing just a pair of shorts and when I glanced up at him, we smiled at each other."

"Sexy," said Jenny.

"Did your other ovary explode?" Beth asked.

Kate gave a surprised laugh. "Yeah."

They cut through Victoria Arcade onto Broad Row, the noise of the fair greeting them. Cars filled the kerbs, ignoring the yellow lines to the delight of an industrious traffic warden.

One of the big rides, a flimsy-looking car filled with screaming teenaged girls on a long arm, loomed over the rooftops and Kate grabbed Beth's arm. "Seriously," she said, excitement making her talk quicker, "that's the Orbiter, we have to go on it."

Beth laughingly agreed as they walked onto the packed Market Square. The kids' rides were still going, little ones yelling with delight as they were spun, dropped and churned. The hook-a-duck and hoopla stalls were busy, children clutching inflatable instruments and cuddly toys. Their parents, some carrying extra loot, all looked ready for home. The smell of frying onions and diesel fumes filled the air.

The queue for the Orbiter was huge so they went straight to the Waltzer. A wooden construction, its walls were covered with airbrush art in neon greens, blues and reds; it held court on the western edge of the square as always. Boasting the loudest sound system of the fair, teenagers gathered on its wide wooden staircase and lined the outer edges of the ride, some watching and some posing – especially the girls. The lads who ran the cars paraded around shirtless, wearing love bites like badges of honour. Beth had been drawn into this pheromone frenzy when she was fifteen but was soon put off when she discovered those fairground heartthrobs smelled of sweat and the fair, their tight jeans covered with greasy handprints.

"I think it's louder this year," Beth said.

"Shelley at school said her cousin leaned on a speaker once," Jenny said, "and the vibration got her off really quickly."

"I heard that too," said Kate.

"So what's the plan?" Beth asked her.

Kate walked backwards for a few steps to address her friends. "Talk to him, of course."

"Even with all those people about?"

"We're only talking."

They went up the steps and found a space against the railing. From her position, Beth could see the woman in the control booth. A small child, no older than Pete, sat on the counter beside her in just a nappy, playing with a rattle.

A group of lads appeared from nowhere as the ride began, moving between cars like a pack of sharks who have sensed blood in the water. They rode the movement with ease as flashing lights on the ceiling painted their slick torsos in a wash of colour. Cars were clearly targeted, ignoring older riders and other lads, homing in on the teenaged girls where one quick spin produced enough screams to draw more punters.

"There," Kate shouted over the music and pointed at a car containing three teenaged girls.

The lad in question couldn't possibly have heard her but looked up all the same, locking eyes with Kate.

Beth didn't read many romance novels, mainly because the boy-meets-girl sequences often made her laugh but this one ticked every cliché in the book and was all the more astounding because of that. Something passed between Kate and him that was so obvious to be almost tangible.

Tall and lean, with thick black hair, a long face with a tight little mouth and dark eyes, he moved sinuously as he spun the car.

"Wow," said Jenny.

Beth's ovaries remained unexploded. He wasn't a knockout but carried himself confidently, like he knew how good he looked to others.

The ride carried him past them and out of sight behind the control booth. Kate grabbed Beth's arm, put her face close to Beth's ear. "What do you think?"

"Hot," said Beth.

"Isn't he?"

The next lap, he watched Kate the entire way, their gazes locked. Out of sight and Kate squealed with excitement. Back into view and this time, as he passed, he dropped her a wink. The girls in the car shouted something and it was like he suddenly remembered they were there. He span the car until their screams disappeared around the control booth.

"Stay there," he mouthed as he went past the next time.

Kate nodded, then looked at her friends. Beth stuck up her thumb.

The ride ended and as the punters got out, Kate's lad crossed the floor.

"Hey," he said as he pulled up the safety bar of the car nearest to them.

One of the teenaged girls in it held out her arm and he pulled her to her feet in one easy motion. She looked at him, eyes wide but he didn't pay her any more attention.

"Hey," said Kate. She was shouting but her voice sounded tiny.

"I've seen you around, who are you?"

"Kate. You?"

The woman in the control booth started pitching for new riders and as they came to the cars, Kate's man held up his finger then moved off to check safety bars and collect fares.

"What did that mean?" Jenny asked with a frown and held up her own finger.

"Wait here?" suggested Beth.

The ride went again, the lad paying attention to spinning his young female riders into happy screams but staring at Kate each time he passed.

At the next change, he walked around the outer rim and stopped in front of her, offering a quick smile to Beth and Jenny. "Hey, Kate," he said, his teeth small and very white, "I'm Blake."

"Hi."

"I get off at ten and I'm meeting up with friends, why don't you stick around?"

"Really? Yeah, sure."

He went back to his job with a smile and Kate watched him go with a dreamy expression. Beth, worrying her hearing was fading with each new song, pulled her out of the ride, Jenny pushing them both from behind. When they got to the bottom of the steps, Beth's ears were whistling.

"Fuck," said Kate, her voice too loud. A women pushing a baby buggy turned to glare. "Did you see him?"

"Uh-huh," said Beth. "I assume we're hanging around until ten?"

* * *

They filled the time easily.

Beth and Kate went on the Orbiter, Kate treated them all to hot dogs – "but no onions, just in case" – and Jenny won a jewellery set on a hook-a-duck stall for Maggie, hoping it might topple Beth's current standing as best person in the world after the ChapStick handover.

Sitting on a bench drinking Slush Puppies, they watched the Waltzer close. As the last riders were shooed away, a huge man worked his way around the cars, draping canvas covers over them.

A young woman, in cut-offs and a white vest, her dark hair loose, crossed the square to sit on the steps, eating candyfloss. The lads spoke to her good-naturedly as they left. The woman from the control booth, carrying her now sleeping child, came down the steps followed by the huge man and Blake. He stole some candyfloss from the young woman and, even though she complained loudly, Beth could tell she didn't mind.

Kate waved to catch Blake's attention and he crossed the square to them with the huge man. The young woman and a teenager followed them.

"You waited," Blake said, as if he'd known she would.

"Uh-huh." Kate tried to play it cool but her voice was squeaky with nerves.

"You didn't tell me who your mates were," Blake said. Away from the noise of the ride, he had a surprisingly soft voice.

As Kate introduced them, Blake nodded then tilted his head towards the young woman. "This is Wendy."

"Wotcha," Wendy said with a wide smile that split her thin face. She had dark eyes and her lipstick had smudged against her teeth.

"The kid behind her is Mouse."

Mouse looked about fifteen. He was pencil-thin with a thick mop of curly hair. He smiled shyly and looked at his feet.

Blake jerked his thumb over his shoulder. "And this is Frankie."

The huge man, who must have been at least six foot five, looked even more imposing close up and younger too, perhaps in his early twenties. Broad-shouldered, his head was shaved and a homemade tattoo of a cross linked his eyebrows.

"We're going to The Candlestick for a swift one," Blake said. "Fancy coming?" He looked at Kate like he wanted to ravish her. "I assume you're all old enough?"

"We're all eighteen," said Kate and shifted her position slightly; head back, tits out.

"That's good to know," Blake said with a smile.

* * *

70

The Candlestick was a small pub Beth had never noticed before on the edge of the docks. Its sign was so battered by the elements it looked little more than a metal sheet. Snug inside, with a low ceiling and dark wood furniture, the bar staff looked bored and the drinkers, mostly male with capillary flowers on their cheeks, looked up furtively when Frankie went through the door. The place smelled of sour beer, sweat and old cigarette smoke.

Beth followed him, anxious about the venue, unable to shake the sensation she was diving into something without knowing where she'd land.

Frankie gestured to a table by the window and they sat on the uncomfortable stools as he went to the bar. He came back a few minutes later with four pint glasses, plonked one down in front of each girl then went back.

"Not much choice," said Wendy, sitting so close to Beth their knees touched. "They think you're a twat if you ask for wine."

Frankie came back with three pints, handed Mouse and Blake theirs, then sat heavily on a stool. He looked at Beth, his gaze drilling into her and she felt her anxiety spike, pulling her scalp tight. Her throat felt constricted. He looked to Jenny, then Kate. "So, you girls live in town?"

"Uh-huh," said Kate.

"Told you I recognised them from school," said Wendy. She looked at Kate. "I was the year above you."

"I thought I recognised you," said Kate.

"Really?" Wendy said sarcastically. "I don't remember you ever talking to me."

Something uncomfortable settled over the table and Beth fought the urge to leave.

"Maybe she didn't see you," said Blake, "not everyone does."

Wendy looked at her drink, pouting as she traced condensation with her finger. She didn't say anything.

"Locals then?" Blake asked.

"Born and bred," said Jenny.

"Still at school?"

"Nope," said Kate, "just finished. Off to uni at the end of the summer."

Blake leaned in towards her and whispered something that made her smile. Frankie, on Kate's right side, looked into the pub as if the conversation at the other tables was more interesting to him.

Wendy leaned in close. "So are you working now, before you go?"

"I work in Ed's Bakery," Beth said.

Wendy seemed surprised. "You're a baker?"

"No, I work behind the counter. Started as a Saturday job."

"Oh." Wendy nodded, apparently disappointed. "Of course."

"What about you?"

"Me?" Wendy seemed surprised to be asked. "I'm a waitress at the Holimarine camp. It's a decent job and pays well; plus some of the holidaymakers tip. The boys crack onto me too and that's nice, boosts my confidence even if I never see them again after their week or fortnight."

"Been doing it long?"

"Since before I left school but yeah, full-time waitress in the summer and cleaner during the off-season."

"How about you?" Mouse asked Jenny. His voice was deep and soft and nervous, as if worried they'd shout at him for asking.

"I work in the Scott's on Yarmouth Road."

"My mum goes in there sometimes," he said with a smile.

"That's nice." Jenny glanced at Beth. "So is Mouse your nickname?"

He chuckled. "No, but you'd be amazed how many people ask me that"

"So what do you do?"

"This and that, to help people out." He smiled again, clearly not going to elaborate.

Blake leaned back, arms behind Kate and Frankie. "So you girls got anything planned for summer?"

Kate, who looked thrilled at his proximity, shook her head. "Not yet."

"Do you like the fair?" Frankie asked, his voice low and rumbling.

"It's okay," said Kate.

Beth nodded her agreement, wanting to join in with the conversation but increasingly uncomfortable with Frankie's presence.

Jenny leaned in close, tapped her arm. "I've seen him before," she whispered.

"Seen who?" Beth whispered back.

"Frankie. I'm not sure about any of this, Beth."

"What do you do?" Kate asked Frankie.

"I do bits and pieces too," he said and looked at Jenny, as if trying to work something out. "Mostly security work for Mr Cowley and that keeps us going through most of the year."

Working for Mr Cowley, the man behind the rebranding of the pier, the one her dad said had some shady connections around town? Beth felt her anxiety notch up enough she thought her scalp would tear under the pressure. What had they got themselves into?

"What about you?" Kate asked Blake.

"Nelson comes in when I need him to," Frankie replied.

"Nelson?" asked Kate.

Beth felt Wendy's leg stiffen against hers.

Blake smiled but it never touched his eyes. "My first name's Nelson," he said slowly, the chill in his voice reminding Beth of the electronic tones on people's answerphones, "but I prefer to be called Blake."

"No problem," Kate said, obviously sensing the charge in the air.

"There's never a problem when we're around," said Frankie and looked at his watch. "We need to get a shift on." He drained his pint and Blake did the same.

"Gotta go, ladies," Frankie said. "Make sure we see you down the fair."

The four of them left, scraping chairs and saying goodbyes.

"Well?" Kate asked expectantly, when they'd gone. "What did you think?"

"I think Frankie is one of the scariest blokes I've ever met," said Beth.

Kate waved away her concern. "Don't worry about him."

"He works for Hugh Cowley," Beth pointed out.

"So do lots of people."

"They evicted one of my neighbours," Jenny said. "It was horrible, her kids were crying and she was screaming at the bailiffs as they dumped her stuff in the street. One of them was Frankie."

"Are you sure?" Beth asked.

"It'd be hard to mistake him for someone else, wouldn't it?"

Chapter 10

"Nick!" Beth's heart raced, adrenaline pumping as she pulled him back to the kerb. "Leave it!"

"What do you mean? We need to help."

Her chest felt tight as she stood in front of him, blocking his way to the alley. "It could be anything and wading into a mugging or a drugs deal is very different to stopping a fight at a funeral."

"But we don't…"

"No, we don't." She put her hand on his chest, a loving gesture as much as a control. Stepping away, her adrenaline faded but seeing Frankie there in the gloom kept her focussed, the memories sparking as tangled and sharp as barbed wire.

"What's wrong? You're as white as a sheet."

"Just startled." She couldn't tell him the truth and, instead, took his hand and led them back along Broad Row.

"Beth? Are you sure you're okay?"

"Uh-huh, bit unsettled that's all." Except unsettled didn't even begin to cover how she felt.

"You and me both."

Turning into Regent's Row, she saw with a surge of relief two PCSOs a hundred or so yards down the hill, chatting to themselves as they watched an old man in front of the shopping centre conduct a puppet show from a suitcase.

"There," she said, "we'll tell them and they can check it out."

The female PCSO looked up and smiled as Beth approached. "Afternoon, love, can I help?"

"On Broad Row," she said, "one of the access alleys. There were two men, one on the ground, the other leaning over him."

Alert, the PCSO looked up the hill. "Which alley?"

"Between a second-hand bookshop and a nail bar."

"We'll take a look," the woman said and tapped her partner's arm. "Thanks for letting us know."

"Feel better?" Beth asked as she watched the PCSOs walk up towards Broad Row.

"A bit. I mean, I'm glad we got the police involved. I just hope the bloke's okay."

"They'll sort it." She looked down the hill towards the seafront. "So after that, did you still want the tour?"

"Of fabulous Seagrave? Of course."

She laughed, happy to be moving away from that man in the alley.

Could it really have been Frankie, whose commanding presence had so terrified eighteen-year-old her during that summer? Apart from the fact he was broader and had heavy scarring on his cheek, it clearly looked like him. Was it likely he'd come home too? He was convicted and sent down after she left for university, partly thanks to her testimony, and she'd worked hard to lock away her memories of him, pushing them back into the darkness where they lingered like a warning but didn't impact on her nightmares. Now, she could feel that work unravelling, his compartment in her head creaking open like a cupboard door.

Would he carry a grudge? She couldn't take the risk of finding out and couldn't discuss it with Nick because he was just another one of those things from that summer she'd kept secret. Regret jabbed at her chest as the same phrase rattled through her mind –marriage is based on trust and secrecy is its enemy. Her secret, her guilty secret, was like a cancer, insidiously working its way into every nook and cranny of her life, waiting to be exposed by the first careless word.

Picturing how hurt he'd look made her feel giddy, her heart racing again, but she had to warn him too. "You know that big man in the alley?" she asked, before her courage faded. "If we see him again, keep well away."

"You know him?"

"Not really." The lie left a sour taste as it tripped so easily off her tongue. "I think his name's Frankie. He was bad news."

"I hadn't planned to try and make friends."

"I know, love, but this place thrives on tourism and some people learn tricks to make life easier."

"You're saying Scarface Frankie from the alley might hustle me?" he asked wryly.

"I'm being serious."

"I'm not mocking you." He stopped and touched her cheek gently. "I understand."

"The seaside isn't all sweetness and light; it can be as rough as any city."

He kissed her. "If I see him again, I'll walk the other way."

"Thank you."

"You're really worried, aren't you?"

"For you, yes. I know nothing's going to happen, but I grew up here."

"You've been hardened by seaside life?"

She forced a laugh. "Something like that." He was so close to the truth it pained her. "Come on, let me show you the delights."

Regent's Row linked the old town to Marine Drive, a tourist trap thoroughfare with every delight and piece of tat the seaside had to offer. The waxworks, however, had finally closed down, paint peeling from windows and walls alike as if the building was shedding its skin.

They walked, holding hands. Small children charged around, parents struggling to keep up while teenagers lounged on benches, laughing and smoking. The shops were filled with cheap toys and clothes, trendy knock-off bags and perfumes and more mobile phone skins and cases than seemed feasible.

"I like it," he said.

"Seriously?"

"Of course, it's so tacky. No" – he held up his finger – "it's fabulously tacky."

"I see what you did there but I'm not sure that's what they were aiming for."

"Are you sure?"

The lower third of Regent's Row had barely changed. St Mary's Church stood proud on the southern side of the street; its small graveyard as immaculately kept as ever though Beth noted with sadness the mesh covering on the stained-glass windows. The clothes shop that sold jumpers with wolves on and other items she'd never seen a local wear sat across from it, keeping a watchful vigil.

They passed the Chinese, now a takeaway, and the Greek place her dad had liked, its menu still barely legible. Back then, the owners only replaced it when the sun had bleached the words away to a plain sheet of paper.

"Anywhere you'd recommend?"

"It's been too long." She didn't want to go into the Greek, knowing the blast of nostalgia would be too much. "There'll be plenty of places along the front, or we could eat in the hotel."

"I could go for some fish and chips, they always taste better at the seaside."

The Sunshine Pub that wrapped around the corner onto Marine Drive had gone, replaced by The Neon Tiger, a gentleman's club decked out in purple and black. Hugh Cowley, it appeared, had won his battle.

"Cool arcade," he said, pointing across the road at The Golden Nugget.

"Always used to be." Facing up Regent's Row and built, her dad had said, when the old pier collapsed, it had seen better days. Two of the three windmills above the huge sign weren't working and the upper floor had been converted to holiday flats.

He pointed at the coffee shop across from The Neon Tiger. "How about a coffee?"

"Good idea." The sky was clearing, dark clouds heading out towards the horizon. "Shall we sit outside?"

"You grab us a seat, I'll get the drinks."

Beth found a table under the awning and sat facing The Golden Nugget. Two teenagers on skateboards came down Regent's Row, weaving around the holidaymakers without breaking their conversation. Two little kids on the next table watched them go, ice-cream running over their fingers.

The kid she'd seen on Market Square rode into view on his BMX, Mohican waving in a light breeze. He freewheeled along the centre line, sitting on the too-low saddle with his knees almost to his chest, his attention divided between his mobile and the pavements, as if he was looking for someone. She knew it was paranoia, but what if that someone was her?

Passing the coffee shop, he glanced at the array of tables and she slipped down in her chair to hide behind the other patrons. He looked frustrated.

At the junction, he stopped in the middle of the road and a car pulled up behind him as he watched the arcade. The car horn sounded and, without looking behind him, the kid raised his hand and gave a one-finger salute. The driver shouted something and pulled around the bike, driving away at speed.

Beth leaned across, trying to keep out of sight but curious as to what he was looking for. Something felt off but she couldn't pin it down. Unless, of course, it was just paranoia, her mind reacting to being back in Seagrave after so long; a delayed shock from the funeral of her old friend?

The kid listened to his phone without speaking then put it in a pocket. He had a last look around – she sank further in the chair and he looked straight past her – then stood on the pedals and rode onto Marine Drive. As he passed The Golden Nugget she noticed a girl walking into the arcade, tall and slim, her blonde hair pulled back into a ponytail. Just like the person she'd seen in the trees at the cemetery.

Just like Jenny.

Except it couldn't be.

* * *

Nick brought the coffees out and sat with his back to Marine Drive.

"I'm sorry about today," he said.

"Why?"

"Booking the hotel, making you stay in fabulous Seagrave – it's not been my best decision."

"You didn't make a bad decision, Nick, it's just this has been emotional in ways I hadn't expected." In ways I couldn't tell you about, she thought. "The fight surprised me and so did seeing how old Richard looked. Then meeting Maggie in the bathroom, those lads on the bikes and the girl with the ponytail…"

"Eh?"

"The kid on the BMX we saw on the square rode past and seemed to be looking for someone. I know it sounds paranoid, but I think him and the kid who made the guns sign are linked. I think he was following us."

"Why would he do that?" he asked, with no sign of mocking in his voice. If she'd heard her story, she'd have laughed at the paranoia.

"I don't know."

"And who's the girl with the ponytail?"

"The one from the woods by the cemetery. I saw her outside The Golden Nugget and she…" She paused, thinking of her phrasing. "She looked familiar."

"How?"

"I don't know, and I know this makes me sound mad but when I figure it out, I promise I'll tell you."

"I trust you," he said and laid his hand over hers, "you know I do."

That didn't make her feel better.

"And what about the thing with Maggie? Who's she?"

"Jenny's sister. I saw her in the toilet at the wake and she wasn't happy to see me. Which hurt, because Jenny was a friend of mine."

Chapter 11

Then

"At the fair again tonight?" her father asked as she sat on the kitchen floor, lacing up her blue Converse.

"Uh-huh, did you want me to win you anything on the shooting gallery?"

Her father laughed and put his cup of tea down. "No, Sprout, you're alright."

"Who are you meeting up with?" her mother asked.

"The girls. Why?"

"No reason. Just be careful."

"Of course she'll be careful, Di."

"I know, Gordon," her mother said irritably, "but it's the Goose Fair."

"Which we both went to for years as kids," said her father patiently. It seemed to Beth he had to speak patiently to her mother a lot about her these days. "We both survived."

"It seems rougher this year."

"You've been?" Beth asked, unable to stop the sarcasm leaching through her words.

"Di, we've taught Beth about stranger danger from the moment she went to school, she and her friends are sensible."

Her mother looked away. "I'm only worried for her. I would hope you could see that, Gordon. You too, Beth."

Her father gestured for Beth to go as he put his arm around her mother's shoulders. "We know, Di, we know."

"See you later," said Beth as she opened the back door.

"Take care," her mother said.

* * *

That week, when Beth and Jenny weren't working, the three met at the beach to top up their tans. In the evenings, they loitered around the Waltzer, chatting with Blake and Mouse on their breaks. Frankie drifted in and out, saying little, which pleased Beth because whatever made her feel uncomfortable about him – his intimidating air, size, the tattoo or his demeanour – didn't dissipate as the week went on.

Blake, on the other hand, was full of charm and although a lot of female riders paid him attention, he only seemed to have eyes for Kate.

One lunchtime, Kate called into Ed's Bakery and she and Beth ate BLTs together, sitting on the wall out the back.

"There's something about him," Kate said, staring intently at Beth as if wanting to make sure her friend understood the sincerity of her words. "The way he looks at me makes my stomach fizz."

"He does seem very interested in you. If he made your ovaries explode, you obviously had a serious effect on his bollocks."

Kate raised her eyebrows. "Oh, I'd like that to happen."

"Ew," said Beth mockingly and held her baguette at arm's length, "I'm eating."

Kate laughed. "You don't think he's got a thing for Wendy, do you?"

"No, but I think Wendy's got a thing for him."

"Oh definitely. What about you?"

"Wendy's not my type."

Kate tapped her arm. "I didn't mean that and you know it."

Beth bit into her baguette and chewed it carefully. "No, Kate, my oldest and loveliest friend, I don't have a thing for Blake. I mean, no offence but…"

"None taken," Kate said, too quickly. "I mean, it'd be bad to fall out over a boy."

* * *

Beth got home from work and walked down to the patio to say hi to her mum. She wasn't there, though a lounger had been set up and a mug of tea sat on the glass-topped table. Beth went into the kitchen and put the bag of rolls Ed had given her into the bread bin.

She frowned, unable to hear humming or singing, both of which her mother did when she was cleaning or pottering about – though it was unlikely she would leave the house without locking up.

No matter. Beth slipped off her Converse and padded upstairs barefoot. She checked her parents' room which she found empty then went into her own.

"Hello, Beth."

She shrieked, lurching back against the wall, heart thudding, pulse points glowing red hot.

Her mother sat on Beth's bed; right leg crossed over her left knee, hands folded primly in her lap. "Sorry, did I startle you?"

Beth took a moment to gather her breath. "Yes, I thought you'd gone out. Is everything okay?" A horrible thought struck her. "Is Dad okay?"

"He's fine," her mother said and nodded. "He just had a bit of heartburn after that curry last night, like I warned him he would." She rolled her eyes. "One day he'll listen to me and live longer."

"So what's up?"

"Clare McPherson saw you yesterday."

"That's nice." This wasn't necessarily a bad thing, though Beth didn't recall seeing Clare. "I didn't see her."

"She didn't think you had."

Beth waited. Her mother obviously had something on her mind and, since her father's heart attack, Beth knew it wasn't best to rush her because that often resulted in raised voices. Recently, Beth often felt she was walking on eggshells and wasn't sure if her mother felt the same way.

"She said you were with the girls and some others."

"Right." Realisation dawned, the heartburn fizzing. "I told you I was going to the fair."

Her mother nodded slowly. "You didn't say you'd be hanging around with fair types – three older men and a scrawny woman."

The heartburn fizzed across her chest and burned her throat. "Wendy's not scrawny, but it was nice of Clare to tell you. Did she also say she saw me last week when I signed her stupid petition?"

"Don't be clever." Her mother uncrossed her legs and sat on the edge of the bed.

"I'm not…"

"Do they work on the fair?"

"The lads do." It sounded worse than it was. "Wendy doesn't," she added, desperately.

"What ride?"

"What's that got to do with anything?"

"Just tell me."

"The Waltzer."

Her mother all but threw her hands in the air in disgust. "Seriously? Come on, Beth, the Waltzer was bad news even when I was a teenager."

What could she say? "I'm not sure what bad news you're thinking of, Mum."

"Really?" Her mother looked like she was about to have a fit. "You know all about blokes who work on the fair, especially the Waltzer."

"Seriously, Mum?" She'd long ago had the lecture on sex. "I'm eighteen not fourteen."

"I know exactly how old you are, Beth."

"So are you telling me off for being friends with them or warning me off for the future?"

"I'm trying to make you understand."

"To make me understand I could make a mistake and not get to university?"

Her mother's stony expression told her she'd hit the nail on the head. Beth groaned and leaned back, her head against the wall.

"You can act up all you like but it's the truth. Look at me."

"You didn't get into trouble with any lads from the fair."

"No, but I had plans, I was going to go off and do things."

"But you met Dad."

"And we fell in love, got together and stayed here."

This was new territory for them and the ground seemed to shift under Beth's feet. "Are you saying that's not what you wanted?"

"Of course I'm not," her mother said quickly, "I've got no complaints about my life but I do sometimes have regrets over what could have been."

"Your regrets or Nan's?" Beth didn't like the direction they were going in.

Her mother watched her hands twist in her lap. "My mother didn't like him at the time."

"She's still not keen."

"That's not true, they just have a difficult relationship." Her mother looked hurt and cleared her throat. "She had this talk with me, told me not to get tied down and live my life. I was winning beauty contests then, I started to do a bit of modelling here and there."

"And I stopped that?"

Her mother bristled, eyes shiny with tears. "You always twist things to make me the villain, don't you? I'm telling you to be careful and you're throwing it back in my face."

"Mum, I…"

Her mother held out her hand. "No, Beth. The lads on the fair have their pick of the girls, it's always been the way. When I was at school, some of them would leave in the fifth form and you'd see them some months later pushing a buggy, a single mum before she's even come of age. I don't want that for you."

Beth took a deep breath, trying to calm herself. "I don't want that either, but I don't fancy any of them. Nobody's going to stop me from going to university. You weren't worried like this when I was seeing Ronnie."

"Because he had ambition, he wanted to do things and he wouldn't have got you in trouble."

Beth bit her lip to stop herself inadvertently blurting out details of her sex life, which she didn't want to tell her mother and, doubtless, she didn't want to hear. "No," she said finally, "he wouldn't."

Her mother got up and smoothed her skirt over her thighs. "I'm glad we had this talk," she said quietly.

"Yes," said Beth, the heartburn in her throat fizzing into anger at how typical of her mother this was. She'd overridden everything Beth said, content her daughter had listened to everything she was told. The unfairness of it all rankled, made worse because it wasn't even as if Beth had ever done anything in the past that would make her untrustworthy.

"So are you seeing the girls tonight?"

"Yes, then meeting the others at the fair but don't worry, I'll make sure to keep my distance from the lads."

Her mother shook her head, frustrated now rather than sad. "I'm doing my best to look out for you."

"I know, but maybe you should trust me a little more."

"Maybe you should give me the opportunity," said her mother and went downstairs.

Chapter 12

"Here's some history for you," Beth said. They were walking back to the Conservative Club, talking about everything and nothing, and passed the mouth of a narrow alley. She pointed into it. "Back in the day, we used this as a cut-through from Market Square. If you were on a bike, you could really get some speed up."

"There's not much space to stop."

The alley extended back the length of the house that formed its outer wall before turning at a sharp angle. "Stopping wasn't the idea, high speed was."

He looked at the road. "Did you ever do it?"

"Of course."

"So what happened if a car was coming?"

"Never happened to me, but I did see a couple of near misses."

"With the driver and cyclist both shitting themselves, I assume?"

"Before the shouting started, yes. We were a health and safety nightmare."

"Most of us were, at times. Do you miss the place at all?"

"Not really." She hadn't at first, while the violence and terror was still fresh in her mind, but did later, remembering the good times. And there were a lot of good times. "I was homesick for a while."

"You were."

"It was before we were going out."

"I knew of you before we went out."

"And you paid that much attention?"

He nodded, looking bashful. "Of course, I fancied you long before I asked you out."

She smiled, held his hand and shook it playfully. "That was so long ago."

"Doesn't feel that way to me. But if you were that homesick, why not come back, even for a quick visit?"

He wasn't fishing but she still couldn't answer him without revealing everything. "Because my best friend went to university and Mum and Dad moved, so there was no one here."

"Your best friend being Kate?"

"Of course."

"But what about Jenny? Where did she go?"

Like a dagger to the heart. She kept walking, hoping the silence would answer him but knowing, of course, that it wouldn't.

"Am I stepping on toes here?" he asked, clearly reading the pause.

"Kind of."

"I'm sorry, I'm just interested."

"I know, love."

"How about Diana and Gordon? Did they grow up here?"

"He did, she lived on the other side of Radnor. They met at a dance and, according to him, fell instantly in love. When I was little, he told me the story in such a way it was almost a fairy tale and I loved it. Mum's version was much more basic."

"So you didn't want to come back because…" He paused, as if trying to think of the right word. "Did you think there'd be ghosts here?"

She thought of the girl with the ponytail. "It crossed my mind."

"And have you seen any?"

"No," she lied.

"Well I'm pleased about that."

* * *

As Nick drove along Marine Drive, she saw the tip of the Winter Gardens, patchy sunlight reflecting off glass, and felt anxiety press on her chest. This was what she'd dreaded, seeing the Empire Pier and Winter Gardens again, the focal points for the brutality that marred that summer.

Heart racing, blood rushing in her ears, her terror became a physical thing. She'd had a few panic attacks about the pier the first couple of weeks she was at uni, frightening enough in their extremes to make her see the campus doctor. He gave her pills, said it was stress and homesickness and would pass. She knew he didn't have a clue but took the tablets anyway and the light-headedness and chest pains did ease off over the following fortnight.

And now she was less than half a mile from the pier. She'd avoided it for fifteen years, done her best to erase it from her mind and thought she'd succeeded but evidently not. If anywhere in this town held ghosts, it was the Empire Pier.

"So," he asked, "has it changed much?"

"A bit."

Seagrave had boomed in the Victorian era and most of the buildings at this end of Marine Drive reflected the grandeur of that time. They passed three-storey terraces, most of them now hotels and B&Bs, with grand bay windows and ornate porches, the ground floors converted to restaurants. Vacancy signs were tucked into the windows, the lounges and dining rooms protected from view by net curtains. People milled along the wide pavement, young families checking the menus, older people walking along content to take the sea air.

Everything seemed the same but also slightly off somehow, like seeing an old friend after too long who'd lost a lot of weight – you knew it was them, but the image didn't quite resonate in your mind.

Beth looked out towards the sea. Even with the sun struggling to break through the cloud cover people had set up deckchairs on the beach and a few hardy souls, most of them children, braved the water.

They passed a horse and cart clip-clopping along in the lane it shared with a land train as the terraces gave way to the Empire Theatre, a cinema that was on its last legs when Beth left. Now shuttered, its heavy ornate doors were plastered with coming attractions posters for the nearby Hippodrome.

The architecture became less grand, sixties-era buildings on both sides of the road with shops and cafes on the ground floor and holiday flats upstairs. The Winter Gardens loomed closer, her anxiety growing.

"Turn right here," she said when they reached a roundabout by the ill-named Excelsior hotel.

Nick did and she directed him along the residential streets that ran parallel to Marine Drive until they reached Oceanview and he turned into it.

Halfway down, the Spar shop that had marked the start of the madness was gone now, replaced by an artisan coffee house.

Ahead, the Oceanview Hotel took up the entire block, hiding the Empire Pier, Sam's Place and most of the Winter Gardens from view. Even though they were coming into the back entrance, it looked as grand to her now as it ever had.

Nick drove into the cobbled car park, the spaces built into the old stables that enclosed most of the back of the building.

"And here we are," he said, "the grandest hotel in all of Seagrave."

She forced a smile to match his, her throat dry, the light-headedness coming back. He leaned over and kissed her softly.

"It is the best hotel," she said.

"You've been here before?"

"Only once, when Dad won a long-service award from work."

He got out, retrieved their case from the boot and they crossed the car park together, Beth being careful on the cobbles with her heels. As they walked down towards Marine Drive, Beth watched her feet to avoid seeing what she was scared of.

At the corner, she looked across the front of the hotel. Dating back to 1841, it had originally been a terrace of houses, four storeys with attics and bay windows, railings and all manner of flourishes.

"Wow," Nick said, "this looks even better than it did online."

They went up four marble steps to the entrance; 'Oceanview' was written in raised letters across the front of the portico. The double doors in the porch were propped open.

The foyer had an air of elegance, with thick carpets, heavy wallpaper and a large chandelier whose jewels glowed. Several chairs, tucked into niches, looked heavy but comfortable. On the end wall were two doors and a wide staircase which led up to the first floor.

The reception area was to the left, with two low leather couches either side of a granite-topped coffee table complete with a spray of upmarket magazines. The desk, apparently made up from dozens of suitcases, had a large sun design clock behind it and a door marked private set off to the right. The three monitors Beth could see were unmanned.

Soft music played, unobtrusive and soothing. An unseen door shushed open.

"Hello, Beth."

Chapter 13

The woman's hair was tied into a neat ponytail, the make-up on her thin face too thickly applied. She had a smudge under her right eye, as if she'd rubbed it too soon after putting on eyeliner.

Beth recognised her immediately and it felt as if the last fifteen years had just been swept away. "Wendy?"

Wendy smiled and pulled Beth into a brief hug. Beth had time to register her hair smelled of jasmine before Wendy let her go.

"It's so good to see you," Wendy said.

"And you."

Wendy wore a brown skirt and blouse, an Oceanview name badge pinned on the left breast of her gold waistcoat. "It's been too long."

"It has." It felt unreal, seeing her now, older but still clearly the woman she'd met that summer. "I looked for you at the service and the wake."

Wendy spread her hands. "I wanted to go but got called in here at the last minute, as there wasn't anyone else to cover." She smiled but it missed her eyes and Beth found her attention drawn back to that smudge. "So how did it go?"

"As well as it could."

"How were John and her dad?"

"Cut up, as you'd expect. I mean, thirty-three is no age, is it?"

"But if she was feeling down…" Wendy paused, as if considering whether to say more. "Sometimes things aren't as simple as they seem."

They looked at one another for a moment that stretched uncomfortably before Wendy rubbed her hands together briskly. "So, I assume you want to check in? Is this your husband?"

"Oh bloody hell, yes." Beth turned to him. "This is Nick. Nick, this is Wendy."

He shook Wendy's hand. "Pleased to meet you."

"Likewise," she said and led them to the reception desk. She slipped behind it and stood at one of the monitors, typing quickly while Nick gave her the details.

"Do you remember the place from before?" she asked as she slipped a plastic keycard into a slot.

"Not really, the Oceanview was far too posh for us back then."

Wendy laughed. "Those were the days, eh?" She handed them each a keycard. "302 on the top floor, a lovely room."

Anxiety raced through Beth like a charge. The top floor meant a view of the beach, overlooking the Winter Gardens and Empire Pier, neither of which she wanted to see. Her throat tightened.

"Thanks," Nick said, filling the silence.

Beth had to pull herself together and face the past down. They were structures, nothing more, and couldn't hurt her. And since she'd buried her guilty secret so far down even her husband didn't know it, she had no other choice.

"Are you okay?" Wendy asked.

"Fine," said Beth, forcing a smile as she tried to snap back into the present. "Sorry, my head's all over the place at the moment."

"It's been a weird day," said Nick.

"I'm sure," said Wendy as she checked the screen. "You're heading home tomorrow?"

"I thought it'd be a nice treat to stay overnight," said Nick, still sounding unsure he'd made the right decision.

Beth rubbed his shoulder.

"Well if you're here, it'd be really good to catch up with you after I finish my shift." Wendy glanced at Nick. "Both of you, obviously, I don't want to hog your wife."

"Old friends should catch up," he said.

Beth wasn't sure. It'd be nice to have a chat and a catch-up but they were never the best of friends and she didn't know how much conversation they'd have to share over a bottle of wine.

"That's lovely," Wendy said and came out from behind the desk. "If you follow me."

She led them towards the stairs at the back of the foyer. "I don't know if you're eating in or out, but our restaurant is through the door on the right. Our chef's won some awards and it's all very swish. Next door is the back bar, for guests only, very nice for a quiet chat."

"I fancy some seafront fish and chips," Nick said.

"I think you should have some," said Wendy, "there're plenty of great places along the front." She stopped beside the staircase. "I'll leave you here, but it's been so good to see you again."

"Likewise," said Beth.

Wendy backed towards reception. "Hope we get a chance to speak later."

"Thank you for your help," said Nick and started up the stairs.

Beth put her hand on the newel post, her chest tightening with anxiety. If their room was at the front, what was she going to do? Yes, they were just buildings but what if there really were ghosts inside?

Nick, halfway up the first flight, stopped and looked back. "You coming?"

"Uh-huh," she said, trying to breathe steadily.

"Are you sure, because it looks like you're staying there."

"Don't be funny," she snapped and immediately regretted it. She wasn't angry at him, but the danger of making him the focus was too high to risk.

"I'm not trying to be." He came down the steps. "I don't know what you want me to do, Beth. I've apologised for fucking up and booking the room, I didn't realise how much it'd wallop you. Maybe we should just go home. I've been an arse, I'm sorry."

"You didn't know."

He pulled her into a hug. "If you want to go, we'll go."

She felt tears threaten. He didn't deserve any of this and she just had to be strong. "It's fine," she lied, "let's go."

* * *

The room was at the front of the hotel.

Nick opened the door for her, she took a deep breath and went in. The curtains were pulled across both windows and she breathed out, slow and shaky.

The room was large and well decorated, lit by lamps either side of the wide bed which faced the windows. The bathroom door, in the far wall, was slightly ajar.

"Impressive," Nick said. He put their case on the dresser and moved towards the nearest window. "Let's get some light on things."

"Don't."

"What?" he asked absently, checking for a pull cord at the edge of the curtain. "Let's get a bit of natural light in here."

"There's enough," she snapped.

"Really?" A frown creased his forehead. "Jesus, Beth, what the hell's going on?"

Anger bristled up her neck and she tried to breathe it back, before this got out of hand. It wasn't his fault but the red mist was making it harder to see. "I'm serious, Nick, leave the curtains alone."

"For Christ's sake, Beth, they're only curtains." He frisbeed his keycard onto the bed and she watched it go, trying to think through the mist. "I don't want us to fight."

"Me either, I just want to have a shower, get changed and grab a bite to eat."

"And I'm not stopping you doing any of them."

She sat on the edge of the bed and slipped off her shoes. "I'm too knackered for this, my emotions are all over the place."

"So talk to me. It feels like there's a lot you're not saying."

She looked away, frightened he'd see the truth in her eyes. She stood and took off her jacket, folding it carefully.

"Tell me about these people who clearly meant a great deal to you but I've never heard of before now."

"There must be people in your life I don't know," she said, clutching at straws.

"No," he said carefully, his voice low, "there aren't. You know everything about me and my life. I thought we told each other everything."

She unbuttoned her blouse, hands shaking.

"It appears I was wrong," he said and dropped his keys on the dresser.

"Oh come on, Nick, I told you that summer was an awful time for me."

"But you either missed out something important or I didn't hear you properly."

"Like you're not listening to me now?" It was a cheap shot but it took the wind out of his sails.

"I am listening to you." He huffed out a breath, as if aware he'd fallen into something it might be hard to get out of. "We've known each other fifteen years and I've never seen you like this before."

"What are you talking about? I'm fucking grieving, Nick."

"I don't remember you being like this after your dad."

"You can't compare the two," she said icily.

"I know." He looked away, deflated. "Tell me what's wrong."

"Nothing." She took off her blouse, folding it on top of her jacket with deliberation, then walked to the bathroom. The hole her secret was buried in was getting deeper by the moment, the opportunity to climb up its sheer sides growing more difficult with every missed opportunity to tell him. If she had a shower now, it would give them both time to calm down.

He shook his head. "You only told me you had a bad time with your friends and I know Gordon was ill, but people I didn't know about have died, I see strange men in alleys and get warned against them. You're seeing a girl with a ponytail and fixating on kids on BMXs."

She felt the walls close around her, escape from this line of questioning narrowing with every breath.

"I thought we didn't have secrets."

Each word hit her like a punch. "I want to go home."

"You said you didn't want to."

"Well I've changed my mind."

"Fine," he said, confusion turning to anger, "so get dressed. I've apologised for this and said about going home and I meant it. I was trying to do something nice to take your mind off everything but it seems like I've somehow made things worse."

"I didn't ask you to do any of this." It sounded colder than she'd meant.

"I know you bloody didn't," he snapped and yanked the curtain.

The rings rattled on the rail as the view opened up and she saw the Winter Gardens and the arcade beyond, the cowboy replaced by red neon lettering.

And the Empire Pier.

Bile rose as memories raced through her, of Kate and Jenny and pain. She grabbed his keys and threw them at him. They bounced off his chest with a dull thud, forcing a grunt.

Time stopped for a moment and she knew she'd crossed the line but her anger burned now and she was helpless to it. "I told you not to open the curtains, I fucking told you."

He stared at her, his mouth fixed in a tight line. "Have you gone mad?"

"You're full of shit." She turned her back on him and strode towards the bathroom.

"Yeah, that's right, walk away."

"Piss off, Nick." She tried to slam the bathroom door behind her but the closer at the top wouldn't let her. "Fuck."

Chapter 14

Then

Beth ate her lunchtime BLT on the wall behind Ed's Bakery, listening to the gulls circling overhead and the people enjoying the beach a few streets away. She only had a couple of hours left on her shift now and hoped to get some reading done if the footfall was light enough before she had to sweep up and tidy away.

Carrying her coffee mug into the shop, she washed her hands at the small sink by the back door and passed the kitchen, where Ed was making a fresh batch of dough.

Just as she sat on the stool behind the counter, the bell above the door signalled a new customer. Beth smiled at the family coming in – parents and three pre-teen kids. As the kids raced to the cakes display, the bell tinkled again as Wendy came in.

"Wotcha."

"Hey."

Wendy moved around the shop slowly, touching a few packets before drifting to the counter. "Do you bake all of these?" she asked.

"Ed does, I literally just serve and tidy up."

"Smells lovely in here."

"Doesn't it just?" said the mother, putting a pack of burned-top rolls on the counter. She smiled, dimples appearing in her cheeks. "Sorry, couldn't help overhearing, I worked in a bakery for my summer job. Lovely smell, though it does get wearing after a while."

"That's true," Beth said.

Wendy walked to a display stand in the middle of the shop. "What're these?" she asked, holding up a pack. "Pain chocolate?"

"Pain au chocolat," said Beth. "It's pastry with chocolate in it."

The mother put some white rolls on the counter. "I'll just see what they're up to," she said and walked across to her family.

"These look nice," said Wendy. She slipped her bag off her shoulder and put the pain au chocolat in it. Beth stared, uncomprehending, and Wendy winked at her. She picked up a pack of croissants and stole them with another wink.

"Wendy?"

"Are we meeting up after the fair?" she asked, as if nothing had happened.

"Wendy, what are you…?"

Another wink. "Okay then, Beth, I'll see you later." With a sweet smile, Wendy turned on her heel and walked out the shop, the tinkle of the bell now almost a mocking sound.

Before Beth had a chance to react, the mother came back to the counter with a cardboard box filled with fresh cream cakes.

"I think this is the lot," she said. "Are you alright? You look a million miles away."

* * *

By the time Ed let her go, Beth had swept the floor, tidied the stock and tallied her till, unable to get Wendy out of her mind. She'd known the bitch for less than a week and now she was shoplifting?

Rather than head home, Beth walked to Jenny's, anger and frustration growing, hoping that talking it through would somehow make sense of this situation.

Jenny answered the door, still wearing her Scott's uniform. "I'm so glad to see you." She called over her shoulder. "I'm just nipping out, won't be long."

Joan said something Beth didn't catch then Jenny pulled the door closed behind her and took Beth's arm, leading her away.

"Where're we going?"

Jenny took them through a narrow alley to a small park that once overlooked the sea but whose view had long since been blocked by the Excelsior hotel. Jenny sat at a bench and pulled Beth down beside her.

"What's going on?" Beth's own frustration had been knocked back, worried at Jenny's behaviour. Had someone been hurt?

"I don't know." Jenny took a deep breath, wiped something Beth couldn't see from the knees of her trousers. "Mouse came into work this afternoon, while I was stacking some shelves."

The girls looked at each other and Beth felt the penny drop. "Shit." Surely they both couldn't have the same story?

"Bugger," Jenny said. "I'm sorry. You came to see me. Are you okay?"

"Sure, you go first."

Jenny licked her lips. "He came into the shop and said hello, then asked what I was doing. It was fairly obvious I was putting bags of flour on the shelf so I didn't really know what to say. He picked up some cake mix and said, 'These look really nice.'"

"Did he wink at you?"

Jenny looked up, surprised. "Yes, then he put the cake mix down the front of his T-shirt and asked if we were meeting up after the fair. Then he left." She looked flustered. "I mean, I work retail, I know people steal but this was, I don't know…"

"Like he was testing you?"

"Yes, that's what it feels like now but it didn't at the time." Jenny suddenly seemed aware Beth was ahead of her. "How did you know? What happened to you?"

"Pretty much the same," she said and told Jenny what Wendy had done.

"I don't understand, why would they be testing us?"

"I don't know, but we'll find out when we see the pair of bastards tonight."

Chapter 15

Nick stormed down the stairs, trying to figure out what to do. Like every couple, they'd argued in the past, of course, but he hadn't seen her this angry in a long time and she'd never thrown anything at him before. He wanted to go back and wait until she finished her shower then confront her over what exactly was going on but what purpose would that serve? Bitter experience had taught him she wouldn't tell him what was wrong until she'd worked it through in her own mind and it seemed this thing had gone unresolved for fifteen years.

He was partly to blame, he knew that, for booking the room in the first place but how could he have known it would have this effect on her? Especially since she'd chosen not to tell him how much the past had clearly hurt her. The realisation she hadn't trusted him enough to share stung badly.

Why hadn't he asked her more questions before about that summer? When they'd first met, it hadn't seemed important since they were both away from home for the first time and reinventing themselves for university life. As time went on, he understood her level of reinvention was steeper than his, especially the first time he met Diana and realised it was his mother-in-law who'd stepped back from Beth and not the other way around. That period of her summer before university became a grey area, which he'd let go. Now, with chagrin, he realised the cost of that.

In the foyer, a tall thin old man came out of the residents' lounge and nodded at Nick. Nick caught the door and went in.

Long, narrow and empty, the lounge looked out to the south; wide windows let in the pale afternoon light. The bar was at the far end, all dark wood and neatly carved inlays. The optics shelf was well stocked and brightly lit. The barman, in his early twenties and wearing the same colours Wendy had, wiped a glass and looked up expectantly. His nametag read 'Stuart – here to help'.

"Evening, sir, what'll you have?"

Nick looked at the pumps, all craft beers he'd never heard of. "Half a lager, please."

After the barman handed Nick the glass, he asked for the room number then tapped it into the monitor of the cash till. Nick sat on a stool, turning slightly so he could see out the window.

A quarter of a mile up the road, a funfair sprawled on the beach side of Marine Drive and young families, clearly calling it a day, were coming away. Fathers carried kids on their shoulders while tired-looking mothers pushed buggies and other children walked, most of them eating a treat.

A row of huts, set against a wooden fence, offered everything from henna tattoos to hair braiding, craft items and artists selling paintings. Madame Rosa, a sign proclaiming her the premier east coast palm reader, occupied the last one.

The Empire Amusement Arcade sat on the edge of a plain wooden pier. On the other side was the decaying splendour of the Winter Gardens, a structure unlike anything Nick had ever seen before. Three storeys high, it almost looked inside out, featuring weatherworn white metalwork holding myriad glass panels which reflected the sunlight. What was it about those three places that had triggered her? What could have happened in them before she left for university?

Nick turned back to the bar and Stuart looked up from slicing lemons.

"Another one, sir?"

"Bit early for that, but could I ask you a question?"

Stuart gave a little shrug. "That all depends."

Nick jabbed his thumb over his shoulder. "I'm curious about the Winter Gardens over the road."

"Not much to tell really. Been there for years but it shut down five or six years ago. Some comedian I'd never heard of owned it and ran out of cash. When I was a kid it was an adventure place, for parties and whatever, but that was it. There's some kind of…" He clicked his fingers, as if trying to remember.

"Preservation order?" suggested Nick.

Stuart didn't look convinced. "Something like that; means they can't knock the place down."

"Is it on the pier?"

"No, it just looks like it from this angle, there's a gap where you can get to the beach. The pier's dead plain, no amusements or food places, but it's good to go crabbing off. My dad used to take me. You sometimes see fishermen out there on the early shift but I'm not sure they ever catch anything."

"What about the arcade?"

"Crummy place, full of old machines and low payouts. Used to be a big cowboy on the roof, like in Las Vegas, but he came down in one of the storms and they never put him back up."

Nothing about this struck Nick as sinister. "Why's it called Empire Amusements?"

Stuart frowned, as if it were the silliest question he'd heard all day. "Because it's the Empire Pier. My mum and dad reckon it was better in their day, they used to meet there then go into the Winter Gardens for discos and stuff."

"How long ago was back in their day?"

"A while, Dad's almost fifty."

"Thanks," said Nick.

He finished his drink with the nagging sense he was missing something. Something about Beth's past was locked across the road but he couldn't see it.

He checked his watch. She'd likely be fuming now, partly from the row, partly because he'd walked out leaving the situation unresolved. He had to go back up, start the ball rolling even if he wasn't sure he should be first to apologise.

Movement caught his eye and he watched a teenager on a BMX cut across the ornamental garden in front of the hotel and brake to a halt at the side of the building. Tall and thin, with spiky blond hair and a bloom of zits on his chin, he wore a T-shirt with a familiar sun design and his bike saddle was so low it looked like the kid was sitting on the back tyre. He put his phone to his ear and looked up at the front of the hotel, spoke briefly, then put the phone back in his pocket. With a last glance up, he cycled away, quickly disappearing from view.

Nick stood up with an uneasy feeling in his belly. Beth had been worried about the kids on BMX bikes earlier and he'd almost ignored her but now even he could see they were similar, with their T-shirts and saddle positioning.

Did she have a point? Could this be something else to do with that summer?

Now was the time to head up and try to make peace.

Chapter 16

Then

Her parents were doing the washing up in the kitchen when Beth sat on the step to put on her Converse.

"So," her father said as he carefully wiped a plate dry, "off to the fair to take advantage of the last night?"

"I fully intend to."

"I remember hoping they'd do longer rides on the last night, but it never happened." He turned to her mother. "What about you, Di? Did it ever happen to you?"

"I wouldn't know, Gordon," she said and then looked directly at Beth. "You just take care."

"Always," Beth said.

* * *

She walked briskly to Market Square, cutting off Regent's Row by the waxworks to come out behind the shopping centre. Past the building, she saw the girls at their usual bench and Jenny waved, Kate oblivious as she ate a fish and chip supper. Beth tapped her on the head as she sat on the bench arm.

"How's it going?" Kate asked and offered her a chip.

"Okay." Beth ate the chip slowly. "How about you?"

Kate dipped a chip into ketchup and ate it with relish. "Living the dream." She leaned back, the neck of her blouse shifting to reveal skin.

Beth saw the mark straight away and leaned forward, moving the material to get a better view. "Is that a love bite?"

"Might be," said Kate, her cheeks filling with colour that spread to her chest.

"Let me see," squeaked Jenny, craning around to get a better look.

"Come on, girls," Kate muttered, "leave it."

"When did you turn into a fourteen-year-old?" Jenny laughed. Kate pulled the neck of her blouse tighter.

"You're at the love bite stage with Blake already?"

"What can I say?" Kate asked, with enough grace to look bashful.

"Seriously?" asked Jenny. "A fucking love bite from the fair?"

"It's not like I asked him to do it."

"How long has this been going on?" Beth asked.

"We got chatting the other day, while you two were working, and then we were kissing and then we were making out and he's sucking on my neck like Dracula."

"Classy," said Jenny.

"What did your mum say?" Beth asked, wondering what colour of puce her mother's face would have turned if she'd gone home with a love bite.

"Why do you think I'm wearing a blouse?"

"So it's just making out?" asked Jenny.

Kate held up her hands. "Yes, Jen, we haven't shagged yet."

"Just checking," Jenny said. The only one of them still a virgin, she was clearly uncomfortable with her status even though nobody ever commented on it. "But I thought Blake and Wendy were a couple."

"Ask her yourself," said Kate, jutting her chin over Beth's shoulder.

Wendy stopped by the bench, stupid grin splitting her face. "Wotcha, girls."

Infuriated, the anger she'd held back since leaving work boiling through her, Beth jumped off the bench. "What the fuck do you think you were doing?" she demanded, jabbing her finger into Wendy's shoulder.

Wendy stepped back, looking frightened.

Someone grabbed Beth's shoulder. "Hey," hissed Kate, "what're you doing?"

Beth shook her off. "Ask her, the stupid bitch."

Wendy held up her hands in surrender. "It wasn't me, Frankie and Blake asked me–"

"They asked you? Well fuck you, what kind of excuse is that? You weren't being friendly in the pub, you were scoping me out, finding out where I worked."

"No, that–"

"You could have got me into real trouble, you stupid shit."

Wendy's eyes were wide. "But I–"

Beth jabbed at her again. "But I nothing–"

"Beth," said Kate abruptly, holding her shoulder, "what the fuck are you doing?"

"She stole from Ed's shop and winked at me while she did it, daring me to stop her."

"That's not–," said Wendy.

"Mouse did it to me too," said Jenny. "He stole some cake mix while I was stacking the shelves. They both winked, like it was some sort of game."

"It was a test," Wendy said, words tumbling into each other. "Honest, I didn't mean anything."

"We could have been sacked," said Jenny.

"I'm sorry, I'm sorry, but it was Frankie and Blake, honest."

"Would you jump off Julia's Point if they asked you to?" demanded Jenny.

"No." Wendy looked on the verge of tears. "I'm sorry."

"So, fuck off then," said Beth.

"No, they sent me over, told me to tell you to meet them at the Waltzer for ten."

"You've got a–" Beth started but Kate interrupted her.

"That's fine," she said and put a hand on Beth's arm as if this was all perfectly natural. She gestured for Wendy to go. "Now piss off and I'll calm things down."

Wendy didn't need telling twice and rushed away, quickly disappearing into the crowd.

"Fucking hell, Kate, I wanted to have a pop at her. She came in, bold as brass, nicked some stuff and winked at me."

"Did you dob her in?"

"No."

"Why?"

Beth paused. "Because I was scared Ed would realise I knew her, then I'd have been in trouble too."

"What about you?" Kate asked Jenny.

"Same thing. I can't afford to lose that job, Kate."

"I know." Kate ate another chip. "None of this makes any sense."

"No," said Beth, "so I'll ask Frankie what he was thinking about when I see him."

"Oh, don't make trouble, Beth."

"Make trouble? Who for? They didn't worry about dropping me and Jenny in the shit."

"I'll figure it out," said Kate. "So long as you two didn't get into trouble, I'll fix it, I promise."

Beth looked at Jenny, who was biting her lips. Neither said anything.

"Please, girls, let me sort it." Kate smiled and rubbed Beth's shoulder. "Trust me."

Beth took a steadying breath. Kate had always sorted things in the past when she said she would. "You do. Now come on, it's the last night, let's try and forget things for a while and hit the rides."

She threw her chip box in the bin and Beth noticed she held the neck of her blouse closed – better to hide the love bite.

* * *

108

The last of the revellers hung on but most of the crowd had thinned out by nine forty-five. The girls passed their time winning a doll for Maggie and a fire engine for Pete, even though Jenny wasn't keen that it made noises.

The Waltzer shut down at ten o'clock and saw off the last of its riders with a puff of dry ice. The woman from the control booth, baby asleep on her shoulder, moved across the boards as her helpers and other men Beth hadn't seen before began dismantling the cars and lighting racks.

The girls sat on the bottom step as Wendy came out the back of a burger van opposite, holding a grease-spotted apron. The cook said something that made her laugh. She handed him the apron then turned to the Waltzer. Spotting Beth, she looked away quickly and went to her left, ducking between two rides.

"I think you scared her," said Kate.

"Good."

"Evening, girls," said Frankie, and Beth spun around. He towered over them at the top of the steps, looking huge from her low vantage point, and she quickly got to her feet to try and balance it out a bit.

"Hey," said Kate and Jenny together.

"I understand there was a problem," he said and gestured behind him.

Beth peered around his mass and saw Mouse and Wendy standing beside the ride.

"There might have been," said Beth, her courage fading at his sheer presence. Standing up to Wendy and Mouse, even to Blake, was one thing but Frankie was so imposing, his face impossible to read.

"You weren't happy with Wendy and Mouse?"

Jenny shook her head.

"How about you, Beth?"

"No," she said, angry enough to summon the courage to take a stand, "I bloody wasn't."

He smirked. "It's just a game, girls." He looked between all three of them. "Do you know the resort at Crozier's Farm?"

"Yes," said Kate.

"Good, be there for ten tomorrow morning."

"Why?"

Frankie shrugged. "Because I asked."

"You're sure of yourself," Kate said with a smile.

"Only sometimes," he said and turned back towards the ride.

Wendy and Mouse drifted away into the night. The girls looked at one another.

"Well that went oddly," said Jenny.

"You're telling me," said Beth. "And what did he mean by a game?"

"Weird and, to top it all, I'm dismissed without seeing Blake." Kate sounded morose.

Jenny squeezed Kate's cheeks together with her fingers. "Come on, lovergirl, I'll buy you some chips."

Kate laughed as she knocked Jenny's hand away. "That's hardly a replacement."

"At least they won't give you a love bite," said Beth.

Chapter 17

Beth tucked a lock of hair behind her ear and stared in the mirror. A tear tracked slowly down her cheek.

She turned, resting her behind against the sink, looking into the shower. She didn't feel like stripping off her underwear now, she wanted to push herself, confront her past and sort things with Nick.

"Shit," she muttered, "what have I done?"

However shocked she was that he opened the curtains after she begged him not to, her shame at throwing his keys at him masked it. Her temper had always been something she fought to control but, however angry she'd been in the past, she'd never gone this far.

She looked at her bare feet and wiggled her toes but nothing came to her other than the need to apologise.

"No time like the present," she said and opened the door.

The room was empty. He'd gone. Exactly as she'd told him to. She sat on the bed, guilt weighing heavily at the thought of the strain she was putting on their marriage.

Maybe a bit of space would be good, it would allow him to calm down a little and hopefully forgive her outburst and the keys. But what if it didn't work? He knew something was wrong, what if he came back still angry, demanding she tell him? Would he understand why she hadn't told him? The thought he might not caused fresh tears and she palmed them away roughly. That wouldn't happen, she'd tell him everything – get it all out into the open.

Perhaps she needed space too, maybe get some fresh air. She walked to the window, pressing her nails into her palms and looked through the ghost of herself at the fading day. Some streetlights were already on, the arcade – not Sam's Place anymore, she noted sadly – a swirl of pulsing neon reds and blues. She felt no reaction to the landmarks and knew she could go out there. The buildings didn't hold any power over her and she remembered something her dad used to say – that worrying was a trait she'd picked up from her mum. "A worrier dies twice, once with whittling about the thing," he said, "then again when it actually happens."

Beth put the suitcase on the bed and took out a Breton T-shirt, a pair of jeans, socks and her trainers. Quickly dressing, she checked herself in the mirror and ran a hand through her hair. She was presentable, though her eyes were puffy and bloodshot, but that was only to be expected. She took her hoodie out of the case, put her wallet in her jeans pocket and picked up the pass key from the dresser. With one last look towards the Winter Gardens, she went down to the foyer.

Behind the reception desk and checking her phone, Wendy looked surprised as Beth walked by and held up her hand.

"What's up?" Beth asked.

Wendy came across the reception. "I was just about to message you, I wanted to make sure everything was okay."

"Why wouldn't it be?"

"I've just come off my break and saw the complaint."

"What complaint?"

"From the room next to yours, about raised voices and people slamming about."

Beth's puzzlement faded into embarrassment. Had they really been shouting loudly enough for someone to complain? They certainly hadn't slammed any doors, as much as both of them had tried to. "I'm not sure what to say."

"Are you okay?"

"I'm fine," Beth said, not wanting Wendy to believe otherwise. "There's no problem."

"I thought that would be the case," Wendy said with a shrug. "We've got thick walls here but some people will complain if they hear so much as a cough."

"That must be the case."

Wendy's expression brightened. "So where're you off to?" She made a show of looking around. "Isn't Nick going with you?"

Beth's cheeks warmed. What could she say? If Nick and Wendy spoke, she'd know Beth had been lying and she didn't want to be caught out. "I'm just going to get some air."

"Good idea, it looks like a lovely evening. Are you planning to retrace some old routes?"

"I hadn't really planned that far ahead."

"Well don't forget I get off at nine, so if you're still about, I'd love to grab a drink and catch up."

Beth felt less like catching up now than she had before, when Wendy first mentioned it, especially since conversation would invariably hark back to the old days. That was the last thing she needed with the raw emotions still rattling through her system.

"I'd like that," she said, hoping her expression looked more sincere than it felt.

"It's a date," Wendy said with a big smile as she walked back to the desk. "See you later."

* * *

Standing under the portico, Beth looked across at the Winter Gardens which, from this angle, pretty much obscured the Empire Pier from view. Without the safety shield of the window, her heart beat a little faster.

"You can do this," she said quietly, trying to rally her earlier courage but it failed. Outside, this much closer to it, she didn't think she'd be able to go onto the pier, touch the railings and step on the planks, breathing in the smell of wood and seawater.

Beth crossed the ornamental garden to the pavement. A woman walked by pushing a stroller, the toddler strapped into it clutching a colourful windmill whose blades turned briskly.

She watched them go, feeling the familiar pang and thinking of the diary in her handbag with stars marking the dates for prime fertility. Maybe Nick's plan to get them away from real life for a few days, to enjoy each other's company and make love because they wanted to, would have worked until she spoiled it.

A horse and cart clattered by, shaking her out of her thoughts. The driver nodded, his customers a young couple so engrossed in each other they probably didn't notice anything around them.

The Winter Gardens loomed over her as she crossed the road and it took a bit of resolve to get closer and look up at it, their shared history suddenly a weight on her shoulders. The place was clearly abandoned. Some of the panes were chipped and cracked and the main doors were secured with a padlocked chain.

"What happened to you?" she asked quietly and looked towards the brightly lit arcade. Empire Amusements was a shadow of Sam's Place, tatty and overly gaudy, though clearly popular with the Seagrave teenagers.

Shouts drew her attention from beyond the low wall to the left of the Winter Gardens. A group of twenty-somethings were making their way around the crazy golf course and she watched them complete a hole then glanced up, breath caught in her throat.

From this angle, the Empire Pier stretched out to sea, ornate lamp posts lit at intervals along its length, pilings hidden in shadow. She grabbed the wall for support, her heart racing as a wave of dizziness crashed over her.

"Come on," she urged herself but it was no use. It seemed the pier still retained some of its power, towering over the beach and full of secrets.

The young woman with the ponytail stood precariously on top of the railings at the far end of the pier. It was far too dangerous a thing to do and Beth felt a rush of adrenaline, heat in her arms as sweat beaded on her upper lip. Her mind flooded with a collage of images, of Jenny laughing and crying, of being under the pier, of everything Beth should have done and didn't.

If the girl planned to jump, Beth couldn't just let it happen, she had to help.

A hand dropped on her shoulder.

Chapter 18

Then

A warm day, the sun had already burned away most of the early mist as they walked to Kate's house.

"What if they just want us to go out there to do stuff to us?" Jenny asked.

"It'd be easier to just drive by in a van and ask if we want to see their puppies," Beth said.

In a town whose population doubled during the summer months, stranger danger had been drummed into them from an early age, even if most of the kids were blasé about it before they finished junior school.

Jenny failed to hold in her laugh. "You might be right."

"You know I am. And if they do stuff to you, I promise I'll tell everyone about it when I run home."

"You wouldn't try and save me before you ran?"

It was Beth's turn to laugh. "No, would you?"

"Probably not."

Kate, as Beth expected, was very enthusiastic about the meeting and met them on the pavement, keen not to waste a minute. They walked to All Saints and crossed the graveyard to the narrow stand of trees beyond, following well-worn footpaths to the meadow that separated the church from Crozier's Farm.

A line of trees marked the edge of the property and Kate led them through to the stile and up a small rise onto the gravel road that ran down to the resort.

Crozier's Farm had never been one, as far as Beth knew, just a big house overlooking the bowl of Radnor Valley, surrounded on three sides by lush woods. The property had been empty for years and big plans had been made to convert part of it to 'The Beeches Resort', a holiday camp offering chalets, camping and outdoor activities. Money issues – Hugh Cowley was said to be involved – forced development to halt with only six chalets constructed, all of them now abandoned.

Beth had always thought the house, shielded from the Radnor Road by more trees, looked sad with some roof tiles missing and most of the upper floor windows broken. Parts of the dry-stone wall surrounding the overgrown garden had collapsed. A steep hill ran from the wall to a fenced paddock just above the bowl. Two beech trees stood sentry over an oval parking area that the chalets surrounded.

"Where exactly are we supposed to meet them?" asked Jenny.

"By the chalets?" Kate suggested.

The chalets were identical, three windows in the back, two in front; the door set to one side. A couple had graffiti tags on the back, one had all its windows broken; all of them looked neglected.

They walked down the hill, the trees cutting out road noise and, apart from their crunching footsteps, all Beth could hear were birds singing. The area felt isolated and dead.

"I don't like this," said Jenny.

"Stop moaning, we'll be fine," said Kate.

As they came level to the paddock, Mouse stepped out from the first chalet, making them all jump.

"Down here," he called, looking nervously at Jenny.

When they reached him, he pushed open the chalet door and ushered them inside, Kate first with Beth at the rear.

The room looked as bad as the exterior had promised. Two doors and a kitchen opened off the living space and the place smelled of bacon, mould and Lynx body spray. Jenny sneezed. Half a dozen deckchairs were set up around a patio table that had seen better days. Wendy sat on a patio chair in front of the door next to the kitchen.

"Wotcha", she said, closing the magazine in her lap. She looked at Kate and her gaze must have caught the love bite because her expression soured instantly.

Frankie stood in the kitchen, eating a bowl of something, and Blake was at the window, topless as he stared out at the turnaround. Mouse stood next to him.

"Girls," Frankie said, "you came."

"Of course," said Kate, looking at Blake as if she wanted to hug him even though he'd ignored her.

Beth felt a pang of sympathy.

"Told you they would," Blake said.

"Sit down," Frankie said – a command rather than a request – gesturing to the table as he put his bowl into the sink.

Kate went but Beth didn't want to move. Nothing seemed out of the ordinary to her but something felt off, as if the world had tilted at a slight angle. Her skin prickled and goosebumps ran up her arms.

"Go," said Jenny, pushing her on.

Beth sat next to Kate as Blake turned to lean against the windowsill, arms folded across his tight chest.

"Welcome to our place," Frankie said, arms wide.

"You live here?" asked Kate.

"Sometimes." He looked at Beth, tilting his head to one side, and smiled. It touched his eyes but still felt like the coldest expression she'd ever seen. "We're a family and look after each other." His attention moved to Jenny. "I'd like to look after you, Jenny."

"Thanks," she stammered.

"All three of you, in fact. My brothers and sister feel the same, that we'd like you to join our squad."

Kate's shoulders dropped, visibly relaxing. "Really? So what does your squad do?"

"A bit of this, a bit of that."

"Does your squad have a name?"

"We're sometimes called the Sunshine Squad."

"As in Hugh Cowley's Sunshine?" Beth asked.

"You know Mr Cowley?" Frankie asked, his voice softer.

"Only from seeing him around, I don't actually know him."

"Thank you for your honesty, Beth. We do sometimes work for Mr Cowley, but not all the time." He rubbed his hands together. "I should tell you, before you decide, that our squad has an initiation process."

Beth glanced towards the open door and wondered what would happen if she just walked out.

"It's not a big deal," Blake said, "and anyway, Wendy and Mouse already partly tested you and Jenny."

"We noticed," Beth said, "and weren't impressed."

"Hey," he said, voice steely, "it wasn't their idea, so don't give her or Mouse any shit."

"It was my idea," said Frankie, "we had to make sure you weren't goody-goodies."

"We aren't," said Kate indignantly.

"But we don't go around doing horrible stuff," Beth said. From the corner of her eye she saw Kate cast her a glare.

"Horrible stuff," repeated Blake, looking amused and pissed off simultaneously. Beth felt her stomach turn and wanted, more than ever, to just walk out. "I only do that when people say my name wrong."

"How do people say Blake wrong?" Jenny asked.

"I hope you never find out," said Frankie and laughed. "So what do you think, are you interested in joining up with us?"

"We're off to uni at the end of the summer break," Beth said.

"In a few weeks," he acknowledged. "Fall in with us and have a good summer before you go."

"But what's the initiation?" Jenny asked.

"It's very simple, we just want some T-shirts."

"You want us to get you T-shirts?" Kate asked.

"Kind of. Do you know BJ's Surf Shed on Marine Drive?" He waited for all three girls to nod. "We want you to get us BJ T-shirts, but we want them with the security tags on."

"You want us to steal them?" Beth asked.

Frankie leaned on the table, the plastic groaning under his weight. "Is that a problem?"

Beth felt the chill in his words. "Well it could be."

Frankie smiled at her, like a shark about to bite a diver in half. "It's the initiation," he said. "It's entirely up to you, of course."

"We can do it," said Kate enthusiastically, pressing her finger into Beth's side. "No problem, is there, Beth?"

Even though Beth couldn't quite put her finger on why, Frankie scared her almost as much as the thought of stealing but the idea of being in his squad, accepted by the kind of man who'd worry her mother so much, gave her a thrill. Was it childish to give in to that and ignore the menace she felt in the atmosphere? Worse, was it worth the trouble she'd get into if they got caught at BJ's?

"No," she said softly, "just clarifying."

Frankie smiled and walked across the room. "Glad to hear it. We're away until Wednesday on business but we'd love to welcome you when we get back. It's all your choice, of course. If you don't want to do it, that's fine." He gestured to the door, clearly dismissing them. "Enjoy your Sunday, girls."

* * *

"Well that was fucking scary," said Beth when she was sure nobody from the chalet would be able to hear.

"It was," agreed Jenny. "That makes sense, them working for Hugh Cowley. I told you I saw Frankie helping evict my neighbour."

"What're you two talking about?" Kate asked. "They were friendly to us. I think being in their squad could be fun."

"The initiation's a bit steep," Beth pointed out.

"Oh don't be a baby," said Kate, "it's not like we're hurting anyone."

"Apart from BJ's," Beth said.

"It's not like they're a little independent. BJ's is a chain, they won't notice. Let's live a little, Beth. Come on."

"So you're definitely up for it then?" Beth asked.

"Of course."

"Gets you closer to Blake," Jenny said. "Did you see Wendy's face when she spotted your love bite?"

"Not my problem. He chose me, I chose Blake. End of story."

Jenny smiled, holding up her hands in surrender. "Okay, okay, don't kill me."

"She looked like she wanted to kill you," Beth said.

"We'll see."

They crossed the stile into the meadow, the spire of All Saints rising over the trees ahead.

"What do you think, Beth?" Jenny asked.

"It might be okay," she said.

"Might be?" Kate sounded incredulous. "Are we really goody-goodies."

"Hardly," said Beth.

"Well we're not exactly rebels, are we?" Kate said. "Have you ever nicked anything, Jenny?"

"I took money from my mum's purse," she said, looking worried they might judge her, "so I could buy cans of pop at school like you two."

"Gangster," said Kate. "What about you, Beth?"

"That summer when they were everywhere, I stole some loom bracelets because I'd spent all my pocket money but felt so guilty, I kept deliberately trying to overpay the shopkeeper but he never let me."

"You see, we're hardly career criminals, are we? I mean, getting a love bite off someone who works at the fair is probably the riskiest thing I've done in ages."

"I could have given you a love bite," said Beth with a smirk.

"And it would have been lovely," said Kate without missing a beat, "but it turned me on when he did it and it felt rebellious. I liked that because we aren't rebellious, are we?"

"What do we have to rebel against?" Jenny asked.

Kate laughed and Beth quickly joined in.

"What?" Jenny looked at them as if they'd banged their heads. "We live in a seaside town full of people getting drunk and getting off with each other, what do we have left?"

"I've rebelled," said Beth.

"How? You tried to pay for what you stole, you told us," Kate said. "And before we say it, getting fingered by Ronnie at school doesn't count because everyone's done it."

"I haven't," said Jenny quietly.

"And how is getting a love bite more rebellious?" Beth asked.

"It isn't and that's my point," Kate said.

"What if we get caught though?" Jenny asked.

"And what if we don't?" Kate stopped, turned to her friends. "Are we just looking for the negative?"

It might collapse like a house of cards if she thought too much about what she'd said but Kate did make some sense. They were leaving, why shouldn't they rebel? And did Beth really want to be the one who poured cold water on it all? "Go on then," she said.

Kate's surprise was total. "Really?"

"So long as we only take what they asked for, nothing else."

"Agreed," said Kate and they both looked at Jenny. "No pressure," Kate said, "whatever you want to do."

"Only what we need?" Jenny asked.

"I promise," said Kate.

"I'm in then."

Chapter 19

Startled, Beth twisted her body to shrug off the hand.

"Hey," said Wendy quickly, "it's me."

"Jesus," muttered Beth, "you scared the crap out of me."

"Sorry, I saw you staring out to sea and got worried. I just wanted to make sure everything was okay."

"I'm fine, honestly, but I was looking at the pier and I think someone's in trouble."

"What do you mean?"

Beth pointed towards the end of the pier. "There, see? Standing on the edge of the railings?"

Wendy looked at her slowly and frowned. "At the very end, you mean?"

"Can't you see them?" Beth asked, frustrated. They were wasting time.

"I see a flag," Wendy said slowly.

Her words didn't compute. "Where are you looking?"

"At the end of the pier are two flags, a Union Jack on this side, the St George's Cross on the other."

But Beth could see the shape of the girl. "How can that be?"

"They're tied up, cinched in the middle. Trust me, I walk past the damned things every day."

To Beth, it still looked like a person. "Are you sure?"

"Are you saying I'm wrong?" A barb in her voice caught Beth's attention.

"No, it's just…" It might have been a flag, tied up and moving in the breeze, but it could easily have been a girl with a ponytail bracing herself to jump into the North Sea. Both made as much sense to her, at that moment.

"It's a flag, I promise you," Wendy said sympathetically. "I'll take you on the pier and show you myself, if you don't believe me."

Her tone pushed away thoughts of the blonde girl she'd seen at the cemetery and The Golden Nugget. "It looked so much like a person." It looked so much like Jenny, she wanted to say but didn't.

"Easy mistake to make, especially after what you went through back then."

Hearing someone else verbalise it ran a chill across Beth's shoulders. "I was probably looking for something."

"Or someone," Wendy said. "But aren't we all? Listen, how about we get that drink now?"

Beth checked her watch. "I thought you didn't get off until nine?"

"I think I can make an exception when an old friend is in town and clearly not doing well."

"I'm doing fine," Beth insisted, stung a little.

Wendy's silence spoke volumes. Maybe she did need to unwind a bit.

"Okay," said Beth, "if you can make the exception, I'll happily go for a drink. Where do you suggest?"

"Anywhere you remember?"

One memory made her smile. "We're close to the Chesty Wanker, is that still going?"

"Of course, where else would the underage drinkers of the town go?"

"It must be under new management by now?"

"Nope, Chubb still runs the place. Come on."

With a last glance at the flag that looked so much like a young woman, Beth stood beside Wendy at the kerb. They waited for an ancient camper van to rumble by then crossed to the central reservation of Marine Drive.

The BMX came out of nowhere, passing so close she felt the draught of it; the shock catching her breath. She pushed back, grabbing for Wendy who cried out as her arm was yanked. The bike skidded to a halt, turning ninety degrees and leaving a thin line of rubber in its wake. Beth's arms tingled with shock.

The teenaged rider sat on his low saddle, wearing skinny black jeans and a yellow T-shirt with a smiling sun on it. Sunglasses were buried in his long blond hair, eyes hidden behind his fringe.

"Stupid bitches, you should watch where you're walking."

Beth turned to Wendy. "Are you okay?"

"He came out of nowhere," Wendy said.

"Like the wind," the teenager sneered.

His attitude stoked Beth's anger, pushed the fear down.

"Nearly caught us there, didn't you?" she said.

"Can't help you two being idiots."

"You can't control your bike either, little boy."

His sneer slipped away. "What did you say?"

"You heard."

The teenager waved his hand dismissively. "Fucking lesbos," he muttered and stepped on the pedals, riding quickly away.

"He nearly hit me," Wendy said, clearly shaken.

"Have you ever seen him before?"

"No, why would I? Seagrave's full of kids who all look the same to me."

"No, I mean kids on BMX bikes like that. I've seen a few of them today and they seem to be watching me."

Wendy laughed and quickly put her hand over her mouth. "Sorry, it's just…" She paused. "You realise how weird that sounds, right?"

"Nick said the same thing but I know they were staring at me."

"Why would they do that?"

"I don't know."

They crossed the road and turned off Marine Drive into a side street. Wendy stopped and leaned on a wall, rubbing her ankle.

Movement at the far end of the street caught Beth's eye and she watched the teenager stop his BMX in the middle of the road. He spoke into his mobile phone, snapped her a mock salute and rode away.

"Did you see that?"

"What?"

"The kid again, at the top of the street. He saluted me then rode off."

Wendy gave her a suspicious smile. "Are you sure?"

Even if Nick and now Wendy didn't believe her, it didn't mean Beth's suspicions were wrong. But why would they be paying attention to her?

"I might be wrong," she conceded.

"You might be paranoid," Wendy said with a big smile.

Chapter 20

As soon as Nick stepped into the room it was obvious from the stillness Beth wasn't there.

He sat on the bed, next to the opened suitcase and saw her jeans, T-shirt and hoodie were missing. Perhaps she'd gone for a stroll along the seafront to clear her mind, or revisited some old stomping grounds. Without wanting to badger her, he thought it best to let her know he was back in the room and dialled her mobile. He felt the first vibration of it before it rang and, surprised, found the handset under the case. His face filled the screen, 'Nick calling' written across his forehead.

Forgetting her phone wasn't unusual but, right now, it might mean she didn't want to talk to him. Either way, he had no way of knowing where she was.

Caught between not wanting to chase her and not wanting to ignore her, Nick expressed his frustration with a growl. Whatever was happening here was at least partly his fault, even if only for not understanding more about this blank slate of time that had clearly hurt his wife so badly.

The only option, it seemed, was to go out and look for her – a search he didn't fancy his chances with.

He checked out the window. The funfair was in full flow, the rides that cleared the fences were brightly lit against the darkening sky. A group of teenagers had gathered at the entrance to Empire Amusements.

Nick changed out of his suit, put her phone in his pocket and left the room. If she'd seen Wendy on her way out, Beth might have told her where she planned to walk.

The reception desk was unmanned and Nick pressed the small 'for attention' bell. The office door opened quickly and a nervous-looking young man came through. His uniform didn't quite fit and his name badge – 'Tony' – was pinned askew over his left breast.

"Evening, sir."

"Evening. I'm looking for your colleague Wendy."

"She's not here I'm afraid, sir," Tony said and clasped his hands in front of his belly, thumbs wrestling. "Can I help at all?"

"I hope so." Nick found a picture of Beth on his phone and held it up for Tony's attention. "This is my wife. Did you happen to see her leave?"

Tony stared with the squint of the short-sighted. "Can't say I have, sir, but I've only just come on duty. Are you guests here?"

"Yes, room 302."

Tony typed the digits and squinted at the screen. "Mr Parker?" He read a little more, then swallowed audibly.

"Oh, it seems there's an issue about your room, a noise complaint for raised voices."

Someone had complained about their argument? "I'm sorry about that," Nick said, "but it's all sorted now. My wife's gone out and I want to make sure she's okay."

Tony looked even more uncomfortable and Nick had the horrible thought he might be suspected of domestic abuse. "It was just a disagreement," he said quickly, knowing this probably made him sound guiltier. "Anyway, Wendy knows my wife and I was hoping they'd spoken."

"She left," Tony said, chewing his lip. "She was called away."

"How long ago?"

"I'm not sure." He paused. "I'm sorry, sir, I don't know what to do, I'm really just training on reception. I'm actually a porter. Wendy rang me and asked a favour and left as soon as I got here, grabbed her coat and said she might not be back." He looked despondent. "She shouldn't have left me on my own."

"I understand, I'm sorry to have bothered you."

"You haven't, sir, please don't think that. I don't want to give you the wrong impression."

Nick offered what he hoped was a reassuring smile. "You haven't, Tony, you've been very helpful."

Tony smiled wanly and Nick wished him a pleasant evening before leaving the hotel. Standing on the front steps under the portico, he looked both ways along the expanse of Marine Drive. It was unlikely she'd head towards the fair and surely, after what happened in the room, she wouldn't go onto the pier.

All that made sense was to retrace their steps back towards town. After all, he had to start somewhere.

Chapter 21

Then

Kate was already leaning on the railing at the pier, three insulated cups at her elbow, when Beth arrived.

"You look as nervous as I feel."

"Then you must feel like crap." Beth's stomach had churned through most of the night and hadn't settled on the walk here.

She took the cup Kate offered her and leaned on the railing next to her friend. BJ's Surf Shed was about a quarter of a mile away and both girls looked towards it.

"We'll be fine," Kate said but, to Beth, she didn't sound any more convinced than she was.

"You're sure?"

"Not at all." Kate gave her a wry smile. "Although, you can still pull out. We all can."

"You won't though, will you?"

"No, because I want to see Blake again." The love bite was barely visible over the neckline of her T-shirt.

"Hey, bitches," said Jenny as she came down the pier towards them. She stood next to Beth at the railing and took the cup Kate handed her. "Thanks. So how're we feeling?"

"Nervous," said Beth, "how about you?"

"Like I could throw up for a year."

Beth looked down at the beach and finished her coffee watching a small child run in ever decreasing circles on the sand. When he fell over and erupted in laughter, his father scooping him up into a big hug, Beth thought of her dad and how he'd feel if he knew what she was doing. She tried to block him from her mind.

"So, are we ready, girls?" Kate asked.

"I think so," Beth said. They'd agreed their outfits, different-coloured plain T-shirts and cut-offs to try and make them blend in, but she now realised they needed more. "We ought to disguise ourselves."

"I don't think a fake moustache would suit me," said Kate.

"No, you dingbat, like sunglasses or hats. I don't know who works in BJ's, but they might recognise one of us."

"Good point," said Jenny. "Three girls in shorts and T-shirts with shades on, that could be any of one hundred or more people."

"Not a bad idea," said Kate as she finished her coffee. "We'll call into Pervy Pete's on the way."

* * *

Peter's News was on Melton Street, just below the Chest & Anchor pub. Its window was shielded by mesh and filled with signs for various deals. Two sandwich boards on the pavement broadcast headlines from the national papers as well as the *Seagrave Telegraph*; and an ancient Coca-Cola sign hung over the street above the recessed door, propped open today by a bag of spuds.

Beth lost the rock-paper-scissors and, with a resigned sign, went in.

A central shelving unit split the shop into two aisles. Fridges and freezers lined the wall on the right, gifts and toys on the left along with the magazine racks.

Pervy Pete sat behind his counter at the end of the shop and stared at her. Tall and thin, with lots of black hair styled into a quiff, he must have been somewhere in his fifties and had a bad reputation among Beth's friends. Unless you wanted to buy single cigarettes or rent a hooky film, it wasn't a shop to go into and he never failed to make her feel uncomfortable.

She picked up three pairs of fake Chanel sunglasses and took them to the counter.

"Morning, love." On shelves behind him were a vast array of cigarettes and some jars of sweets. A tall fan, in front of the backroom door, blew over them as it lazily rotated. "Haven't seen you for a while."

Did he really recognise her or was this just something he said? "I've been about."

"I don't doubt it," he said and dropped her a wink.

She swallowed her distaste as he checked the prices on each pair of glasses.

"All for you?" he asked and rang the sale into the till.

"No, buying for friends."

"You should have asked them in."

"I might do that next time."

He looked up. "I'd like that."

"I'm sure."

The till did its thing and he held out his hand. His index finger traced across her palm as she gave him the cash and she pulled her hand back quickly, making an "ew" sound.

"Don't be like that," he said as he sorted her change.

Holding the coins in his fingertips, he gestured for her to take them. She held out her hand and as the last one dropped, he stroked her palm again.

She put the money into her purse without checking it and grabbed the glasses.

"Call again," he said as she rushed out into the sunshine.

* * *

BJ's Surf Shed was double-fronted and covered with plastic wood lengths, its windows displaying a range of beachwear. The shop assistant, a skinny, tanned white bloke in his early twenties with untidy dreadlocks, priced T-shirts behind the counter as a family browsed through hoodies on a table just inside the door.

Kate went through the plan as they stood across the road. "We want four T-shirts; XXL for Frankie, large for Blake and Mouse and an XL for Wendy, that'll fucking teach her. I'll get the large ones."

"I'll get the XXL," said Jenny.

Kate nodded. "Spread out and take from different areas, because the bloke can't chase all of us. If he does stop one of us, turn on the waterworks while the other two get out. There are two cameras – one in a dish on the ceiling in the middle of the shop, one pointing in from the front door – so block them as best you can."

"I don't exactly feel gangster with this," said Beth.

"Or me," said Kate. "Good luck, girls."

She put on her shades, crossed the road and once she was in the shop, Jenny counted to ten and followed her. Beth counted to ten then went into the shop, her heart racing.

Kate was at the back, Jenny on the right beside the changing room. Neither looked up as Beth browsed her way to a small shelf of tie-dyed T-shirts on the left. With her back to the cameras, she slipped off her rucksack and picked up a T-shirt as if to examine it. She felt even less gangster now. Her heart hammered and cold sweat gathered in her hairline. She turned the T-shirt over, considered putting it down and walking out, then dropped it into her bag. The bloke behind the counter didn't shout. Had she got away with it? Taking a deep breath, she glanced at him and found he wasn't paying any attention to her – his gaze was fixed on Chrissie Ford as she came into the shop.

Hair casually piled up and glowing in the light, she wore a vest top and short shorts under an almost transparent overshirt; a white tote bag was draped over her shoulder. She nodded at the assistant and he smiled, clearly taken with her.

A weight settled over Beth's chest. Today, of all days, she had to be in here at the same time?

Chrissie saw her immediately and came over, standing on the other side of the shelf. "Taking up surfing, Beth?"

"No, just looking."

"I'm surprised you can see anything in those cheap glasses."

Beth pulled them down her nose slightly. "I sometimes find it's better not to see everything."

Chrissie's lip curled. "You want a change of scenery, that's all. Me and Ronnie just got back from staying up the coast at a friend's place. It was lovely. Plenty of privacy and…" She stopped, as if suddenly aware of who she was talking to. "Oh, I'm sorry," she said with a fake smile, "you don't want to hear that, do you?"

Beth's stomach turned over as her mind assaulted her with images of Ronnie smiling and laughing and kissing her. She thought of how he looked when he talked about running; the way he smelled straight after a shower; the way he looked after they'd made love; and it made her sad. "Not really, because I don't want to think about your skanky arse."

Chrissie looked like she'd just sucked the sourest taste in the world. "Fuck you, Beth."

"No, Chrissie, fuck you. Why are you revelling in this?"

"Because it's funny?"

"Only as funny as you thinking you're going to be something in the real world." Beth felt a small surge of triumph as Chrissie's smile dropped slightly. "In fact, where are the other Barbies?"

"Shut up, Beth."

"What happened to the wit?"

Chrissie looked like she was thinking of a retort then turned on her heel, walking over to a display stand of hats. As she watched her go, Beth suddenly realised how they might make this whole enterprise work. She walked to the back of the shop and sidled up to Kate.

"What're you doing?"

"Don't look, but Chrissie's in here."

"Shit, did the bitch say anything to you?"

"Just the usual, but she's given me an idea."

"I'm listening."

Beth told her the plan, picked up another T-shirt and went around to Jenny.

"Have you got yours?"

"In my bag," whispered Jenny, as if she was in the middle of a spy film.

"Good, pass me another."

"Why?"

"I'll tell you later."

With the two T-shirts, Beth went to stand at the same table Chrissie was browsing at.

Chrissie looked up with a smirk. "Trying to find the cheapest, Beth?"

"I think I'm looking at that."

"You're a cow."

"Not as bad as you. You do realise that one day Ronnie'll see the real you, under all your fluff and shite, and he's not going to be happy?"

"I haven't heard any complaints yet."

"I'm sure."

Beth walked behind Chrissie, made her move and crossed the shop. The family had left and she stood at the hoodie table. Chrissie browsed on, occasionally glancing over and smiling when she saw Beth looking. After what felt like an eternity but was probably two minutes at most, Chrissie walked towards the door.

"I'll tell Ronnie I saw you."

"I'm sure he'll love that."

The alarm sounded as soon as Chrissie went through the door. Surprised, she stopped. The assistant raced around the counter as if he'd been in training for this moment his entire life.

"Hey, sister, stop there please."

Chrissie turned, her mouth a perfect 'O' of surprise and touched her bag, unconsciously. Her cheeks were crimson and Beth bit her lip, trying not to smile.

The assistant pointed at the camera above the door. "Look up there," he said and she did. "Have you got anything in your bag you shouldn't?"

"What?" Clearly confused, Chrissie glanced at Beth as the alarm continued to ring. "What do you mean?"

Jenny left the shop, shaking her head at Chrissie and Kate followed her.

"You set off the alarm," the assistant said. "It might be a glitch but I need to check."

"You don't need to check me."

"Please, sister, just put your bag on the table and open it for me."

Looking numb, Chrissie did as she was told and her face dropped.

"Oh dear," said Beth as she left, "how embarrassing."

Her friends waited a few yards away from the doors, grinning like Cheshire cats. Once she was on the pavement, they grabbed Beth's arms and pulled her along Marine Drive laughing, drawing curious looks from passersby that just made them laugh all the more.

Chapter 22

Time had been unkind to Melton Street.

A handful of terraced houses on the south side had their doors or windows covered with hardboard and small bushes grew out of broken guttering. Pervy Pete's and the shop next to it had gone completely, concrete footprints in waste ground their only legacy, while two houses were sealed with steel sheeting. The factory on the north side had been converted into flats, a cluster of 'to let' signs growing like ivy around the main doors. The road wore an air of abandonment like a heavy coat.

Beth felt a wave of melancholy, picturing herself and friends on this road years before, their lives unmapped, walking the same steps towards the Chest & Anchor pub.

The Chesty Wanker, as everyone called it, now had spotlights above the bay windows, casting a sickly glow over the lime-green wall. A tattered Sky Sports banner hung lopsidedly under the windows of the upstairs living quarters.

"Do you still drink in here?" Beth asked.

"Not often."

"I can't believe Chubb still gets away with serving kids."

"Well, the drinkers when we were regulars are now councillors and coppers, so they probably let him off out of a sense of nostalgia."

Wendy stopped by the pub steps. An upright ashtray next to one of the propped open doors was overflowing, butts scattered across the pavement. The area stank of cigarettes, body odour and weed. "Don't worry, it's safer than it looks."

"Street's taken a beating, hasn't it?"

"It's off the beaten track, Beth, it's always been pretty shitty."

Following Wendy into the lounge, Beth felt like she'd stepped back in time. The sturdy wooden tables and chairs were just as she remembered them. The drinkers were of all ages, most looked closer to retirement. A dartboard hung over the fireplace, the wall around it a trypophobic's nightmare, and three fruit machines stood in the corner, all flashing enticingly although only one was being fed patiently by an old man in a hi-vis jacket. Two barmaids chatted with customers; the older one with a sour expression like she'd heard every sob story and chat-up line in history. She stood with folded arms while the younger woman, enjoying the lion's share of attention, almost spilled out of her vest top.

"I'll get them in," Wendy said. "What did you want?"

"Dry white wine, please."

"Okay, you find us a seat." She gestured vaguely as she walked towards the bar.

Some men shifted in their seats to watch her go, while others looked at Beth with no pretence of doing it secretly. She found a small empty table off to one side and sat with her back to the wall. The long table in front of the bay was surrounded by a group of men with shaved heads, all wearing polo shirts a size too small, a game of dominoes snaking between their pint glasses. One player looked at her and she smiled. He scowled and went back to his game.

Tension filled the air, crackling like a static she could feel in her bones. Back in the day, there'd been a sense of fun in here but now the atmosphere was oppressive, filled with barely contained violence.

She put her bag between her feet and looked towards the bar. Wendy said something to the older barmaid who laughed and leaned forward, looking at Beth. She said something to Wendy and they both laughed again.

An old man in a shabby brown suit wandered over and leaned on the back of the chair across from her, broken blood vessels roadmaps on his cheeks.

"How are you, love?" His front teeth were missing and air whistled through the gap as he spoke.

"Not bad, yourself?"

"Can't complain," he said with a broad smile. "Did I see you earlier?" The stink of alcohol came off him in waves, barely covering another more unpleasant smell.

"Maybe, I've been in town since this afternoon."

He nodded. "Thought so. Went well, didn't it?"

Had he been at the funeral or wake? "Yes," she said, rather than ask him to explain.

"You're right pretty, love."

Tension tightened through her core. "Thanks."

He grinned. The edges of his teeth at the gap were nicotine-stained. "I think they're playing our song, did you want to dance?"

"Not right now." She could barely hear music and there was no room to dance even if she wanted to. "But thanks."

He pouted. "Really?"

"Uh-huh, really."

"Evening, Jello, how's it going?" Wendy put Beth's wineglass in front of her.

Jello's face lit up. "Wednesday, my girl, so lovely to see you."

"And you." She sat across from Beth, half turned away from him. "He always calls me Wednesday."

"So you two fillies know each other?"

"We're old friends."

"Very nice." Beth saw a flash of tongue in the gap as he smiled. "Are you going to introduce me?"

"Maybe later," said Wendy firmly.

Her tone pulled him up short and he took out a tatty leather wallet, selected a ten-pound note and gave it to her.

"Lovely to meet you," he said to Beth, dipping his head in a small bow.

"And you," she replied automatically.

He winked at Wendy then walked towards the bar, his balance suspect.

"Sorry about that," said Wendy, putting the tenner in her purse. "He wasn't inappropriate, was he?"

"No, he thought he knew me, and I wondered if he'd been at the funeral."

"I doubt it, he wears that suit all the time." Her nose wrinkled. "In the middle of summer you smell him before you see him."

"I can imagine." Beth sipped her wine. It wasn't the best she'd ever tasted. "It was a shame you couldn't be at the funeral."

"I wish I could have made it but the thing with Kerry was all last minute."

"Kerry's the lady you're covering?"

"Yes, the head receptionist at the hotel. She got mugged this morning by a couple of scrotes who cut her." Wendy's matter-of-fact tone added a chill to her news.

"What?"

"She was out on her run and they came up behind her – cut her arm badly."

"That's terrible."

"I know. I mean she was running; she only had her phone on her."

Beth, who kept fit power walking around Hadlington, felt terrible for this woman she didn't know. "Did she see them?"

"No, the arseholes came up behind her on bikes, took her by surprise."

Beth felt a chill pull her shoulders tight. Her mind raced. "I wonder what kind of bikes?"

Wendy leaned forward. "Calm down, Miss Marple, there's loads of kids on loads of bikes, I doubt it's any of your BMX squad."

She was right, of course, but that didn't shake Beth's nagging suspicion. "I know. So how is she?"

"The coppers reckon they were using matchstick Stanleys."

"I don't know what that is."

"It's where you put a matchstick between two blades in a Stanley knife so the wound can't be sewn up properly."

Beth felt icy fingers run up her back. "Jesus, this gets worse."

"It happens but she's home now and recovering." Wendy shrugged and picked up her glass. "Enough of the gloom and doom."

Beth touched her glass to Wendy's and they drank.

"It's good to see you," Wendy said. "Coming back can't have been easy, I don't suppose?"

"It's brought back some memories, mostly good but bad ones keeping popping up."

"That's why you were staring at the pier?"

Beth stroked away some of the condensation on the stem of her glass. "I've spent so long thinking about that summer, Jenny and the pier, I'd kind of made it a monster in my head."

"I get that," Wendy said, eyes curious. "So tell me, how did you cope back then?"

The abruptness of the question surprised her but now, in her old hometown, if felt more answerable, as if time had been swept away.

"I think I went a little bit mad because I'd always assumed, even with uni, that she'd always be at the end of a phone or email." She sipped her wine, mouth dry as emotion gathered in the base of her throat. "I thought she'd be there forever."

"What do you mean, you went a bit mad?"

"I was away from home, which was a wrench for a lot of reasons other than Jenny and I hit freshers' week hard. I went to too many parties, I drank far too much and I slept with more people than I should have. It beat going back to an empty room and my thoughts."

"How long did that last for?"

"About ten days, I think." She laughed, a sour chuckle without humour, and traced some of the scores in the tabletop with her thumbnail. "I made myself ill. The uni health team sent me to A&E where a nice doctor said it wasn't unusual for new students to burn the candle at both ends but I'd pushed it too far and nearly given myself alcohol poisoning. Once I sobered up properly, I realised the excess hadn't wiped away what I'd intended it to."

It was the most she'd ever told anyone about that period and the act of it felt both exhausting and liberating. The sex and heavy drinking hadn't been ideal conversational subjects with Nick and, since they were tied in with Jenny and that awful summer, it was easier just to bury them. Except now, of course, when fifteen years later she was paying the price for keeping the secret.

"What happened after that?"

"I was very lucky. My doctor listened properly and prescribed me anti-depressants that worked, I connected with my flatmates and got on with things." She sipped more wine, aware she'd nearly drained the glass. "What about you, how did you cope after that summer?"

Wendy sat back, downing half her drink. "It was really hard. With the boys gone, I was suddenly alone, especially when you and Kate left." Her voice cracked and Beth felt a pang of guilt.

"I'm sorry."

Wendy shrugged. "It was always going to be that way, but some of us didn't have the opportunity to leave."

"What do you mean?" Beth asked, annoyed to hear the echo of Maggie in Wendy's comment.

"We weren't all born lucky."

"Who was born lucky?"

Wendy smiled sourly. "We were different people, right from the off, Beth. You all had nice houses and families, I had a mum who didn't give a shit and a damp flat on the Duncan Jackson estate."

Beth took a deep breath. This wasn't a conversational warren she wanted to run down and Wendy wasn't simply being provocative, she clearly believed her version of history. "That's how you saw it?"

"Was I wrong? I understand why you joined us, for the thrill of it, but you were always going to leave Seagrave and I couldn't. My life never changed."

"So what did you do?"

"Not much was open to me. I got some attention during the trial but Mum didn't like it and kicked me out. I literally had no one and nobody wanted to be my friend, so I bashed about for a few months and ended up in a hostel."

Beth felt worse with every word, a proper sob story to counter her woes of leaving home, drinking too much and fucking too many people.

"They put me in touch with housing people," said Wendy, "so I got a little flat and started rebuilding."

"I'm sorry," Beth said. It felt weak and massively inadequate but what else was there to say?

"If I was in your position, Beth, I'd have legged it out of here. I wasn't smart enough to get into university, I wasn't that kind of girl."

Chapter 23

Nick tried to take in every face he saw around him on Marine Drive, his frustration growing the further he got from the hotel without finding Beth. He wasn't even sure he was going in the right direction.

He reached a row of Victorian townhouses. Neither he nor Beth had eaten since breakfast, so he looked through restaurant doors as best he could, on the off chance she'd decided to grab a bite. He didn't see her inside any of them.

As he walked, he thought about what he'd do when he found her, if she hadn't calmed down and didn't accept his apology. What if his turning up made her angrier?

No, thinking like that wouldn't get him anywhere.

He saw The Golden Nugget ahead, a beacon of familiarity as it shimmered in a rainbow of colour against the evening sky. Teenagers on bikes and skateboards stood outside, laughing and pushing each other. He checked for BMX bikes with low saddles but didn't see any.

A homeless man, a cardboard sign gripped tightly in one hand, sat against a telecoms box, his legs wrapped in a sleeping bag. Two young women, their skirts almost an afterthought, stood over him as they smoked and talked excitedly on their phones.

Nick stopped at the corner of Regent's Row. Marine Drive ran on for a couple of hundred yards, with hotels and a couple of rowdy pubs lining the pavement, so he decided to head up towards the old town.

Three drunk women wearing hen night sashes queued with two nervous-looking teenaged lads outside the entrance to the Neon Tiger gentleman's club. Nick walked past them into Regent's Row as two women came out of an alley in front of him, their heels echoing. The one nearest to him, a blonde wearing a tight vest and leggings, stumbled. Without thinking, he grabbed her arm to keep her upright.

"Thanks love," she slurred, beaming a lazy smile. "It's these heels on those bloody cobbles." She gestured vaguely towards the alley. Nick couldn't see to the end of it. "I wouldn't go down there, lousy bloody bar."

With another smile, she grabbed her friend's hand and they tottered across the road. Nick looked quickly down the alley and walked on. He had no interest investigating down there.

Most of the souvenir shops had closed but the restaurants were doing a good trade. Through windows he saw people enjoying pizza, curry or Thai and the fish and chip place had customers queuing onto the street. The mixed smells made his stomach rumble and he resolved to bring Beth here when he found her, so they could eat together and make sense of their situation.

That brief shot of positivity felt good and lifted him out of his worrisome state of mind. He knew they could work it out, that there was probably some simple explanation for everything.

An alley cut between a small bar and a pizza place and laughter drifted out from the darkness. Was it linked to the one the drunk woman told him about or did all these alleys have drinking holes at the end of them? Did the alley perhaps open onto another street full of pubs and restaurants? Beth could be anywhere.

He'd reached the church, railings protecting it from the street. Spotlights at ground level lit the small Gothic building, gravestones casting crosses against the stonework.

Passing the open gate he caught a sense of movement in the shadows of the porch, accompanied by what sounded like a small sob.

Nick stopped. "Hello? Is anybody there?"

Another sob. He couldn't just walk away but remembered Beth's warning when he'd tried to wade in this afternoon.

"Is everything okay?" he asked again, staying on the path. "Do you need help?"

"No," said a deep male voice from the darkness.

Startled, Nick stepped away from the gate and moved along the railings. From this angle, the frame of the porch was lit by the spill of a spotlight and a hi-vis vest glowed brightly as someone moved. Beyond it, he could see a young woman on the step, head bowed, hair obscuring her face. The man turned, his bald head catching the light as he glared at Nick. A homemade cross was tattooed between his eyebrows and another, bigger cross had been scarred into his cheek.

Nick's breath caught in his throat as he recognised Frankie, who'd frightened Beth enough that she had warned him to keep away.

"I hurt my leg," the woman said, to him or Frankie he couldn't tell.

The man got up and came to the railings, looming over Nick in the glare of the spotlight, his vest glowing. "She's fine."

Nick couldn't think straight, his pulse racing and roaring in his ears. He looked away from Frankie and saw the woman in the porch had one bare foot, the other clad in a flip-flop.

"Are you really?" he asked her.

"Yeah." She looked up, shielding her eyes from the glare. "My own stupid fault."

She sounded genuine. Nick glanced at Frankie and the bigger man looked at him impassively.

"Thanks though," she said, offering Nick a weak smile.

He backed away, content she was okay, and walked up Regent's Row. Adrenaline sped his pace as he glanced over his shoulder. Frankie stood on the pavement, hands on hips as he stared after him and Nick kept moving until he reached an alley on the left and turned into it.

The narrow passageway between buildings led him to a small square marked Paseo Place. A post office, craft shop and baker's were all dark while a woman wiped down tables in an otherwise empty coffee house. A metal bench, backed against a raised flower bed, was in the centre of the square and another alley across the way cut between the post office and the baker's.

Nick leaned on the bench as the adrenaline deserted him, taking deep breaths.

He heard footsteps and looked up as two men came through the alley across from him, one short and blond, the other tall and painfully thin. They stopped when they saw him and Blondie crossed his arms.

"Alright there, mate?"

"I think so," Nick said.

"You look like you're about to keel over," said Skinny.

"I'm fine."

Blondie moved to his right while Skinny edged in front of the coffee house. Nick, caught in the middle of them, felt his heart race again. Surely he couldn't have walked away from one horrible situation straight into another?

"So where were you headed?" Blondie asked, stepping even closer.

"Just out for a walk," Nick said.

"Nice night for it," said Skinny. "Now give me your wallet."

Fear pinched his shoulders as Nick realised he had, indeed, walked into something much worse than he'd left. He could try and run back the way he'd come, but they'd be on him in an instant. He might get further heading for the alley they'd used but he had no idea where it finished and what if he took a wrong turn or ran into a dead end?

"We don't want much trouble," Blondie said reasonably, "so hand over your wallet and we're sorted."

Nick couldn't take a full breath, as if his ribs were constricting his lungs. "Just leave me alone." If they found his hotel passkey, would they head there? What if they went in and Beth was back, taking her shower? He couldn't risk that. "I'm not handing it over."

"Hoped you'd say that," said Skinny and he lurched forward.

Nick sidestepped but Skinny caught his arm and yanked him off balance. Nick kept to his feet as Skinny spun him until they both faced Blondie. The shorter man rushed at them, teeth gritted, and threw his punch low. It caught Nick in the belly. Winded, he folded forward, trying to catch his breath.

"Now give us your fucking wallet."

Nick shook his head, more to clear it than show contempt, and Skinny pulled him upright. Nick ground his heel down the man's shin but his attacker kept a surprisingly firm grip.

"Hey, brothers." The voice took them all by surprise. "This looks like something I'd like to get involved in."

"Nothing to do with you, street preacher," Blondie called, "just keep walking."

Skinny wrenched Nick around until he faced the way he'd come in and his heart sank instantly. "Shit."

The scarring on his cheek catching the light, Frankie stood in the mouth of the alley, looking huge and menacing and Nick realised that whatever trouble he was in before, things had just got a lot worse.

Chapter 24

Then

When Beth got to the Jupiter, Jenny was already at their usual table. Mrs Jones had left for the day and Titus, who covered the evening shift, was making a sandwich behind the counter. Half a dozen tables were occupied, the conversation and laughter loud.

"Alright?" Jenny asked as Beth slid into the chair opposite her.

"Better than you seem. Why so sad, Eeyore?"

"Don't make fun," said Jenny as she fiddled with her necklace, "I feel terrible."

"Oh, bloody hell," Beth said, worrying she'd put her foot in it, "what's happened?"

Jenny looked as if she was going to cry. "I'm so sorry, but I broke my necklace somehow." She held up the pendant and the bottom swoop of the R was missing so now the shape looked like JP.

"Don't worry about it," Beth said, relieved nothing had happened to Jenny's family.

Jenny shook her head, eyes glistening as they caught the light. "But I do, because you bought this and your friendship means so much to me."

"And yours means so much to me too."

"People don't often buy me things and I feel terrible."

"Well, most of it's still there."

"You're not mad?"

Beth put her hand over Jenny's. "Why would I be mad? It's yours. I only bought it because I thought it'd get me into your knickers."

The comment took her by surprise and Jenny's laugh was loud and sharp. "That thought never entered my head."

"Well, that was a waste of money then, wasn't it?" She saw Kate come out of Victoria Arcade and wave. "Anyway, JP, let's go."

* * *

Kate had the T-shirts in a carrier bag and scrunched it between her hands as they walked to The Candlestick. She stopped by the pub door, her hand on a brass plate so filthy it looked like it'd been painted puke yellow.

"Nervous?" Beth asked. She was.

"Why should I be nervous when we're such master criminals?"

"I wouldn't go that far," said Jenny.

Kate pushed open the door and the others followed her in. The same bar staff as the other night looked up with disdain at the girls.

"Over here," Frankie called.

They were at a small round table next to the window. Wendy was sitting on Blake's lap, her arm draped over his shoulders. She grinned at Kate – the cat who got the cream.

"Wotcha."

Kate ignored her and sat across from Blake, annoyance coming off her in waves. Jenny rescued two stools from the next table, handed one to Beth and they sat slightly back from Kate.

"Girls," said Frankie.

Kate put the bag on the table and Frankie pulled it onto his lap and took out a T-shirt. He checked the label and the security tag then looked at them each in turn.

"Nice work," he said as his gaze lingered on Jenny.

"Thanks," Kate said.

"Any problems?" asked Blake.

Wendy shifted on his lap, her smile getting wider.

"No," said Kate, ice in her voice.

"So how did you do it?" he asked.

Kate didn't answer so Jenny leaned forward. "It was mostly Beth. She got us some shades as a disguise from Pervy Pete's then her ex's new partner came in and gave her some shit, so Beth dropped a couple of T-shirts into her bag to set off the alarm and we just strolled out while she got into trouble."

Blake and Mouse laughed and Frankie nodded his head, acknowledging the success. "Well done girls and that's good thinking, Beth."

"You did well surviving Pervy Pete," said Wendy.

"Who the fuck is that?" asked Blake.

"Surely you've heard me talk about him in the past?"

"Wendy, I try my best not to listen to you."

Her face fell. "That's not nice."

Nobody else spoke.

"So are you going to tell me or shall I ask Beth?" Blake said.

"I'll tell you," Wendy said with a quick smile. "Pervy Pete's a lecher. When I used to go into his shop, he'd check out my rack and stroke my palm and make me feel really uncomfortable."

"Is this true?" Blake asked Beth.

"Yeah, he's gross. Not many fifteen and sixteen-year-olds go in there wearing bikini tops more than once."

"So, Pervy Pete being a pervert aside," Kate said, a little too loudly, as if to draw attention back to their success, "the rest of it went well." She looked at Frankie. "So did we do okay?"

He scratched his chin and glanced at Blake, who nodded, then looked at her. "I think you showed real balls."

"Great, so we're in the squad?"

"Uh-huh." He looked at Beth. "Your idea for escape was good and cold."

It felt like the worst backhanded compliment ever and suddenly Beth didn't want to be in that grubby little pub anymore, surrounded by people who put her on edge. As pleased as Kate was to become part of this squad, nobody had told them what it entailed. Nicking T-shirts from a chain shop was one thing but what would come next, especially since Frankie's squad helped out the likes of Hugh Cowley? Her mother's irrational worries about Beth getting pregnant by the blokes from the Waltzer would pale if she knew she'd passed the initiation test into a criminal gang.

"Now you're in," Blake said, "let's head down to the front, drink our body weight and see what we can turn up."

Beth felt her stomach roll with the sick feeling that if she did, something unpleasant would happen. "I think I'll head back, actually."

Kate turned so quickly Beth was surprised she didn't hear her neck creak. "What? A few drinks won't matter."

"You go, I'm feeling a bit weird."

"Oh shit," said Kate, "did your dad have a turn or something?"

"No, it's just…" She stood up, giving her friend a weak smile.

"I'll walk you back," said Jenny.

Kate's disappointment sounded complete. "You're going as well?"

"You'll be fine, Kate, I'll look after you," said Blake.

"I'll bet you will," muttered Wendy.

Beth put her hands on Kate's shoulders. "Speak to you tomorrow."

"Uh-huh, you take care." Kate patted Beth's hands.

"I'll see you all later," Beth said, looking around the table without catching anyone's eye.

Jenny said her goodbyes then they left the pub and walked back towards Broad Row.

"Did that feel weird to you?" Jenny asked, hooking her arm through Beth's.

"Uh-huh. Weird and uncomfortable."

"Phew, thank God for that, I thought it was just me. I know Kate's being led by her desires but I really don't want to get pulled into anything heavy."

"I don't want to steal anything again," Beth said.

"Me neither, though I wouldn't mind seeing more of Frankie."

"You've got the hots for Frankie?"

"Haven't you?" Jenny asked. "He's ripped and big and scary. Wow."

Beth, looking at the affection in Jenny's expression, was glad she hadn't confided how uncomfortable he made her feel. "You go for it."

"As if you had any more chance than me," Jenny scoffed good-naturedly.

"Dream on, Jenny." Beth laughed.

"Wait!" Blake called and they both turned.

"Oh no," said Jenny.

Beth felt her stomach drop.

They waited while Blake jogged to them. "This Pervy Pete," he said, "who the fuck is it?"

"You really don't know?" Jenny asked.

"If I did, I wouldn't be asking."

"He's the newsagent on Melton Street."

"Fuck, I used to buy my fags from him. I can't believe that I didn't know he was a pervert."

"We're not making it up, Blake," Beth said.

"I get that but the thought of him letching after young girls makes me…" He couldn't express himself but made a fist, his hands shaking. "Meet me outside his shop at ten tomorrow morning, just you two."

"Why?"

"Because maybe I can teach him a lesson."

Chapter 25

"Why don't you fuck off down to the pier, street preacher, and sing Kumbaya and save the pretty girls who've had too much to drink?"

"Glow gently, brother," said Frankie as he shook out his arms, the biceps big and tight.

"Fuck's sake," muttered Skinny.

Nick dropped his shoulder and ducked down. Skinny lost his grip and Nick dodged forward, out of his grasp but not close enough for Frankie to grab him.

"Bollocks," muttered Blondie then he rushed Frankie, arms spread as if he intended to rugby-tackle him.

Frankie stepped out of the way with surprising grace and pushed Blondie into the wall. He hit it with a grunt and pushed away quickly, his face full of rage.

"Take the piss, eh? We'll fucking have you, Jesus-freak."

Frankie didn't move this time and the smaller man bounced off him, fists swinging wildly but barely connecting. Frankie elbowed the back of his head and Blondie went down like a sack of potatoes, slumping against Frankie's legs. He stepped back, carefully laying Blondie's head on the ground before turning to Skinny.

"Be calm, brother."

Skinny either didn't hear or didn't care and ran for Frankie, pulling his fist back as he closed the distance between them. At the last moment, Frankie slapped Skinny hard across the face, the crack echoing around the square. Skinny staggered towards the baker's but collapsed in a heap before he reached it.

Frankie turned to Nick and held out a hand in a calming gesture. "Are you okay?"

Immediate danger over, Nick's pain came back into focus though he could breathe easier now. He nodded. "Got winded."

"It'll pass," said Frankie, "just breathe."

Keeping an eye on him, Nick tried to take ever deeper breaths as Frankie rolled Blondie into the recovery position then moved to Skinny. The thug groaned and Frankie knelt beside him, closed his eyes and put a hand on Skinny's forehead.

"What're you doing?" Nick asked.

Frankie regarded him carefully, touched a finger to the cross between his eyebrows. "Reflecting."

"On what?"

Frankie stood up and shrugged off his backpack. "Working through the cycle. Reflection leads to understanding, understanding leads to improvement. Violence is never the right answer and I'm not a fan of hitting people, even if it's just that they'll wake up with headaches."

"Serves them right."

"That's not very charitable."

"You hit them."

"I did what was necessary, causing as little pain as possible." Frankie sounded sad. He took a bottle of water from a side pocket on the rucksack and offered it to Nick.

"No thanks."

Frankie shrugged, took a big swig then put the bottle back into its pocket and pulled the rucksack on. "My name's Frank. What happened?"

Nick's swirling confusion made him feel giddy. Far from the threat Beth had suggested, it appeared Frankie – or Frank – wasn't going to be a problem to him.

"Sit, brother, you might be in shock."

"No," said Nick, "it's just…" How could he explain himself?

"You have nothing to fear from me, though I understand why you wouldn't believe that. After all, you saw me earlier on Broad Row, didn't you?"

Oh shit, Nick thought, so he had seen them.

"Worry not, you did the right thing. You didn't know what was happening so you took action and that's admirable. I wish more people were like you."

"What did the police do?"

Frank smiled. "Officer Maria and I have history. She came to check and took over the situation. I was trying to rouse the unconscious gentleman and she called for assistance."

"What about the girl just now, at the church?"

"I found her crying on the step, she'd lost her shoes and purse so I provided her with flip-flops and gave her a couple of pounds and she's now on her way home."

"I thought…"

"People often do." He pointed to the badge on the left breast of his vest. "My name is Frank Collins and I'm part of the street ministry for the Glow Church. A group of us travel the town, helping our weary fellow travellers, providing water and food and flip-flops, as well as advice if asked."

Nick's head spun, trying to reconcile this man to the person who'd frightened Beth so much. "Glow Church?"

"It's a charity, brother. Now, you didn't tell me your name."

"Nick, Nick Parker."

"Thank you, Nick. Can I trust you now realise I'm on your side?"

"Uh-huh."

"Well since our friends here will be recovering soon, let me take you for a coffee to settle your nerves."

As much as it would calm him down, he couldn't afford the time. "Thanks for the offer but I need to do something."

"You're looking for your wife?"

Another surprise. "How did you know?"

"Is she in trouble?"

"I hope not. We had an argument and she left the hotel and I need to find her."

Frank's eyes widened. "With no knowledge of Seagrave?" He smiled.

Nick, in spite of himself, smiled too, suddenly aware of how stupid all this was. "Not a bit."

"Then let me settle your nerves and help find your wife."

Had Beth mistaken this man for someone else altogether? Other than how he'd dealt with the muggers, Frank didn't project any sense of threat at all, his tone as benign as could be.

"I see you're conflicted, Nick, but I give you my word."

Nick made a decision quickly. He had to find Beth but didn't know where to start and this man might have the knowledge to do so. "Okay," he said finally, "help me find her."

Chapter 26

"Have you and Nick been together long?" Wendy asked.

"We met at uni, had a couple of classes together and one thing led to another." It was the barest essentials of the truth but sounded better than her being on the brink of chaos and Nick providing her with an island of calm so she could settle.

"Family?"

"Not yet."

Wendy seemed surprised. "Any planned?"

"Oh yes, we're practising well." She'd endured enough conversations with people who thought a childless woman in her early thirties was selfish, to keep it light, because trying to explain the pain to them was often like talking to a brick wall. How did you get across the frustration of seeing friends and colleagues falling pregnant at the drop of a hat, or the anger at news stories of people having babies they couldn't afford and mistreating the ones they already had?

"I'm sure it'll happen," Wendy said, after looking intently at Beth for a moment too long. "It often does when you least expect it."

Except in their case, Beth wanted to say. She thought of Nick, beside her in those offices and cubicles waiting for test results, squeezing her hand as he shared the pain, and felt bad, all over again, for her behaviour in the hotel. She had to speak to him, had to apologise, try and get things back to some semblance of normality. She reached into her bag for her phone, wanting to at least let him know where she was, but couldn't find it. She put her bag on her lap and searched it again, checking all the pockets but it wasn't there.

"What's the matter?"

"I was going to ring Nick but I must have left my phone in the room."

"I'm sure he won't worry, we've only been out half an hour."

"Oh no, he'll be fine," Beth said, trying to convince herself.

"I would think so."

"So how about you, do you have any family?"

Wendy's smile was humourless. "A son called Philip. He's thirteen, which seems amazing to me." She looked into her glass. "He lives with his dad in Norwich."

"Do you see him often?" Beth knew the answer as soon as she saw the little wobble in Wendy's chin.

"Not really, me and his dad didn't part on the best of terms and he got full custody. I was still in a bad way, wasn't focused on things like I should have been and wasn't looking after myself." She stared into her glass. "Or Philip."

"Oh." What was she supposed to say to that?

"My ex turned out to be a real shit and made sure all my visits got fucked up for one reason or another. He was ill one week and couldn't drop him off or Philip was poorly, or something was up with his new partner. All kinds of shit, whatever he could think of. In the end, I got so fed up, I caught the bus to Norwich."

The pain in Wendy's voice was tangible enough Beth couldn't meet her gaze.

"I'd cleaned myself up by then and went there on the bus. I'd won a little cuddly toy, some stupid black and white cat thing, on a grabber in an arcade and wrapped it in some paper I found. I spent the whole journey rehearsing what I was going to say."

Wendy took a sip of drink, her eyes red with unshed tears. "I couldn't afford a taxi from the bus station and the shuttle bus wasn't much cheaper, so I got a one-way ticket, banking on my ex bringing me back." She laughed, humourlessly. "It took forever."

"Wendy, you don't have to…"

"I'm fine, honestly," she said but her chin wobbled again. "I checked the address on my phone for the hundredth time and started walking." She took a deep breath and let it out slowly. "I ran out of road before I reached the number." A tear fell and she rubbed it away quickly with her index finger.

"When was this?"

"Ten years ago."

"You haven't seen Philip for ten years? That's awful, what did the courts say?"

"Not much, I was an unfit mother, remember?"

"I'm so sorry. How did you come back from that?"

"I slept with too many people and drank too much for a while." Wendy smiled wearily. "Is that how you put it?"

"Something like that. So are you seeing anyone now?"

"On and off but no serious relationships down the years and I haven't had any more kids either." She winced. "Sorry, that sounded shitty."

Beth held up her hand. "I know what you meant."

They were quiet for a few moments, Wendy drawing circles in the condensation on her glass. Beth glanced over at the domino match, not sure of what to say.

"I've missed this," Wendy said finally, "having friends that understand. You can't imagine how pleased I was when you answered my message."

"I'm glad you got in touch."

"Shame it couldn't have been with better news."

"Absolutely. It was such a shock, I couldn't believe it. The bits I've read online since seem to think it was suicide but John didn't take that well at the funeral." She gave Wendy a quick rundown of what happened.

"That was fucking tactless," Wendy agreed but her sentence tailed off as her lips pinched together. Beth waited and Wendy went on, "People get down though, it happens. Kate lost her mum, maybe she wasn't coping and ran out of ways of hiding it."

"But would she leave everyone, especially her little boy?" As heartbreaking as losing her father had been, it never once occurred to Beth to take her own life. "Did you ever talk about it, how she felt?"

Confusion puckered around Wendy's eyes. "Why would we do that?"

"Why wouldn't you?" Beth asked, confused.

"Would you, with your friends?"

"I'd like to think so."

"We didn't." Wendy picked up her glass and cleared her throat. "But then, I didn't tell you the whole truth. Kate and I weren't what you'd call close."

Beth's confusion grew. "What do you mean, you weren't close?"

Wendy shrugged. "Exactly what I say, we were from different worlds, you know?"

Beth had the sense there was something missing in what Wendy was telling her but couldn't quite grasp it. "But you asked me to come on her behalf."

"I'm sure it's what she'd have wanted." Wendy put down her glass, her expression a mixture of defeat and annoyance. "I didn't mean to lead you on, but me and Kate, we just chatted if we met in the street. Last time we spoke, she said she was thrilled you two were talking again and I thought you'd want to know about the funeral."

"Well I'm glad you told me," Beth said, forcing a smile. It was as pointless to try and understand why Wendy had led her on as it was to be annoyed by it. "You did the right thing and, regardless of the situation, it's good to see you again."

"And you." Wendy put on a big smile, pressed her hands on the table. "I'm so pleased you're not annoyed with me. Let's have another drink to celebrate."

Beth, wanting to get back to the hotel, didn't have time to decline. The dominoes table erupted in aggressive shouts and the man who'd scowled at her jumped to his feet. Another man, taller and wider, stood up too and very soon they were pointing into each other's faces. The scowler said something about "the slag you're fucking married to" and the taller man swung a punch. Chaos broke out with more shouts and random punches. A man fell onto Wendy, who shrieked and stood up quickly.

"Oi, oi, oi." It took Beth a moment to recognise Chubb, a lot heavier and balder than she remembered, as the man charging around from behind the bar.

Wendy moved around to Beth's side of the table as he waded into the fight. There was the loud percussion of smashing glass and the atmosphere felt more oppressive as the rest of the pub turned to face this new entertainment.

Literally backed into the corner, Beth wanted out. If the fight came their way, they wouldn't be able to avoid it and she grabbed Wendy's arm. "We have to go." Wendy wasn't easily distracted and Beth had to shake her arm. "Wendy!"

More glass smashed and a man screamed in pain, the fight gaining momentum as Beth pushed her way to the door gripping Wendy's hand tightly.

Chapter 27

Then

"Are you ready for this?" Jenny asked.

"Nope," said Beth. All last evening and again this morning, she'd debated whether to turn up or not. Pervy Pete made her uncomfortable, he always had, but she had no idea what Blake planned and that was worse. Very much an unknown quantity, she didn't know him well enough to understand what kind of lesson he planned to teach but he had an air about him that he might do something rash and not worry about it. "What about you?"

"I don't think I slept a wink last night for worrying about it."

"Girls!" Blake shouted and ran across the road to them. His red T-shirt had a sun logo and his sunglasses were pushed back into his hair. "What's happening?"

"Waiting for you," Beth said.

"Nice. Anyone in the shop?"

"Nobody's gone in or come out since I've been here."

"Good," he said and rubbed his hands together, bouncing on the balls of his feet. "So here's the plan, you and me go in and pretend we don't know one another. I'll go round by the drinks, you grab a magazine and go to the counter."

"What do I do?" asked Jenny.

He regarded her for long enough without speaking that her shoulders tightened and she looked uncomfortable. "Stay outside, keep watch."

"Keep watch?" she said. "What for? You're not going to do anything serious, are you?"

He grinned, pointing both hands at his chest. "Would I?"

"We don't know," said Beth.

"Trust me, I just want to teach him a lesson." He sounded sincere but there was an energy to him she didn't like, a coiled spring waiting to go off and hit someone in the eye. "Count to ten then follow me."

"I'm not sure about this," she whispered to Jenny, as he crossed the road.

Blake turned. "Ten," he said and went into the shop.

She and Jenny crossed the road and she counted to ten standing by the mesh window. Jenny stuck her thumbs up. "Good luck."

Against her better judgement, Beth entered the shop. The door was propped open by a pack of bound comics. Blake was looking in a fridge and she stopped by the magazine rack, the covers blurring into one mass. Aware of Pervy Pete watching her from behind his rampart of newspapers, she grabbed a magazine at random, picked up a bag of crisps and went to the counter.

"Alright, love?" His smile quickly slipped into a leer. His plain grey shirt was faded and his waistcoat had seen better days. "I don't see you for ages then it's twice in as many days. I feel like all me Christmases have come at once."

"Well, there you go," she said, so ill at ease she couldn't think straight.

His eyeline dropped to her chest. "You're a real treat for the eyes."

Even though she was instigating this and knew Blake was listening, she didn't feel any less grubby as he gazed at her. "Thank you."

"So what do we have here?"

He reached out and, fearful he'd stroke her palm, she dropped the magazine and crisps on one of the piles of papers.

He prodded the packet. "Not so good for you, these, they won't help you keep that lovely figure. Unless, of course, you're getting a lot of exercise?" He winked. "You have a boyfriend, I take it?"

"Just split up."

"Idiot didn't realise what he had." He lifted the magazine. "*Mechanics Monthly*, eh? Like getting your fingers dirty, do you?"

Beth felt a shudder run through her. "How much do I owe?"

His greasy smile slipped away as he looked over her shoulder.

"Alright, mate?" Blake asked.

Pete sat upright. "I'm just serving this young lady."

Blake stood beside Beth and Pete looked him up and down. "I heard you being nasty with her."

"What're you talking about, we were just chatting. Tell him, love."

She felt the power shift. "You were being gross."

"What?" Pete shook his head. "She doesn't know what she's saying, mate."

The atmosphere had changed and she could see in his face Pete felt it too.

"Are you like this with all the girls, you old pervert?" Blake asked.

"Like what?" Pete stood up. "I don't like your attitude, mate. You're barred. Go on, clear off."

Blake looked calm, comfortable with the unease. "What would the police say?"

"Yeah, good luck with that," Pete sneered, "your word against mine and I've been here longer than you."

"Maybe, but I could always sort you out myself, pay you back for all the young girls you've had a pop at."

"Don't fucking threaten me, boy." Pete reached under the counter without taking his eyes off Blake and straightened up, holding a cricket bat. "This thing tends to make a dent."

Panic rattled through Beth. This was taking a turn for the worse.

"You haven't got the balls to hit me with that, you old perv."

Pete squinted at him, as if trying to place this stranger. "I know you, don't I?" He clicked his fingers in Blake's face. "No, I knew your mum. How is she these days?" He smiled, licked his lips. "Proper council house she was, back in the day."

Beth saw Blake tense, his fists opening and closing. "Stop," she said to both of them.

"Dirty old bitch, she'd do anyone for the bus fare home."

"One more word," Blake said, teeth together, jaw set.

"I'll give you plenty," said Pete, tapping the bat into his left palm. "How many do you want?"

"Seriously," said Beth, her panic rising, "don't."

"If he comes over this counter, love, it's assault." He smirked. "Did you think I wouldn't recognise you, little Nelly Blake?"

Blake vaulted the counter, scattering newspapers as he went. Beth, surprised, let out a yelp and stepped back. Pete swung the bat but didn't have enough room and Blake slapped it down onto the counter. It clattered onto the floor. Pete went to his right but there was nowhere to go and Blake grabbed his lapels, spinning him around.

"Say that again!"

"Blake," Beth called, "what're you doing?"

Blake pushed Pete towards the backroom door, lips twisted into an angry snarl. Beth grabbed for his arm but missed and clambered over the counter herself.

"Jenny," she called, "get in here."

162

Blake shoved Pete into the wall, his head bouncing off. "Nobody calls me that name."

He pushed Pete through the door and Beth followed them into a narrow corridor, lined on both sides by boxes of crisps, packs of toilet rolls and cases of canned drinks. A small desk, cluttered with paper, stood next to a filing cabinet. The door at the far end was closed.

Blake pulled the chair out from under the desk and pushed Pete down into it. He tilted back briefly, the mechanism groaning, and tried to get up but Blake stood over him.

"Fucking sit down," he said, jabbing a finger into Pete's shoulder.

"What're you doing?" Beth asked urgently.

Jenny appeared in the doorway and made her jump. "What's going on?"

"I don't know."

Blake slapped Pete hard, snapping his head to the right then backhanded him. "Nobody calls me that name."

Beth grabbed his arm. "He didn't call you a name, you said this was about the girls."

Blake tried to shake her off but she held on tight, more scared of letting this go further than him having a pop at her.

"Blake, it's about the girls."

Glaring at her, he shook his head and took a deep breath, hissing it out, his hands making fists. He looked at the ceiling, chewing on his lips.

"Blake," Jenny said desperately, "the girls."

"Okay," he said finally, his voice softer. He looked at Pete. "Leave them alone, you old pervert, or next time I won't have anyone around to hold me back."

Pete, his cheeks red with livid handprints, looked astonished. "Are you fucking nuts?"

Blake was shaking. "Say anything to them again, I'll come back and kill you."

Pete made a sound Beth mistook for being a sob then realised he was laughing. "You have no idea how much trouble you're in, do you?"

"And you're a nonce, so I win."

"You're also an idiot, Nelly."

"Nobody calls me Nelly." Blake punched him, the impact loud in the confined space and Pete's nose was instantly bloody.

Blake shook with anger. Beth, too terrified now to grab him, backed away.

"Did your mum call you that after one of her johns when she was on the game?" Pete licked blood from his lip and spat it at Blake, who didn't flinch.

"I wore red for a reason," he muttered.

"If you were so tough, you'd let me stand up."

Blake kicked the chair and Pete fell over the back of it. He scrambled to his feet and grabbed a pencil off the desk.

"You're not the sharpest tool in the box, are you, Nelly?"

Blake went for him. Pete swung a fist and the pencil buried deep into Blake's arm but he didn't seem to realise as he grabbed the newsagent around the throat and drove him into the desk. Pete struggled but Blake had the better angle and punched him in the face again and again. Pete's face became a mass of blood and he stopped struggling. Blake punched him again, the impact sound wetter now.

"He's going to kill him," Jenny shouted.

Beth grabbed his arm to stop him swinging punches but Blake turned on her angrily. Fear made the edges of her vision shimmer black and red and, for a moment, she thought she was going to faint. When it cleared, Blake was staring at her.

"Leave me alone, Beth," he said. "I mean it."

But she couldn't, this was her fault. "You're going to kill him," she screamed.

He tried to push her aside but she stood her ground and screamed again, stepping between him and the desk, blocking his view of Pete.

"You're going to kill him," she shouted, grabbing his wrists.

For a moment, she thought he was going to hit her but something shifted in his face. She didn't know what it was, but it slowed him up.

"Blake," she shouted, "you have to stop."

He took a couple of deep breaths, letting them out slowly. Blood had flecked across his lips and cheek and he wiped it away. "He needs to learn a lesson."

"Look at him," she shouted, "he already has."

"Nobody calls me that name and gets away with it."

"He didn't get away with it, look at all the blood. You let him wind you up and half killed him." If this had ever been a gallant gesture to help young girls, that ideal had long since gone. "It's done."

"He's learned his lesson," said Jenny.

"I doubt it, pervert motherfucker."

Pete coughed and spat on the floor. Blake turned away, pulling his wrists free of Beth.

"Leave it," she said, "it's not worth it. You'll go to prison."

"I doubt it," he said and pushed his way through the door into the shop.

Jenny stepped smartly aside to let him by. "You've still got the pencil in your arm," she said but he'd already gone.

Pete grabbed one of the filing cabinets for support and pulled himself up so he sat on the edge of the desk. He groaned and leaned forward, spitting blood onto the carpet.

"What do we do?" Jenny asked, panic making her voice rise. "I don't know what to do."

Beth stepped towards Pete cautiously. A blood bubble had formed in his left nostril.

"Get away from me," he said, waving his hand. "Just get out of here."

"We need to call someone," she said, "you're not okay."

"I've had worse," he mumbled. He pressed a finger against a tooth and groaned again. "Just fuck off and leave me alone."

"But you need–"

"Fuck off!" he shouted, blood spraying. "I don't need your help, I don't want you telling anyone."

Jenny held her arm. "What do we do?"

Beth couldn't focus, her mind was whirling with thoughts and guilt, all impossible to pin down.

"I already told you, leave me the fuck alone," Pete said and spat bloody saliva that just missed Jenny's foot.

Beth snapped back to attention. "Right," she said and grabbed Jenny's hand, "we're going."

She peered around the door frame. Blake leaned on the counter, breathing deeply, clutching the bloodied pencil in his hand. She was uncertain about walking past him, not sure what he might do.

He glanced at her. "It's okay."

"Have you calmed down?"

He nodded. "I fucking warned him, you heard me, I warned the stupid bastard." He threw the pencil across the shop.

"You beat the shit out of him, Blake."

"I know." He bit his lip. "Don't say anything to anyone."

"Is that a threat?"

"No, I'm just telling you both. I can sort this, Beth, just walk away."

"How can we? He's going to report it."

"I'll sort it." He abruptly pulled up the hatch and the girls followed him, at a distance, out of the shop. "Seriously, just pretend you weren't here."

None of this made sense. "He saw us."

"And you helped him and he told you not to tell anyone. You're out of it."

"You're not going back in there," Jenny said.

"No, I'm not," Blake said as he walked away.

Jenny and Beth exchanged a glance, equally astonished, as they watched him go.

"Do you think you can you leave it, Beth?"

She closed her eyes as the adrenaline deserted her. Feeling sick, she leaned against the wall. "I don't know."

"Did he deserve it?" Jenny didn't sound like she wanted to ask the question but needed to process the answer, which was exactly what Beth was doing. "I mean, he was a pervert."

"He was," Beth conceded, "but it's not what got him the beating."

"Pete kept pushing him, even after Blake warned him."

"Did it justify that?"

Jenny shrugged.

Something dragged in the doorway, startling both girls and they pushed away from the wall. Pete, on his hands and knees, squinted at them. He'd wiped away the worst of the blood but his mouth and cheeks were already puffing up. "What're you two looking at?"

"Pete, we just…"

He shook his head. "Fuck off, the pair of you."

"But you're hurt," Beth insisted.

"And I told you before, I've had worse. This isn't about you, it's about me and Nelly Blake. So be good girls and fuck off, right?" He shoved aside the comics pack and slammed the door, locking it and flicking over the 'closed' sign.

"Well," said Jenny, "that told us."

Chapter 28

"Let's just have one more, yeah?"

Beth didn't want another drink, she wanted to head back to the hotel and try to mend some fences with Nick. But as Wendy seemed so determined, so eager to take her somewhere else, it seemed churlish to blow her off.

"Just the one," she said.

"That's the spirit." Wendy hooked her arm into Beth's. "I've got just the place, let's go."

Instead of turning towards the seafront or heading straight towards the old town, Wendy went left instead.

"So where're we going?"

"Trust me, you'll enjoy it. And it can't be worse than the Chesty Wanker, eh?"

They walked until Beth saw the high window-filled walls of the flats marking the outer edges of the Duncan Jackson estate. Whatever memories she had of Seagrave, not many of them centred around here, the only place her dad specifically advised her to steer well clear of once she started going out with the girls.

"Are we going into the estate?"

"That was my plan."

"But I haven't got my phone. I'll need to head back to the hotel first."

"Why?"

"Well, I don't want Nick to worry."

"How do you know he'll be worried? He's the one who left after your argument. Maybe he's gone for a drink and forgotten the time."

"Wendy, he doesn't know anybody here."

"I'll take you back if you want," she said, sounding wounded. "But I thought since we haven't seen one another for years, you'd enjoy catching up."

It seemed reasonable except, like in the pub, Beth got the sensation there was something going on behind Wendy's words, even if she couldn't quite grasp what it was.

* * *

The Duncan Jackson estate had weathered better than Melton Street but only just. For every two houses a resident took pride in, another was missing a fence or a window, and glass shimmered in the road like diamonds waiting to embed themselves in the soles of their shoes. 'For sale' signs, listing at angles, clustered around repossessed properties; doors and windows were shuttered with steel sheeting. One front garden held three cars in varying states of completeness, a massive Union Jack mounted on a broom handle stuck through an upstairs window.

"Looks worse than it is," said Wendy. She sounded embarrassed. "Do you remember much of it?"

"Not really, though I did come in to see a pub burn down once."

"The Jolly Roger," Wendy said with a nod. "I'd been out with Blake and Frankie and we saw the flames before we were even in the estate. Three fire engines, loads of coppers and then all the stories afterwards about them finding the body in the bins." She smiled wistfully. "Seems like a different life."

"It was."

"For you, maybe." She turned in a slow circle, arms wide. "I mean, look at it. You got away, made something of yourself and here I am, in the same fucking town and living on the same fucking estate and what do I have to show?"

Beth, thinking of Wendy's son, didn't say anything.

"You three were like fairy-tale princesses to me, which I know sounds stupid, but it's true and I so wanted to be part of that world; to have a chance." She rubbed her hands together, as if trying to rid herself of the resentment. "I'm not sure what I'm trying to say."

It felt like whatever she was going to say could go two ways, either bonding them over their past selves or unleashing a storm of vitriol that had been shut away for too long. Beth didn't want to go through either of them, particularly. "You don't have to explain yourself," she said, hoping it sounded kind.

"Of course." Wendy laughed. She walked a few paces in silence then took a deep breath. "You and Jenny were always nice to me; it was Kate who was the bitch but she had the thing for Blake and I was kind of in the way."

"For what it's worth, her thing for Blake put a wedge between us too."

"And then the shit hit the fan."

"That was hardly Kate's fault."

"In my head it all comes back to her."

Laying the blame at Kate's feet wasn't anywhere close to the truth, even if it sounded logical from Wendy's view of the situation. "But you were at the court with me, you know it was all down to Blake and Frankie."

Wendy shrugged. "Whatever, it all changed after that. You and Kate left, the boys went to prison and I'm left on my tod." She shook her head and tried a smile that didn't quite connect. "I'm going over old ground now, aren't I?"

"It's our past."

"Our shit past." This time the smile connected. "I'm sorry, I don't want us to fall out."

"We don't need to fall out, Wendy."

"I just can't switch off, you know? It's always here for me, whichever way I turn."

"I understand," Beth said and sympathised.

Leaving Seagrave gave her the distance to re-examine things relatively objectively, but any sifting through the details only ever came back to the three villains of the piece being Blake, Frankie and herself. Time couldn't erase that guilt and she felt it surface again, a sharp edge ready to cut her at any moment.

"I'm always doing this," Wendy said, sounding defeated, "ruining things when they're going well."

"You're not, I'm just a bit tired. It's been a long day."

"I'll stop talking about it, I promise." Wendy's shoulders folded in, her anguish making her smaller. "The pub's just around the corner, we'll have a quick drink and clear the air then I'll walk you back."

"There's no need to clear the air, you've not ruined anything."

"You see what I mean, about you always treating me right?"

They walked through a narrow passage, the walls crawling with graffiti, and onto a path with terraced houses on one side and a blank wall three storeys high on the other. On the corner, a deformed wheelie bin, its lid gone and one side half melted away, stood guard.

"It's all gone downhill," Wendy said as they cut across some garages. "They put a lot of foreigners here who work on the docks, so most of the original crowd moved out. Bit rough and ready at times."

The street they came out on had small houses packed along both sides of the road, cars crammed in at the kerbs, some on front lawns. The carcass of a tyre-less kid's bike rested against the buzzing lamp post it had been chained to. Dock cranes rose out of the darkness over the roofs, warning lights flashing at the end of the arms.

The houses on the south side ended at a small parade of shops, of which only a Chinese restaurant was open. A newsagent, bookie's and cafe were locked up and dark, the remaining unit was empty, posters plastered over the window grills.

Behind the shops, standing in the middle of a half-empty car park enclosed by a waist-high brick wall, was a pub, the big sign on the gable end identifying it as The Rising Sun. It was long and wide, with an extension protruding from the side like a bricked hernia; two big bay windows faced the street, the curtains open to show the busy bar. A single-track road led down beside the car park and lights from the docks showed through the scrubby trees and bramble bushes beyond the wall.

"Here we are," Wendy said with a big smile.

Beth couldn't even recall coming this far into the Duncan Jackson before. "I really don't remember this pub."

"Well, that's weird because we came here a lot back in the day. Doesn't matter though, you'll know it when you get inside."

Beth wasn't sure she would. She had a decent memory, of that summer particularly and she could describe The Candlestick down to its door plates but she was convinced she'd never been here before. Worse, the pub logo looked far too much like the one on the T-shirts the BMX riders wore. The ringing in her ears was getting louder, the sense that something wasn't quite right.

"Anything?" Wendy asked as they crossed the car park.

"Nope."

"Oh bloody hell, how could you not?"

"Because I don't. I've never been here before, Wendy."

"I thought it might have made an impression on you," she said, sounding hurt, "but clearly not. We can go somewhere else if you want?"

"That might be an idea," she said, hoping that didn't mean the night would drag on as they searched for another pub.

Now Wendy looked hurt. "Really? But we're here now. I'll get the drinks in."

"I think…"

"I know," Wendy said quickly, "but come on, one more drink then we'll head back."

Not convinced, but not wanting to upset Wendy, Beth angled towards the main doors but Wendy walked by them.

"Not in the bar," she said, glancing over her shoulder, "we go in the locals' lounge. It'll be quieter and we can chat."

They walked alongside the extension, sounds of a working kitchen drifted through an open window set too high for Beth to see into. The car park extended beyond the end of the building a dozen or so feet, the back lost in darkness, some of the bramble venturing into the vacant spaces. A small wooden stall full of wheelie bins seemed popular with seagulls judging by the amount of shit on the floor.

Beth heard footsteps from around the corner and felt a quick, sharp twinge of worry stroke her shoulders.

The person moved in front of the wooden stall, cast in shadow, his gait unsteady due to a limp.

"Trust you to be fucking early, Wendy," he said.

Beth recognised his voice almost immediately.

Chapter 29

Then

Beth walked to the Jupiter in glorious sunshine, her stomach tying itself in knots as she tried to figure out how to tell her best friend what Blake had done to Pervy Pete.

The lunchtime crowd almost filled the cafe and Mrs Jones was busy taking orders, the kitchen noisy through the serving hatch.

"Hey," said Kate. She'd poured her Diet Coke into a tumbler; Beth's unopened can wore a glass like a hat. "You look chirpy."

Beth smiled, in spite of herself, as she sat down and wished Jenny hadn't had to work, so they could at least back each other up. Kate had always been able to see through her and Beth believed the reverse to be true, though things seemed to have shifted out of alignment slightly since the Goose Fair. Whether that was due to Frankie and Blake, or the girls withdrawing from each other slightly to make the parting in September less painful, she didn't know.

The bell over the door tinkled and Kate looked over Beth's shoulder. "Shit," she said, stretching the word. "It's Wendy."

Beth turned as Wendy held the door for two women. The older one, in her late sixties, had a dome of white curls while the other, who could have been thirty or fifty or anywhere in between, was scrawny with sharp cheekbones and darkly shadowed eyes. Wendy waved at them, smiling broadly.

"Wotcha, girls," she said too loudly when she got closer. Several customers turned to look but she didn't seem to notice. "How are you?"

"Okay," said Beth, "you?"

"Not bad, just brought my nan out for lunch." The older woman sat at an empty table and smiled at Beth. "She likes it here," Wendy said, sitting across from her grandmother and pulling a face, as if eating here was the weirdest thing in the world.

"Fair enough," said Beth and turned back to Kate.

"It's so nice of her," Kate said sarcastically, "to bring out her nan and her alkie mum. I wonder if she's following us around, trying to make friends?"

"She's harmless."

"She's after Blake, is what she is." Kate tapped her glass with one slim finger. "Anyway, what's up with you?"

"I'm fine."

Kate smiled. "Tell your face that."

Beth poured her Diet Coke and touched her tumbler to Kate's. "All for one."

"All for one."

"So how's it going with Blake?"

Kate's smile turned coy. "You remember what you were like with Ronnie in the beginning, driving me and Jen nuts? Well, we're heading into that stage."

"Into?"

"We haven't done it yet."

"His fault, your fault or lack of privacy?"

"Him, maybe all three, but it'll happen." She glared over Beth's shoulder. "Assuming that bubblehead keeps out of it. I was ready to spit nails when I saw her all over him in the pub the other night."

"I noticed."

"It's a shame you two pissed off early, it ended up a fun evening. And why did Blake follow you out? Wet Wendy asked him and he blanked her in front of everyone. Such a stupid bitch." She leaned forward, fingers knitted, elbows on the table. "So what happened, what did he want?"

The door was open, all she had to do was step forward. "He wanted to know about Pervy Pete."

"Why?"

"Because we met there the next day. Him and me and Jenny."

"What?" Kate's face clouded. "Why didn't you ask me?"

"He only told us to meet him there, I assumed he'd ask you." A blatant lie but there was something in Kate's expression that made it feel like the right thing to say. "It wasn't good."

"What do you mean, what happened?"

Beth took a sip of her drink to buy a couple of moments, knowing that things would change after this.

"He wanted to hear Pervy Pete say something to me so he could step in and have a pop."

"That's not so bad."

She saw Blake in her mind's eye – his anger and violence. "Kate, it was awful. Pete called him Nelly and Blake went off the deep end and smacked the shit out of him."

"Bollocks."

"It's true. He pinned him down and kept punching him in the face."

Kate shook her head and leaned back. Beth could almost hear her defensive walls going up. "You're lying."

There wasn't the hint of humour in her voice, just cold accusation. It was a tone Kate had never used with her before.

"Why would I lie? Ask Jenny, there was blood everywhere, he must have broken Pete's nose."

"Fuck off, Beth."

Each word felt like a slap. "What?" Had Kate really just said that?

"Don't fuck this up for me, Beth."

"What are you talking about?"

"All this bollocks. I like him, alright, we've only got a few weeks before uni, let me enjoy myself."

"I'm not trying to stop you getting with Blake, I just wanted you to know what happened."

"Well thanks, but not interested."

Had she not explained it properly? "Kate, he went nuts, I've never seen anything like it."

"And what did Pervy Pete do to you? Did he stroke your hand, say anything?"

Surely Kate wasn't going to try and justify the violence? "He said stuff, he was grubby."

"And that was the plan, right? That's what you and Jen and Blake cooked up together."

"No, that's not–"

"Beth." Kate pressed her palms against the table. "Pervy Pete's been a proper weirdo since we can both remember, we've both experienced it and Blake doesn't like that kind of thing. Maybe Pete got what was coming to him."

Beth sat back, smiling vacantly in amazement. Not only had Kate attempted to justify it, she'd found an angle to make Beth sound unreasonable if she disputed it. "Well," she said finally, because it seemed Kate was waiting for a reply, "that's one way of looking at it."

"There's another way?" Kate's eyes were hard, flinty and she bit her lower lip, as if trying to stop herself from saying something she'd regret.

"I'd have said so."

Kate put a hand over Beth's, her skin warm, the contact seeming to calm the air. "I know it was hard breaking up with Ronnie and Chrissie being a shit didn't help but let me enjoy this, alright? It's been a while for me and I want him."

That's not it, Beth wanted to say. She wasn't trying to be a bitch, she wasn't trying to ruin Kate's romance, she was trying to warn her best friend. "I'm not saying you shouldn't see him, I just wanted you to know," she said, ashamed at how lame it sounded.

"Uh-huh," said Kate, not sounding entirely sure. "Be happy for me, Beth."

"I am," she said, wondering if she'd ever regret the lie.

"Anyway, speaking of Chrissie, I wonder what happened to her at BJ's?"

Kate's expression lightened and Beth welcomed the change, even if it left too much unresolved.

"I'm sure I'll find out the next time I see her," Beth said.

"Did you want an escort?"

"Nah, I could take her."

Kate leaned across the table and punched Beth's arm. "You go for it, tiger."

"Wotcha." Wendy stood between them and tapped her fingertips on the tabletop, a nervous twitch as she looked from one to the other. "You did really well at BJ's."

Kate shushed her loudly enough that a woman at the next table turned to look. Kate smiled sweetly at her and then, when she'd turned away, glared at Wendy. "Are you trying to get us into trouble?"

"No, why would–"

"You can't just go around blurting stuff out like that, for fuck's sake."

"I didn't mean anything."

Kate glared at Wendy then shot a glance to Beth, who could see her friend was enjoying this. Even if Wendy was just trying to be friendly, this was a stupid conversation starter.

"All we know," Beth said, "is that there was a shoplifter in BJ's the other day."

"That's right," said Kate solemnly. "The thief was someone we went to school with, who we didn't think was a criminal."

"It's awful, her parents must be beside themselves," said Beth. "Though we clearly blame them."

Wendy's brow furrowed until the penny dropped. "I was only trying to be friendly," she said, clearly hurt.

"We get that," said Kate, "but I think your mum needs topping up."

"What?" Wendy glanced over her shoulder, looking flustered. "I'll go, I just wanted to say hi."

"And you did it well," Kate said and smiled sweetly until Wendy said "See you later" and went back to her own table.

"Harsh," said Beth, finishing her Diet Coke.

"She bloody deserves it, the fucking drip. I mean, why the hell would she think Blake sees anything in her?"

"Maybe they've got history?"

"Wants to pretend they have, you mean. Now are you buying me a drink or do I have to splash out again?"

As Beth made her way to counter, both Wendy and her nan looked up expectantly. Beth smiled at them. Wendy's mother, if it really was her mother, stared into her coffee cup.

Beth watched Kate stare out the window, her chin on her palm, the sister she'd never had, whom she loved dearly. They rarely argued, had only ever seriously fallen out once – their parents got them back together, fed up of them moping about so much – and yet now that bond seemed to be fraying. It wasn't like the separation anxiety as they made their uni choices, which had been devastating and resulted in floods of tears, but harder almost.

"Never fall out over a boy," Mum told her once and it made perfect sense then as it did now. Maybe Kate couldn't picture what had happened to Pervy Pete but surely she trusted Beth enough to know she was telling the truth?

Beth couldn't allow their friendship to founder so close to them leaving their old lives and decided she'd do whatever was needed, even putting up with the gang for a few weeks.

The decision made her feel slightly better and, as if she could sense it, Kate looked over and smiled, waving with her fingers. Beth waved back.

Chapter 30

Nick quickly lost his bearings as he followed Frank away from Paseo Place. Pedestrians on Regent's Row paid the big man a lot of attention, eyeing him with barely concealed worry and even though he knew better, Nick understood it. Standing a good five inches taller than

Nick's six foot and broad with it, Frank looked like a problem just waiting to happen.

"I'm sorry about before," Nick said.

"For what?"

"I judged you by the way you look."

In the orange cast of the streetlight, the Xs scarred into his cheeks looked deeper than ever.

"I appreciate your honesty," Frank said without a hint of irony.

They turned a corner and Pinocchio's Cafe was in front of them, sandwiched between a bookie's and a mobile phone shop. The window, brightly lit, showed a dozen or more tables, most of them occupied.

"As promised," Frank said. "I want you to glow, brother, and a hot drink and a chat will help."

"Finding my wife would help even more."

"Coffee and composure, then we seek your wife. Order through chaos."

Frank opened the door for Nick and the woman behind the counter, her hair short, purple and spiky, raised a hand in greeting.

"Good to see you, Frank!"

"You too, Jules!" he said.

Several customers looked up and, unlike the people on the street, responded positively to his presence, greeting him warmly as he led Nick to a table by the window.

"It may not look like much," he said as they sat down, "but Jules is a good sister to all, keeping this place open and helping out when she can. Plus, she has great coffee."

The cafe was compact and tidy, with posters for local events displayed haphazardly on the tiled walls. The kitchen area and counter took up the entire back wall and the place smelled of bacon and coffee.

"You're in early tonight, Frankie," Jules called.

"Taking a break from the streets, as brother Nick is jaded and your coffee, as always, is the path to resolution."

"I'll see what I can do."

"Let me get it, it's the least I can do." Nick reached for his wallet but couldn't feel it. He stood and patted his back pockets, then checked the front ones. "Shit, it's gone."

Frank closed his eyes and put his hands together in silent prayer. "Tell me, you came by the Neon Tiger, didn't you?"

"How did you know?"

Frank opened his eyes, his expression weary. "A blonde woman fell in front of you?"

"Yes," Nick said, realisation dawning. "Bollocks, I've been had, haven't I?"

"Fear not, I know Vicki well and we'll probably see her later."

"Later?" Surprised at how calmly Frank had reacted to the theft, Nick shook his head. "I want to get my wallet back now. And find Beth."

"Everything in its time and a time for everything. Your first impression of my town hasn't been good, has it?"

"Not really. I broke up a fight at a funeral, got into an argument with my wife, almost got mugged until you rescued me and now I've been robbed."

Jules brought two mugs to the table; the one she put in front of Nick filled to the brim with coffee. Frank looked like he was drinking green tea.

"You, Jules, are a star."

"And so, dear Frank, are you."

She went back to the counter and Nick took a cautious sip of the coffee. It was very hot and very strong and tasted wonderful.

"See?" said Frank.

"You were right." Nick put the mug down. "So how do you know this Vicki?"

"My calling brings me into contact with a lot of people, from most walks of life. I may not look it but I'm friendly and I like to help people achieve their glow and potential. If people can look past this," – he gestured vaguely at his face – "they allow me into their space and that prevents, as

Matthew said, the seed falling on rocky ground. I saw that I worried Vicki so I smiled and let her see me talking to others."

"And she allowed you in?"

Frank clicked his fingers. "I listened to her troubles, which were many, and she listened to me and I assisted her until she glowed."

"Like your church?"

"The Glow Church is a mission following the basic tenets of the Church of England's teachings, but also taking what is needed from other formal religions. Our hope is to allow people to glow and make the best of their lives. Hope, after all, is everything; so no one worships at our centre, we go to those who need us."

"Like the girl with one shoe?"

"Indeed. I work with the church but follow my own path." He cleared his throat and drank some of his tea. "I was once on the wrong path, until things came to a head and I was imprisoned. I deserved to go, without doubt, but it was my turning point and I used the time to lose myself in books."

"And found religion?"

"Not in the way you mean. I recognise and respect all religions, believing in them all, while not necessarily believing in all they teach. Omnism. Every religion contains a truth but not all the truth."

"Isn't that like having your cake and eating it too?"

Frank gave a slight smile as he nodded. "You're not dismissing what I'm saying, brother Nick, not slamming the door in my face. That's unusual and I appreciate it."

"I'm trying to understand."

"As I do. I reflect, I read, I restore and I get to help the lonely and the fallen. I see the glow as a life force, a person's essence, and helping restore that is my ultimate achievement. I don't glow if you don't glow."

"And how do you square that with violence?"

Frank steepled his fingers under his chin. "I don't. Violence, in itself, is wrong, but it's a question of degrees; religion and violence have always been mutual companions. How I choose to react is the key and having my epiphany in prison meant I saw a lot of things happen that clearly contradicted the teachings I was reading. So I adapted. If someone threatens me with a knife, I ask him to put it down. If he doesn't, I neutralise the threat in a way that minimises his pain. If that doesn't work, I also carry a cosh."

"Why didn't you use the cosh on those thugs in Paseo Place?"

"Because I neutralised them with minimal harm." He smiled, the scarring on his cheek crinkling and he caught Nick looking. "You wondered about these?"

"I'm sorry," Nick said, feeling the heat of embarrassment, "I didn't mean to stare."

"It's only natural."

"So what happened?"

"In prison, I was an easy target since anyone taking down the big man would instantly increase their status. I knew it was going to happen and I was terrified but kept my head up and tried not to show the fear." He stared into his mug. "The man who did it was my cellmate, a pot-bellied mugger who wasn't at all repentant. Three of them jumped me in the shower and I gave as good as I got until I slipped and that was it. Pot-Belly had a shiv and the other two held me down."

"Fucking hell."

"I struggled, of course, but they pushed my face into the tiles and I couldn't move because the showers were running and I didn't want to drown. Pot-Belly cut an X into both cheeks, deep enough on the left side the blade actually nicked my tongue. I couldn't scream because of the water but I have never, before or since, experienced pain like it. My anger and adrenaline got me to my feet, I grabbed the shiv and stabbed him twice in the ribs. By then, alarms were ringing and people were shouting and hands pulled me away and hit me until I was on the floor again."

"So what happened then?"

"They took us to the infirmary, but Pot-Belly had made such a mess of my cheeks they couldn't sew the wounds up properly. Sadly, HMP doesn't employ the best plastic surgeons."

"So did people target you after that? Did you get a longer sentence?"

Frank shook his head. "The inmates gave me a wide berth because I'd walked away from being shivved and although it was obvious I'd stabbed Pot-Belly, nobody could prove it. He was transferred out just before I was put to work in the library. What happened in that shower was the last time I ever allowed anger and fear to guide my actions."

"You didn't have a lot of choice."

"There's always a choice, if only to turn the other cheek. Isaiah said 'they shall beat their swords into plowshares, and their spears into pruning hooks' and I didn't, I used the sword against him."

"He pinned you down and scarred you for life."

"I caused him damage, which has preyed on me ever since and part of my explorations was to find a way to put it into context to try and gain forgiveness."

"And have you?"

Frank shook his head. "Never. All I can do is try to be a good person every day, to accept I made the mistake and live with it." He slowly rotated his mug with his fingertips, silent for a moment. "Do you have a picture of your wife?"

"Yes," Nick said and found one on his phone. He turned the handset to Frank. "She knows you."

"I know her too, brother."

"She was very worried to see you."

Frank looked sad, a frown knitting his forehead. "I feared she might and I'm sorry for that."

"She hasn't been back here in fifteen years, hasn't talked about any of this to me."

"I'm not surprised to hear that."

"What the fuck did you do to her, Frank?"

"Nothing, I give you my word. We were friends once but my impact on her world was clearly worse than I'd thought, so I have further amends to make for my past." He stood up. "You have no idea where she went after leaving your room?"

"No and I couldn't find Wendy to ask if they'd spoken."

"I know of Wendy," he said slowly, in a tone Nick didn't like.

"Is there a problem?"

"Not as yet." Frank wished Jules a good evening and walked to the door, holding it open for Nick.

"What do you mean, not as yet?"

"'Do not be anxious,' Philippians 4:6."

"You're quoting the Bible at me?"

"I'm telling you not to be anxious."

Chapter 31

"Be nice," Wendy said, "we've got company."

Mouse stepped out of the shadows wearing a smart blue suit, his left leg stiff. "Fuck me," he said with a smile, "Beth Kennedy? Bloody hell, it's been years and they've treated you well."

He held out his hand and Beth shook it. "You too, Mouse. Are you hurt?"

"Not recently," he said, his tone suggesting he didn't want to talk about it.

"Nasty business," Wendy said, leaning close to Beth but saying it loud enough for him to hear. "Had it done to him."

"What do you mean?"

"I got a bit out of line," he said with a resigned air.

"Bit more than that," Wendy chided, sounding like she was enjoying this.

"Beth doesn't want to hear all that."

"I'm just glad to see you again." Beth looked at Wendy. "We've all had water flow under the bridge."

"He got kneecapped," Wendy said.

Beth shuddered with revulsion. "Are you joking?"

Mouse sighed. "It was a long time ago. Blake and Frankie were in prison and I was trying to get on. I made a mistake, ran foul of Mr Cowley and this was the price I had to pay."

"Cowley had you kneecapped?"

"He was lucky," said Wendy. "I heard some people got their fingers snipped off with pliers."

"Jesus, Wendy," Mouse said, "give it a rest."

"They caught up with him in the Chesty Wanker," Wendy said gleefully. "Dragged him around the back of Pervy Pete's and put a railway spike through his kneecap."

"Bloody hell," said Beth, shuddering again.

"I messed up," Mouse said and rubbed his hands together. "Life goes on. So what brings you here?"

"I came up for Kate's funeral," she said, happy to focus on something other than his injury.

"Bad news that, such a shame." He shook his head. "So where are you two off to this evening?"

"In here," Wendy said.

He looked at her as if she'd told him the sky was green. "You can't."

"Yes, I can. We're going in."

"No," he said and, with a quick smile at Beth, held Wendy's arm. "What're you doing?"

She shook his hand off. "I'm taking Beth in for a quick drink. Do you have a problem with that?"

"We can head back," said Beth. Something was clearly wrong. "Have a drink at the hotel."

"No," said Wendy sharply, "we're here now. Get out of the way, limpalong."

She shoved him but he held her wrist and didn't let go when she tried to shake him off.

"Excuse us," he said to Beth and pulled Wendy towards the wooden shelter.

They spoke tersely for a moment before he let her go and she came back, hooked her arm through Beth's and walked her to the corner.

"What was that about?"

"Mouse being fucking Mouse, just getting onto me like he's the big I-Am."

"You were harsh on him."

"Harsh?" She seemed surprised. "He fucked up, I didn't. We both got left behind and had to make choices, it's not my fault he went wrong. I heard later people could hear him screaming from the seafront."

The thought of it turned Beth's stomach, not helped by Wendy's clear pleasure in recounting the details. "You don't have to sound so happy about it."

"He's a twat, like he's always been; hanging around Blake."

"He seemed alright to me."

"You're too kind."

The bins, this close, smelled like something had died in amongst them. Four of the half-dozen parking spaces were occupied, one by a large Audi with foreign plates. The car park was closed off by a high wall that ran from the pub into the bramble. A door was midway along the back of the pub, a weak light shining above it.

Wendy pulled the door open. She gestured for Beth to go into a small vestibule with a ratty carpet and woodchip wallpaper. A large sign, peeling at the corners, asked patrons to be gracious to neighbours. Wendy opened the next door to reveal a large man, almost as wide as he was tall. His nose had the flattened quality of a career boxer and his dark hair was buzzed short, a long line of scar tissue running up from behind his left ear.

"*Ja?*" he said.

"Hey, Cas."

Cas's face relaxed. "Wendy, *hoe gaat.*"

"Feeling good."

"Who's this?"

"An old friend, she used to live here." Wendy introduced them and Cas nodded his head at Beth.

"You should be here?" he asked.

"Just coming in for a drink," Wendy said.

"Hokay."

He stepped back to allow them in. The locals' lounge wasn't a big room. The bar, a right angle of dark wood with taps glowing in the lights from the ornate pelmet, was set up in one corner, the mirror behind the optics tarnished by age and cigarette smoke. Half a dozen tables were dotted around and a dilapidated dartboard hung between two uncurtained windows. It all felt old and barely loved, the ceiling stained with blossoms of nicotine. One of the posters on the wall advertised an East Of England show from the nineties.

"Small but friendly," Wendy said.

A woman who might have been in her early twenties sat at the bar. On the floor, by her stool, was a baby's car seat and she rocked it gently with her foot. Four men, the woman's age, played darts and two much older men, somewhere in their sixties, sat at an adjacent table.

All of them turned to look and Beth felt uncomfortable at the scrutiny. Wendy smiled and raised a hand to the older men, ignoring everyone else.

"Go on," she said, making shooing gestures. "Find a table and I'll get the first round. White wine again?"

Self-conscious, Beth chose a table tucked up against the side of the vestibule and sat with her back to the outer wall of the pub. Deep scars marked the tabletop and four drip mats were set around a big plastic Heineken ashtray that looked like it had survived from the seventies with only minor burns.

The young woman, still rocking the car seat, looked over her shoulder at Beth, her lank blonde fringe dropping into her eyes. She wore a bomber jacket and tight jeans and a mobile phone had almost worked its way out of her back pocket. After a few seconds appraising Beth, she turned back to the bar.

From this angle, as she looked around trying to find something that would spark a memory, Beth could see another table in the far-right corner, two men in overcoats sitting with their backs to her.

Wendy put their glasses on the table and sat across from Beth, smiling broadly. "Okay?"

"Not really."

Wendy's smile faded into a frown. "Why, what's up?"

There was no point in lying. Beth didn't want to be here so why endure it? "This place is…"

"Not brilliant, I know but…" She turned to look around the room. "It has history."

"Not for me, I've really never been here before."

"Of course you have. Not often, I'll give you that, but we had a couple of heavy sessions in here."

Even if those sessions had been the heaviest ever, surely she'd have recalled something about this place? That summer was seared into her brain. "No, Wendy, I'm sorry."

"So you want to leave?" Wendy looked hurt and annoyed at the same time.

Beth's ingrained need to be polite had worn away. "I wouldn't mind."

The side of Wendy's mouth creased and she sipped her pint. "Okay," she breathed, resigned. "We'll finish these then head back."

Beth nodded her agreement, debating necking her glass in two.

The darts game ended, one player being pummelled on the back by his friends and they went to sit at the bar next to the woman with the baby seat.

The two men in the corner stood up, scraping their chair legs as they rose, revealing another man who leaned back into the shadows.

One of the men, short and slim, his grey hair combed to hide a bald spot the overhead light made obvious, adjusted his overcoat as he glanced around the room. He stopped when she saw Beth and Wendy and said something to his companion, who was much taller and broader, with thick dark hair and a wide face. The first man turned back to the table and spoke while the second watched her as he did up his coat.

Beth looked away.

"What's the matter?" Wendy asked.

"Nothing, just a bloke staring at us."

Wendy twisted around in her seat as the two men crossed the pub. "Oh I know them. Dutch blokes – they're with Cas."

"I thought he was the doorman."

The shorter man nodded a greeting to Beth and she smiled. Neither of them spoke or glanced at Wendy as they walked out of the pub. The door closed and Beth was suddenly aware of conversation starting up.

"Who were they?"

"The shorter fella, the good-looking one, is Dahvit and Floris is the big guy. They have an import-export company at the docks."

Beth was aware of a third man from the Dutch table coming towards them, walking with a pronounced limp, his left leg at an odd angle. As he came closer, her sense of unease quickly became something else and her shoulders pulled tight, heart thudding. "Fuck."

Wendy's eyes opened wider. "Now what?"

The man stood behind Wendy and leered at Beth. "Fancy seeing you here," he said.

Chapter 32

Then

"Nasty business," said her father. Reading last night's *Seagrave Telegraph*, he tapped the page as Beth finished her bowl of Cornflakes. "Did you read this?"

"Not really." Beth thought the *Telegraph* was a local paper for local people and she wasn't interested if Mrs Smith from Boring Avenue grew a whopper of a melon or Mr Billabong of Stupid Street painted his house with baked beans. "Why?"

"A shopkeeper got attacked."

"Attacked?" she asked, attention caught. "Who?"

"Peter's News, on Melton Street. Doesn't ring a bell for me."

Her mouth went dry. Did the article go into detail? Had Pervy Pete talked? Was she in trouble? "I think I know it," she said, hoping her voice didn't betray her by wavering. "What happened?"

"A robbery, apparently, he got badly beaten up. I don't get it. If you're going to steal someone's takings for the day, why beat the crap out of them as well?"

"It's terrible," she said, staring into her bowl, afraid to meet his gaze in case he saw her guilt.

Her mother, of all people, saved her as she came downstairs, putting on an earring. "What's that?"

"The bloke who runs Peter's News got robbed and beaten up." Her father held up the paper to underline his point.

Her mother barked out a little laugh and pulled a face. "I'm surprised that pervert hasn't been shut down before now."

Beth looked up from her cereal. "Did you know him?"

"We all knew Pete the pervert, always touching your palm or making some lewd comment. Horrible man and it was always to younger girls. We used to buy single fags off him."

"Sounds like a charmer," her father said. "I'm surprised you never mentioned him before, Di."

"I'm sure I did, Gordon, you just didn't listen."

He didn't rise to her dig. "I wonder if that was behind this business?"

If only you knew, Beth thought.

"I wouldn't be surprised if it was," her mother said. "What does surprise me is that he was still open." She dropped a kiss on top of her father's head then Beth's. "I'm off to work." She went into the kitchen, put on her shoes and left.

"I don't know what the world's coming to," her father said and folded the paper. "Get yourself sorted," he said to Beth, "and I'll run you into work if you want."

* * *

"Mum says you've found some new friends to knock about with."

"Kind of." Had he made the connection between her and Pervy Pete? Was her guilt a neon sign, crackling over her head? "We met them at the Goose Fair."

"Roughnecks, eh?" He sounded mildly surprised. "Not from the Waltzer, surely?"

"Oh don't you start."

He laughed. "Mum been giving you some hassle?"

"You could say that."

"She's only thinking of you."

"She thinks I'm about twelve," Beth said, not liking the sound of bitterness in her voice.

He pantomimed a nod. "I'll speak to her, tell her there's nothing to worry about."

"There really isn't."

"I understand and I trust you, you'll always do the right thing."

"Thanks, Dad." The crackling of that neon sign got louder. "How about you?"

"I haven't made any new friends in years."

She smiled, indulging him as he played for time, knowing he'd understood her question. He stopped at a junction, waiting for a gap in the traffic. Seconds ticked by before a driver flashed his lights to let them out. She counted to twenty. "Dad?"

He tapped his fingers on the steering wheel, a tune only he understood. "I'm feeling fine."

"It didn't look like that the other day."

"Honestly, I'm fine."

"Did you speak to the doctor?"

"No need, Beth. Lots of people have heart attacks and cope okay, there's no reason why I shouldn't."

He pulled up outside Ed's Bakery and she put her hand on his.

"I just worry," she said, "that's all."

"And I appreciate it, but that's not the way it's supposed to be. I should worry about you."

She felt a spike of guilt, heard more of the crackling neon. She wanted to tell him what she'd got mixed up in but daren't, in case it scared him enough to push his blood pressure through the roof.

"We worry about each other," she said quietly.

"I can handle that."

* * *

The morning rush over, her mind flashing back constantly to Pete's shop, Beth was absently re-arranging the fresh cream cakes when Ed came through from the kitchen.

"You've got a visitor."

There were three customers in the shop, two old ladies comparing the prices of unsliced loaves and a young girl picking through the sandwiches in the fridge, reading the labels carefully.

"Really?" Beth said.

Ed jerked his thumb over his shoulder. "Out the back. Big bloke, probably lovely but looks mean."

Her stomach sank. "Did you tell him I was here?"

"Shouldn't I have?" Ed frowned. "If there's a problem I can tell him to bugger off."

"No, that's okay. Do you mind if I go out?"

"Of course not, I can man the fort for a few minutes."

She went into the back and past the kitchen to the door. Open to let out the heat, a metal mesh curtain stopped birds and insects getting in and she paused in front of it, her anxiety growing. She couldn't see the person from here, who must surely be Frankie, only the big shadow he cast on the small courtyard.

What on earth could he possibly want? Shakily, she pushed through the curtain and he turned at its rattling. She gasped.

He'd been badly beaten, the skin black around his swollen left eye and a deep cut gouged the bridge of his nose. His right cheekbone was buried in puffy flesh and his lower lip was split in two places.

"Bloody hell," she said.

"Nothing to worry about."

"Bumped into a door?"

He groaned, held a hand to his mouth gently. "Something like that."

"What happened?"

"I made a mistake, but this isn't about me, I wanted to speak to you."

She crossed her arms, suddenly defensive. "Right."

"A little bird told me you were concerned."

"Did they?" Kate had blabbed? Why would she do that? Beth felt angry her friend had dropped her in it like this. "What about?"

"About us and the business at BJ's." He looked at her impassively, clearly not trying to be intimidating but everything about him, his bulk, the bruising and blood, made him so. Dare she say anything? "Is that true?"

"I didn't like stealing."

"It's not all about stealing."

"Is that what these are for?" she asked, gesturing at his face.

"I've told you I sometimes work security."

"You got that working for Hugh Cowley?"

"You ask a lot of questions."

"Sometimes."

"The three of you, you're all very different, aren't you? Kate knows what she wants and how to get it, especially with Blake. Jenny knows too, I think, but she's shy and holding back on something. You, though, you're a perfect balance of the two and feisty with it."

Was that a compliment? She was confused by this intimidating man who scared her, yet seemed to think before he spoke and only spoke when he had something to say.

"Thank you," she said, "I think."

He smiled then winced, touched his lip again. "I know you were at Peter's News."

Shit. Her stomach plummeted. Had the same little bird told him? She was going to kill Kate. "Yes."

"Blake asked you and Jenny to go?"

"He did."

"Did you witness everything?"

She relived it whenever she closed her eyes. "I did."

"Someone has been made very unhappy by this because Peter, whatever his failings, shouldn't have been touched."

Beth's mind reeled as she tried to take this in, her anxiety growing. Was there a mafia in Seagrave?

"There were penalties to be paid," he said carefully and suddenly she knew it was Cowley who'd had him beaten.

"He did this? But you weren't there."

"I took it to cover for the guilty party, who is fully aware. But I need you and Jenny to keep your mouths shut, otherwise the payback might hit you."

He'd covered for them? She looked at the wounds, wondering what level of pain had been inflicted to create them. "What do I have to do?"

"Nothing. The less people who know the better, for you and Jenny and for Blake too."

"You're protecting us?"

"I lead the squad, it's what I'm supposed to do. Blake stepped over the line and knows that if it happens again, I can't and won't protect him."

"And the same for us?"

"No, because you didn't do anything wrong. But it's best that people don't know you were there."

"Of course."

"Good." He nodded. "We're having a party on Saturday at the resort. You should come."

The issue had clearly been addressed and closed and she felt suddenly deflated, her adrenaline fading. "I will."

He smiled as best he could and turned to go. "I hope so," he said and walked away.

* * *

The remainder of her shift moved at glacial pace and even though she turned on the smiles and charm for her customers, all she wanted to do was ring Kate and scream at her. That chat in the Jupiter was just between them, so why the fuck would she blab?

When Ed told her to clock off, she walked to the pier, wanting to calm herself before confronting her best friend in the world. The best friend who, it seemed, was slipping ever further away. What she'd thought in the Jupiter, she felt even more keenly now. Maybe it was too melodramatic to say she'd been betrayed but this indiscretion felt like it. She and Kate shared everything on the implicit understanding nothing ever went beyond them, even to Jenny on occasion.

It was ten minutes before she felt ready to call.

"Hey, you," Kate said, "I thought you were at work today."

"Just got out."

"Is everything okay?"

"No. Frankie came to the shop. He knew I wasn't comfortable about BJ's and he knew about Pervy Pete." She paused. "Why did you tell him, Kate?"

"What?"

"It had to be you, I haven't spoken to anyone else but it's been eating me up inside and then Frankie turns up at my work to tell me he knows everything and I shouldn't tell anyone else."

"I swear I never said anything, Beth."

"Then how the hell would he know? It was just us at that table, Kate, Jenny was at work."

"You have to believe me, Beth, I didn't say anything. Why would I?"

Because we've been slowly unthreading since the holidays started, she wanted to say. Because you told me to fuck off when I explained what happened at Pervy Pete's, that you essentially didn't believe me. "How else could he have known?"

"It wasn't me, Beth, on my mum's eyes."

A childish phrase they'd used forever but it was enough that Beth knew she wasn't lying, their friendship too rich for Kate to be able to pull the wool over her eyes like this.

And the guilt came in then, that she could have even thought it. "I'm sorry, Kate."

"Don't be. I understand completely, I'd have thought the same."

"What's happening to us, Kate?"

Her friend paused long enough Beth thought she'd lost the connection.

"I don't know," Kate said. "Maybe it's nerves, we're scared for the end of the summer and what it means."

"I don't like it."

"Neither do I. We need to figure out what it is and stop it." And she needed to find out who'd told Frankie.

Chapter 33

Frank walked briskly along the middle of Regent's Row and Nick followed in his slipstream, passing the alley to Paseo Place and the church. Ahead, the Neon Tiger sign – red and black neon in the shape of legs with garter belts – glowed against the dark sky.

"Wait here," said Frank as he cut between two parked cars, the people on the pavement giving him plenty of space.

"Where are you going?"

Frank didn't respond as he worked his way through the crowd, clearly watching someone further down the street. Nick kept pace with him on the road, going onto the path when Frank stopped by a hole-in-the-wall kebab seller almost opposite the gentleman's club.

"What're you doing?"

Frank pointed to the end of the queue for kebabs. Nick followed the direction and saw the blonde woman who'd stumbled against him earlier. Deep in conversation with her friend, she hadn't noticed either of them.

"It's her."

"I know. If you need to follow me, don't do or say anything."

Frank walked slowly along the queue, Nick beside him, until they reached the woman. Frank took her elbow gently and, startled, she turned, her snarl evaporating when she saw him. She glanced at Nick and her face fell.

"Evening, Vicki."

She bit the inside of her cheek. "What's up, Frank?"

"I need a word," he said and pulled her, gently but firmly, out of the queue.

"I'm hungry, Frank."

"I'll get you something after we talk."

She grabbed her friend's hand, pulling her out of the queue too, as Frank led them to a narrow alley between the kebab place and the darkened shop next door. Frank and Vicki went in first and Nick gestured for her friend to go, then followed.

The alley, gloomy and pungent, ended in a blank brick wall just beyond the door that cast the only light. Through a metal mesh fly curtain Nick could hear conversation, muted music and the clatter of people preparing food.

Frank stopped Vicki beside the door, next to a pile of stinking, stained fruit boxes and leaned against the wall across from her. She glanced at Nick, as if trying to figure out whether she could escape past him. Her friend bit her nails anxiously, staring at the ground.

"I fucking knew you were trouble," Vicki said to Nick, lips tight. She didn't sound mad, more scared.

"I don't even know you," Nick protested.

She shook her head, as if that didn't matter.

"Vicki," said Frank carefully and repeated her name until she looked at him. "Brother Nick here lost his wallet earlier this evening. Would you happen to know anything about it?"

"No," she said quickly.

"Then why say I was trouble?" Nick demanded. "Just give me my bloody wallet back."

Frank held out a hand to silence him. "Vicki, you're not in trouble, my sister. I don't intend to hassle you, nor does Nick."

"Doesn't feel like it."

"Vicki, you know me, we understand each other and I hope you trust me. Just tell me."

She looked at Frank for a moment, glanced at her friend and sighed. "I took his wallet."

"Marvellous," said Nick.

"Thank you for being honest," Frank told her.

"I didn't want to do it."

"But the compulsion spoke to you, I understand. There's no harm done, so long as you give it back."

She looked at her feet. "I don't have it," she muttered, the words almost lost to the sounds from the street.

"Seriously?" asked Nick, his stomach dropping.

Frank glanced at him and shook his head briefly. Nick held up his hand in apology.

"Why don't you have it, Vicki?"

She didn't look up but Nick saw her body stiffen. "Because it wasn't a random snatch, Frank. I've turned the corner, I really have." Now she looked up, imploring. "Someone gave me money, told me what to do."

Nick's annoyance turned to surprise. "But nobody knows who I am."

Vicki looked at him. "Somebody does."

"Who?" Frank asked gently.

"I don't know. A kid stopped me and showed me a picture of him." She pointed at Nick. "He gave me an envelope and I thought he was taking the piss but there was fifty quid in it and a note saying to lift his" – again she pointed at Nick – "wallet. I was to give it to the kid, who'd be at The Nugget, and that was it."

"Who was the kid?"

"I don't know his name, but I've seen him around, just some kid on a bike."

Nick had a sudden sinking feeling. "Was he on a BMX with a low saddle?"

"How did you know?"

"Lucky guess," he said. None of this made sense but it did prove Beth hadn't been paranoid and he felt bad for not believing her.

"I didn't mean any harm, Frank, honestly. I'm trying to get myself straight."

"I believe you." He motioned Nick to move aside. "Take care, sisters."

Nick didn't move, glaring at Frank. "Don't let her go, I still haven't got my wallet."

"She doesn't have it."

"And you believe her?"

"Brother Nick, let them go."

Reluctantly, Nick stepped to one side. As soon as he had, the friend rushed to the mouth of the alley without waiting for Vicki.

"Take care, sister. Remember to glow."

"Thank you, Frank." She looked at Nick, said "Sorry" then rushed down the alley as quickly as her heels would allow. He watched until she'd been swallowed into the crowd on the pavement.

"Seriously?" he thundered.

"Be calm, brother," Frank said and took Nick's elbow. Nick shook him off. "I think 1 know where your wallet is and I'm sure we'll find Beth there too."

Chapter 34

Nelson Blake leaned on his cane, grinning. Beth couldn't swallow, her throat dry and cold sweat prickled on her upper lip.

"So, how've you been?"

She could barely hear him over the roaring of blood in her ears and dark curtains fluttered at the extremes of her vision. She blinked them away quickly, determined she wasn't going to pass out. It felt like someone had punched her in the sternum.

"I asked how you'd been."

He looked gaunt, dark rings around his eyes, his lips little more than tight lines and his hair was shaved so short it looked like a five o'clock shadow. He stepped back, arms wide. "Beth? You're being very rude."

Someone laughed lightly. She tried to speak, couldn't, managed to swallow and licked her lips. "I'm fine." She couldn't draw a full breath. "You?"

"Couldn't be better," he said and put his hands on Wendy's shoulders. She smiled, like the cat who'd got the cream and Beth suddenly understood. This wasn't a coincidence; it wasn't a chance in a million she found herself in a room with the man she'd helped send to prison. She'd been betrayed.

Blake slid his long thin fingers through Wendy's hair. "Unfortunately," he said, "you're early."

"I thought you'd like it," Wendy said, her voice almost childlike, desperate to please a distant parent.

"Yeah?"

He closed his fingers into a fist and yanked his hand up. Hair caught, Wendy went with the movement, face contorted with pain. She made an "urk" sound and was then on her feet, hands clutching his.

Blake swept his arm wide, dragging Wendy around. He twisted her back towards him until they faced one another, faces a few inches apart.

"Blake," she whimpered, trying to prise his fingers out of her hair, "please…"

"You stupid fucking bitch, you don't even know what you did." He turned to the people at the bar who looked as terrified as Beth felt. "What do you say?"

None of them said anything and the woman stopped rocking the baby seat.

"Come on, boys and girls," he roared, "everybody make some noise."

One of the men looked away to the dartboard but didn't say anything. The baby snivelled and the young woman slipped off her stool, shushing the infant.

"So what do you say, Wendy, any clue at all?"

She shook her head, throat hitching.

He tilted her face up to his, his finger under her chin. "Don't make me ask again."

"I don't know what you want me to say," she whimpered, her voice full of tears.

Putting his hand over her face, Blake pushed her back. Her head bounced off the corner of the vestibule wall with a loud crack. She didn't cry out but her eyes rolled up.

"What do you say?"

"I'm not… what… how do…?"

He pivoted on his good leg, spinning her around into one of the bar stools. It toppled, the man on it falling on top of her. Keeping his eyes on Blake, he scrambled to his feet, treading on Wendy, and stood to one side, hands clasped in front of him, clearly not knowing what to do.

Wendy moaned, slumped against the bar.

The sheer violence paralysed Beth and she felt hopeless and helpless, stuck in a moment so terrifying her mind was a kaleidoscope of images, none of them helpful. Her stomach churned and her throat tightened.

"Do you know, Beth?" Blake asked.

She shook her head.

Wendy groaned, drawing his attention. He knelt beside her, stroked her cheek. "Hey, you took a tumble."

"Yeah," she muttered.

He helped her to her feet, standing close while she got her balance. "Feeling better?"

"I think so."

He slapped her face hard. Beth flinched, but nobody else appeared to move a muscle.

Wendy kept to her feet, crying openly. "What did I do wrong? I did what you asked me to do."

He pinched her cheeks together. "You didn't think to fucking check, did you? You come swanning in and think you can just sit down and carry on like nothing's happening?" He jabbed his left index finger at her forehead. "Now I've got to explain to the Dutch why you're bringing unknown people into the bar."

"I'm sorry, Blake," she said, the words garbled.

He pushed her away and she staggered back. The woman jerked the baby seat onto her lap and the infant squawked its displeasure. She rocked it, making hush noises.

Wendy slid down the bar until she sat against it, chin against her chest.

"Where's Ziggy?" Blake asked the darts players.

One of them, wearing a peaked cap, mumbled something.

"Well, go get him then."

"Okay, boss." The man rushed out of the bar like he was escaping a fire, watching Blake until he'd gone into the vestibule.

Beth heard the door open and close, the sound as loud as her heartbeat. She tried to take a deep breath but couldn't, as if the violence had somehow charged the air.

"Fuck," Blake muttered, shaking out his hands. "Fuck, fuck."

He was distracted and everyone was watching him. Could Beth make a break for it? She might get around the table before anyone noticed and the woman with the baby probably wouldn't chase her. If she got to the car park, she could make a run for it, but what if they caught her? Being dragged back to face an even angrier Blake was almost as terrifying as the thought of sitting here, waiting to find out what he had planned.

"Right," he said, clapping his hands as he came towards her table, "on your feet."

"What?" Beth asked.

"Get up. I know you haven't been around for a while so I'll warn you, I don't like to ask things twice." He leaned on the table. "Get out of your fucking seat."

She stood up, the chair tipping back and clattering against the wall. She held her bag against her stomach.

"Come here," he said.

She edged around the table, each step too far and not far enough at the same time, until she stood in front of him. He shifted his weight, wincing slightly, and she looked at his left leg, pitched out at an angle, his foot twisted.

"Admiring the view?"

"No."

"It's pretty, isn't it? Had it a while, I'll tell you all about it later." He grabbed her upper arm, pinching the skin in her armpit between his fingernails.

The pain made her whimper. He pulled her across the room towards the table by the dartboard and shoved her into a chair between the two older men.

"Keep her there, Laurie," he said.

"Right," said Laurie. He had a bulb of a nose, dotted with broken blood vessels, and his eyes were pale and watery.

"If she moves a muscle, break her fucking arm."

Chapter 35

"What exactly did you do?" Laurie asked her.

"Nothing." Except, of course, something damning fifteen years ago. "You have to help me."

Laurie's head rocked back in a silent little laugh. "No chance, lass. I don't know you, I don't drink with you and I'm not scared of you. Nobody else is going to help you either. You're really up shit creek."

Blake dialled his mobile, staring at Beth until she had to look away. "Mouse? Bring them in."

He slipped the phone into his pocket and limped to the vestibule as Wendy got to her knees, using the nearest stool to help her up.

"Let Mouse in," Blake said to the big doorman.

When Mouse came into the bar, he was carrying three large cardboard boxes. Each was white, a flower outline printed on the top, 'Bloemen Bakker' written in heavy cursive script along the side. He put the boxes on the table Beth had originally sat at.

Mouse sliced the seal on the uppermost box with a Stanley knife, reached in and took out a small plastic bag filled with what looked like white pills. He handed it to Blake who smiled as he shook it.

"Looks good," he said and Mouse nodded.

Blake went behind the bar, picked up a slim black attaché case and handed it to Cas. "Tell Dahvit thank you," he said.

Cas nodded and left. Blake came out from behind the bar, smiling.

"Mouse, sort these out, I'll be back in a minute." He looked at Beth and she felt something curdle in her belly. "Laurie, keep an eye."

"Will do," said Laurie, raising his thumb.

Blake limped through the lounge door, pulling it shut behind him and the current in the air seemed to ease slightly, though not completely.

"Don't make life difficult," said Laurie. He leaned in close and put a hand on her knee. "It'd be an awful shame to see you get hurt."

She looked pointedly at him, then at his hand.

He followed her gaze. "Don't you like this?"

Although terrified by Blake to a degree that was almost paralysing, Beth wasn't about to let this little shit take advantage. Laurie moved his hand a few inches up her leg.

"I'm not scared of you," Beth said through gritted teeth.

Surprised, he did a little double take. "You should be, lass."

She shook her head. "If your hand moves another inch, I'm going to break your finger." She stared him down, her bravado running on fear and adrenaline. She didn't know how to break someone's finger, but he didn't know that.

He moved his hand.

"Thank you," she said.

"I hope he throws you off Julia's Point," Laurie muttered and picked up his pint.

Beth took several deep breaths, exhaling slowly to calm herself as she looked around, trying to figure out her next move. Laurie's mate stared off into the middle distance and the three remaining darts players sat next to one another at the bar. Wendy leaned against the bar next to them, the baby seat next to her head. The robust little boy strapped into it had a mop of blond hair and round cheeks. Food was smeared around his mouth and his all-in-one had dirty marks on the sleeves and a brown stain across the chest. The kid tried to grab Wendy's hair while the mother watched Mouse making piles with the pill packets.

He looked up. "Chelle? Bring it over."

The woman carried the seat to the table, setting it down in front of Mouse, and lifted the baby out, holding him absently. The kid looked around and his eyes briefly met Beth's.

Mouse peeled back the padding on the chair arms and slipped several packets of pills into the gaps. Once he'd folded them back into place, he lifted the seat and slipped twice as many packets there. He finished off with three packets in the backrest then smoothed down all the padding. "Okay," he said, "take off."

Chelle strapped the baby in and let him squirm for a moment before picking the seat up and leaving, as Mouse put unused packets back into the cardboard box. No one else moved and Beth felt the weight of anticipation push up her anxiety, the suspense almost a living force.

"What happens now?" she asked Laurie, but he didn't even spare her a glance. She cleared her throat. "What happens now, Mouse?"

He ignored her and carried on sorting the packets.

The lounge door opened and Blake limped in, glaring at Beth as he made his way to Mouse's table.

"She's gone," Mouse said, looking up.

Blake nodded. He clicked his fingers and the darts players all sat up to attention. "Where's Ziggy?"

"Palmer's not come back yet," said one of them.

"So where the fuck is he?"

The man who'd answered started to shrug then thought better of it. He didn't say anything.

"Two of you get out there, track him down."

The three men looked at each other and all of them stood at once. The older of the group pointed at the younger one and he sat back down. The other two edged around Blake and left.

Mouse closed the box and carried all three out through the lounge door. Wendy watched him go then turned her attention to Blake, who stood in the middle of the room and leaned on his cane.

"I've known people be late for their own funeral, Beth, but never early for their murder."

She felt the room shift as he limped towards the window.

"It's been a while, hasn't it?" His tone suggested they were old friends, meeting up after years apart, but his gaze drilled through her. "So what brought you back?"

"Kate's funeral."

"Ah, another blast from the past. Bit of a shame what happened to her. I understand she was married, had a kid."

"That's right."

He shook his head and looked out into the car park briefly before turning back to her. "Did she move, Laurie?"

Beth felt him jump.

"No, not really," he stammered.

"Shame you didn't have to break her arm, eh? Now do me a favour and fuck off, yeah?"

Laurie quickly stood up, grabbed his pint and cap and reached across Beth to tap his mate's arm. "Come on, Perce, we're going."

Perce looked up as if he hadn't heard anything. "Same again."

"No, come on, you daft twat, we gotta go."

"Eh?"

Laurie stood in front of him, pulled him to his feet. "We're going."

"Not ready."

"Don't care."

Holding Perce's elbow, Laurie quickly crossed to the lounge door and went through it.

"And then there were five," said Blake.

The darts player shifted uneasily, looking as scared as Beth felt.

Blake stretched out his bad leg with a sigh. "So, how're you doing?"

She couldn't find her voice.

"Cat got your tongue?" Blake asked.

She licked her desperately dry lips but there was no saliva in her mouth. "No," she managed.

"Then talk to me. I asked how you were doing."

She struggled to think of the best thing to say. "I didn't expect this."

"Had you forgotten about me?" He waited until she shook her head. "You think about me a lot then?" He waited for another shake. "So you didn't expect to see me because…?" He let the sentence dangle, like a fisherman who knows he's got a great catch and it's only a matter of time. "Did you think I'd still be inside?"

She'd hoped so. "I didn't think we'd be in town long enough to catch up with many people at all."

"Except those at the funeral, eh?"

She nodded and he held his hand against his ear, mouthing 'what?'

"Yes," she said.

"I saw you," he said quietly and she felt a chill spread across her chest. Had he really been there or was it a lie to disorient her? "I wasn't paying my respects, you understand, none of you bitches deserve that, but I just wanted to make sure you came." He jerked his chin towards her. "Are you scared?"

She nodded.

"You haven't got the first fucking clue what it's like to be scared." He laughed joylessly. "I've changed a lot since you knew me, since you did the dirty deed."

So everything she'd experienced today, that she'd assumed was paranoia, was just glimpses of the workings behind the curtain, as elements of his revenge lined up.

She took a deep breath, tasting something metallic and her mind raced, desperate for a plan to get herself out of this.

"Do you ever think about what you did?"

She'd walked right into his trap. She was a helpless pawn in this terrible game.

"Do you?" he repeated.

Knowing that what she'd seen and worried about was real pushed the terror back somehow, her mind clearing slightly. She was undoubtedly in trouble but it didn't mean she had to accept his plans. If she let fear take over, he'd already won and she wasn't going to accept that – she would fight back however she could. If he was going to hurt her anyway, why not go down standing up for herself?

She looked him in the eye and shook her head slowly. "No."

"I think about it a lot, getting caught in a situation where I couldn't just dust off my hands and carry on because a friend had dropped me right in the shit. Do you know the kinds of scars that gives you?"

"I do," she said, her stomach turning at the scars she'd earned hearing Jenny on that last night, the tears and the pleading.

"Can't get rid of them, can you?" He gestured towards his ankle.

"I didn't hurt your ankle."

"No?" He limped to the bar and leaned on it, next to Wendy. "What about you? Do you think Beth ever thinks about what she did?"

"I don't know."

"Wrong answer."

Blake swung the cane so hard it whistled, before connecting with Wendy's leg, above her left knee. The loud crack might have been the slap of wood on flesh or something breaking. Wendy screamed and fell to her knees, forehead on the floor.

Startled, Beth gasped and gripped the seat of her chair so tightly she thought her fingers would snap.

Blake limped towards her.

Chapter 36

Then

Richard dropped them at Crozier's Farm.

The three of them had decided it wasn't the kind of party for little black dresses, especially since they might have to traipse across the meadow to get home but Kate ignored this in the end, wearing one she'd designed as part of her A level studies. Beth opted for a pale blue summer dress with spaghetti straps her mum had warned her wasn't a good idea with her bust size, and Jenny wore the summer dress Kate helped her make when the round of eighteenth birthday parties had started in earnest a few months ago.

"Can I just say you all look very nice, girls," Richard said as they got out.

"Surely we look nice all the time?" Beth asked, mock seriously.

"Whoops." He looked down the driveway. "Are you sure about this place?"

"Yes," said Kate, "it's in the resort."

"I thought that had closed down?"

"Oh, Dad, you're so dread…" Kate leaned in to kiss him quickly on the cheek. "See you later."

"How're you getting back?"

"We're getting a lift," said Kate and shut the door.

Jenny and Beth said their goodbyes and Richard waved as he drove down the hill back into Seagrave.

"Do you think he was concerned?" Kate asked.

"A deserted farmhouse in the middle of nowhere and the assurance we've got a lift?" Beth laughed.

"That sounds like most horror films Beth tries to get me to watch," said Jenny.

"And on that," said Kate, "we'll brave the walk past the abandoned building to get to our party."

Laughing, they pushed through the rusting gates but none of them looked into the dense woods on the left of the driveway. They walked by the house, Kate in the centre carrying the bottles they'd bought in a carrier bag, the glass chinking to accompany the clicking of their heels on the tarmac.

The resort was bathed in sunshine and, on the turnaround outside the squad's chalet, sat an old Fiat van, the previous owner's livery badly stripped.

Music drifted up, loud and bassy. A man shouted, a woman laughed and something crashed.

"Sounds good," said Jenny.

Mouse came out of the chalet and waved, waiting patiently until they reached him. "Good to see you," he said, his tight black jeans and pale shirt highlighting just how skinny he was.

Frankie stood in the doorway, filling it, his arms holding the frame above his head. He wore cargo shorts and the BJ's T-shirt, the security tag pulling the neckline down. He looked at each of them in turn and winked at Beth. She smiled, still slightly unsure. The skin around his eyes was so dark now it looked like he was wearing a domino mask and the bruising on his cheeks had turned purple.

"What happened to your face?" asked Kate. Beth hadn't told her or Jenny about Frankie's injuries.

"Had a run-in with some people."

Kate handed him the carrier bag. "That looks painful."

"It was," he said and handed the carrier bag to Wendy who took it into the chalet.

Blake came around the side of the van, the one person Beth hadn't wanted to see. It felt like a bad idea to spend time with a man who had such obvious anger issues.

"Hey, girls," he said with a grin. The sleeves of his dark shirt were rolled up to show off his muscles.

Kate's voice got breathy. "Hey, Blake," she said and Beth realised how far she'd fallen for him. Kate had never acted like this around a boy before.

He slipped a hand around her waist and kissed her. "Did you miss me?"

"Of course."

Blake said "Hi" to Jenny, who looked equally ill at ease, then he was looking at Beth, his smile growing wider.

"Hey, Beth."

"Hi." She could see his distrust of her in his eyes. He didn't seem to have any marks or bruises and she wondered why Frankie hadn't passed at least some of his beating onto Blake.

"Do you like my van?"

"It's a van," she said.

He laughed. "No, it's unlimited possibilities."

"Of course it is," said Kate, nudging Beth's arm.

"Do you like it?" Blake asked Jenny.

"It's alright." She looked uncomfortable and crossed her arms, shutting him out.

"It's more than alright, Jenny. Would you like a ride in it?"

Surprised at his innuendo, Beth glanced at Kate and saw murder in her eyes.

"No, thanks," Jenny said.

"It's cute, how quiet and shy you are."

She glanced at Beth with a 'help me' look. "Thanks."

Kate stiffened, as if annoyed with her boyfriend's wandering attention. "So, Frankie, what happened?"

"I ran into the wrong people at the wrong time."

"I'll bet you took some of them out though, didn't you?"

"You'd like to think so."

"I'll bet," she said. "So, what's the party in aid of?"

"You three, to welcome you into our squad."

Wendy touched Beth's arm. "Come on, we'll get a drink," she said. "They're in the chalet."

Beth grabbed Jenny's hand and pulled her through the door. Someone had hung tinsel off the light in the middle of the room and it turned gently in a breeze, light reflecting off the red tassels onto the ceiling. The table was by the front door with several bottles, six-packs and plastic cups on it.

"I did that," said Wendy, pointing at the tinsel, "we didn't have a lot of stuff."

"I like it," said Jenny, "it's different."

Wendy smiled. "I like your dress too."

"She made it," Beth said.

"Did you really? Wow. I had a go at making my own once, but my mum wore it on a date and I never saw it again."

"Oh," said Jenny.

Wendy smoothed her bold orange and white A-line dress against her thighs. "I picked this up from a shop on Munro Street, proper vintage it is."

"Very retro," said Beth, "which shop was it?"

"The horses charity shop, do you know it?"

"I do," said Beth, watching the pride in Wendy's face that they were discussing her dress seriously. "It suits you perfectly." It didn't come out as sincere as she'd intended but Wendy beamed as if she'd just received the best compliment ever.

"You're so lovely, I'm glad you've joined the squad. I mean, the boys are great, even if Frankie acts like my dad sometimes, but it's nice to not be the only girl."

"How long have you known them all?"

"Since school. I was in Blake's class and he helped me when I was getting bullied." She poured generous measures into three plastic cups from one of the wine bottles Kate had brought. "Very nice," she said, after taking a sip.

"Kate likes the best brands," Beth said. "So what happened at school?"

"The usual, I was poor and didn't have a dad, so the popular girls made my life hell. One lunchtime, they were going to flush my head down the toilet but Blake overheard them and helped me. He didn't hurt any of them but they reported him and even though I told the teachers what happened, he got suspended. Nobody believed me."

"And you've been friends ever since?"

"Uh-huh." She leaned in, as if about to break a confidence. "I know he's got the hots for Kate and she's younger than me and smarter, but if Blake asked me to go with him, I absolutely would." She refilled her cup. "Come on, we'll go and see the others."

As she left, Jenny held Beth back. "Why do you think she told us that?"

"Solidarity perhaps?"

"When Kate makes her move, Wendy's going to get hurt."

"There's not much we can do if Kate's made up her mind, but it won't last long, will it?"

"She and I aren't so different, except my dad's still about, but it was you and Kate who stopped me getting much shit." Jenny shook her head, as if trying to dislodge a thought. "My mind seems to be all over the place at the moment and I keep thinking of things I need to say or do."

"Like what?"

Jenny's eyes glistened. "Like making you realise how much you mean to me."

Beth felt the heat of tears build behind her eyes and nose, wanting to say the same thing to Jenny; wanting to express all of her worries about leaving behind friends. "I know."

"Maybe…" Jenny's smile didn't quite work, her lips quivering slightly. "I don't say this enough or, when I do, I don't think you pay enough attention but I love you, Beth, I really do."

"I love you too, you nitwit, but you're going to make me cry."

"No, I'm not," Jenny said, "but I need you to know. With us all going away, even though we're going to see one another–"

"Loads," Beth interjected.

Jenny smiled at the interruption. "Even though we're going to see one another loads, I'm scared about moving on without you there."

"You'll be fine."

"Yeah, yeah." Jenny smiled but it quickly wavered. "Just know that I love you, okay?"

"I love you too." Beth wanted to pull Jenny into a hug but was scared it might make them both cry. "We'll always be there for each other, whatever happens."

"Always?"

"I promise. Whenever you need me, all you have to do is shout."

* * *

They spent the afternoon listening to music and chatting, while Frankie supervised the BBQ.

"We're almost out of booze," Wendy said, stumbling out of the chalet. Clearly annoyed with Kate fawning over Blake, she'd tried to drink her way out of caring.

"We didn't have much to start with," said Frankie as he put the burgers on. "Nip out and get us some more, Blake."

"No problem." He rubbed the back of his head. "Fancy coming along, Jenny?" He grinned and licked his little teeth.

"I'll come with you," said Wendy, "I don't mind."

"I didn't ask you."

"I'll go," offered Kate.

"I asked Jenny."

"Take Beth," Frankie said, in a tone that offered no compromise. "She'll keep you on the straight and narrow."

Beth felt her stomach drop. Kate and Wendy glared at her, as if she'd somehow engineered this.

"Fair enough," said Blake, "come on then."

* * *

The van stank of diesel and pot, a heady mix that, combined with Blake's driving ability, made Beth feel queasy. He sped away from the chalet, something clanking hard under the van as it hit the slope, and barely braked as he drove through the gateposts onto Radnor Road.

"Do you always drive this fast?"

"Only when I'm drunk." He drove with one hand on the vibrating steering wheel, his elbow on the windowsill.

"What if something had been coming?"

"They'd have had to move." He laughed. "You need to chill out, Beth, take it easy."

She bit her lip to avoid saying anything that might rile him up. Having seen him in action, the last thing she wanted was him going off on one in the car.

He approached the junction by All Saints too quickly and she pressed her feet into the footwell.

"Brakes are on this side."

"I know," she said bitterly.

He tailgated a taxi for a few hundred yards then turned towards the seafront, tyres squealing. Something came loose in the back of the van, rattling as it crossed sides before clunking to a stop.

"Jesus," she said.

"You're safe with me, Beth." He grinned, his eyes dark. "You know that don't you?"

His tone was wrong and she wondered if Frankie had told him her version of the Pervy Pete incident. If so, why would he send the two of them out now, or had Blake suggested this – a chance to get her alone so he could threaten her?

"Do I?"

"I thought you were cool but you're a bag of nerves."

"Wouldn't you be?" She couldn't tell if her stomach felt unsettled because of his reckless driving or being alone with him.

He looked at her for a moment too long. "What have you got to be nervous about? Are you scared of me?"

She knew, from the amusement in his voice, he was playing with her. "A little."

"That makes me sad, because you shouldn't be."

"Then I won't."

He laughed out loud. "You've got a lot of spirit, Beth, I like that." He put his hand on her knee and she moved her leg to break contact. "I like you."

"I think you've got your hands full with Kate and Wendy."

"You don't miss much, do you?" He did a drum roll on the steering wheel. "I quite like Jenny, actually, she's a bit shy but I'll bet she's a firecracker when she's all riled up."

"Something like that."

He took a turn too fast, tyres protesting. The car behind honked its horn and Blake gave the driver the finger. He pointed at a Spar shop. "That's where we'll go," he said and drove down past the Oceanview Hotel onto Marine Drive. At the first roundabout, he doubled back and parked close to the entrance of the Winter Gardens.

"Why are we parking here?" Beth asked as she got out.

"Do you mind walking?"

"No."

"Then don't worry about it."

They walked up by the hotel, Blake pulling on a peaked cap she hadn't seen him carrying. He stopped outside the Spar and looked both ways but the pavements were virtually empty, few holidaymakers having any reason to come up this far from Marine Drive.

219

"Ready?"

Beth followed him into the compact shop. The shelves in the narrow aisles were filled to overflowing and Radio 1 played loudly. Three television monitors above the dairy fridge showed different angles of the shop and she watched herself walk through them.

At the drinks fridges, Blake picked up three six-packs of lager and a couple of oversized bottles of cider. "What wine did you want?"

She selected four bottles and carried them to the till at the front of the shop. The assistant, a young Asian man in an Adidas T-shirt, smiled when they reached the counter. Blake put his purchases on the pile of newspapers between the sweets rack and the till and Beth balanced her bottles next to them.

"Alright, mate?" Blake said. "What's your name?"

"Harmi," he said and rang through the items.

When he told them the total, Blake stepped back and tapped his pockets.

"Sorry, mate," he said, looking sheepish, "I've forgotten my wallet."

Brilliant, thought Beth and reached into her handbag for her purse.

"I tell you what though," Blake said. "You seem like a decent bloke and I'm a decent bloke, so rather than kick your head in, we're going to walk out of here and you're going to watch us go, yeah?"

Beth stared at him, unable to believe what she was hearing and angry he'd dragged her into trouble again. "I can pay," she insisted.

"Ignore her, Harmi, I just got her to bring the bottles down."

"Oh man," said Harmi, "why you got to be like this? I'm doing a favour for my uncle; he's going to kill me when he gets back."

"He'll be insured and I'm sure he'd rather come back and find you with all your teeth, don't you?"

"I wouldn't bet on it."

"I'll take that bet." Blake handed Beth her bottles then picked up his lager and cider. "If I hear anything other than that door chime as we leave, Harmi, I'm coming back in for you."

Harmi held up his hands. "Yeah, sure."

Blake pushed Beth out the door and she went, head down, seething. He started walking down the hill as if nothing had happened. "Another successful mission."

"What's your fucking problem?" she demanded, anger brushing aside any concerns about how he'd react. "I could have paid."

His smile only infuriated her more.

"Why pay when you can take?"

"Did you not see all the cameras in there, you fucking idiot? All Harmi's uncle has to do is run back the CCTV and there we both are."

Blake laughed. "I know, it's cool isn't it?"

"No," she said, disgusted. "I'm not a thief."

"Well…" he said and held his hand flat, wobbling it from side to side.

Her stomach churned because he wasn't wrong. "BJ's was because Frankie asked us to. This time I had no idea you were going to do that."

"Great defence," he said and mimicked her. "I only took that T-shirt, your honour, because the big boy told me to."

"You're an arse."

"Oh, diddums, is the little rich girl not enjoying real life?"

"I'm not rich," she insisted, stopping. "And this isn't real life. I could have paid, none of that needed to happen."

Blake kept walking, striding towards the hotel and she followed, deliberately slower, hoping he'd leave her stranded. That way, she wouldn't have to go back to the resort and be a part of the shit squad that had now seen her break the law three times in a week. Except she had to go back, even if only to protect Jenny from Blake's attentions.

A hundred yards from the back of the hotel, he turned on his heel, waiting for her. Her stomach flopped again and she walked with the same deliberate pace, glaring at him as he glared at her, not sure what was going to happen.

"You really do have spirit," he said, his tone almost admiring.

"I don't care what you think."

"Hey, Beth, I'm just trying to be nice."

"Why?" Maybe Frankie had threatened him, in lieu of a beating.

"Because I don't need the hassle, alright? I genuinely don't have my wallet, but I'll come back later and square up with him."

"Are you serious? I can go and pay for it now."

"No." He chewed the inside of his cheek for a moment. "I need to do it."

So Frankie had threatened him then, she decided. Maybe Blake was already on his second strike and couldn't afford for her to drop him in the shit.

"If I don't," he continued, shifting from foot to foot, "you can tell Frankie and he'll deal with me."

"Fine."

"What're you going to tell him?"

"Nothing, if you come straight back. But don't do this to me again."

"Thanks," he said with a smile that didn't touch his eyes. "Come on."

They crossed Marine Drive together, angling towards his van until he grabbed her arm.

"Shit."

"What?" She shook his hand away.

"Willis," he said, pointing beyond the Winter Gardens.

Beth only saw holidaymakers and a couple of PCSOs.

"I had a run-in with him a little while ago." He crossed the pavement and, not quite sure what to do, she followed him into the Winter Gardens foyer.

The woman behind the ticket counter didn't look up from the magazine she was reading. Blake stood behind a Space Invaders cabinet that had seen better days as he looked out to the street. He motioned for Beth to keep back.

"Who's Willis?"

"One of those coppers, he's after me."

"What did you do?" she asked without thinking. "No, don't tell me."

"Fuck me, he's coming in." Blake rushed across the foyer. "Come on."

"What? He doesn't want me."

"If he sees you with me, he will."

Feeling a mixture of anger and fear, she followed Blake into the central aisle. Lined with craft stalls it led to the busy atrium where exposed ironwork arches and girders towered over the people sitting at tables as they admired the view of the beach and Sam's Place. The space looked impossibly bright and airy, hundreds of metal grids holding panes of glass in place. On some summer evenings they held formal dances in there and her parents often came.

Blake cast a quick glance over his shoulder and grabbed for her hand.

"Enough," she said but he held tight and pulled her between two stalls then peered around the edge.

"I don't think they've seen us."

"Will there be trouble if they do?" she asked.

"One way or another."

At the other end of the stalls, a drape rippled slightly in a breeze. She moved away from Blake and looked around the end of the stalls into a narrow walkway. The drapes ran the length of the central aisle, the entrance end blocked by a yellow A-frame that read 'No Entry' in big letters. The atrium end seemed clear.

"We can go this way," she said but he was still at the other end, watching for the PCSO. "Blake," she said, as loudly as she dared. The great glass and metal building seemed to swallow her voice. "Blake!"

"What?"

"We can get to the atrium through here."

"Hang on, I want to see which way Willis goes."

If she went now and waited for him at the van, the PCSO wouldn't connect them straight away. And if Willis caught Blake, she could ring Jenny and head home.

Taking her chance, Beth stepped into the walkway and bumped into Ronnie, her ex.

Chapter 37

"How come my fucking wallet has anything to do with where Beth is?"

Frank stood on the corner of Regent's Row, looking towards The Golden Nugget. "History and taking the time to pause always shows the way."

"I'm not in the mood for riddles, Frank."

"I'm trying to help."

"By staring at an arcade? The kid who got my wallet has long gone."

"Maybe," Frank acknowledged, "but maybe there's more."

"More thieves or kids on bikes?" He wished again he'd taken seriously Beth's worries about the kids she'd seen on BMX bikes. "She saw them, you know? I thought it was all just a coincidence."

"Why didn't you tell me?"

Frank's careful phrasing annoyed him. "Because it wasn't relevant until your friendly pickpocket brought it up." His sense of impotence, that he couldn't sort this, fed his frustration. "This isn't my town, how the hell am I supposed to know if they're important or not."

"You aren't, but they're a part of this place I don't like."

"Meaning what?"

"Those lads have fallen from the path, exploited by others, sometimes causing mayhem, sometimes not, but organised. They run the dope between dealers and clients."

"Beth has nothing to do with drugs."

"That's not it, I think it's history."

Frank started walking in the direction of the pier and Nick rushed to catch up, falling in step beside him as they weaved between people coming away from restaurants and pubs.

Nick's worries echoed through him, as if he'd been hollowed out. How had it come to this? Yesterday, he was a husband concerned for his wife's feelings, preparing to take her back to her hometown to mourn a dead friend. Today, they'd had a fight and now he was searching a town he'd never been to before, accompanied by a man his wife appeared terrified of, learning things about a summer she'd never told him about.

"Where are we going?"

"We'll know it when we find it."

Nick grabbed Frank's arm, pulling him to a halt. "What aren't you telling me?"

"I know no more than you, I just have a suspicion."

"So let me in on it because I'm going mad here. I've known Beth fifteen years and didn't know she'd been carrying any secrets until today."

Frank started walking again. "How did you meet?"

"You're asking me this now?"

"I'm asking for the reason Beth didn't tell you."

"What reason could that be?"

"That's what you need to tell me."

"We met at university, okay? A couple of weeks after starting."

He'd seen her around campus and fancied her straight away but hadn't managed to speak to her until they bumped into one another in the library. Reading a book, she was inadvertently blocking the aisle he wanted to get through and he had to ask her to move. As soon as she smiled, he was smitten.

"Was your love immediate?"

Thinking about that first meeting reminded him of the heady rush he'd experienced. He loved the way she carried herself, her sensuality, how she laughed, what she talked about. "It was for me and now I just want to hug her and make sure she's safe."

Frank stopped beside a telecoms box and spoke briefly to the homeless man Nick had seen earlier, before giving him a bottle of water and two lollipops.

"It pays to have eyes and ears," he said to Nick. "Sometimes, the way a man looks isn't the worth of him. This is brother Malcolm's spot and he sees what happens here."

"He saw Beth?"

"I don't know, I asked if he'd seen Wendy."

"And did he?"

"No, which means what we seek isn't here."

He walked back towards a junction and turned abruptly off Marine Drive, taking Nick by surprise.

The road they walked up was narrow and gloomy, filled with shadowy doorways. At the next junction, Frank crossed into another street, the sign on a post covered in such thick graffiti it seemed someone had tried to hide its identity. Another sign, attached to a terraced house whose back wall had fallen into the garden, identified it as Melton Street.

A large patch of waste ground had two islands of concrete in its centre, as if the premises there had been spirited away. Frank stopped outside the Chest & Anchor, which looked like the kind of pub where everyone would stop talking and stare when you opened the door.

"I'm going to check in here."

"Why?"

"Because this used to be a place…" He paused.

"What?" A horrible thought crossed his mind. "Was this sexual? Were you and she an item?"

"No, not at all but this was once a place to congregate. Feel free to come in but it's not the most welcoming of taverns in the town."

Let alone welcoming, the place looked like a shithole. "I'm happy out here, but if she's in there, come and get me."

Frank was only inside for a few moments and brought a smog of weed and body odour out with him. "They were here but left a little while ago."

"Well, that's a start. Do you know where they went?"

"No, a fight broke out before they left so people were distracted."

"Jesus." He glanced at Frank. "No offence."

"None taken." He looked up the hill. "We'll head that way, towards the Duncan Jackson estate, to check the other pubs where Wendy might drink."

Nick heard the rhythmic tick of a bike chain and turned to see a kid on a BMX cycling up the hill. He wore skinny black jeans, a pale top with a shining sun on it and white trainers that looked too big for him. His saddle was set low. Keeping his distance from them, the teenager rode by affecting a casual air but, once passed, sped up and leaned over his handlebars, as if eager to get away.

"Frank?"

"I saw."

"Do you think he was watching for us?"

"Possible. Did Beth ever mention Nelson Blake?"

"Not that I recall. Who was he?"

"Someone else. Another problem from that summer."

"Did he hurt her?"

"Not in the way you think."

"Just fucking tell me, Frank."

"Beth clearly had reasons for her silence, so I can't betray her. But we will resolve it together."

"How?"

"Trust me, brother. And understand that, back then, your wife did the bravest thing I ever saw."

Chapter 38

"So what're we talking? A husband, nice little house, a good job? Am I close?" Blake said.

"Sort of."

"Kids?"

"Not yet."

Blake stroked his chin, a pantomime of thinking. "Any reason for that?"

"None of your business."

"Are you one of those career-bitches, too focussed on yourself to drop any?"

"No."

"Husband can't get it up?"

She tried not to let him rile her, which was clearly his intention. "No," she said, hearing her indignation and realising she'd given something away.

"I always knew you were frigid." He laughed again. "But that's not it, is it? Something doesn't work, you're faulty."

She took a deep breath, trying to let his words wash over her. Losing her temper wouldn't help. "No."

"Do you lie and say it's his fault? I remember you were a good liar. In fact, I remember your lies giving me this."

He gestured at his left foot. "Aren't you curious about the limp?"

"Not at all," she lied. The thought of pointing out his disability was a bad idea in a night already overflowing with them.

"Your lies hammered me. I had a reputation from working with Hugh Cowley and thought I could cope with prison life but I was arrogant and made some enemies on my first day."

He sat heavily in the chair across from her. "They pinned me down," he said, his voice steady. "Said I needed to learn a lesson and they snapped my ankle against a block of wood. Hurt like a bastard then and still does when it's cold and damp. Turned out the infirmary doctor was one of the biggest junkies in there, and in their pocket, so when they told him to reset my ankle wrong, he did. Can you imagine? No, course you can't because that kind of thing doesn't happen in your world, does it?"

Blake lifted his leg so his calf rested on the tabletop and pulled up his trousers. Beth looked away, concentrating on her knees.

"He reset it at an angle and the bones fused. They'd have to be broken all over again, to make it right." He paused. "Look at it."

His foot was twisted at an uncomfortable angle to his leg, scar tissue streaking around his ankle. The skin was blotchy and dark. "Doesn't look good, does it?"

Beth shook her head.

He lowered his leg to the floor. "The pain was overwhelming in the early days and I blamed you entirely. My hatred for you kept me going. Still does, really, because the pain only fades, it doesn't go away. I'm on so many pills I could probably break a finger and not realise."

He got up and limped towards the bar. Wendy, eyeing him warily, covered her injured knee with her hand.

"Prison breeds anger; focuses on the strongest bits of a personality. I made mistakes, but I also learned to play the game and realised the parole board only released the charming motherfuckers. They're a bunch of nasty bastards who enjoy their power and after the first few knock-backs, I figured out what they wanted and pretty soon I could turn on the charm like you wouldn't believe. During my last panel, they couldn't sign the papers quick enough for me."

Beth tried to imagine how he could possibly have charmed a parole board. He looked manic now, eyes wide as he limped around the room. "What kept me going was the idea of paying you back for the fifteen years of my liberty that were robbed." He tapped the cane on the floor as if checking for landmines. "And you owe me, big time, for my ankle."

Beth knew, her stomach turning, that she was never going to get out of the pub alive.

"Come over here," he ordered Wendy.

Her colour drained. "Why?"

"Because I want you to. Or shall I drag you over?"

"No, I'm coming." She slipped off the stool, wincing when she put weight on her injured leg.

Blake looked at Beth as he waited for Wendy. "You don't seem scared."

She didn't look at him, instead watched Wendy's slow progress. "I am," she said, feeling the terror in every fibre of her being.

"Lie down," he said to Wendy.

She got to her knees.

"How scared are you, Beth?"

Beth gripped the edge of the table so tightly it felt like her knuckles might burst. "I'm terrified, Blake. Is that what you want to hear?"

Blake stood astride Wendy and she brought her knees up, as if scared he'd tread on her. He whipped the cane around and hit Wendy's thigh. She sobbed and bit the side of her hand to keep quiet.

"You've proved your point, Blake, let her up."

Using his cane for support, Blake squatted over Wendy's chest and shifted his leg, sighing quietly. He dropped onto her belly and Wendy woofed out her breath.

"Can't…" she gasped.

"She can't breathe," Beth shouted.

He smiled as Wendy punched at his chest, trying to unseat him. He swatted her hands away and leaned back, taking off his jacket. Wendy gasped, sucking in air. A crude spider's web was tattooed around his left elbow. He caught Beth looking.

"Like my prison ink?"

"No."

He pointed at ACAB, etched into his forearm. "All coppers are bastards." He smiled and took a Stanley knife out of the inner pocket of his jacket. Beth felt a lurch of nausea. "Fear is a currency, did you know that?"

She shook her head as he opened the knife and she saw the match separating the two blades.

"Of course not, little miss everything-handed-to-you-on-a-plate. Growing up how me and Wendy did, it just becomes second nature. I got dragged up on this estate by a single mum who sold our fucking telly to buy booze. I had no life, no prospects, I earned my first money selling other kids' lunches and felt like somebody then." He laughed, sourly. "Prison was full of it, and I learned quickly. You could buy people with fear, make them do things they didn't want to or miss things they should have seen."

"What're you going to do?"

"You," he said, examining the blades closely, "but first I have to deal with this one."

"Please don't cut me," Wendy pleaded.

He mimicked her. "Listen to yourself."

"I did what you asked."

"And what time did I say, you stupid bitch?"

"You said…" She stopped, panicked and shook her head. "I can't remember."

He leaned down until his face was inches from hers and licked his lips. She flinched.

"You knew how important tonight was, how big this deal is, how hard I've had to work to get Dahvit to trust me and this operation. That's why I fucking told you not to be early. You know what he's like, he's very particular about people turning up and yet you saunter in like you own the fucking place." He leaned closer, a hair's breadth from kissing her. "Do you have any idea what it took to calm him down?"

"No, Blake, I don't."

He sat up and jabbed his finger hard into her chest. "He wanted a piece of you, to prove I'd disciplined you."

Wendy gasped and began to cry.

"You know the rules," he raged and spun the Stanley knife in his palm. "I told you not to come before ten, Wendy, I fucking told you. You know he takes his privacy seriously, I mean, what does he keep saying?"

Still crying, Wendy tried to speak, her voice clogged by tears and phlegm.

"What does he say, Wendy?"

She reached for his face and he slapped her hand away.

"What does he say?" Beth asked, wanting desperately to stop whatever was about to happen.

"Loose lips need to go," he said and pinched Wendy's lips together. She tried to scream, rocking and bucking her torso but he dug his knees in. She twisted her head and he lost his grip on her lips. She screamed as he tried to pinch them again, snapping her teeth at him. A heavy slap rocked her head to one side and, before she could move, he grabbed her lips again.

"Stop it, Blake." Beth was almost out of her chair.

He laughed. "Why are you protecting her, haven't you got it yet? She's not your friend, she betrayed you because I told her to."

She looked at Wendy who stared back, eyes wide and imploring.

"She sold you out, Beth, just like you did me and the cavalry isn't going to come and rescue you."

He was right. Whatever happened next was down to her, but she couldn't sit and watch this. "Maybe."

"So what're you going to do?"

She looked at him without saying anything because they both knew the answer was nothing.

"Didn't think so," he said and turned his attention back to Wendy.

Beth looked around, trying to find something she could use as a weapon. On the next table over, where the darts players had sat, three of their darts were in the ashtray. If she could grab one, would she be able to use it as a weapon?

Checking Blake wasn't watching her, she slipped off her chair and edged around the table. She grabbed one of the darts, adrenaline pumping. Blake leaned over Wendy, taunting her. Beth could run past him easily now but could she leave Wendy, even if the bitch had dropped her in the shit? No, she couldn't.

"It's no use fighting," Blake said and pressed the blade against Wendy's top lip. She reacted with fury, spitting blood at him. He pressed his arm against her throat. "Do that again and I'll cut them off slowly."

Beth ran into Blake full force, grunting with the impact, and wrapped her arm around his neck. Her momentum dragged him off Wendy and his knife slid away, thudding into wood. She tightened her grip, forearm in his throat until he gagged. Blake twisted and she struggled to hold on, the adrenaline keeping her going.

"Stop it, Blake, I mean it."

He gagged again, and said something she didn't understand.

She stabbed him, digging the dart into his right side. It went in much easier than she'd expected and he made a horrible noise, jerking sideways.

Chapter 39

Then

"What're you doing back here?" Ronnie asked.

He and his friend, who she didn't recognise, were carrying large boxes.

"I'm just…" She couldn't think of a lie quick enough and let the sentence tail away.

"I'll come back for yours," his friend said and walked around Beth.

She raised her eyebrows at Ronnie.

"Doug," he said. "His mum has the papercraft stall near the entrance, we're shifting some stuff for her."

It was the first time they'd been this close in months and it felt awkward, more so because he looked so tanned and healthy.

"You look good," she said.

He smiled and something pinged in her belly. "You too, I always liked that dress."

Another ping, lower this time, a growing sensation she couldn't act on. "I haven't seen you around for a while."

"I've been away quite a bit with training."

"Yes, Chrissie told me."

"I understand you two have had some run-ins?"

"She's been a bitch, to be honest – rubbing my nose in it about you."

"That's not how I heard it, she told me about BJ's."

"Oh," Beth said, feigning innocence. "Yes, that was odd. We were talking, or at least she was gloating, then she left and the alarms went off."

"They found stuff in her bag."

"Did they?" Beth hoped she was giving a convincing performance. "That's terrible, has she been a klepto for long?"

"She isn't a klepto, somebody planted the T-shirts on her."

"But who'd have done that?" She paused for dramatic effect then let her mouth fall open. "Surely she doesn't think it was me?"

"Kind of." He didn't sound convinced. "She said you talked then she left and all hell broke loose."

"It's a bit rich saying it had to be me, though."

"I know." He looked at his deck shoes. "I said the same thing."

She laughed, without meaning to. "I'll bet that went down well."

He pulled a face. "Yeah, like a lead balloon and that's why I'm a single man again."

"She finished with you?"

"Chrissie made it quite plain I was a weak idiot who'd never got over you."

Beth felt her breath catch. "What?" Had she heard him right?

"And you know what? She was absolutely right."

"She was?" Her world shifted, altering the future to one where she and Ronnie had a chance again.

"Yeah and then–"

Blake rushed out from between the stalls, reaching for her arm. "They're doing a tour, come on."

The delight of a reawakening magic with Ronnie soured instantly. She didn't want to look at Blake but Ronnie was staring at him. "You go, Blake," she said.

"What're you talking about?" He reached for her hand. "Beth, we need to go."

"I'm not going," she said, reassured by Ronnie's presence.

"What's going on?" asked Ronnie.

235

Blake seemed to finally see him. "What do you fucking care?"

Ronnie's eyes widened and he took a half-step back, shifting his weight. Beth saw him do it and felt her anxiety level shoot up. The last thing she wanted was a confrontation.

"Because Beth said she didn't want to go."

"And who're you, her dad?" Blake got a hard glint in his eyes.

"I remember you from school. Blake, isn't it?"

"Well done, you win, now just fuck off."

"You beat the shit out of one of my friends."

Blake dropped his shoulders. "I can do the same to you, if you want."

Beth stepped between them and put her hand on Ronnie's chest. "It's okay, I'll catch up with you later."

Ronnie put his hand over hers, gently moved it off his chest. "Do you remember Martin Clemens, Blake? He was part of the swimming squad at school, you tripped him in the canteen."

"Nope, can't remember."

"I can," said Ronnie. "You were king of the hill at school and now you're what, running around in the Winter Gardens, hiding from someone."

"Leave it, Ronnie," Beth said.

"Yeah, Ronnie," taunted Blake, "just leave it."

"I'm not afraid of you, we're not in school anymore."

"Please," said Beth.

"No," Ronnie said to her. "I'm not intimidated by him."

Blake shoved Ronnie towards the drapes. Surprised, Ronnie staggered back but kept to his feet and squared up to Blake.

"I'm not scared of you, Nelly."

For a split second, Beth's world went silent, as Ronnie stood his ground and Blake's lip curled. The sound came rushing back with a fury.

Blake grabbed Ronnie's neck, pushing him back. Ronnie twisted to one side, knocking Blake off balance, and kicked at his thigh. Blake landed heavily, glaring at Ronnie.

Blake sat up, rubbing his leg. "Think you're tough, do you?"

"Just defending myself."

"Blake," said Beth, desperate to break this up, "pack it in, don't forget Willis is in here."

"You, of all people, know what happens when people call me that."

She felt sick, feeling the pressure of the situation weighing on her. She'd never stop Blake and if she couldn't convince Ronnie to run, this was going to end very badly. "Ronnie, you have to go."

He stood over Blake. "It's under control, go and find someone."

"Please, Ronnie, just leave it."

"Yeah, Ronnie," Blake sneered, "just leave it."

"Fuck off, Nelly."

As if he'd been shocked, Blake was on his feet instantly. He threw himself into Ronnie and as they staggered back, Blake landed quick hard blows to his stomach. Ronnie couldn't break free and Blake got his balance first, driving a knee into Ronnie's thigh. It had little effect so Blake followed up with more vicious jabs, focussing on Ronnie's ribs.

Beth wrapped her arms around Blake's neck and pulled, making herself a dead weight. He gagged and staggered back, knocking her aside.

Ronnie threw some punches and Blake went forward. He tackled Ronnie to the ground and sat on his chest, punching his face and neck, Ronnie desperately trying to block the blows. Beth grabbed Blake's hair and pulled. He twisted, body all at bad angles, falling onto Ronnie's legs. Ronnie kicked out and Blake rolled onto his feet, kicking at Ronnie's thigh, the blows hard and loud. Beth screamed at him to stop. Ronnie screamed in pain.

She heard raised voices from the central aisle.

"In here," she screamed, "he's killing him."

Blake glared at her as footsteps pounded in the gap between the stalls. "Fucking traitor," he hissed.

He grabbed the carrier bags and ran as the PCSOs came into the walkway. Willis looked at her and his colleague raced after the fleeing Blake.

Beth went to follow her, wanting to pound Blake until he lay in a crumpled heap but PCSO Willis held her arm.

"You stay here until I find out what happened." He looked at Ronnie and took his radio out of his stab vest. "Shit, he's in a bad way."

Beth knelt beside Ronnie's head, her vision swimming. There was so much blood on his face she could barely see his lips, his teeth smeared with the stuff. He groaned, reaching for his leg gingerly.

"Ronnie, it's okay," she said but knew she was lying.

Chapter 40

Blake lurched forward.

Terrified he'd spotted where the Stanley knife had fallen, Beth jabbed him with the dart again. He howled with pain but she couldn't pull it back out. He twisted to one side and she lost her grip on his throat, rolling away as he got unsteadily to his feet. She jumped up, backing towards the vestibule.

He leaned against a table, blood in an ever-widening circle staining his shirt around the dart.

Mouse came through the lounge door, took one look at their face-off and pulled out his own Stanley knife. "What happened?"

Blake gingerly touched the dart flight and winced. "She fucking stuck me in a rib."

Mouse glared at her then saw Wendy. "Shit." He knelt and touched her cheek. Wendy swatted his hand away. "It's me, it's okay." He looked angrily at Beth. "What the fuck did you do?"

"I didn't do anything."

Blake howled as he prised the dart out, his face creasing into a wince. He sagged, holding the table for support, blood running off his hand.

"Her lip's cut," Mouse said and pulled a handkerchief from his pocket.

"She fucked up with Dahvit," Blake growled, taking deep breaths. "He wants an example made."

Mouse looked startled. "Of Wendy?"

"Oh fuck off, Mouse," she said and slapped his hand away.

He backed away as his phone rang. "Yes?" He listened without speaking then finished the call. "Frank's coming into the estate."

Blake shook his head, watching Wendy. "You make all these plans then people keep getting in the way."

"What do we do, boss?"

"I need to think," Blake snarled. "Jesus, I'm surrounded by fucking idiots."

Mouse slipped the phone back into his pocket. "This thing with Wendy," he said, "what did you mean, Blake?"

"She broke the rules and Dahvit wants penalties. You know how these things work, Mouse."

There was a loud knock at the door and Blake let out a frustrated growl. The knock came again, in a pattern. Mouse went into the vestibule and Blake pointed at Beth. "Stay there."

She held her hands out and nodded.

Mouse came back into the room with the teenager who'd saluted Beth earlier.

"You wanted me, Mr Blake?"

"I did, Ziggy," said Blake. The darts players filed in, looking nervous. "Took your time, didn't you?"

"They split up," said the player who'd been sent out last. "I pulled everyone back together."

"You left your darts on the table."

"Did I?" The player shrugged and checked his pockets. "I must have done."

"That's what I said." Blake threw the dart Beth had stabbed him with. His victim didn't have a chance to move and it struck just below his collarbone. He yelped in pain, falling back into his friends. One of them tried to support him until Blake bellowed, "Leave him." He fell to his knees.

"Mum?" said Ziggy and stepped around Blake. "Mum?"

Wendy covered her face and Beth couldn't tell if she was shielding herself or perhaps protecting him. The kid was the right age but that meant the whole sob story about her son was yet another lie she'd spun.

Blake grabbed Ziggy's arm. "She got injured," he said and jerked his head towards Beth. Ziggy glared at her. "We're sorting her out, but I need you to pay attention, I have a job for you."

"What's that?" Ziggy looked like he hoped it would be hurting Beth.

"You know Frank Collins, the preacher with the scars?" He waited for Ziggy to nod. "He's coming here and we need him stopped. Take these four as your crew and intercept him."

Now Ziggy looked at Blake. "You want him hurt?"

"As much as possible without killing him." Holding Ziggy's shoulder for support, Blake turned to the darts players. "If you kill him, I'll kill you. Frankie is mine, got it?"

The darts players nodded in agreement as their fallen friend got to his feet and pulled the dart out. He looked at it, as if he didn't know what to do for the best, then put it on the bar.

"Got it?" Blake asked Ziggy.

"Yes, boss. But Mum…?"

"You deal with Frank Collins, I'll sort out your mum."

Ziggy took one last look at her then nodded and left, the darts players trailing behind him.

"What next, boss?" Mouse asked when they'd gone.

"I don't know," Blake snapped. He limped to the window and looked out.

Beth felt the atmosphere in the room cloud a little, uncertainty adding to the danger.

Mouse's phone rang again. "It's Dahvit," he said, looking at the screen.

"For fuck's sake." Blake took the phone, pressing it to his chest. "Keep these two quiet, I'm going to the office." He limped to the lounge door and put the phone to his ear. "*Hoi*, Dahvit."

"Come over here," Mouse said to Beth as the door closed.

"Why?"

"I'm keeping you two together," he said, lips tight. "I don't trust you at all."

"Mouse, I promise I didn't do anything."

"Liar." He pointed at the chair across from Wendy. "Sit there."

When she did he leaned down to her eye level, jabbing a finger in her face. "If you move, I'll hurt you."

"I won't move."

He looked as if he didn't believe her but went behind the bar without saying anything.

Beth tilted her head back, feeling the tendons in her neck creak. A small nicotine bloom stained the ceiling above her and she stared at it for a moment or two, breathing deeply to try and calm herself. Her adrenaline was wearing off and she felt sick, her legs ached and her head swam. She tried to shake it away because now wasn't the time to collapse, she had to keep it together.

"I'm sorry," muttered Wendy.

Beth didn't even want to look at her. "You're a fucking bitch."

"I had to do it."

"You had to betray me?"

Wendy sniffled. "He made me. You don't know what he's like."

"No, I don't know what you're like." She thought of the lads on the bikes. "They were watching me from when we arrived, weren't they?"

"I don't know, I just had to meet you at the hotel and bring you here, I promise."

"Your promises aren't worth shit. And what about Ziggy, is he really yours?"

Wendy didn't speak for what felt like thirty seconds. "Yes."

"Has every word out of your mouth been a lie?"

"You don't understand what it's been like, you weren't here."

"That old chestnut again? This is my payback because I got out?"

"No, not at all." Wendy cleared her throat. "What I said was true, I admired you for getting out and wish I could have done it. But I got so wrapped up in things, my world fell apart and when I got pregnant things just got worse. As much as he could, Blake stood by me."

"Are you defending him?"

"No, just trying to explain. He told me things would work out for us and I kept myself for him." She wiped her nose on her sleeve. "I didn't get many offers but turned them down, thinking it'd just be me and Blake and the baby."

The realisation was a punch. "Ziggy is his?"

"Of course."

"He called for his son to show how badly his mother had been beaten?"

When Wendy broke eye contact, Beth knew it wasn't the first time Ziggy had seen it.

"I was vulnerable and he fed me lies I wanted to hear. I would have done anything for that man but then he started getting visits with Chelle and knocked her up."

"The one with the baby seat, where Mouse put the drugs?"

Wendy nodded. "I passed up any chance for a normal life because Blake promised we'd be a family but his sentence kept getting increased because he was always hurting someone. Fifteen years later he comes back, taking over what he'd had Mouse laying the groundwork for and she already had her legs open. I was cast off."

"But you're here."

"What choice do I have?"

"You could have chosen not to do this to me."

"Because you're little miss perfect and didn't deserve it?"

"I don't deserve any of this."

"You came willingly enough."

"Fuck off," Beth muttered.

Wendy said something else but Beth shut her out, trying to focus because the cavalry really weren't coming. Blake was clearly unhinged, his desire for revenge pushing him past the depths of depravity he'd shown against Pervy Pete and, later, in the Winter Gardens. No one was going to help and, unless she used an ashtray or threw a chair, there weren't any weapons to hand, which meant it would have to be a dirty fight. If he came close she'd go at him with her nails, scratch his eyes, kick his balls or his bad ankle.

"I'm as good as dead," Wendy muttered, impinging on her thoughts. "You don't mess up like I did with Dahvit. He even makes Blake shit himself."

The thought of how violent someone would have to be to have that effect on Blake wasn't worth contemplating. "I don't care."

"People have been hospitalised after Dahvit's finished with them."

"My heart bleeds." Did Wendy really expect her to feel sorry about this?

Wendy sighed. "I'm trying to help you."

Beth laughed. "Are you kidding me? I don't need any more help from you."

"Beth, he'll split us up. If he takes me first, you can make a break for it."

"That's your plan, you fucking idiot? You think I hadn't thought of that? I was going to run down to the docks and take my chances."

"That's good, but I can also give you a weapon."

"Like what?"

"Can you grab my handbag from the table?"

Beth got up and Mouse glared at her. "Sit down," he said sharply.

"Wendy needs a tissue; I need to get her bag."

"Hurry up then."

She got the bag and dropped it into Wendy's lap. Wendy rooted through it and took a short metal nail file from a make-up bag. She handed it to Beth, watching Mouse, who was looking at his phone screen. "It's not nice," she said, apologetically, "but if you stab him like you did with the dart, it might give you a bit of a head start."

Beth turned the nail file in her fingers. Three inches long, it might do enough damage to distract someone but she'd have to be quick getting away. "What about the door?"

"Bolted at the top but you'll reach it."

It wasn't much, but it was a plan, however paper-thin. "What about you?"

"I don't know."

Wendy sounded defeated and scared and Beth knew even after the betrayal she couldn't leave Wendy to an unknown fate.

"Can we go together?"

Wendy looked surprised. "After everything, you want me to come?"

"I still hate you, if that's what you're asking, but I can't leave you here alone."

"Thank you." Fresh tears tracked down Wendy's cheeks. "But then what? You'll go home but Blake's got a lot of people in his pocket, not to mention the Dutch, and I won't be safe."

There was no answer to that and while she was trying to think of something to say, Blake came back into the room. Beth's anxiety flooded back.

"Let's get this started," he said. "On your feet, Wendy."

Fingertips tingling, Beth gripped the nail file tightly, terrified it would slip through her sweaty fingers before she could use it.

Mouse took Wendy's elbow, looking at her sympathetically as he led her to the bar.

Blake licked his lips slowly. "Your turn, Kennedy."

He was five paces away, if that. Beth clenched her fist, the nail file digging in and walked towards him. Should she aim for the bloodstain, hit the same spot again or go for his neck?

"Blake, watch out, she's got a blade!"

Stunned by Wendy's shout, Beth jabbed at Blake but he moved easily out of the way and jerked his cane up. It hit her hand with a loud slap and the file clattered out of sight.

His momentum twisted him sideways and she took her chance, running for the vestibule. Blake grabbed her wrist and she tried to wrench it free but couldn't dislodge his grip. She spun into Mouse, who grabbed her shoulders.

"Where'd you get that?" Blake asked, breathing heavily.

Beth glared at Wendy. "She gave it to me."

"Is that right?" Blake said. He slapped Beth, the impact ringing in her ears like a peal of bells playing against the ribbon of black that bled across her vision. "Let her go," he snarled at Mouse and slapped her again.

Beth fell and darkness took her before she hit the floor.

Chapter 41

Then

Beth wanted to cradle Ronnie's head in her lap but there was so much blood on his face, she couldn't tell how badly he'd been hurt. He winced every time he tried to move his leg and made a pained sound that seemed to come from the bottom of his chest.

PCSO Willis put his radio away and pulled on a pair of latex gloves. "Can you mind away, miss?"

She moved away slightly and he nodded, as if aware she wouldn't go further. "What's your name?"

After she told him, he asked, "Do you know him?"

"Yes, he's Ronnie Martin."

"How old is he?"

"Eighteen."

"Okay. It looks like his tooth went through his lip, which might account for all the blood."

"Is that bad?"

"Could be worse. Do you know what the fight was over, Beth?"

"Ronnie called Blake a name and he went nuts." Reduced to this, it sounded like a playtime fight at an infant school rather than a beating.

"Oh aye, I've had a run-in or two with Blake. Did Ronnie shorten his name?"

"Yes."

Willis nodded, grim-faced. "So how are you, Ronnie?"

"Dizzy." He blinked slowly.

"That's fine, you're safe now. I see blood on your face but do you have pain anywhere else?"

Ronnie made a broad movement over his ribs.

"Blake went mad," Beth said, desperate to be helpful. "Ronnie tried to defend himself but…"

Ronnie convulsed, tilting his head towards the ground and threw up. The vomit was watery and rancid. One of the onlookers behind Beth said "that's gross" and made retching sounds of her own.

"Does your leg hurt, Ronnie?" asked Willis.

He nodded.

Willis's partner came back, breathing heavily, her face shining with sweat. "He got away." She panted her words out and gave Beth a quick tight smile. "Jumped into a van out the front and took off, didn't see the registration."

"It's okay, Leigh," said Willis, "I know who it is."

"How's it going?" she asked.

"I think it's a category three, but can't be sure. Call for an ambulance then get these people out of the way and find some towels."

"Will do." Leigh herded the ghoulish onlookers back towards the central aisle. As she did, Doug came along the walkway, forehead twisted into a frown.

"Holy shit," he said, "what happened? Is he okay?"

"He got beaten up," Beth said.

"By that bloke you were with?"

Willis's attention turned to her. "Blake was with you?"

"Yes," she said, knowing how this must look. "I'll tell you everything after we get Ronnie sorted out." She wanted to drop Blake in it good and proper, even if it meant the worse for her too.

"I didn't take you for part of that crowd," Willis said with a withering look her mother would have been proud of.

Leigh came back with an armful of towels and gave one to Willis, who rolled it tightly and slipped it gently under Ronnie's knee. She laid two over the puddle of vomit.

"You're in with Blake?" asked Doug.

"No," Beth said, annoyed. "Of course I'm not."

"So how come Ronnie got beaten up?"

Doug was the outlet her anger needed. "Fuck off, I didn't get him beaten up."

"Well, if he hadn't seen you, he wouldn't have seen Blake, would he?"

Shocked that Doug was absolutely right, Beth began to cry.

* * *

The paramedics swept in about ten minutes later and Willis conferred with the leader, a woman who listened intently as she knelt beside Ronnie. Her colleague asked Beth a quick series of questions and then seemed to dismiss her from the scene. Beth edged away, letting them work.

"You okay?" asked Leigh.

"No," said Beth. "There's something wrong with his leg."

"He'll be okay," said Leigh, without sounding confident.

"He runs for the county."

"Oh."

The paramedics carefully lifted Ronnie onto a stretcher and wheeled him out of the Winter Gardens, Leigh following them. Doug left then, staring daggers at Beth. Willis spoke into his radio.

"My DS wants to speak to you," he told Beth.

"Okay." Her fingers felt tacky with drying blood.

"I'll bring her through," Willis said into the radio and led Beth to the main entrance.

A tall thin woman wearing a dark trouser suit, her hair the colour of rust, waited for them in the cluttered office behind the counter.

"DS Chisholm," Willis said. "This is Beth Kennedy, she was witness to the beating."

"Thank you. Have you been checked over, Beth?"

"I'm fine."

"You have blood on your hands and leg."

"It's not mine," she said and her voice cracked. She looked at the spray of blood across her knee, a bloody handprint on the hem of her dress.

Chisholm sat behind the desk and gestured for Beth to take the chair opposite. Willis closed the door quietly and stood in front of it. Chisholm opened her pad. "Let's get started, shall we?"

* * *

The evening grew dark as Chisholm took her statement. Beth's phone vibrated with several messages and she was glad she'd turned the ringer off.

After asking specific questions, Chisholm let Beth talk and she told the DS everything, from meeting at the resort to Willis arriving on the scene. Chisholm made notes and listened without speaking but when she closed her pad, her expression spoke volumes. Beth felt utter disappointment in herself, for everything she'd allowed to happen.

"So what happens now?" Beth asked.

Chisholm pursed her lips in a shrug. "We'll pick up Blake for questioning and once we establish the situation with Ronald Martin, we'll know how best to proceed."

"Do you need me to do anything else?"

"No, you've been very helpful, Beth, and you strike me as a level-headed young woman whose disgust at this is all too clear. But with an obvious bright future, why are you hanging around with the likes of Nelson Blake and his associates?"

Beth looked at her shoes. "I don't know anymore."

"You have your whole life ahead of you, Beth, don't let that scum drag you down."

"I won't."

"Did you want a lift home? I'd prefer you not to walk, until we've picked up Blake."

She hadn't thought of him lying in wait for her but felt too sick about the situation to be scared. "I'll call my dad."

"Fine. PCSO Willis will take you out to the reception and if I need you again, I'll be in touch."

"Thank you," Beth said, feeling like a schoolgirl who'd been excused by the headmaster.

* * *

Night had settled, stars bright in the almost cloudless sky. People around her were dressed up on their way out to drink or eat.

"How're you feeling?" Willis asked.

"I've been better."

"You made a bad choice," he said, his voice soft. "We all do it but sometimes it catches us out."

"Thanks."

She had half a dozen texts on her phone, one from Kate with a simple 'What's going on?' and the rest from Jenny, ranging from 'Where are u?' to 'I'm worried now, what's happening?'

She ignored them and rang her dad. "Hey, Sprout, what's up?"

"Can you come and get me please? I'm at the Winter Gardens."

"I thought you were…? Is everything okay?"

"I'm fine, I just need a lift."

"I'm halfway out the door," he said, "I'll see you in ten minutes."

* * *

Her dad shaved three minutes off his estimate. Willis went inside the Winter Gardens as he pulled up and she got into the car.

"Was that policeman with you?"

The tears came then and she hugged him awkwardly over the handbrake. He did his best to hug her back. When she let go, he got a napkin from the glovebox and gave it to her.

"What's happened?" he asked gently.

She told him, talking through the tears, using more napkins to wipe her eyes and face. "It didn't look good, Dad, his leg was really hurt."

"It wasn't your fault," he said and touched the top of her head gently, like he used to when she was little. "Come on, let's get you home."

* * *

Jenny texted again – 'r u ok? I need you!' – as her father pulled up at home. The streetlight cast shadows on his face and made him seem gaunt.

Her mother stood in the hall, looking flustered and her black dress shimmered as she pulled Beth into a tight embrace. It was the first time she had hugged her like this since the night her father came home from the hospital after his heart attack.

"You're bleeding!" she said. "What happened?"

"It's not my blood, Mum, Ronnie got beaten up really badly."

"Ronnie?" Her mother held Beth at arm's length and Beth noticed she was wearing eyeliner and lipstick. "You went out with the girls. You and Ronnie broke up weeks ago."

"He broke up with me," Beth corrected her. "I went to get some drinks, we were in the Winter Gardens, there was a fight, it was…"

"Hold on, I'm not following."

"I'm fine, Mum, just upset. It's Ronnie that's hurt."

"So who beat him up?"

"A bloke called Blake."

Her mother frowned. "One of your new Waltzer mates?"

Beth couldn't think of a way to say "yes" without starting a fight. Her father came through the door then, moving slowly, his actions deliberate. He looked so grey her stomach turned, a medicine ball of guilt and nerves pushing into the base of her throat. This was her doing, making him worry.

"Bloody hell, Gordon," her mother said and put her arm on his shoulder. "You look terrible."

He tried to smile but it faltered. "I've felt better, Di."

"You need to lie down," her mother said.

"I'll make you a cuppa," offered Beth.

"But what about the do?" asked her father.

With an inward groan, Beth remembered. Her mother was supposed to be co-hosting a charity evening at the Cons Club tonight, she'd been planning and talking about it for ages.

"Well, we obviously can't go, can we?" Her mother scowled at Beth. "I'll ring Maureen and tell her. I just hope I catch her in time."

"I'm sorry, Mum."

"Yeah. Make him a drink, I'll see him upstairs."

"I'm not an invalid, Di," he said.

"Not saying you are, but you're looking pretty grey, love."

Beth went into the kitchen while they made their slow progress up the stairs, her stomach knotting with worry as she waited for the kettle to boil.

Her mother came downstairs a minute or so later, a chilly temperature following in her wake. "I thought you were making tea," she said, as if she couldn't hear the kettle doing its business.

"I am, I've just—"

"Enough!" Mum held her finger up, face contorted with anger as she paced to and fro, never once looking away from Beth. "What the hell do you think you're doing?" She kept her voice level and quiet but the steel in her words was clear. "I told you what would happen if you got mixed up with the lads from the fair and now, look at all this. Just look at it. Your ex-boyfriend in hospital, you've been interviewed by the police and, worse, you've made your father feel poorly too."

The medicine ball blocked her airway again and Beth tried to swallow it away. "I didn't do any of this on purpose."

"Are you sure?" her mother asked bitterly.

Wounded by the implication, Beth fought to hold back tears. "How could I have known this would happen?"

"Because this kind of shit is always what happens with the wrong crowd. For once in your life, couldn't you have listened to me?"

"I always—"

"No," her mother said and came towards her, holding up that finger again. "Don't even try that, young lady. I don't know if you've noticed, but things are a bit strained here at the moment and your dad is struggling, I'm struggling. He doesn't need stuff like this, coming from you."

None of the words seemed to connect with reality. Yes, tonight was down to her but the idea of making her father feel worse made her physically sick. Everything spiralled then, anguish and worry turning to anger and frustration until it was all Beth could do to not shout at her mother. She tried to keep her expression on the contrite side of blank, to defuse the situation before her father heard raised voices.

Her mother took a step closer and Beth smelled the musky scent of her perfume. "You're rebelling against the wrong people, Beth, and your new friends are going to get you into serious trouble, one way or another."

Beth swallowed, thinking of Harmi in the Spar shop and wondered how far DS Chisholm would push that. "I know."

"Your dad can't cope with it and I'll tell you this for nothing. If your activities get too much and kill him, I will never forgive you."

Beth felt like she'd been punched. "I'm not trying to kill him," she said, staggered at the betrayal. How could her mum even suggest something like that?

"I don't know why you're being a selfish little bitch but think of what you're doing to him. He looks terrible because you thought it'd be fun to get involved with beating someone up."

"That's not what happened."

Her mother turned away. "I don't want to hear it," she said and stormed upstairs.

Beth's phone beeped with another text and she checked it. 'I really need you' from Jenny. She switched off her phone, not wanting to talk to anyone.

Chapter 42

"Welcome to the Duncan Jackson estate. Tread softly, we may be expected."

Frank led Nick into a walkway, a graffiti war waging over its poured concrete walls. Two bollards at the end were heavily dented and scratched, glass around them like a carpet of jewels.

The walkway opened onto a small square and Frank stopped in the middle of it to adjust the straps of his rucksack. Nick turned in a slow circle, taking in the typically sixties estate, with the same Brutalist architecture as those in Hadlington.

Towering over them were four storeys of flats, narrow walkways overlooking the square. A few bikes were propped against the railings and some washing, grey in the poor light, hung from a makeshift line that sagged in the middle.

A heavy beat grew in pitch and then faded, the cause of it not coming into view. A woman shouted from somewhere and a child started crying.

Frank led them through a warren of streets. Cars passed, a couple of people walked dogs that looked like they wanted to be at home and a group of young people stood in the shade of a large bush, whispering loudly, the air smelling of weed. Three old men, drinking cans of beer, sat on a leather sofa someone had dumped on a piece of waste ground. The man in the middle, his belly straining his shirt, lifted his can as they walked by.

"God be with you, street preacher," he called.

His two companions looked up and one of them shushed him. Frank raised his hand in acknowledgement but kept moving.

"It doesn't matter how often I tell him, he thinks I'm religious."

"You are wearing your Glow Church vest."

Frank glanced at him and smiled. "I know," he said.

Two teenaged girls came towards them, wearing football shirts and shorts. One, a white girl, was absorbed in her phone but the other, a black girl, smiled.

"Hey, Frank," she said.

"Good evening, sister," said Frank. "How did practice go?"

"Okay, we're going to smash Lowestoft Ladies at the weekend."

"You go for it."

The girl turned as she passed so she ended up walking backwards briefly. "Got to keep up the glow, eh Frank? Take it easy."

They went through a passageway that cut between two houses, a bedroom overhead. Stars Wars and Marvel characters crowded the window as Darth Vader and Luke Skywalker battled it out across the curtains.

Nick heard a whisper of voices and mechanical clicking, but couldn't see anyone. "Did you hear that?"

"That and everything else," Frank said quietly as a far-off shout echoed around them.

Beyond the houses were half a dozen garages, enclosed by the three-storey walls of surrounding flats. A wide car entrance stood to the left, a streetlight next to it.

Nick heard the mechanical clicking again and glanced over his shoulder but the path and passageway were clear. Someone laughed and it echoed off the garages, chilling in its isolation.

"We need to be cautious," said Frank.

The clicking seemed to surround them now. Nick turned as two people, silhouetted by the streetlight, cycled through the passageway. They stopped before reaching the houses.

"Shit," he said.

Two more cyclists, both teenagers with sun logos on their T-shirts, came through the car entrance, blocking that escape route. Fear charged through Nick until his fingertips ached with it.

"Brother?" Frank said.

It took Nick a moment or two to find his voice, his mouth dry. "What?"

"Be ready."

"Uh-huh," Nick said and stepped onto the garage apron.

The bikers in the passageway freewheeled down and as they got closer Nick could see they were perhaps in their mid-twenties. One wore a dark peaked cap pulled low on his forehead.

"Here they come," Nick said.

"Breathe," Frank said quietly, "and stay behind me."

Stay behind him? Did he really think they could take on four people on bikes?

Another biker came through the car entrance, his white trainers looking as ridiculously big as they had when Nick saw him in Melton Street. "It's him," he said.

Frank nodded. "I thought as much."

The newcomer looked around, as if taking everything in carefully. "You ready, lads?" he called.

"Ready, Ziggy," said Peaked Cap.

Ziggy wheeled down the slight incline onto the apron, the other two riders following him. "So, street preacher, what brings you out here?"

"We're looking for someone, little brother."

"You've found five of us, I'd say."

"Looking for a lady."

"Not many of those around here." Ziggy laughed and, after a moment, his cronies joined in. "Does she have to glow?" He made quote marks as he said "glow" and the biker next to the garages sniggered.

"We all glow, little brother."

"I'm not your fucking brother, man, you need to get that through your thick head. You wander around with your flip-flops and lollies, talking about glowing but you're just a fucking dummy."

Everyone looked at Frank, who absorbed the criticism with the smallest of nods.

"You hear me, street preacher? This isn't your area, so fuck off back to the front and pick up those young girls, you fucking paedo perve."

Frank didn't react which seemed to rattle Ziggy more. "So take your boyfriend and fuck off, yeah?" he said.

"I'm only seeking." Frank eased the rucksack off his shoulders and set it gently between his feet. "Not spreading discord."

"Could be a problem there, preacher." Ziggy tilted his chin at the teenaged bikers and they set off as one, racing towards Frank. The one by the path held something that flashed in the light.

"Watch out," Nick shouted.

Frank grabbed the rucksack and feinted to his left, as if he was going to throw it at the armed biker. That kid went wide, riding up onto the path.

His mate went straight at Frank, who stepped aside and held out his arm, the kid riding straight into it. Knocked off, he landed heavily, the bike rolling on for a few feet. Frank picked the kid up and banged his head against the nearest garage door. The impact echoed dully as the kid crumpled in a heap.

The two older bikers came off the path.

"Frank!" Nick called.

Peaked Cap pointed his mate towards Frank then rode at Nick.

"Stay by the garages," Frank shouted.

Nick, terror slowing his reactions, glanced over his shoulder and realised he was by the edge of the last garage. Between it and the wall was a small patch of wasteland. Peaked Cap came quickly, a blade catching the light.

"Stanley knives," Frank called, "be careful."

Knives? Nausea rushed through him, a dizzying wave that left him light-headed, white flowers skidding across his line of vision. He was in a knife fight?

Peaked Cap brought his arm up and Nick's adrenaline kicked in. He backed onto the wasteland, tripping over a pile of bricks. More bricks and building debris littered the small space along with the ruins of a sofa.

Peaked Cap caught his hand on the garage wall and the impact threw him off balance. He tried to keep the bike upright but the front wheel turned sharply, knocking him into the wall. The bike hit the sofa.

Nick edged forwards, stumbling over bricks and bits of wood as Peaked Cap got to his feet, anger twisting his face.

"Where you going?" he demanded, holding the knife in front of him.

Nick could barely breathe, fear like a rock on his chest. A cold sweat bathed his forehead and upper lip.

Peaked Cap lunged but stood on a brick and something cracked as he fell. Gritting his teeth, he struggled to his feet.

Nick reached for half a brick. "Leave me alone."

"You gonna take me on?"

"If needs be." He knew he couldn't take the thug in a straight fight; he'd never been in a situation like this before and didn't have a clue what to do, but showing weakness had to be bad. Nick hefted a brick and considered his limited choices – throw it or charge him.

Watching the youth grimace as he came closer, Nick knew what to do. "Stay here or I'll throw this at your ankle."

Peaked Cap laughed and took another step.

Nick threw the brick as hard as he could and realised it would miss as soon as it left his hand. It bounced up against the garage wall with a loud crack and ricocheted back, hitting his assailant in the thigh. He fell to his knees, the Stanley knife clattering into the shadows.

Nick ran at him and drove his knee into the biker's chest, connecting with a loud crack. He went down hard, his legs bent under him. Nick kept to his feet, abuzz with adrenaline, and after making sure the biker didn't get back up, went out onto the apron.

Frank, just around the corner, raised his fists.

"It's me," Nick said, hands up.

Frank unclenched his fists and put his hands together as if in prayer. "Brother Nick, I was coming to find you."

"Are you okay?"

Frank shook his head gently. The younger biker was still in a heap against the garage door, his mate now spreadeagled on the apron next to his bike. The other was sitting against the wall, chin on his chest. Nick couldn't see his bike anywhere.

"How did you do all this?"

"They forced me to make a choice I would not have otherwise taken." Shaking out his hands, Frank rolled the spreadeagled biker into the recovery position. After touching his forehead, he went to the biker by the wall, checking his airways.

"What happened to Ziggy?"

"He left as soon as it was obvious we were on top of the situation. Are you hurt?"

"No." Nick saw the cuts in Frank's shorts. "What about you, did they stab you?"

"They weren't trying to stab. They put matchsticks between the blades, to make it harder to stitch wounds together. Thankfully, they missed." He checked one of the holes in his shorts. "Did you deal with your cyclist?"

"Uh-huh."

"Feel sick?"

"Not sick so much as…" Nick couldn't think of any way to finish that sentence.

Frank touched his shoulder. "Reflection leads to understanding, understanding leads to improvement."

"I threw a brick at a man then kneed him in the chest," Nick said sourly. "I don't want to improve on that."

"Later will be time to work through it, brother." He took a bottle of water from his rucksack and handed it to Nick, who rapidly drank half of it. "Now we need to move."

Nick handed the water back. "Do you know where to go?"

"I pray so."

Chapter 43

Then

Beth felt like she'd barely slept.

Guilt sat heavily on her chest while her anger at her mother's furious, cutting words manifested itself as acid in her throat. Accusing her of trying to hurt her dad was beyond cruel.

Cutlery rattled on a plate. Beth checked the time, realised her mother had probably gone to church and got up, pulled on her dressing gown and went downstairs, wondering how her father would look. Thankfully, he had colour in his cheeks as he ate toast at the dining room table, reading the paper. His eyes were bright as he smiled at her.

"Hey, Sprout."

"How're you feeling?"

"Better than yesterday."

She sat down. "I'm sorry about all that, I really am. I didn't mean to make you feel bad."

"It's not you, love, I've been up and down for the past couple of weeks."

"Mum doesn't seem to think so."

"I think she was disappointed."

"You must have been too?"

He gave a little shrug. "I wasn't best pleased but sometimes even good people find themselves in situations beyond their control, it's called being human."

Beth wondered if Ronnie, Harmi or the assistant from BJ's – or even Chrissie Ford – would agree she was good. "But it upset you."

"As terrible as it was, you didn't instigate what happened to Ronnie."

He was right, of course, but she couldn't quite convince herself of the fact. "I didn't mean to scare you or wind Mum up." She kept the threat to herself. If her mother hadn't said anything to him and Beth mentioned it now, she'd be opening doors that should be kept firmly closed.

"I feel better after a good night's kip and Mum seemed fine before she headed off for church. How do you feel?"

"A bit sick, very guilty."

"Have you heard anything?"

"No, I turned my phone off last night."

"Well you might have some messages."

"Good thinking."

She went back upstairs and switched on her Nokia. Ten texts binged in, one from Kate and the rest from Jenny.

Kate's was first – 'Party pooper :-)'. Beth frowned. Maybe Blake hadn't gone back to the resort, so Kate didn't know?

'u ok b, where r u?' was Jenny's first text and the next five were variants of it. It saddened Beth, her friend trying so hard to get in touch but she'd had her own problems to deal with. The next read 'please get in touch' and was followed by the ominous 'fuck b, I need you, where are u?'. She opened the last message with a real sense of trepidation.

please b, I need you to help me

Beth rang but it went straight to voicemail. "Hi, Jen, I just got your messages, it's been a weird night. Ring me back when you get this."

Since Jenny's texts sounded desperate, and Beth needed to talk to someone who understood the situation, she got dressed.

* * *

The Sunday morning streets were relatively empty. A few young families walked to the beach, laden with bags, windbreaks and toys while old people came back from the seafront. A few spoke to her, commenting on the fine weather and she smiled at them all, wondering if the expression looked as dead to them as it felt to her.

At Jenny's, she pressed the doorbell and a few moments passed before the door opened.

"Hello, Beth," Joan said with a weary smile.

"Bethy," said Pete, sitting happily on Joan's hip.

"Hey, Pete." Beth tickled him under his chin until he squirmed. "Hi, Joan, everything okay?"

"Hopefully now," she said and stepped back, giving Beth space to come in. "Jenny's been a real grump this morning."

"Shouted," Pete said.

"And made poor Maggie cry. I know Maggie gets on her nerves but she really had a go. Was there a lot of alcohol last night?"

"I don't know."

Joan frowned. "I thought you went with them?"

"I nipped out to get some more drink and got involved in a fight at the Winter Gardens." Joan's eyes widened. "Not me personally, but I got interviewed by the police."

"I'm sorry to hear that, love. How awful."

"Awful," mimicked Pete.

"Go and see her, she might cheer up for you. If not, come down and I'll make you a cuppa."

"Me go up," said Pete and reached for Beth but Joan turned herself away slightly.

"I think Beth and Jenny want to talk."

"Play with me."

"Maybe later," said Beth. She kicked off her shoes by the door and went upstairs. Jenny and Maggie's bedroom door was closed and she knocked on it lightly.

"Go away, Maggie."

"It's me."

"Come in then."

Beth pushed the door open and knew, instantly, something was wrong. Nothing about the sun-drenched room was different – Maggie's side still untidy, Jenny's full but neat – but Jenny sat at her narrow desk, a dressing gown wrapped around her as if she was in the depths of winter. The air felt stale and old.

"Blimey, what did you do last night?"

Jenny glanced at her. "You don't want to know."

"Maybe not." Beth opened the window to let in some fresh air. A gull circled somewhere nearby, its cry loud. "What time did you get in?"

"I don't know," Jenny murmured, "late."

Beth sat on the edge of the bed. Jenny pulled her knees tight to her chest, bare feet on the seat. She twirled the broken pendant of her necklace with her left hand and looked without seeing at the desk. Everything about her seemed just askew enough to be noticeable.

"How much did you drink?" Never a big drinker, Jenny was a happy drunk whose hangovers barely troubled her.

"Not much."

Maybe Blake hadn't gone back after all. "It's just that…"

"Where did you get to?" She said it so softly, Beth wasn't quite sure she'd heard properly. "You told me you'd always be there for me, Beth. You promised. I needed you but you weren't there."

"I'm sorry, but something bad happened with Blake and…"

Jenny made a strangled noise, somewhere between a snort and a sob. A tear caught the light on her cheek.

"What's going on?" Beth put her arm over Jenny's shoulders.

At the contact, Jenny leapt up as if Beth had touched her with a heated roller. "Don't touch me," she shrieked, pulling the dressing gown tight and seeming to curl in on herself.

Startled, Beth backed away. "Okay, I won't."

Jenny stood at the window and cried. Beth felt as scared as she had in the Winter Gardens.

"What's going on?"

Jenny's hands made fists and she pressed them into her thighs. Without thinking, Beth took a tentative step forward.

"Don't."

Beth began to cry. "Jenny, you're scaring me, what's going on?"

Jenny bit hard into her top lip then licked away a tear as it ran past the side of her mouth. "You promised me," she said and pressed the pendant against her sternum. "Why did you leave me, Beth?"

"I didn't. Blake freaked out and beat Ronnie to a pulp and broke his leg. The police interviewed me and it took ages so Dad came to fetch me."

"I needed you." Jenny's voice was small and wounded.

"Everything okay, girls?" Joan asked through the door.

Beth looked at Jenny, who just stared back. "I think we're okay."

"I heard a noise."

"I tripped on the chair and stubbed my toe, sorry. I'll keep it down."

Joan chuckled. "You are so accident prone, Beth Kennedy."

"I know."

Jenny didn't speak until they heard Joan walk downstairs. "Thank you." The interruption seemed to have calmed her a little, though tension still came off her in waves.

"Are you going to tell me what's up?"

Jenny wiped her cheeks. "I hated being on my own. After ages, Blake turned up and said you'd got lost somewhere and he couldn't find you."

"He ran off," Beth said indignantly.

Jenny shook her head as if it didn't matter. "I wondered where you were, I texted you."

"I saw them this morning, I wasn't paying attention last night."

"I noticed," Jenny said without inflection, a comment rather than a condemnation. "Blake drove us home in his horrible van." Her hand shook and she pressed it harder into her thigh. "Everyone was laughing and messing about. I sat in the back with Mouse and Wendy and just wanted to walk home."

Jenny reached for a tissue and blew her nose.

"All I could smell was diesel and weed and I think that's why we were laughing but I felt sick too. We dropped the others off then Kate. She wanted me to get dropped off first and gave me daggers when she got out. I felt really sick by then but Blake drove off before I could get into the front and I knew we were going the wrong way because it doesn't take that long to get from Kate's house to here."

Beth heard the horror in Jenny's voice and wanted to reach out to offer comfort but was scared to. "Are you alright?"

Jenny shook her head briskly and stroked the pendant. She started to say something but her voice broke and she stopped, took a couple of deep breaths. "He took me down to the docks."

Beth felt the weight of the story crush her as she understood how much she'd let Jenny down.

"I don't know where he parked but it was dark. He climbed into the back and…" Her voice broke again, tears streaming. She stroked the pendant like she wanted to summon a genie who could turn back time. "I tried, Beth, but I couldn't fight him off. He told me he liked me because I was shy and wanted a challenge. He asked if I'd ever fucked anyone before and when I said no, he told me to take my dress off. He pulled me to him and I screamed and the sound, oh my God, it echoed and hurt my ears and

I kept screaming and he put his hand over my mouth really hard. I thought I was going to suffocate and when he let go I screamed again and he laughed, saying I could make as much noise as I wanted on a Saturday night in the middle of the docks."

It took every ounce of Beth's self-control not to hold her friend, even as her hatred of Blake built into a fury.

"He pulled my dress off, Beth, and I fought as best I could, I hit him and gouged him with my nails and kicked him and he seemed to like it, he kept laughing and then he had his hand in my knickers and…"

A sob cut off her words and Beth tentatively put her arms around Jenny, feeling the steely vibration in her friend's limbs as she stood rigid. When she began to cry, with wracking sobs that came from deep within, Beth held her tighter. After what felt like an age, Jenny snaked her arms around Beth, holding her tightly as if afraid she'd disappear.

"He raped me," she said between hitches of breath, and sobbed into Beth's neck.

They stood that way until the tears stopped.

Chapter 44

They left the garages and walked along several streets before they came to a small parade of shops next to a pub called The Rising Sun.

Surrounded by a wall, lights from the docks were visible through the trees and bramble that marked the end of the car park. The pub sign, high on a slim pole, showed the same logo as the one the BMX kids had on their T-shirts.

"You think Beth's in there?"

"Ziggy's part of Blake's crew and this is where I've heard he operates from." Frank stepped over the low wall around the car park. "Let me do the talking."

He walked along the side of the building. The main doors were wide open, letting out the sound of music, conversation and laugher, the smell of alcohol and stale bodies. Frank stopped at the far corner where a foul smell coming from a small wooden stall contaminated the air.

"Jesus," Nick muttered, wrinkling his nose.

"They do a nice Sunday dinner here," said Frank, without irony.

"I believe you."

A door, set into a porch, had a few BMX bikes propped haphazardly against the wall beside it. A wide window above them was dark.

Frank went up the porch steps, knocked and pushed the door. It didn't budge. He knocked again.

"Nobody home," he said and walked back to the main doors.

Nick followed him into a narrow corridor with a sticky carpet. In the lounge bar, a pool match was in full swing, the teenaged players egging each other on and jeering when one of them missed an apparently easy shot. A short man, who might have been in his sixties or seventies, stood by the raised bar flap. His face suggested a lifetime of heavy drinking and the elbows of his black Harrington jacket had been worn grey. His eyes lit up when he saw Frank.

"My boy," he said, "come let me buy you a drink."

"No thanks, Barrie, but I appreciate your offer."

Barrie didn't look at Nick. "So what brings you here?"

"Looking for a friend."

"You've found one, I think."

Frank smiled. "Indeed." He patted the man gently on the shoulder. "Be safe, brother."

"Aye," said Barrie and went back to his drink.

"What are you looking for?" Nick asked as they walked further into the lounge.

"A contact."

"What about old Barrie there?"

"You should ask him about the little green men who help him on his way home."

"Ah."

"Some people live in their own worlds and that's perfectly fine, but we need something more solid."

Frank moved around the semi-circular bar. Two barmaids stood at the far end, chatting to customers as one pulled a pint. Above the cash till was a pinboard full of postcards and foreign banknotes.

One of the pool players shouted a greeting and Frank waved but kept moving, heading toward a table in the furthermost bay window. Two men sat on a bench seat; a snake of dominoes spread in front of them. They looked up as Frank got to the table and one of them, his drinker's nose dotted with broken blood vessels, smiled.

"You're a long way from home, Frank."

"Nice to see you, Laurie."

The man raised his pint glass in a toast, took a sip and put it down gently on the beer mat. His friend, pale and thin, offered a watery smile and stroked his domino chip like a rosary.

"And you too, Perce."

"So what brings you here, preacher man?" Laurie looked Nick up and down. "And who's this?"

Nick raised his hand in greeting. "Nick Parker, friend of Frank."

"Never seen you around before," said Laurie and Nick could almost see the wall going up as he was judged an outsider. "And I know most folk."

"Well, you know me," said Frank.

"Aye. So what's happening?"

Frank gestured to the two empty chairs across the table and Laurie nodded. Frank sat down, waited for Nick to do the same and then leaned forward, careful not to nudge any of the dominoes. "I'm looking for someone, Laurie."

Laurie and Perce exchanged a glance. Perce sipped his drink, seeming to struggle with the weight of the pint glass.

"Anyone we know?" Laurie asked.

"A woman."

"Come on now, laddie, this is a port town. You know where you need to go to find a woman."

"Our sister is a friend of mine and Nick's."

Laurie sucked in his lips, eyes wide and Nick knew they'd come to the right place. He found the picture of Beth on his phone and gave it to Frank.

"Have you seen Beth?" Frank asked, holding the phone so Laurie could see it.

Laurie put on some reading glasses, his eyes seeming to fill the lenses. His mouth set in a thin line as he checked the picture.

"It's not my intention to get you into trouble," Frank said quietly. "As far as anyone needs be aware, we're just old friends chatting."

Laurie nodded, played with his pint glass and looked at Perce.

It was so obvious he'd seen her, Nick wanted to reach across the table and grab him; force him to say yes. To his surprise, Frank put a hand over Nick's and shook his head once, almost imperceptibly.

"You really know her?" Laurie asked.

"Yes," Frank said.

Laurie exhaled slowly. "If you say anything, we're dead."

"I understand."

"She was here, in the back room, but I don't think she is now."

"On her own?"

"Wendy was with her."

"Okay, thank you, brother." Frank got up.

"Wait," said Nick, "is that it?"

"That's it." Frank gestured for him to stand up. "I appreciate this, Laurie."

"If he ever finds out…" It sounded like a threat but Nick could tell from the look on Laurie's face that it was anything but.

"He won't. Take care, both of you."

"Remember to glow," said Perce as they walked away.

* * *

"Why didn't you get him to tell us where Beth is?" Nick asked once they were outside.

"I got as much as I could. Things aren't quite so simple here, brother, this is Nelson Blake's pub."

"You never told me what this Blake did."

"And I won't. He and I have not spoken since he went to prison but I've heard stories."

"What stories?" Nick's worry escalated. "She's not just missing, is she? You think it's something else. This brave thing you said she did, was she somehow involved in him going to prison?"

"You have to trust me."

"You could have pushed Laurie."

"To what point? He couldn't talk. If we went straight to where Beth is, Blake would ask questions and one of the drinkers here, in an effort to keep in the good books, might mention us talking to Laurie."

"So why did he help you at all?"

"Because he thinks he owes me."

"What does that mean?"

"His brother Perce has led a troubled life, mostly not his fault though he's no angel. One day, I happened to see him climbing up on the pier. I talked with him and reasoned with him and in the end, grabbed his legs as he jumped and held on until people came to help. He was livid, as you could imagine, but got some treatment and a new direction. I met Laurie when Perce brought him to the Glow Church to thank me. I said neither of them owed me anything but Laurie said if he could ever help me, whatever it was, he would do his best."

"And now he has?"

"Oh, he's done it on a few occasions but yes, tonight was one such."

"So now what?" Nick tried to shake away the pins and needles fear had filled the tips of his fingers with. "If Beth's in trouble, we haven't got time to waste."

"And lo, the universe provides," said Frank, looking over Nick's shoulder, who turned to see Ziggy ride into the car park. Frank pulled Nick into the shadows.

"Are we going to beat up a teenager for information?"

Frank looked aghast. "No."

Ziggy rode one-handed, looking at his phone screen and when he reached the corner, Frank stepped in front of him. The teenager, surprise unbalancing him, braked and the bike wobbled to a stop. Frank blocked his exit route and Nick stepped into the light.

"Evening, Ziggy," Frank said.

"What're you doing, let me go."

"We're not holding you," Nick said.

"I'll call the police, this is intimidation."

"We merely want to ask a question or two," said Frank.

"I'll tell the police you're a couple of nonces, got me down here in the dark and tried to touch me up."

"Your word against mine."

Ziggy laughed sourly. "You're the one with the prison record."

Frank nodded in acknowledgement. "And I've been clean since I was released. How many times have you been picked up?"

Ziggy's bravado fled. "Let me go, Frank mate, come on."

Nick tried to control his growing anger. "Where's my wife?"

"Dunno what you're talking about."

Frank stepped forward and Nick matched his pace, backing Ziggy into one of the parking spaces. His rear tyre caught something and the bike twisted. He stepped away as it fell over and backed towards the high wall.

"We won't hurt you," said Frank and picked up the bike. "We just want some answers."

"If either of you touch me, I'll get the police on you."

Frank put his foot on the front wheel and pulled hard on the handlebars. Metal groaned as the wheel buckled, one spoke pinging free.

"Fuck."

"Were you trying to ring him? Is he at his flat?"

Ziggy licked his lips, eyes darting as he tried to find a way out. "I ain't talking."

"Give me your phone, Ziggy," said Frank. He threw the bike into the bramble and held out his hand.

"Fuck off, get your own."

"Ziggy?" Frank was now a step or two away from the teenager. "We have to find this man's wife."

"Maybe she ain't with Mr Blake."

"Is your mum?"

Nick saw the teenager deflate. "Wendy's his mum?"

Frank nodded without looking away from Ziggy. "Is she okay?"

"Was it you that hurt her?" Ziggy suddenly sounded much younger.

"Why would you think that? I haven't seen her in weeks."

"You're lying. Mr Blake says people lie all the time and you are now. You hurt her and she had to come here with that woman, that's why Mr Blake told me to sort you out." He paused, as if he'd said too much, then carried on anyway. "I had to hurt you to get my revenge."

"I don't lie." Frank took a step closer, towering over Ziggy. "Let me see your phone, I'll give it straight back."

Ziggy backed against the wall, the bramble to his left, with no way out. "You're a prick."

"You're not the first person to tell me so."

"Fine," Ziggy said, annoyance making his voice rise and handed the phone over.

"Thanks," said Frank and gave the handset to Nick. "Don't know how to work them, brother."

Nick activated the iPhone screen. "Passcode?"

Ziggy told him. The keypad faded to reveal an image of a young woman posing nude, Ziggy visible in the mirror behind her. Nick opened the call log. "Last three calls to Mr Blake."

Frank nodded. "So now we know and you didn't betray your boss because Nick told me. Okay? So where might they be, if not here or at Blake's flat?"

Ziggy shrugged. "I don't know."

"Where would you go, as your next option?"

"Probably out to the resort."

"That makes sense." Frank turned to Nick. "I know where it is, we have what we need. Give Ziggy back his phone."

Nick looked at him, incredulous. "What? He'll just ring Blake and warn him."

"I made him a promise."

"I didn't," said Nick and threw the phone as hard as he could into the bramble.

"Fucking arsehole," Ziggy muttered.

Frank walked over to the three bikes by the porch. He lifted the first and swung it hard into the wall, buckling the front wheel. "Whoops," he said and threw the bike towards Ziggy, who quickly stepped out of the way. Frank held the second bike by the saddle until Nick took the handlebars.

"Don't be a fool forever, Ziggy," Frank said as he picked up the third bike and got onto it. His huge frame dwarfed it. "You'll live longer if you try to see the good in people around you."

Ziggy shook his head in disgust.

Nick got on the other bike, the saddle so low as to be useless. "I hope you have a very unpleasant life, you little scrote," he said and cycled out of the car park.

Chapter 45

Then

"We need to report him."

"I can't," Jenny said quietly.

"What do you mean?" Beth didn't want to upset Jenny but her rage at Blake was peaking. Hurting Ronnie was terrible but this, what he'd done to her best friend, was unforgiveable.

"He said it was all my fault because I stayed in his van when he got in the back, that I led him on."

"That's bollocks, Jenny, he forced himself on you. You didn't lead him on any more than Ronnie asked to get beaten up. The bloke's a nutter who needs to be stopped."

"I can't." Jenny leaned against her, as if already beaten. "Even if the police believe me, it'll be my word against his. It'll go to court, it'll be awful."

"I reported him to the police yesterday, they knew all about him." Why hadn't she told Chisholm about Pervy Pete? "All that combined, it has to go against him."

Jenny looked at her, eyes wide. "You believe me, don't you?"

The question shocked the air out of her momentarily. "Of course I believe you! Why wouldn't I?"

"Maybe he said those things often enough they got snagged in my brain."

"Well unsnag them, never think them again. I'll always believe you and stand beside you."

Jenny looked at her with a wounded expression and, even though Beth was convinced the police should be told, it wasn't her decision. Whatever happened next was Jenny's choice.

"If nothing else, Jen, you need to get checked out."

Jenny looked away, in disgust or distress Beth couldn't tell. "I will."

"Have you had a shower?"

"Of course, I wanted to wash that bastard off me the first chance I got."

Beth didn't know a lot about this kind of thing but was sure that wasn't the right action. "What about your clothes?"

"In the wash basket."

"We can get them out, they can be evidence."

"Of what?" Jenny sounded exasperated. "If they find his spunk it'll still be his word against mine."

Beth's frustration bubbled up. "We can't let him get away with it," she said in desperation. She touched Jenny's cheek. "I'm so sorry I wasn't there."

"You couldn't have known."

"Except I'd made him angry."

"He seemed fine when he got back, which made it all the worse."

Beth's thoughts chased themselves into endless dead ends. "Let me take you to the hospital."

Jenny sat and fiddled with the pendant again. "I'll get Mum to take me."

"Do you want me here when you tell her?"

Jenny shook her head. "No, thank you. I'm sorry to put all this on you."

"Don't be silly, that's what I'm here for."

"I feel better for telling you, the thoughts aren't running around in my head like ants. But please don't tell anyone else – not Kate or your mum and dad or the police."

Overwhelmed with sadness, Beth agreed to her friend's terms even though she knew, deep down, someone else would have to know to make sure Blake didn't get away with it. "I won't."

"You promise?" Jenny sounded insistent, as if she could sense Beth's indecision. "Please, Beth, let me sort it. Promise you won't tell anyone."

They sat for a while without speaking and Beth watched the dust motes dance. Feet up on the chair again, Jenny looked at her toes whilst stroking the broken pendant.

"I think I'm ready," she said finally.

"Are you sure you don't want me here?"

"No," she said, so softly Beth almost didn't hear it. "Thank you."

"All for one." Beth hugged her awkwardly. "If you need me for anything."

"I know."

Beth opened the bedroom door. "I love you."

"I love you too," said Jenny and gave her a weak smile.

It was the last thing they ever said to each other.

Chapter 46

Water shocked her awake.

Beth spluttered, coughed the liquid away and opened her eyes. She tried to wipe her face but her hands wouldn't move. Sitting on an uncomfortable chair, she saw a room she hadn't seen in a long time and a sense of dread settled over her. If she was this far from town, nobody was going to find her.

Blake leaned in close, grinning, his breath meaty and sour. "You're awake."

She shook her head to get rid of the water but couldn't take a full breath. Her chest ached and her wrists were bound behind her by something thick. "What's going on?"

He stepped back, still grinning. "Still asking stupid fucking questions then."

The chalet had the same layout as the one the squad used fifteen years ago except this had a wide shelving unit between the front windows, filled with what looked like horse-riding tack. A chicken coop, three feet tall and perhaps six feet long, sat in the corner.

There was no overhead light, just several lanterns on the floor that cast a weird orange glow into the room. The front door was closed and Wendy lay in the doorway across from it, her back to Beth.

Mouse came in, stepping over Wendy, wiping his hands on an old cloth. He looked distracted and his expression darkened when he saw Beth awake. Her panic rose with a horrible sense of defeat, that whatever she'd wandered into she was never going to get out of.

"Enjoy," Blake said and dropped a rough fabric sack over her head, cutting the light instantly. "Can you see me?"

She didn't answer, not wanting to tell him no so he could take advantage, scared that if she said yes he would make the situation worse.

Water hit the sack, the shock of it making her breathe in sharply. The fabric stuck to her face, plugging her nose and mouth as the water seeped through. She choked, tipped her head forward, tried to blow to clear her face. The material released itself and she took in a deep breath before more water hit.

She swallowed some, more went up her nose. She coughed and gagged.

Fear overwhelmed the panic. She pulled on her hands, trying to breathe, her lungs on fire as she choked. She kicked her legs, tried to twist her body on the chair, doing anything that might help.

"She can't breathe, man."

"I know." Blake pulled the sack off and Beth gasped, sucking in air greedily.

Blake grabbed her hair, pulled her head up and leaned in close. "Didn't like that?"

She coughed in his face.

He smirked, wiping the water away. "Dirty girl." He unclipped something from her wrist and pulled her to her feet, holding her hair. "Do you know where you are?"

"In the resort?"

"Bonus point for Kennedy. I'm surprised you remember it, seeing as how quickly you legged it once you'd sold me down the fucking river."

He pulled down, her scalp burning until she dropped heavily to her knees, her bound wrists not giving her any options.

Blake unlatched the door of the chicken coop. It was empty but patches of the matted straw were stained with shit, and feathers clung to the wooden supports and chicken wire that formed the cage. "Either go in nicely, or I rip out your hair then shove you in anyway."

"I'm not going to fight."

"Good," he said and shoved her in, closing the door behind her.

She shuffled back against the wall.

"All trussed up and ready," Blake said as he fastened a padlock over the hasp.

She didn't want to think what for and, instead, focussed on moving her hands. The binding on her wrists creaked, like an old belt. If she could rip it on something, then…

"You have no idea how long I've dreamed about this moment," Blake said. He picked up the chair she'd been tied to and set it down in front of the coop. He sat, heavily.

Watching him, Beth felt in the straw and, after a while, her index finger snagged on something metallic.

"Everything was your fault, from Pervy Pete to your boyfriend in the Winter Gardens and all the shit with Jenny."

"An odd way to remember it," she said, investigating her find with her fingertips. It seemed to be a small screw, half-lodged in a floorboard. She wiped her fingers on her jeans and tried to twist it. After a moment, the screw finally turned, giving with a little groan.

"It took three years to get back at the doctor who set my ankle wrong. I was top dog by then and had the run of things, so he paid dearly. I cleared the infirmary and paid off the guards so it was just me and him in his operating theatre with a claw hammer and a scalpel." He gazed at the ceiling, a strangely delighted expression flitting across his face. "I always used to think the idea of delaying revenge was a load of bollocks but it really isn't and building up to this, over the years, has really kept me going."

"You deserved everything you got, for what you did." The screw came free and she palmed it.

He looked over his shoulder at Mouse. "Can you hear this? Says I deserved it."

"I reckon she's remembering it wrong," Mouse said, without looking at Beth.

Blake laughed, his eyes dead like a shark about to attack. "You never came back, did you? I mean, I get it, not much was left. Jenny was gone, the squad was scattered to the winds and things were bad with you and Kate. It's such a shame you didn't see her at the end. You'd have laughed, actually. She fell for the oldest trick in the book."

"What do you mean?" Beth asked.

"She was driving over Julia's Point, going to see her old man. I wonder how her suicide plays on him, or her lad for that matter. Nice kid, by all accounts, but you've got to imagine it'll weigh heavily on his mind. On the bright side, though, it brought you home."

"Her funeral was hardly a bright side."

"But if she hadn't died then…" He let the sentence dangle and widened his eyes, as if prompting her to connect the dots.

She felt things falling into place but badly, like a jigsaw where the pieces were jammed in regardless of whether they fitted.

"She was stupid and got out of her car," he said, "so intent to check the baby seat she didn't hear me."

"What did you do to her?"

"Pushed her across the road into the wall and she just tipped right over it."

The revelation was like getting hit by a car. "You killed her?"

Blake leaned back, a faint smile playing at his lips. "Didn't you realise?" He laughed. "God, you're dumber than I thought."

She felt winded. "Why would you do that?"

"Because I needed you here, on my terms, and she was my only link to you."

Beth gagged on the realisation. "You killed her for that?" Tears blurred her vision. "How could you?"

"Lack of empathy, social dysfunction, prison life, take your pick. Murder isn't difficult once you've done it a few times."

She gagged again and spat out the bile.

"You have to pay for the past, Kennedy."

"But Kate didn't have to." She blinked away tears. "You're a monster."

"And you're locked in a chicken coop in the middle of nowhere."

She felt the terror reducing her. Even if she managed to get free of the bindings, the coop and the resort, it was a long way into town and there were probably plenty of BMX riders between her and safety.

He stood and limped towards the coop, pulling a dark wallet out of his back pocket. He sifted through it, notes and receipts dropping out. "Ah-ha," he said and pulled out a piece of paper, unfolding it. He dropped the wallet and leaned over the coop, slipping the paper through chicken wire and holding it steady so she could see.

"Recognise this?"

It was a photograph of her and Nick, looking impossibly young, standing outside Covent Garden market. They hadn't been going out long when it was taken and Nick, a huge fan of the film *Frenzy*, took every opportunity to visit the place whenever they were in London.

"I took care of the cavalry too," he said and laughed.

Beth's world collapsed around her.

Chapter 47

Then

Beth shut herself away in her bedroom for the rest of the day, her thoughts tangled. Her mother ventured up to see if she wanted anything for tea, clearly trying her hardest to be nice. Beth made an effort, agreeing to toast and a cup of tea, weak smiles exchanged as the start of mending some bridges.

DS Chisholm rang as Beth watched twilight fall. "We haven't picked Nelson Blake up yet so if it's possible, I would stay in this evening."

"I hadn't planned to go out."

"Quite. I could also do with asking you a few more questions, just to clarify a couple of things. Could you come to the station at nine tomorrow morning?"

"Uh-huh."

"I'll see you then."

Night fell. Her parents went to bed, both saying "love you" as they walked by her door. She replied to them both.

Her phone stayed silent. Kate had probably heard about Blake's situation, which would explain her distance, but nothing from Jenny was troubling. Twice Beth wrote her a text but scrapped it, thinking the last thing Jenny would want was Beth chasing around after her.

She dozed, vivid and unpleasant dreams of Ronnie's beaten face merged with Jenny's full of tears, startling her into waking. She checked her phone as dawn lit her window and saw she'd somehow missed a text from Jenny. "Shit, shit, shit."

Hi B, spoke to mum and really, really need to speak to you. Please ring me asap. Love you x

It had been sent last night – how could she have missed it? She rang, the call going to voicemail.

Beth got dressed and went downstairs, made a strong cup of coffee and drank it sitting on the patio. She tried Jenny again, but the voicemail cut in.

"Jenny, it's me. Sorry I missed your text last night, really wish I hadn't. Hope everything went well with your mum, let me know. I have to go and see the police this morning but I'll keep our promise." Even if it kills me, she thought. "See you, love you."

* * *

She decided to call in to see Jenny on the way to the police station, cutting down onto Marine Drive once she was well past the Winter Gardens. She rang Jenny twice and only got voicemail.

A sleek black Jaguar passed her and stopped at the corner of Regent's Row, outside the Sunshine Pub. A tall man in a black jacket got out the nearside rear door and disappeared from view around the corner. Frankie got out the other side, carrying a suitcase. He looked around, saw Beth and stopped.

Her stomach dropped but she was too close to turn and run the other way. "Going somewhere?" she asked, keeping her distance.

"What?"

"The suitcase," she said, jerking her chin towards it.

"Coming back actually." He took a deep breath. "I'm working, Beth, leave me alone."

"Carrying a suitcase? What've you done, shat on someone's day?"

His eyes flicked away briefly, as if he'd been caught in a shameful lie. "You could say that."

Realisation dawned. "You've been collecting, haven't you?"

"It's common policy," he said with a shrug. "Grab them on a Monday and it fucks their week up."

If she'd had breakfast she'd have thrown it up, her stomach curdling at the thought of some poor sod opening their door to Frankie demanding their valuables. "That's disgusting."

"That's life," he said and shifted his hands on the case. "One you're clearly not cut out for. Wendy told me what you'd said."

"What?" It was Wendy, not Kate? That argument with her best friend had been pointless? "That fucking snake in the grass listened to our private conversation and tattletaled it straight back to you?"

"She did what she thought was right, as I'm sure you did last night, after the beating."

"What do you expect, the PCSO was right there. Blake's mad, he lost control with Ronnie like he did with Pervy Pete."

"I told you I'd deal with it."

"But you didn't, Frankie, and now someone who was in the wrong place at the wrong time has had his leg broken. Did you know he was a county runner?"

Frankie shook his head. "So what did you tell the police?"

"Everything and when I see them this morning, I'm going to tell them what happened to Pervy Pete."

He shook his head, looking hurt and lost and it made her angry because it was his fault, he was supposed to keep Blake under control. And people had been hurt because of his failure, especially poor sweet Jenny. Beth felt energised by her rising anger.

"I was frightened of you when we first met and the thought of being part of the squad scared me too."

"I didn't twist your arm."

"No." She shook her head. "It doesn't work like that, though, does it? Kate wanted in because she wanted Blake, and you wanted us because, what, people perhaps wouldn't believe we were thieves? Is that it? I thought people in the squad protected each other."

"We did."

She barked a laugh. "Are you kidding me? You knew what Blake's trigger was and yet you sent me out with him on Saturday and then let him take Jenny home. What were you doing, waiting for something to happen?"

"I'll deal with Blake."

"It's too fucking late for that. You were supposed to protect us, but you're pathetic."

His cheeks coloured but he didn't say anything.

"You don't scare me, Frankie, because you're nothing. You couldn't even save your friends." She managed to stop herself just in time but he noticed.

"What does that mean?"

"Nobody should have been attacked, Frankie."

He frowned, tilted his head. "Did Blake touch you?"

"No." She shook her head, frustrated. "It'll come out."

"What did he do?"

"Fuck off, Frankie."

He took a step towards her but she stood her ground, heart thumping. "You don't scare me."

"Who did he touch? Was it Kate or Jenny?"

"I'd like to think it'll worry you," she said and walked past him, "but I doubt it will. You already knew he was dodgy, you bastard."

"Beth," he said but she ignored him, turning to Regent's Row and walking away as steadily as she could, even though she wanted to be sick.

He said something else she didn't quite catch it, though it sounded like "I'll sort it". At the first junction, she risked a glance over her shoulder and saw him go into the pub, head down.

* * *

Nobody answered the door at Jenny's.

Beth cupped her hands at the front window but couldn't see anyone and a chill of concern joined the upset of her stomach. Even if Joan had taken Maggie to school and Len had left for work, Jenny should still be there.

* * *

Kate rang as Beth made her way across Market Square towards the police station.

"What the fuck did you do?"

The tone and ferocity of the question startled her. "What?"

"Don't come the innocent with me. I texted you on Saturday, I was worried when Blake came back on his own and said you weren't feeling well."

"Kate, that's not–"

"I fucking know," she snapped. "He told me everything yesterday."

"You saw him?"

"I can't, can I, because he's got the coppers after him. I fucking told you not to mess this up for me but you just had to do it, didn't you? You selfish bitch, you couldn't stand to see me happy, could you?"

Angry tears pricked Beth's eyes. "Do you know what he did?"

"He told me you led him on then bumped into Ronnie in the Winter Gardens and it all kicked off, with you making it worse."

"That's not what happened at all."

Kate laughed, a sour sound like she was chewing something she'd much rather spit out.

"Did he tell you about the Spar shop?"

"What the fuck does a Spar have to do with anything? I can't believe you let me down, Beth."

"I didn't," she insisted, tears clogging her voice. She'd never heard Kate this angry before and could feel her whole life unravelling. "He stole booze from the Spar and we ended up in the Winter Gardens to avoid the police. I wasn't coming onto him."

"You must think I'm an idiot. I know the Ronnie thing is real because his mum told mine everything – that his leg's broken and he might not run for the county anymore and it's all your fault."

"How can it be my fault? Ronnie called him Nelly and that was–"

"I don't care," Kate said and repeated it until Beth stopped talking. "I told you not to fuck this up for me and now you have, you jealous poisonous cow."

The words stung. How could her best friend have got things so wrong? And what would she say when she found out about Jenny?

"I'm glad we're all going off at the end of the holidays so I don't have to see you ever again," Kate said.

Beth's eyes were hot with unshed tears, as much for Jenny and the three of them as for her friendship with Kate. All those years, destroyed so quickly. "Kate…"

"I loved you, Beth, but this is it, you've ruined everything."

"It's going to get worse," she said softly.

"And what's that supposed to mean? What else have you done?"

Beth could feel the words pushing for release but couldn't betray Jenny. "I can't tell you."

"I hate you."

Beth listened to the dead line for a while. A little girl stopped and stared at her. A woman rushed towards them, pushing a stroller.

"Sammy, leave that lady alone."

Sammy continued to stare, even when the woman got close enough to take her hand.

"Sorry she bothered you, she's just really…" The woman paused. "Are you alright?"

Beth rubbed her eyes. "I'm fine, just had a shitty…" She stopped herself, looked at Sammy. "Had a crappy call."

The woman nodded, as if she understood perfectly. "Don't let them get to you," she said and turned the stroller around, dragging Sammy with her. "Keep your chin up, love."

"I doubt that'll make much difference."

* * *

Seagrave Police Station was on Howard Street. Beth stood outside the main doors and looked at her pale reflection. What if they asked about Jenny and she collapsed under the questioning and accidentally betrayed her friend? Worry and guilt laid heavy in her stomach and she felt sick.

Beth went into the reception. The walls were an unpleasant green, the dark floor tiles looked scuffed and a pot plant stood at death's door in the far corner. The desk sergeant looked up.

"Can I help you, love?"

"I'm here to see DS Chisholm."

He took her name and rang someone. "Tell the DS a Miss Beth Kennedy is in reception." He put the phone down. "She'll just be a minute, take a seat."

"That's okay," she said and stood where she was, reading the public notices on the wall behind him.

DS Chisholm took at least five minutes and came into reception wearing the same clothes as Saturday. She looked tired, her rust-coloured hair pulled back severely into a ponytail.

"Beth." She had a pad and thin folder clasped to her chest and shook Beth's hand. "Thank you for coming in."

"That's okay."

"Come through." Chisholm guided Beth through a door that led onto a narrow corridor. Several doors opened off it and Chisholm walked briskly, Beth having to rush to keep up. Chisholm knocked on the door of Interview Room 1 then went in. Beth followed her into a small featureless room with four chairs around a desk, a tape recorder and a window overlooking a car parked dotted with police vehicles.

Chisholm walked around the desk and dropped her pad and folder onto it. "Please," she said and indicated the chair opposite her.

"Am I under arrest?"

"Of course not," said Chisholm with a soft smile. The expression made her seem younger, her eyes less steely. "Sorry, I forget the effect police stations have. I'll bet even the Pope would feel guilty if he ever went in one."

Beth laughed nervously as she sat down. She laced her fingers to stop them dancing.

"Relax, Beth. There's nothing to worry about, I just have a few things I'd like to clarify about Saturday night. I can get someone in, if you'd prefer, but we're really just talking. I'll make some notes but I won't be recording anything."

"That's fine." She wouldn't dare bring her father here and her mother would probably refuse.

"Good." Chisholm uncapped a pen and tapped it against her teeth. "I'll be honest, I'm a little curious about your link to Nelson Blake."

Beth's nerves felt like a flock of panicking butterflies. "Okay."

"He moves in very different circles to you and has something of a reputation."

Beth took a deep breath, her butterflies getting worse. "I met him through my friend Kate."

"I see. And have you known Kate for long?"

"Years."

"So she's the same kind of young woman as yourself?"

"Uh-huh."

"And again, I'm curious."

"Kate saw him working at the Goose Fair and fancied him. We kind of fell in with his little squad."

Chisholm raised her eyebrows and Beth wondered if she had the same thoughts about fair workers as her mother did. "Fell in?"

"That makes it sound bad." The butterflies pushed against the base of her throat. "Look, I know it was stupid but it seemed like a fun thing to do for our last summer here. Nothing like this was supposed to happen."

"I believe you but it got me thinking and seeing you on Saturday night sparked a memory." She opened the folder. Inside were several photographs copied onto sheets of A4 and she picked up the top one. "Have a look," she said and slid the page across the desk.

Beth slowly untangled her fingers as she looked at the grainy monochrome image showing her and Jenny outside Pervy Pete's, Beth's face clearly visible. "That's me and Jenny."

"It was recovered from the CCTV at Peter's News last week. There was an incident there, the proprietor was badly beaten in an apparently motiveless attack where nothing was stolen. The victim isn't pressing charges, which isn't unusual because, between you and me, he had a reputation when I was a teenager." They locked eyes, as if sharing an understanding. "On the day of the incident, you and your friend Jenny were photographed outside the shop with Nelson Blake having already entered."

Beth stole a glance at the tape recorder and Chisholm caught her. "You're not being recorded."

"I know, you told me."

"So talk to me, I know something's wrong."

When the tears came, they stole her voice. Chisholm dug out a packet of tissues from her jacket and handed them to Beth. As she pulled herself together, Chisholm went to the door and called for someone. She closed the door but waited by it and, a few moments later, opened it when someone knocked. They handed her a glass of water and she put it on the table in front of Beth.

"I'm sorry about this," Beth said.

"Don't worry, do you want me to call someone?"

"No, I want to talk."

She sipped the water and told Chisholm everything, from Pervy Pete to the BJ robbery, from the Spar to the Winter Gardens, implicating herself completely and not caring because she deserved it. The DS made notes but said nothing, waiting until Beth had finished.

"So Nelly is the trigger then?"

Beth nodded, feeling like a weight had been lifted off her.

Chisholm shook her head. "I knew he was trouble."

"He is," Beth said, pressing her hands together, the urge to tell the DS about Jenny's rape almost too much to bear.

"Is there something else, Beth?"

She couldn't break her promise and let Jenny down, not again. Her head ached. Chisholm seemed to have some empathy, if not sympathy, and apparently understood the situation with Blake, so perhaps the best thing to do was get justice for her friend. Even if that went against Jenny's wishes.

"Beth?"

She pressed her fingers together. "I promised," she said, angry at herself for dithering. "I know that sounds stupid but…"

"Who did you promise?"

"Jenny."

Chisholm checked her notes. "Your friend from the newsagents?"

"Yes, Jenny Reid, she's one of my best friends."

Chisholm looked as if she'd just got a shock. "Jenny Reid? Have you spoken to her recently?"

"She left me a message last night but I didn't get it and I've been trying to call her all morning. Her house is empty too."

"Where does she live?"

"New Street."

"Would you excuse me a moment?" Chisholm left the room and when she came back, she had another folder in her hand. She sat down. "Is this Jenny?" she asked and slid a picture across the desk.

Beth recognised it instantly because she saw it every time she went into Jenny's house, where it normally sat, pride of place on the sideboard alongside pictures of Maggie and Pete. "Yes. How come you've got this picture?"

Chisholm leaned forward with a pained expression. "I'm sorry to have to tell you this, Beth, but Jenny is dead."

Chapter 48

The moon sat high and heavy over Crozier's Farm, casting a pale blue glow on everything.

Nick stopped in the driveway, legs aching from cycling up Duncan Hill.

"We need to be cautious," Frank said quietly.

"We should just call the police."

"No." Frank's voice sounded hard. "Even if we're correct and convince them, what happens when they go in all lights and noise?" He laid his bike down. "We'll go on foot."

Nick laid his bike next to Frank's. An owl in the trees hooted and a wave, crashing off to the left, seemed to answer it.

Frank led them through the stone gateposts onto a road darkened by overhanging branches. The trees to the left were so densely packed Nick couldn't see more than a few feet into them, the undergrowth a combination of bramble and bracken. The lights of Seagrave were visible through the thin line of trees to the right.

The owl hooted again, making Nick jump.

"Be calm, brother."

"I'm trying."

Something crashed in among the trees, the sound followed by a frustrated "Fuck".

"What's up?" asked another voice.

"Fell over this fucking tree," came the muffled reply. "Can't see a fucking thing."

"Keep your fucking voice down."

"Fuck off."

"Shall I tell Mr Blake that?"

"No," came the muffled reply.

"Then get up, you twat, and keep moving."

The men, at least two of them, moved off through the wood away from the gate.

"We're in the right place," Frank whispered.

The idea of guards being posted scared Nick more than he was willing to admit. If Blake had people lying in wait then his intent for revenge was clearly very serious.

"They're very noisy, this isn't their normal space."

"It's not mine either."

"No," said Frank, keeping to the edge of the road, "but it lends us equality."

A branch snapped somewhere to the right. "Someone's there," Nick whispered.

"Into the trees," Frank said.

Once off the road, darkness settled over Nick like a heavy cape, the high branches cutting out most of the moonlight. He felt alone and vulnerable, the air heavier, his breathing too loud. Sounds surrounded and disorientated him.

His shoulder bumped a tree and he stopped beside it, waiting for his night vision to set in. Soon, he could see Frank a few paces ahead, standing beside a tree himself.

The person across the road reached the tarmac and came into the trees on this side. Looking around frantically, knowing he probably only had a moment, Nick ducked behind a trunk.

He wasn't quick enough. An arm wrapped around his throat and pulled back. Nick staggered and saw a flash of movement, moonlight on metal and felt heat on his forearm. His attacker's breath was loud and hot in Nick's ear and then, suddenly, it was gone.

Nick turned quickly, his forearm warm. Shafts of moonlight picked the fighters out of the deep shadows. Frank's shorts, his vest, another man in dark colours being shaken like a rag doll, making a horrible gurgling noise.

Frank lifted the attacker and drove him back hard into a wide and unyielding trunk. When he let go, the attacker slid into to a heap among the roots.

"Are you okay, brother?" Frank asked, barely out of breath.

"Yes, he took me by surprise."

"How's your arm?"

Nick held it up, saw the blood. "Oh." That explained the pain.

"Be careful of their knives," Frank said. He shrugged off his backpack and took out a bottle of water and a white T-shirt. "It's not too deep," he said.

He ripped the T-shirt in half, wet it and gently dabbed at the wound. Nick winced with the pain. Frank dressed the wound with the dry half of the shirt, tying it off tightly.

"That'll do for now. Are you feeling okay?"

"I feel a bit giddy."

"Breathe steadily," said Frank and handed him the water.

Nick drained the bottle as Frank checked the attacker's pulse and put him into the recovery position. After touching his forehead briefly, Frank came back and held Nick's shoulders.

"Ready, brother?"

"Yes and thanks, you saved my life again."

Frank's appreciative nod was barely visible in the gloom. "Keep glowing, brother."

Suddenly, it seemed very quiet, the crashing progress of the other men either far enough away the sound didn't carry, which was unlikely, or they were hiding – a terrifying thought. Nick held his breath, the sound of the woods growing. Animals called and skittered in the undergrowth, branches shifted. A bird landed in a tree high above them, sounding like a percussionist warming up.

Frank jolted away from the tree, a dark shape against his side. Another shape, a slice of moonlight revealing a man in dark clothes, went with them. The trio landed noisily and Frank cried out. One man hissed "stay down" and the other made a guttural sound.

The shock of the assault stopped Nick for a couple of seconds and then he rushed forward, bramble grabbing at his legs and feet. The men writhed on the ground, flashes of moonlight glancing off blades. One was lifted high and brought down quickly. Someone grunted in pain.

One of the attackers sat on Frank and Nick threw himself at the man, driving his shoulders into the man's back, knocking him sprawling. Nick kept to his feet and the man got up slowly, breathing heavily. Nick waited, not sure what to do next.

"Shouldn't have done that," said the man.

"You shouldn't have attacked my friend."

"You shouldn't be here." He reached into his pockets and shook his head. "It's your lucky day, can't find my blades."

Nick's arm throbbed in sympathy. "So now what?"

The man came at him low and Nick stepped aside, pushing him into the undergrowth. Reaching blindly, Nick grabbed a broken branch as thick as a baby's arm. As the man got to his feet, Nick swung the branch and it connected with the attacker's temple. The man fell, holding his head.

"Fucker," he muttered.

"Stay down."

The man stood unsteadily and looked at his hand. "You made me bleed," he said, angry and incredulous at the same time. He grabbed for Nick and slipped.

Nick quickly sat on his chest, pressing the branch into the man's throat. The man's eyes bulged and he made a terrible gurgling noise, clawing at Nick's fingers.

"Can't breathe…"

The man rocked his body and threw ineffectual punches but nothing worked. Nick watched him weaken, heard his breathing become reedy and light and realised he was going to kill him.

The man's eyes rolled up and his arms dropped.

Nick let go, sick to his stomach. The man, once the aggressor but now clearly the victim, breathed in deeply and coughed.

A shout from behind drew his attention and Nick turned to see Frank on his back, dark patches dotting his T-shirt and shorts as his attacker stabbed him. Nick raced to help his friend, swinging the branch as he did so. It hit the attacker's arm and as he cried out in pain, Frank twisted, rolling the man into a tree. Nick stood over him, waiting to hit him if he moved. Frank got slowly to his feet, dark trails running down his legs.

"You're bleeding, Frank."

"I know," he said, breathing heavily, "and it would be worse, if not for you. Thank you, brother."

When Frank's attacker got to his feet, he had the Stanley knife in his left hand, his right stiff by his side. "Looks like I'm back in control," he said, teeth dark with blood.

Frank glanced at Nick. "I can't deliberately hurt him."

"I know."

"Your arm is broken," Frank said to the man. "We don't have to do this, there is always another way."

"Fuck you, Frank. You picked me up off the streets a year ago, got me on my feet and told me to look after myself, how to keep myself clean. Don't you remember?"

"I see a lot of people."

"I did what you said and nothing happened until I met Mouse and he introduced me to Mr Blake. All you fucking do-gooders say the right thing, but Mr Blake gave me money and a roof over my head."

"I'm sorry."

"You will be," the man said and closed the space between them.

Frank grabbed his left wrist and yanked it down. The man jerked backwards, trying to free himself but Frank kept his grip.

Nick swung the branch, aiming for the man's head. It caught his shoulder instead and he went down, pulling Frank of top of him. The thump as his head hit a root sounded horribly loud.

As Frank checked the man's pulse, the other attacker came in low out of nowhere. He and Frank tangled and a blade glinted in the moonlight. Frank cried out.

Nick hit the man between the shoulders and, when he turned, Nick hit him across the jaw. The man slipped off

Frank and Nick followed, hitting him until he stopped moving.

Breathless, Nick went to Frank. "Hey."

"My leg."

Even in the dim light it was clear something was terribly wrong. Nick activated the torch on his phone, shined it on Frank's lower leg. One look and he turned away, throwing up what little he'd eaten.

"What is it?" Pain added a hard edge to Frank's voice.

"I'm not sure," said Nick, wiping his mouth with the back of his hand. He steeled himself to look again. Blood oozed from a deep crescent-shaped wound, a flap of skin standing proud.

"He's cut your leg really deeply."

"My tendon?"

"I don't know." Nick got a bottle of water from Frank's backpack. "This might hurt."

"Couldn't be worse."

Nick gently washed the blood away and Frank made a noise like he was trying to suck a golf ball through a hosepipe. The flap of skin flopped back into place but didn't seem to fit, the gash deeper than he'd originally thought.

"He's cut my Achilles, hasn't he?"

"I think so. I'll call an ambulance."

"No, you need to find Beth."

"Are you mad? You've got an open wound."

"Then cover it." Frank sounded angry. "If you call an ambulance, you'll alert Blake. My leg's not going to drop off and I can work through the pain to find my glow."

"Frank, I–"

"Nick." So much rage in the four letters. "I know this world. You don't have the time you think you do. I've been stabbed before, I can clean and dress this when you get out of here."

Frank was right. Nick didn't want to leave him alone but he had to find Beth.

"Okay," he said and pulled a T-shirt, more water and some paracetamol out of the backpack. He gave them to Frank, who held his hand tightly.

"Thank you, brother."

"I'll get help as soon as I can."

Frank twisted until he could sit up, injured leg in front of him. "Fuck off, Nick." He shook his head. "Now you've made me swear and undone years of my own good work. Please don't stay and watch me squirm."

"I see your glow."

Frank pointed over Nick's shoulder. "Follow the road past the farmhouse to the resort. Beth will be in one of the chalets." He shifted his leg, grimacing with the movement. "And be careful. Blake isn't a nice man."

Chapter 49

How could Blake have Nick's wallet and, worse, what did it mean? Had Nick paid the same price as poor Kate – a means to an end to fulfil Blake's twisted desire? Fresh tears spilled down her cheeks.

Her world was crumbling, that awful summer coming back to tear her life apart as Blake's hatred scorched everything it came into contact with. She hadn't killed Kate but if her actions in the past had guided his hand, was she not somehow responsible? And now Nick? The stress was too much, her anxiety was peaking.

"No," she said, sobs breaking her voice, "this can't be true."

Blake turned to Mouse. "Told you I'd have her on her knees."

How had she fallen for all this? How could she have led Nick to his death? If he'd stayed home, he'd be safe. A widower, almost certainly, but safe.

She tipped her head back, trying to relieve the pressure on her sinuses and stared at the ceiling. Would those damp patches be the last thing she ever saw? What was the last thing Kate saw? Were her last thoughts of her son, husband and dad as she realised she was going over Julia's Point?

What had Blake done to Nick? The idea of him suffering, of being tortured or tormented, pushed back the sadness and made her angry. She felt its heat in her chest, zipping through her synapses, making her fingers tingle. She had to resolve this, get out of here and tell the police everything; let Kate's family know she hadn't taken her own life; get revenge for Nick.

The decision felt physical. She blinked rapidly, clearing her vision. Her head ached, her nose and throat felt clogged but her mind was clear.

"So how're you feeling now, Kennedy?"

"Not good," she said, playing up to him, making her voice crack. If she could convince him he'd broken her, he might get careless.

"That's what I like to hear." His mobile rang and Blake pulled it out of his pocket. "Dahvit?" He checked the screen, put the handset back to his ear. "Dahvit?" He limped to the door. "Keep an eye on her, I'm going out to find a signal."

Leaning against the wall with Wendy's body at his feet, Mouse avoided Beth's gaze. Watching him, she tried to manoeuvre the screw into a better position, so she could use it to saw through her bindings, but couldn't get a decent angle.

Frustration bubbled up, feeding her anger. "Mouse?" she called, making her voice crack again.

He ignored her.

"Mouse? We were friends, weren't we? I'm trapped in here; I've just found out my husband is dead." Her voice cracked for real then and she swallowed the emotion.

Now he looked at her and she saw the discomfort in his face.

"I don't want to get you into trouble, because Blake's clearly nuts, but at least give me a fighting chance."

Mouse fiddled with his fingers like a kid caught stealing money from the school tuck shop. "You were always nice to me, Beth." He glanced towards the front door. "But I can't. I'm sorry, he'd kill me."

The front door clattered open and Blake limped in, face like thunder. "Fucking signal," he roared. "Fucking Dutch bastards."

"What's happened now?" Mouse asked.

"This is all your fucking fault." Blake jabbed a finger at Beth and she shrank back against the wire. He kicked Wendy's backside and glared at Mouse. "He's pushing me for the proof."

"Shit."

Blake shook his head. "She fucking knew the rules." He gestured into the room. "Drag her through."

Mouse grabbed under Wendy's arms, her head lolling back, and pulled her out of sight. Blake followed him, closing the door. Sounds drifted through the thin walls – thumps and bumps. Mouse said something and Blake replied, their voices rumbling, the words indistinct.

If Beth couldn't get away, she could put herself in a stronger position and getting her hands in front of her would be a start. Pushing away from the frame, she laid as flat as possible, soles on the floor, and lifted her backside up. Edging her shoulders back, she pushed her hands under her bum, then looped her arms up her legs.

A thin leather belt had been wrapped several times around her wrist, then tied. Even if she'd had a whole day, she would never have been able to saw through it with the screw. She dropped that, sat up and bit at the knot. Roughly made, she quickly loosened it.

A loud thump came from the room and Beth's pulse spiked, expecting Blake or Mouse to come out and catch her. Neither did. A sharp metallic sound rang out, like a child hitting a ladle on a saucepan. Blake said something and Mouse retched. There were three more thumps, each louder than the last.

Beth worked on the knot and it started to undo, far too slowly. Pausing at every sound, it took a minute or more to open the belt enough so she could move her wrists within the confines. Bathed in sweat, she worked her right hand free, wiggling her slick wrists against the cheap leather. As soon as it was clear, the loops sagged and she pulled the belt off, rubbing at the welts it had dug into her wrists.

Blake backed into the room, awkwardly holding Wendy's legs. Beth quickly put her hands behind her but he didn't look over. Mouse came through, holding under Wendy's arms, his body shielding her head and shoulders, her body sagging at the middle; a dead weight. There were dark stains on his trousers. Blake dropped her legs with a thud as he opened the front door. His trousers had similar stains and a red spray ran across the belly of his shirt. He grabbed her legs again and they went out into the night.

What had they done to her? And were they going to do it to Beth next?

Chapter 50

Then

DS Chisholm's lips moved but Beth couldn't hear the words, the sound distorting like she was listening underwater. Her headache got worse and it felt like her eyes were full of grit.

"I'm sorry, Beth."

"How did it happen?" She blew her nose, wiped her eyes, her chest tight.

"I'm not sure I…"

"Please tell me," Beth pleaded, her voice too high. She had to know. Would Jenny still be here if Beth had responded to that last message? Had she let her friend down again, after promising she never would?

"It looks as though Jenny took her own life."

"No." She coughed the word out and sobbed. "That can't be possible." It was all her fault, she hadn't been there when her friend needed her. "When?"

"Last night. A fisherman found her under the pier this morning. He called an ambulance immediately and he and the paramedics did everything they could but unfortunately she was already gone. I'm so sorry, Beth, I wish I didn't have to be the one telling you this."

Beth shook her head, her world in tatters. If only she'd replied to that text.

"Do you want me to call someone for you – your parents perhaps?"

She shook her head and tried to get herself under control, calm her breathing. If she'd failed before, now she could really make a difference. She stared at the desktop and ran her thumbnail along a narrow trough someone had scored in the surface. "I promised Jenny I wouldn't tell anyone this, but I have to. I saw her on Sunday and she told me this and I believe her. After Blake went back to the resort, while I talked to you, he gave everyone a lift home."

Chisholm bit her cheek, as if already ahead of the story but didn't say anything. Beth followed the groove on the desktop with her thumb again. "He took her to the docks." A stray sob rocked through her. "He raped her."

Chisholm leaned forward. "Did she report it, do you know?"

"I told her she should and she was going to speak to her mum but I don't know any more than that."

"Okay. I need to get a colleague to come in but would you be willing to repeat this for the tape?"

In her mind's eye, Beth saw the hurt and loss in Jenny's face yesterday morning. "Very willing."

* * *

Beth walked home in a daze to an empty house and wished her dad was there to give her a hug and tell her everything was going to be alright. It wasn't, could never be, but she was willing to believe the lie for a moment if it lifted the weight from her chest.

Kicking off her Converse and socks, Beth sat on the patio. The sun was high, the heat baking and she closed her eyes but saw Jenny huddling in her dressing gown and quickly opened them again. How could she have let her friend down so badly? Jenny would never see an almost cloudless sky again, wouldn't hear birdsong, wouldn't be able to explore the sights and sounds the world had to show.

Her phone rang. An unknown number. "Hello?"

"It's DS Chisholm, I'm just ringing to let you know we've picked up Nelson Blake at Crozier's Farm, as you suggested. He's been taken directly to Seagrave General and my colleague has gone to see him."

Had she heard that right? "Why's he at the hospital, what happened to him?"

"He'd been severely beaten and his attacker was taken into custody at the same time and is currently waiting interview."

"Who attacked him?" she asked, but knew it was Frankie.

"I'll let you know as soon as I'm able." Chisholm paused. "Thank you again for your bravery, Beth, you've done a very good thing today and honoured your friend."

It still didn't feel to Beth like she'd done enough.

* * *

Her mother came home at lunchtime and held out her arms. "I heard the news in town, love, I'm so sorry."

Beth willingly allowed herself to be swallowed up in her mother's embrace, soaking the shoulder of her blouse with tears. She stroked Beth's back. "I'm so sorry, baby."

It was almost the last time mother and daughter would ever enjoy an embrace.

Chapter 51

Nick found his way back to the road using the torch app. His phone had taken a battering, the screen cobwebbed with cracks. The signal icon, showing he only had one bar, was barely visible.

Slipping the phone into his pocket, he kept to the edge of the road as he made his way to the farmhouse. The place was a ruin and he walked by cautiously, watching for signs of movement. Beyond it, the skeleton of a swing set stood in the middle of a thin patch of grass.

A sign, driven into the ground and listing at forty-five degrees, had a slice of wood attached to the top of it. 'The Beeches Resort' had been painted on in a cursive script.

The land sloped sharply down to an empty paddock. Beyond that, six chalets were arranged around a wide turning circle from which a narrow concrete ribbon led back uphill to where Nick stood. This must be the resort Frank had meant.

It looked knackered. A chalet on the far side was burned out, leaving only some jagged uprights and part of the roof hanging on with stoic determination. The unit furthest left had been flattened by a large beech tree, its branches spreading into parking spaces, the trunk edging a pond that reflected back shimmering moonlight.

The chalet across from it was the only one with light at the window. A pile of wooden beams, for horse jumps perhaps, were stacked against the back wall.

After checking no one was around, Nick crossed the road and crouched in front of the hedge. He could see the corner of a car parked in front of the chalet with the light.

Now what? Would there be more guards hidden somewhere? Other than Blake and Beth, who knew how many people might be here? He couldn't just wade in but Frank was right, if he called the police and they came in mob-handed, what would her captors do?

Knowing he couldn't take any chances, he started down the hill. Car locks thunked and a startled Nick jumped onto the verge.

Two men came out of the chalet, struggling as they carried what looked like a body. Nick felt a jab of fear then realised the person was dressed in the brown skirt and gold waistcoat uniform Wendy had been wearing at the Oceanview. His fear subsided slightly, though it made no sense why they would be carrying Wendy.

The first man had a really bad limp. His partner was tall and skinny. Both men wore dark suits and Nick hadn't seen either of them before. Conversation, discernible only as mumbles, drifted up to him. The men bundled Wendy's body into the boot, locked the car and went back into the chalet.

Keeping as close to the verge as possible, Nick ran down the hill and stopped behind the first chalet. His heart thudded with the terror of what he was doing.

He peered around the corner, careful not to lean out too far. Nobody moved in the turning circle. The dead leaves of the downed beech rattled against the block paving, sounding like rainfall.

Nick glanced over his shoulder. The hill was clear and nobody moved around the old farmhouse. Unless other thugs were hiding in the chalets, it was only him and the two men here. And Beth too, because he had to believe that.

The ground dropped away slightly behind the chalets and a drainage channel formed a narrow bed that ran towards the pond. Nick slipped into it and walked slowly, bent forward, head down. It wouldn't make him invisible but might hide him from a cursory glance.

The middle chalet smelled bad, the wood soft and damp. Something scurried through the channel bed, hidden in shadow, and Nick tried not to think about it as he moved forward.

At the end of the chalet, he leaned against the rotten wood, trying to breathe steadily. Still nothing moved around the farmhouse and the hill was clear. His own heartbeat seemed louder than the world around him.

The last chalet was set at a sharper angle to this one as if to make it fit in the space. Just around the back wall, he could see fencing around the pond.

Now or never.

He cleared the space in seconds, crouching low when he reached safety, and looked along the back of the chalet, trying to figure out a plan. There was no door but three windows, the one nearest with a crack in the top fanlight. The middle window was dark, the one at the far end showed light leaks around the casement, as if the glass had been covered by something from inside.

A door opened and Nick pressed himself against the wood. Footsteps crunched on grit.

"Fucking phone," a man said angrily. His footsteps went a distance, the limp clear in the rhythm.

A phone rang. "Yes?" he said quickly, no anger in his voice now. "Dahvit?"

Nick, holding his breath, heard the faintest murmur of a reply.

"It's done," said the limping man. "You have my word." More murmuring from the handset. "I always deliver on my promises, Dahvit, I hope you know that."

More murmurs, then silence. A second later, the man exploded. "Fucking signal!"

As the man limped away from the chalet, Nick made his move. On tiptoes, he reached through the crack in the fanlight, angling his arm so the glass didn't press into his wrists and strained for the handle. It was just out of his grasp.

The footsteps came back, sounding softer on the grass as if the man was coming into the gap between the chalets.

Nick pressed harder and even though a shard pushed against the temporary bandage Frank had applied, he managed to twist the handle and pull the window open. The mechanism moved silently.

Relieved, he pushed the fanlight up and boosted himself onto the windowsill, adrenaline giving him the extra strength. He slipped through the window and dropped into the dark room without making too much noise. He landed in a crouch and stopped still, breathing heavily.

Nobody shouted. The door didn't clatter open.

He'd landed in the bathroom, obvious from the smell of human waste, mixed now with something vaguely metallic. The only light came from the fanlight, something taped over the other panes. He could see a bath across the room and his elbow knocked the toilet pan as he stood up.

The window was covered by thin card taped to the frame and he pulled part of it away. Moonlight flooded in.

Nick pulled the window closed and when he turned back, moonlight glistened in the eyes of the person staring at him.

Chapter 52

The person stared at him over the rim of the sink.

Nick looked away quickly and threw up beside the toilet. He wiped his mouth, eyes watering and turned back, not wanting to look but knowing he had to.

Wendy's hair was spread over the taps and the sides of the sink, a spray of blood up her left cheek and temple. Her wide-open eyes stared flatly.

He moved away from the wall, giving the sink as wide a berth as he could but it wasn't far enough. The smell of blood made him retch. Wendy's mouth was fixed in a startled 'O', a wide swathe of blood across her top lip and around her nostrils. Her head sat in a gory puddle.

Nick rubbed away the tears. What had she done to deserve this? Had they done the same to Beth?

He pressed his ear to the thin wood of the door but couldn't hear anything. He tried the handle and it moved without protest, unlatching with a soft click. Nick's heart raced. No footsteps, no shouting.

* * *

A latch clicked, the sound as loud as a whip crack to Beth's heightened senses. The front door didn't move, even though a hinge creaked. Was somebody else in here?

The front door clattered open then and Blake limped in, wincing with every step. He glanced towards the coop, as if to check Beth was still there. "Make sure she's secure," he said.

Mouse, following him in, rubbed his hands as if trying to get rid of some noxious substance. There were more stains on his suit but it was impossible to tell what they were in the weird orange light.

"Her or the cage?"

"Both, I'm just going to get something," Blake said and pulled open the door of the room Wendy had been half-lying in.

* * *

Nick stepped back as soon as he heard the front door open, his heart beating so fast he was surprised it didn't burst. He looked around quickly, knowing if someone came in now they'd see him straight away and with him caught, no one would help Beth.

That moment of clarity cut through the terror squirming in his head.

If he went out the window he'd be back to square one, or he could get into the bath. As hiding places went, even with the shower curtain as a shield, it wasn't brilliant but it might give him a moment of grace.

He stepped into a dark pool in the base of the bath, stains along the sides, as if Wendy had been beheaded here. He pressed a hand tight to his mouth, leaned against the tiled wall and pulled the shower curtain around him.

The door opened.

* * *

Mouse knelt in front of the coop, pulling roughly at the padlock and didn't look at Beth.

"Please," she said, "just give me a chance."

"I can't," he said, focussing on his task, brow furrowing.

"He's in the other room, just undo the padlock."

Blake came out of the room and hefted the axe he carried, raising it above his head as he limped quickly towards the coop. At first she thought he was going to bring it down on top of her then realised he wasn't.

"Mouse!" she cried. "Watch out!"

He looked up as Blake brought the axe down in a savage arc. It buried in Mouse's shoulder with a heavy thump.

Mouse's mouth opened wide but no sound came out. He fell against the coop and blood sprayed across the straw. Beth scrambled out of the way, screaming.

Blake got his balance and pulled on the axe, yanking it hard to try and free it from Mouse's shoulder.

* * *

Beth's scream charged Nick and he jumped out of the bath, catching something that clattered against the base of the sink. A walking cane with a metal grip, he picked it up thinking any weapon had to be better than nothing.

She screamed again.

Nick pulled open the door and walked out into carnage.

* * *

Mouse pulled the shelving unit down around him as he fell, bits and bridles clattering to the floor.

Running on shock and adrenaline, Beth kicked at the door. It barely moved. She kicked again and again, concentrating all her energy into the spot where she thought the padlock was. The wood gave slightly.

Blake planted his good foot in the middle of Mouse's back and pulled sharply on the axe handle. Mouse howled in pain.

Seeing movement from the corner of her eye, Beth looked up as someone came out of the back room.

* * *

Nick couldn't quite fathom what he was looking at.

Beth was kicking at the door of a cage she'd been padlocked into. The limping man was standing on his partner, who howled in agony. It took Nick a moment to see the axe buried in his shoulder, blood covering the back of his jacket.

Which was Blake? Where was the danger?

Beth saw him, looking scared and surprised and happy. For the moment, she seemed safe and he had to stop the two men before he got her, that much made sense. "Blake!" Nick shouted.

The limping man glanced over his shoulder and Nick swung the cane as hard as he could, aiming for Blake's head. Blake raised his shoulder for protection and the cane hit his upper back with a solid thump, almost jarring it out of Nick's hand. Blake cried out and fell into the remains of the shelving, which came down on him as his head connected hard with the wall. He landed heavily beside his partner.

Nick dropped to his knees in front of the coop.

"Oh my God, oh my God," said Beth.

"I'll get you out." The padlock was heavy and locked but the hasp, where Beth had been kicking at it, had come away slightly from the wood.

He dropped the cane and pressed his fingers into the gap as best he could, pulling hard. The screws squeaked against the wood. "Push with your feet," he said.

Between the two of them, the hasp came away quickly and Nick pulled the door open.

Beth scrambled through, grabbing his shoulders. "How did you find me?" she demanded then kissed his lips and cheek, his neck and lips again. She buried her face in his shoulder and sobbed and he dropped his own kiss on top of her head.

"You're safe, are you okay?"

She looked at him and cupped his cheeks. "He had your wallet, said he'd dealt with you, I thought…" Another sob. "I thought you were dead."

"No," he said and pulled her to her feet. "Someone stole my wallet, that's how we found you. Or how Frank did."

"Frank?" She looked confused. "I can't believe you're here, I thought I was never going to see you again."

"Are you sure you're not hurt?"

"Yes, but what about you? This is all my fault, I dragged you into it."

"What happened, how did you even get here?"

"It was Wendy, she betrayed me."

He thought perhaps he'd misunderstood her. "Wendy's in the bathroom."

* * *

Beth's mind turned cartwheels, trying to make sense of everything. The shock of being able to touch and hold Nick, still a part of her life, was overwhelming and she shook her head, trying to focus herself.

"I saw them carry her out."

"So did I, but her head's in the sink."

Everything clicked into place, the price Wendy said she'd have to pay, the evidence Blake needed to present to Dahvit.

"I threw up," he said.

She felt like throwing up too but there was no time, they had to get out.

A floorboard creaked.

"So you must be the husband."

Chapter 53

Blake, tall and thin to the point of being gaunt, stepped away from the wall. There were stains on his suit and he leaned on the cane he had picked up, his left foot at an unnatural angle to his leg.

"You found us then, Nick?"

Malignancy came off the man in waves and Nick's heart raced. Why hadn't he kept hold of the cane? He moved in front of Beth as Blake backed towards the door. "That's right."

"Seems a long way to come just for your wallet, or were you thinking of trying to take Beth away?"

"I am taking her."

The life bleached out of Blake's smile. "You're not taking her anywhere."

Beth squeezed Nick's hand and he returned the gesture without looking at her. "So you say."

"You won't get by me and, at most, you've got Frank as back-up. Where is he, by the way?" He raised his eyebrows. "He's not here, is he? Did my boys get him?" He paused. "So it's just you, me and Beth, out here in the middle of nowhere?" He smiled. "I endured a lot of shit for this moment and you're not going to take her away from me. She's mine now."

Nick bit the inside of his cheek, willing himself to stand his ground and not show weakness. "I am."

Blake laughed, a quick hearty burst. "Have you ever been to prison, Nick?" He stepped in front of the door. "It was an experience your wife gifted me."

"You did that to yourself," Beth said, her voice loud and steady.

Blake ignored her. "I saw and did things in prison that would turn your hair white, Nick. I've enjoyed a breakfast after watching a man get his throat cut and watched someone bleed out after being stabbed in the gut, listening to him beg for help. The smell was bad. Life really is cheap and any of us could go down at any minute, so take what you want and enjoy it." He leaned forward, resting heavily on the cane. "Do you know what the most frightening thing in the world is?"

Nick shook his head.

"A person with nothing to lose." Blake lashed out with the cane and Nick didn't have a chance to get clear. It hit below his right shoulder, the crack echoing as his arm exploded with pain.

Beth screamed as Blake came forward, raising the cane again. She pulled Nick towards her and the cane thudded harmlessly against the wall.

His arm on fire, agonising pain radiating from his bicep, Nick tried to push Beth out of harm's way but she shook his hand off and rushed at Blake, arms extended. The impact knocked him into the wall and he backhanded her away. She bounced off the front door and slid down. Blake rubbed his throat, coughing.

Anger surging, Nick threw a punch at Blake. It glanced off his temple and something popped in Nick's hand. Blake stayed on his feet and Nick punched his shoulder repeatedly until Blake dropped the cane. They both dived for it but Blake was closest, his stretching fingers inches from the prize.

Nick punched Blake's ankle. It hurt, his knuckle singing with fresh pain but Blake rolled away. Nick went with him, punching the ankle until he could barely feel the blows.

Blake kicked Nick off and rolled onto his knees. He grabbed the cane and got unsteadily to his feet.

Nick got to his hands and knees as Blake stood over him.

"I fucking told you," Blake shouted and raised the cane, gripping it two-handed, as if he intended to stove Nick's head in.

* * *

Winded, Beth tried to catch her breath.

Blake had his back to her, cane high above his head. She pushed away from the door, her chest aching, and forced herself to her feet. "Nick?"

Blake brought the cane down hard enough for Beth to hear the impact. Nick cried out. Blake laughed viciously and raised the cane again. She yanked it down and he staggered back, stumbling on his bad ankle and falling against the wall. Leaving him, she checked Nick. His eyes were closed, his breathing heavy and erratic.

"Fucking spoilsport," Blake said, pushing away from the wall.

She stood by Nick's feet, making herself a barrier. Anger and adrenaline warmed her blood. "Leave him alone, or I'll kill you."

He snorted out a laugh. "You haven't got it in you."

"Try me," she said, making fists, willing to do whatever was needed to save Nick and herself.

"I've missed you," he said and licked his lips.

The sick bastard was enjoying it but maybe that gave her a way in. If she made him react to her rather than drive the situation, she could perhaps use that. And she knew just what button to press.

"I haven't missed you one little bit, Nelly."

He bristled at the name. She smiled sweetly, which just made it worse.

"You have." He tapped his temple. "I've been in there, all those years, eating away at you."

"Not once," she lied, hoping the untruth didn't show in her face as he found yet another chink in her armour. "Sounds like I've been in yours, though."

"Oh, you have," he said with a rueful smile. "Some days, it was just the thought of slicing the skin from your body and listening to you scream that kept me going."

The back of her neck prickled at the chill in his words.

"Right from the start, I knew you were going to be a problem, slumming it with the council house kids but too fucking good for us. Is that how you got your cheap thrills, rebelling against mummy and daddy?"

She bit her lip to stop herself from saying anything.

"Thought so," he said, as if her silence was the answer he'd expected. "Was it the violence or the thieving? Did I get you wet when I kicked the shit out of your boyfriend in the Winter Gardens?"

Her fists tightened, nails digging into her palms. "You nearly killed him."

"Was he ever the same? I like to think he's still knocking about, dribbling into a cup and asking if people want fries with their burger."

"All because he called you Nelly?" She smiled when he blanched. "Still gets to you does it, Nelly?"

"Uh-huh, but have your fun now, Beth, because you're not going to walk out of here."

"Who's going to stop me? You and your gimp ankle? Did you cry when they broke it?"

He came towards her and winced as he put weight on his ankle. She laughed and he gave her a dead-eyed smile. "That's not nice."

"Neither are you."

"Do you wear jewellery?" he asked, loosening his tie. "I see a wedding ring and watch, how about a necklace?" He undid the top button of his shirt. "I like to keep mementoes, don't you?"

She didn't say anything, not following his point. He limped around her, keeping a good distance, and she shifted so she constantly faced him, careful not to step on Nick.

"I do and read up about it when I was inside. Seems like I'm a textbook case."

"What are you talking about?"

"Have a look at this," he said and laughed. He pulled a necklace over his head and tossed it to Beth.

She caught it and looked at it but her mind refused to make the connection. It felt like she'd been punched hard in the belly.

The pendant, JP in a cursive script tarnished now with age, blurred with her tears. She gripped it tightly, the rough edges of the broken letter digging into her skin. "Where did you get this?"

"From her."

"No." Beth shook her head, refusing to believe. "That's not true, she'd never give you this."

"She didn't, willingly."

Beth remembered Jenny's tears, in her sunny bedroom with the dancing dust motes. "Did you steal it from her, after you raped her?" She thought back to that awful day, Jenny's beautiful face and sad eyes, fiddling with the necklace as the story came out. "No, she had it then, when she told me."

Blake leaned against the kitchen wall, lifting his leg slightly. "It was later, when we got serious."

"There wasn't a later." She pressed her fingers against her temples in a futile attempt to stave off the headache threatening to crush her skull.

He grinned. "The look on your face, this is exactly what I've dreamed it would be."

Each word was a finger angrily prodded into her chest, the weight of his ruthless drive behind each one. Now was the time to make her stand. He might be stronger but she wouldn't go down without a fight.

"Oh, I have a shit home life," she said in a mocking singsong voice, "and mummy doesn't love me so I'm going to be cruel to animals and people." She shook her head. "You're pitiful, Nelly."

"You have no idea," he sneered but she could see in his eyes she was getting to him. If he lost his temper, he might make a mistake.

"All this shit about being top dog in prison and running your empire in Seagrave, it's a dream. You're Dahvit's lieutenant, doing what he says and swanning around pretending you're king, knocking up teenaged girls who want to call you daddy."

He shook his head. "I took it from her."

"I'm not surprised, she's what, eighteen at best? Was she underage when you knocked her up? Did you slap her around? Is that the only way you can get your dick hard?"

"Right at the end," he said, looking away as if remembering past crimes.

"And now you use your kid to cover up the dealing?"

"She cried."

"What?" Beth suddenly realised they were having a different conversation.

"The necklace," he said and jerked his chin towards it. "I got to watch her face as I took my memento."

Beth felt the chill run up from her feet, freezing her stomach, chest and heart. "When did you take this, Nelly?"

"This is the story I want you to hear, Beth, before I rip your fucking head off your shoulders."

Chapter 54

"Are you going to talk me to death, Nelly?"

"You were dead as soon as we put you in the car to bring you here. I just want you on your knees, begging me to kill you. I want to destroy you, cave in your world, because that's what you did to me."

"That's not going to happen, Nelly."

"I saw her again."

"You couldn't have," she said, fighting back her confusion. She couldn't let him in now, couldn't let him see he was getting past her defences.

"I knew where she lived and I wanted to have a word."

"Threaten her, you mean."

He smiled. "She wasn't at home, but I knew where you all hung out so I decided to go and have a look-see."

She didn't want to listen, to give him the pleasure of revelling in her discomfort.

"It was a proper summer's night, clear sky full of stars and nobody around to see me. She was under the pier with her back to me and the tide was coming in."

His eyes bored into her and Beth felt a rush of nausea.

"I crept up on her but could have gone down there with a marching band, she had no fucking idea." He paused. "You know how she died, don't you?"

Beth's tears came then, silently tracking down her cheeks.

He nodded. "There were all these old bits of rope, stuck on the pilings and the boards of the pier. It didn't take much to pull one of them down."

"What?"

"I grabbed her and clamped my hand over her mouth and nose. She really fought for a while then went kind of limp, but that was okay, it saved me some aggro. I looped the rope around one of the metal supports in the sand. I knew the water would wake her up so I took off my T-shirt and wrapped it around her head as a gag. Then I tied the rope around her wrists as tightly as I could."

Beth's stomach turned, feeling the anguish of her best friend who clearly hadn't wanted to die, who had just wanted a few moments of peace as she waited for Beth to tell her everything would be alright.

"I knew she'd never get free, wet knots are a bastard to undo and with her on the sand it would only be a matter of time, so I sat and waited."

"You watched her?" Beth's disbelief was a lead weight around her neck.

"I had to make sure. The first wave woke her up pretty damned fast, I can tell you. When she realised what I'd done, she tried screaming but the gag made it sound like somebody shouting from miles away. As the water rose, she kept looking at me, as if I was going to start laughing and untie her, like it was all a big joke. By the time the water was up to her waist she knew I wasn't kidding."

Beth's revulsion made her feel sick and angry in equal measure, Blake's nonchalant cruelty was beyond anything she could even imagine. "You murdered her."

"When the water was at her neck," he said, as if Beth hadn't spoken, "her eyes were wider than you'd believe. She was frantic, like a cat dropped in a bath."

It was too much. "Shut up," she cried, "shut the fuck up."

"It wasn't peaceful, Beth, she really suffered. And as much as she struggled, there was nothing she could do."

Anger coursed through Beth, misting her vision, roaring in her ears. Her heart thumped so hard she could almost feel it rattle against her sternum.

"And the worst thing for her? After everything else, my face was the last one she ever saw."

Anger extinguished all rational thought and Beth rushed him, screaming. He tried to move but she was too quick and hit him, hands on his chest, her momentum driving him backwards.

They fell against the wall and the wood cracked and split.

Blake tumbled out into the night and she fell after him.

Chapter 55

Beth landed on Blake, driving her elbow into his belly. Breath whooshed out of him. His knee caught her stomach, winding her as she rolled away.

She lay on her side, knees against her chest, desperately trying to quash the pain. White blossoms flared across her vision as she stared at the moonlit sky, temples throbbing. After a moment, she managed to get on all fours, lungs protesting. She glanced at Blake who lay where he'd landed, head to one side watching her.

Pain had sapped some of her anger and brought clarity to her thinking. The dynamic had shifted and she could make an escape. If Nick could walk, she'd take them across the meadow to All Saints, since the uneven ground would clearly slow Blake down.

"You won't get away," Blake gasped.

I only have to outrun you, she thought but didn't say. Her lungs felt like they were being squeezed but she could breathe without wheezing.

"Can you hear me, you bitch?"

She pushed herself up onto her knees, hands on her thighs, head back. He'd rolled onto his side, reaching for her though the gap between them was too big.

"Fucking kill you," he wheezed.

"Yeah, yeah," she said and got unsteadily to her feet. Looking around, the view towards Radnor looked wrong and it took her a moment to realise the beech trees were missing. One had come down on the brook, less than twenty feet away, creating a pond that reflected the moonlight on its dark surface. The other had flattened one of the chalets.

Blake struggled onto all fours. Beth felt the fire return to her veins, thinking of what he'd done to poor Jenny, who didn't deserve anything that happened to her.

She could give in to the anger, kick him while he was down or stick to her plan, get her and Nick to safety.

Blake crawled towards the chalet.

"Give me your phone," she said.

He glared at her. "Fuck off."

She covered the short distance between them, stopping just far enough away that he couldn't grab her. "It's over."

Holding the side of the chalet, he started to pull himself up, favouring his good ankle. "Not until I say so." He coughed and spat at her. "You're as worthless as Jenny, I decide how this ends."

Acid bubbled in her throat and she kicked him so hard in his left thigh her foot hurt. With a grunt, he dropped to his knees. The deep shadow of the chalet sliced his face, the moonlight making his eyes blaze.

"Is that your best shot?"

She held her arms wide. "I'm not scared of you, Nelly."

"You will be," he muttered. "Place has gone to the dogs, hasn't it? Do you think Jenny would like it down here now? I think she would, she was a dirty bitch."

The red mist descended. "Enough," she roared and shoved him.

Wincing as his legs bent under him, he grabbed for the edge of the chalet but missed and fell into the stack of horse jump poles. She watched him writhe, trying to push the shifting poles off his legs.

"Bitch."

Blood rushed in her ears. She'd never felt this angry before and wasn't even sure how far she was willing to go as she embraced the red mist.

Blake finally pushed the poles away and he dragged himself backwards as Beth advanced on him. The ground angled away and she lost her footing, slipping into a narrow channel behind the chalets.

He pulled himself upright, grabbing a windowsill to help. The broken fanlight reflected moonlight like a kaleidoscope.

"Now what?" he taunted, staring her down.

"I'm going to pay you back for Jenny."

He almost tripped and looked down. With a grin, he quickly bent to pick up half a brick, hefting it in his hand like it was a sponge.

She stood where she was. If he threw the brick, she might be able to duck from this range and perhaps even throw it back. If he hit her, he'd probably brain her and then get away, literally, with murder. And she couldn't let that happen.

She backed along the channel, careful not to tread on any of the poles. Blake came towards her, hobbling badly now.

"I'm going to make you suffer, Beth."

He threw the half-brick and, for the briefest of moments, she lost sight of it in the gloom, her heart thumping hard in her chest until it whistled past her ear and landed in the grass beside the paddock.

Blake bent to grab something else and she ran, ducking as another brick clattered into the back of the chalet.

* * *

Nick coughed, the stink of old straw and rot clogging his throat. There was another smell too, as if someone had emptied a jar full of pennies next to him, a metallic scent he could almost taste.

Everything came back in a rush, including the burning pain in his left shoulder that ran down his arm and across his chest.

He opened his eyes with a start, terrified Blake might still be looming over him with the cane, but he appeared to be alone. He put his hand down to push himself up and fresh pain flared. His knuckles were swollen, the skin tight enough to burst and badly discoloured.

He got slowly to his feet, gritting his teeth against the nausea. Giddiness made him light-headed and white stars filled the room. He stood still until they'd almost faded then slowly looked around. The thin man lay on the floor in the ruin of shelves, an axe buried in his shoulder. Blake wasn't anywhere to be seen and, more frighteningly, neither was Beth. A large, jagged hole had been punched into the wall next to the chicken coop.

Had they gone through there somehow? Had Beth fought him? Nick had to get outside to see what was going on. If he couldn't find them, he needed to locate the sweet spot on the turnaround where Blake had got the mobile signal. He'd call the police, the news about the decapitated head would surely be enough to get them here in double-quick time.

Something banged against the back of the chalet and Blake shouted, his voice pained and distant.

Nick tucked his left hand into his jeans pocket, hoping that might help with the pain but it barely made a dent in the sensation as he crossed the chalet.

A shape ran past the hole in the wall. In a flash of moonlight, he saw stripes and knew it was Beth in her Bretton T-shirt.

Adrenaline shoved down the pain in his shoulder and hand as he edged his way through the hole.

* * *

The pond lay in front of her. Someone had tried to make the area safe by enclosing it in a fence but most of the posts were unlinked now.

Beth intended to cut through to the turnaround but a chunk of concrete landed in front of her. She veered towards the pond as a stone bounced near her feet, Blake's aim improving.

The third missile, small and jagged, hit her right thigh hard. Stumbling, she hit the ground and slid a few feet, arms outstretched, coming to a halt with a fencepost less than a foot from her fingertips. Two strands of barbed wire hung from it, the top snipped to a nub, the lower one looped loosely around the wood.

Beth got up slowly, her chest heaving and leg burning with pain, and turned to face Blake. He came at her quickly, his bad leg scuffing the ground. She had to get away but didn't think her leg would hold her. Angry tears stung her eyes and she grabbed the fence post to steady herself. A stone ricocheted off the ground a foot to her left, splashing noisily in the pond.

Blake ran into her. Legs tangled, they toppled forward and she landed on her belly. Her upper body slid over the lip of the pond, the water a foot or so away down a slight incline littered with half-buried lumps of hardcore. Blake was on her legs, locking her in place, and she kicked as best she could, connecting with a body part that made him grunt.

He pulled himself over her, moving enough to shift her centre of gravity so she tilted towards the water. As panic set in, she tried to think. If she dragged them down the slope, it might catch him unawares. She could grab a lump of hardcore and he'd slide into the pond, giving her a chance to get away, even if she had to drag her leg.

She stretched, reaching for the edge of a brick and pulled herself towards the water. With a lurch, her body moved a few inches.

"What're you doing, you mad bitch?"

She grabbed for a lump of battered concrete half-buried in the mud at the water's edge and pulled towards it, feeling the strain in her shoulders. He didn't slide down her back.

Her plan had failed and now the dark water was inches from her face.

Blake pushed her head forward, fingers in her hair. "Stupid bitch."

She tried to brace her neck but he had leverage and her face went under.

The cold shocked her, stagnant water rushing into her mouth. She coughed and choked and pushed against his hand, trying to break the surface, rocking her body as she did so.

He pulled her up and she gasped as soon as she felt the cool night air on her face. He pushed her back before she'd got a proper breath and she dug her nails into the back of his hand. He released his grip and she pulled her head clear of the water, lungs straining.

Gripping the concrete for all she was worth, she gasped for air, water stinging her eyes. He shouted at her, the words a jumble and she shifted, flinging her arm back to try and hit his face.

326

He pushed her head under again.

Water rushed up her nose. Her fingers slipped on the concrete and panic rippled through her. Her throat constricted, noises popped in her ears. She tried to blow the water out her mouth as more ran up her nose. Blake pushed her further down.

This was it.

She wasn't going to get out of the water.

He'd won, again, having taken her friends' lives and ruined hers by filling it with grief and guilt. If he killed her now, Jenny's parents would never know she hadn't committed suicide and Kate's son would forever believe his mum had killed herself. It wasn't fair.

Her lungs felt like they were collapsing in on themselves. Sparks lit up her eyelids like fireworks and she could almost hear the pops of the explosions, blood pounding in her ears.

Desperate for breath, she wanted to open her mouth, even though it'd be suicide.

Suicide.

Jenny hadn't killed herself.

Beth hadn't let her friend down and Blake was going to get away with it all because there was no one left to tell the truth.

She had no air left, but enough energy for one last effort.

Desperately, she threw her arm back, fingers reaching blindly, slipping over his forehead. She pressed her nails in but he shook her hand free.

The explosions in her head got louder.

Her arms were tired and heavy. Her fingers brushed his eyebrows and she pressed a thumb into his eye. Instantly, he let her go. She brought her face up and breathed deeply, coughing out the foul pond water. Her head pounded but the fireworks tailed off.

Blake slipped off her and screamed, jerking to a stop. With his weight gone, she pulled herself away from the water, her lungs and bicep on fire. She dug her toes into the earth, bracing herself as she gulped in air.

His screams tapered off. She put both hands on the concrete, relieving her left arm at last, the palm bereft of sensation. Letting her head drop, the damp smell of earth filled her nostrils.

Blake reached for her and she punched his hand away. He still hadn't slid away and she glanced over her shoulder at the fence post, silhouetted against the sky. The lower piece of barbed wire was pulled taut, looped around Blake's bad ankle and digging in deeply, blood glistening on his calf.

Beth grabbed his leg and he cried out as she pulled herself around, planting her feet on the concrete. Safe for the moment, she lay back, exhausted, chest heaving and throat burning. When he moved his leg, the wet grinding sound of the barbed wire turned her stomach.

He pushed himself up the slope slightly, away from the water. The barbed wire rattled against the post. "I'm going to kill you," he muttered.

"Fuck off and die, Nelly." She reached for the wire and, holding it carefully between barbs, yanked it down quickly. "You're pinned here and I'm going to call the police and you'll go to prison, again."

"Who says? Nobody knew about Jenny and with Kate, it'll be your word against mine."

She tried to let his words wash over her but they needled, finding soft parts of her to stab. She bit her lip, determined not to be drawn in.

"Why would I risk my liberty? I'll tell them you and Kate were at each other's throats, that you hated her and have been plotting this for years, waiting for me to be released."

"You're insane."

"And you're weak. All I have to do is talk about Jenny." His jibes were like a finger pushing at a rotten tooth. "Think how she suffered."

Beth pressed her hands over her ears but couldn't shut out his words.

"She begged me to let her go, said I could do whatever I wanted to her. Can you imagine being so scared you offer yourself to the man who raped you?"

"You're a fucking liar, Nelly." Each word hit its target, stoking the anger that fired through her all over again.

"You weren't there, Beth, were you?"

That hit her throat, made her gag.

Blake didn't stop. "She said I could have her little sister too and I would've done. Her sister, then Kate, then you – fuck the batch. I could have tied you to the same strut, choked you with my cock and then pushed your head under the water."

Her world went red. Beth climbed onto his back and pressed his head forward. He tried to resist but she used her position to her advantage, anger giving her strength. She pushed his face under and he reacted instantly, writhing as she clung on with grim determination. Bubbles rose around her hands, his waterlogged screams like the exotic night call of some bird in the trees.

She should have done this years ago, as soon as Jenny told her. They could have gone through university life together, enjoyed a happy friendship, seen those teenaged laughs into their twenties and thirties, enjoyed all the things Blake had taken away.

Pain filled her head as someone said her name softly and repeated it.

Beth looked up. Jenny sat across the pond, a teenager at the water's edge, her blonde hair pulled up in a ponytail. She looked sad. "What're you doing, Beth?"

A hand grabbed her arm and pulled her back. Blake broke free of the water with a gasp. She turned, full of venom, and saw Nick, his eyes wide as he looked from her to Blake and back again.

"What're you doing?" she demanded.

"You were going to kill him."

"I will, if you let go of my arm."

"He's not worth it, Beth. He really isn't."

"You don't know what he did, Nick."

"No," he said, voice level and firm, "you can tell me. But he needs to be arrested."

"He'll get away with it."

"He won't. Beth, please…"

Blake grabbed her wrist and pulled her towards the water. Wrenched out of Nick's grip, she fell onto Blake and he twisted around, baring his teeth as he reached for her throat. She elbowed his face and heard something crack. She did it again and again, until Blake slumped back.

Nick pulled her back. "He's finished, Beth, you broke his jaw. It's over."

She allowed herself to be pulled up onto the grass without looking away from Blake. He didn't move, his face inches from the water, his right forearm submerged.

Beth looked across the pond. "I'm sorry," she said.

"You don't have to be," Jenny smiled. "All for one."

Tears burned her throat.

"Don't be sorry," Nick said. "You're safe, he's wrapped in some barbed wire."

Beth wiped her eyes. Jenny had gone.

Holding Blake's bad ankle, Nick yanked backwards twice, pulling him clear of the water's edge. When he sat on the grass next to her, Nick was breathing hard.

Beth draped a hand over his good shoulder and kissed his cheek. "I'm so sorry for dragging you into all this," she said and started to cry. She kissed his cheek again. "I should have told you."

He nodded. "Maybe."

She felt sobs building. "I wanted to, at the beginning, but it was never the right time. I didn't want you to think I was damaged."

"That'd never happen," he said and patted her hand awkwardly. His knuckles were dark.

"But you've got hurt so much and it's all my fault."

"Beth," he said gently, "we both got hurt, but we can sort it."

"There's so much I need to tell you."

"And you can, let's just get ourselves away."

They helped each other up, both of them wincing. Every exclamation of pain from him hurt her because whatever he said, his injuries were her fault.

He reached for her hand and she took it gently.

"Doesn't this hurt?"

"So long as you don't squeeze."

"I won't," she promised.

She led Nick onto the turnaround and wondered where Blake's men were. Nick looked up the hill towards the farmhouse and raised his arm. She followed his gaze and felt a jolt of shock when she saw the tall, bald-headed man in the long grass.

"Oh no," she said. If Frankie came at them now, they were properly finished. Nick was broken and she was knackered, though she'd fight like a wildcat to the end.

"What?"

"I'm putting you in danger, all my past is coming back to haunt me tonight. Blake wasn't the only problem I left behind, that's the man we saw in town earlier that I told you to avoid."

"No, he helped me, Beth. How do you think I found you?" Nick checked his phone as they walked. "Frank helped me."

"What?" Nothing made sense anymore. "What're you talking about?"

"He's a good man." Nick pressed the phone screen. "Yes, a signal."

"What do you mean, good?"

"He reformed himself, he got the glow." Someone answered the phone. "Police please."

Beth looked at Frank. He raised his hand haltingly as if unsure of how she'd react and gave her a brisk wave. She looked away.

"Yes, I'm sure," Nick told the operator. "We're safe." He listened. "Okay, thank you." He put the phone back in his pocket. "Five minutes," he said.

She touched his cheek and he smiled. "I'm so sorry you got hurt."

"We have a lot to tell each other."

"I suppose we do."

"But not here. I understand now why you didn't want to come home."

"Don't worry." Beth kissed him gently on the lips. "I won't be coming back again."

Acknowledgements

To Mum and Dad, for their constant love and support; Sarah, Chris and my favourite bookworms Lucy and Milly; Nick Duncan, Julia Roberts, Caroline Lake, Jonathan Litchfield and Kim Talbot Hoelzli; Sue Moorcroft for her friendship and advice; Laura, Barry and Bob Burton; Ian Whates for his belief; my pre-readers who are more helpful than they could ever imagine; Steve Bacon and Wayne Parkin; Peter Mark May and Richard Farren Barber; Steve Harris, Phil Sloman and James Everington; Alison Littlewood, Gary McMahon and Gary Fry; and everyone at the NSFWG Writers Group. I'm also indebted, for their friendship and support, to The Crusty Exterior as well as my convention gangs at FantasyCon and Edge-Lit.

David Roberts and Pippa have been a tremendous help (I'm not even sure they realise just how much), with both our Friday night walks and all the plotting sessions which helped make this book what it is.

Thanks also to Matthew, my Dude, who lets Dad go off to write every now and then and always tolerates with good humour the occasions when I ask him "Hey, what do you think of this idea…?" And, of course, to Alison who's never doubted me and always been supportive, knowing when to listen and when to give me a kick. Writers' spouses sometimes seem to get lost in the shuffle but she's been with me every step of the way and had to endure some odd conversation topics over the years. I hope I've done you proud.

If you enjoyed this book, please let others know by leaving a quick review on Amazon. Also, if you spot anything untoward in the paperback, get in touch. We strive for the best quality and appreciate reader feedback.

editor@thebookfolks.com

www.thebookfolks.com

Printed in Great Britain
by Amazon

77229658R00209